A j...
A hus...
Stirring ti...

THE STEEPWOOD

Scandals

VOLUME TWO

When the debauched Marquis of Sywell won
Steepwood Abbey years ago at cards, it led to the death
of the Earl of Yardley. Now he's caused scandal again by
marrying a girl out of his class – and young enough to
be his granddaughter! After being married only a short
time, the Marchioness has disappeared, leaving no trace
of her whereabouts. There is every expectation that yet
more scandals will emerge, though no one yet knows
just how shocking they will be.

The four villages surrounding the Steepwood Abbey
estate are in turmoil, not only with the dire goings-on at
the Abbey, but also with their own affairs. Each of the
eight volumes in THE STEEPWOOD SCANDALS
contain two full novels that follow the mystery behind
the disappearance of the young woman, and the
individual romances of lovers connected in some
way with the intrigue.

THE STEEPWOOD

Scandals

Regency drama, intrigue, mischief...
and marriage

THE STEEPWOOD
Scandals

Volume 2

Meg Alexander & Nicola Cornick

*Harlequin Mills & Boon Limited, Eton House,
18-24 Paradise Road, Richmond, Surrey TW9 1SR*

First published in Great Britain in 2001

THE STEEPWOOD SCANDALS © Harlequin Books S.A. 2006

The Reluctant Bride © Harlequin Books S.A. 2001
A Companion of Quality © Harlequin Books S.A. 2001

*Special thanks and acknowledgement are given to Meg Alexander
and Nicola Cornick for their contribution to
The Steepwood Scandals series.*

ISBN-13: 978 0 263 85496 1
ISBN-10: 0 263 85496 5

052-1206

*Printed and bound in Spain
by Litografía Rosés S.A., Barcelona*

The Reluctant Bride
by
Meg Alexander

After living in southern Spain for many years, **Meg Alexander** now lives in Kent, although having been born in Lancashire, she feels that her roots are in the north of England. Meg's career has encompassed a wide variety of roles, from professional cook to assistant director of a conference centre. She has always been a voracious reader, and loves to write. Other loves include history, cats, gardening, cooking and travel. She has a son and two grandchildren.

Chapter One

1811

The elder of the two ladies seated by the fireside in the tiny cottage was visibly distressed. Tears fell unheeded down her cheeks as she looked up at her brother-in-law.

'Tell me it isn't true!' she pleaded. 'Must Isham take everything? Oh, please, not my dowry too and the portions for the girls?'

Sir James Perceval hesitated, hating the task ahead of him, yet knowing that it must be done.

'There is no help for it,' he said at last. 'Isabel, my dear, it is better that you face the worst. I tried to save what little I could, but the debt is too great. When I said that everything was gone I meant not only the house, your carriage, and the horses...'

'I don't care about those,' Mrs Rushford cried, waving aside the comforts which had sustained her for a lifetime. 'But my girls! I had such hopes for them. Who will take them now, and how are we to live?'

She reached out a hand to the silent figure of her

daughter. 'India, we are destitute…quite ruined!' Then, to the horror of her companions, she burst into hysterical laughter.

India rose to her feet and rang the bell. Then she took her mother's hands and began to speak in a low voice.

'Mama, you are very tired. Let me take you to your room. Martha shall bathe your head with Hungary water, and make a hot brick for your feet. Uncle and I will see to matters here. There may be something we can do…'

Slipping an arm about her mother's waist, she supported her distraught parent from the room.

It was some time before she returned, much to Sir James's concern, but India was quick to reassure him.

'Mama is resting,' she said quietly. 'But I have sent Letty for the doctor. A sedative will give her some respite. It was the shock, you see, coming on top of all she has had to bear just recently.'

'I would have spared her if I could, my dear, but it wasn't possible. This is a bad business, and I am sorry that she has taken it so hard…'

India nodded. 'I'm afraid that the news about her dowry was the last straw. These last four months since Father's death have been a nightmare. And then, you know, she had such plans for us.'

'I know it, my dear child. God knows I tried at least to save your own portions, but the debt was too great. Your father's vowels committed him to the hilt, and a debt of honour must be paid.'

'Honour?' India cried harshly. 'Forgive me, Uncle, but I see no honour in any of this. Isham must have known that Father could not pay such sums. He is a cur. If I were a man I'd call him out myself.'

Sir James's face grew stern. 'You don't understand, I fear. If a man sits at the tables his companions do not question his finances. It is taken for granted that he will be able to meet his obligations. To do otherwise would be fraud.'

India was silent. In her heart she knew that Lord Isham was not solely to blame for the disaster that had overtaken them. For the first time in her life she was beginning to realise that her adored papa, for all his charm and gaiety, lacked any sense of responsibility for his family. To face the truth squarely, as she must now do, he had gambled away not only the roof above their heads but monies which he might have considered were not his to spend.

The law would not agree with her. She knew that well enough. Where her own property was concerned a wife had no rights. Her husband might dispose of it as he willed. But how could Papa have left them destitute? Something of her despair must have shown in her face, and her uncle saw it.

'I wish I could make you understand,' he said more gently. 'Tailors, grocers, even builders may be left to whistle for prompt settlement of their accounts, but gambling debts must be paid at once.'

'Very well then,' India told him stiffly. 'He shall be paid, and much good may the money do him. He, above any man in London, is in no need of it...'

'That's not the point, my love. Try not to be bitter. His lordship has been accommodating. He gave you three months' grace in your old home when he might have turned you out at once.'

'That was kind of him!' India would not be placated. 'He must have been waiting with impatience to take possession of the Grange. After all, a hovel would be an amusing change from one of his so-called palaces.'

'Your home was scarcely that, India.' Sir James looked about him sadly. 'Now this, I fear…'

India was at once contrite. 'Uncle, I am a wretch! Pray do not think we are ungrateful to you for giving us this place. We shall be happy here…' Her voice wavered a little but she pressed on resolutely. 'I have such plans for the garden. We shall grow fruit, and vegetables.' She managed a brief smile. 'I am even learning to cook.'

Sir James looked shocked. 'My dear, there is surely no need for that? I thought that Martha…'

'Martha is an excellent housemaid, but she has no gift for cooking. My own efforts are in self-defence, and it is not so very difficult. Hester has brought me a copy of Mrs Rundle's book, and I follow it to the letter.'

'Even so, it is an unsuitable task for you. I'll send someone over from the Hall.'

'No, please! I beg that you will not. We are too much in your debt already…'

'I wish I could do more. You shall have coals, and food of course, and the use of a carriage when you need it. I'm sorry about the house in London, but the rent was beyond my means, otherwise you might have finished your Season… That I do regret.'

'Please don't. How could we have stayed? After Father's death, rumour alone would have driven us away. It would have been unthinkable.'

Sir James regarded her set expression with unease. How much had she heard? He'd done his best to protect his wife's family from the worst of the London gossip, but rumour had raced through the Ton like wildfire, and had lost nothing in the telling.

Even without it India had been badly hurt. Described always as 'the child of his heart,' she had been her father's favourite, and to her he had seemed a godlike creature. Now her uncle sensed that much of her anger towards Lord Isham stemmed from that hurt, and the realisation that her idol had feet of clay. Gareth Rushford's death had come as a shock to all of his family, but what had followed had been worse.

Damn the fellow, Sir James thought savagely. He had known for years that that charmer's carefree lifestyle had rested upon a pyramid of debt. It had taken only that fatal evening at White's to bring the whole edifice crashing down. The result had crushed his family.

Now India spoke with difficulty. 'Have you heard nothing more? About the accident, I mean?'

'Nothing!' her uncle said mendaciously. India must never learn the truth. Gossip had not lied, as he had taken the trouble to find out. Knowing that he was ruined, Rushford had stayed on at the club, drinking heavily. In the early hours of the morning he had staggered out of White's and into St James's Street. Would they ever discover if that lurch into the path of a racing curricle had been deliberate? He himself suspected it. Had Rushford tried to spare his family the shame of an obvious suicide? Perhaps. As it was he had died instantly beneath the flying hooves.

There was little he could say to comfort his niece, but he tried. 'It was very dark, you know, my dear. We suspect that your father did not see the carriage until it was upon him. At least he did not suffer.'

'Even so...I wonder that he did not hear the horses. It is very strange...'

'My dear child, you must not torture yourself. Perhaps your papa was thinking of something else...'

'His gambling debts? Oh, Uncle, how I hate the practice! It should be outlawed...'

'There, at least, we are in agreement, India. As you must know, my own estate is heavily encumbered and has been so since my grandfather's day. He had to sell much of it to settle his losses at cards. I have been trying to buy it back, a little at a time.'

'I know it,' she cried warmly. 'Hester has told me how you've struggled. It is selfish of me to think only of our own concerns, but I cannot help wondering how men can risk their substance upon the turn of a card.'

'Not only men, my dear. It is the vice of our time, and the ladies play their part. You must have seen it when you were in London.'

'I didn't pay much attention,' she confessed. 'There were so many other things to do. It was one long round of parties, balls and concerts...'

Sir James's hand reached out to her. 'Your life now will be very different,' he said sadly. 'Tell me now...during your Season, was there no one...I mean...?'

'You mean did anyone offer for me?' For the first time India managed a slight smile. 'No, they did not. Uncle, look at me! In the first place I am much too tall. I towered over most of the men who danced with me. And then, you know, I cannot be described as ethereal. I believe that statuesque is the kindest word. My hair is not exactly carrotty-red, but it is certainly a ruddy chestnut, and blue eyes are much preferred to hazel.'

Sir James smiled his dissent, and India dimpled. 'I did, however, create one sensation,' she admitted. 'I had the misfortune to offend George Brummell, who promptly snubbed me. I was expected to be crushed, but I'm afraid I laughed aloud. He won't forgive me for it.'

'You seem to have borne that fate with fortitude,' Sir James said drily. 'He is another, I fear, who lives beyond his means.'

India was silent. That last remark was much too close to home.

Her uncle sensed it and made haste to change the subject.

'How is Letty?' he enquired. 'I hope that she is a comfort to you at this time.'

'She is upset, but not because of our losses. Letty is in love. We had hoped that Oliver Wells would offer for her, but now? Well, I don't know.'

'Wells?' Sir James considered for a moment. 'One of the Wells of Bristol? Money can be of no consideration there, so it cannot signify if Letty has no portion. I married for love myself, you know...'

'I know it, Uncle dear, but Oliver is a younger son and his mother is as proud as Lucifer. She is hoping for a splendid match for him. Now Letty has sent word that all must be at an end between them. She tries to hide it, but I know how sad she feels.'

'And your brother? Where is Giles? I had hoped to find him here with you today. There is so much to be decided. Have you news of him?'

'Giles is gone into Derbyshire,' India faltered. 'He stays with the Cromfords. It was a long-standing invitation...'

'Indeed!' Sir James's voice was stiff with disapproval. 'The invitation might have been declined. His place is here with you.' He did not trouble to hide his anger. His fear always was that Giles might follow in his father's footsteps.

India bit her tongue, though her instinct was to fly at once to her brother's defence. She was saved from further strictures upon his conduct when Letty entered the room.

Her sister looked pale and tired, but she managed a smile for her uncle. Then she turned to India.

'The doctor has gone up to Mama,' she murmured. 'I caught him as he was about to start his rounds, and he brought me back at once.'

'Good!' India smiled encouragement at the younger girl. 'Mama needs rest above anything. Then, when she is feeling better, we shall tell her of our plans.'

'What plans are these?' Sir James bent a keen gaze on his nieces, thinking as he did so that they could not have been less alike. No one would imagine that they were so closely related.

Letty was a full head shorter than her sister, and so slender as to appear almost elfin. That look was emphasised by her crop of fashionably short blonde curls atop a pair of dark blue eyes. A beauty, he decided, but to his mind India cast her into the shade.

Beside those of the younger girl, India's looks were striking. There was character in that face, with its strong jaw and noble brow. The much-despised auburn hair was drawn back smoothly into a chignon, beneath which surprisingly fine black eyebrows soared above the great hazel eyes, framed as they were by sooty lashes.

Sir James smiled to himself. India had no trace of vanity, believing herself to be so plain.

Yet in one respect she had seized correctly upon the reason for her lack of offers. Even at first glance it must be clear to the most casual observer that this was a woman to be reckoned with. There was resolution in those sweetly curving lips, and a stubborn tilt to her chin. He sighed. Such qualities were scarcely at a premium in the marriage market. As a wife India was unlikely to be biddable.

Not for the first time he regretted the close proximity of Mrs Guarding's Academy. So many of the local girls had gone there. Had he known that his own daughter would be exposed to the radical thinking of that redoubtable educationalist he would have sent Hester to a more conventional school for the children of the gentry. Greek, Latin and philosophy indeed! Of what use could those subjects be to any sensible woman? And that was not the worst. Both India and Hester had now what he could only describe as an odd kick in their gallop. Both were inclined to speak out as boldly as any man. These notions of independence would never do.

With a sigh he returned to the matter in hand, addressing Letty. She, at least, had some notion of what was acceptable feminine conduct.

'What plans are these?' he repeated.

Letty returned his smile, but she shook her head. 'India will tell you,' she said shyly.

'India?'

'Uncle, we are trying to decide on something,' India admitted. 'We cannot continue to rely upon your help.'

Sir James was not altogether surprised. He could understand her dislike of what she must regard as charity.

'And what have you considered?' He was determined to press her, knowing better than she that there were few options open to delicately nurtured girls thrown penniless upon the world. 'You will not, of course, wish to leave your mother?'

'We may have no choice, but I heard yesterday that a teacher is to leave Mrs Guarding's Academy. There may be an opening there.'

'Teaching, my dear? Shall you enjoy that way of life?'

'Enjoyment cannot be our first consideration,' India said quietly. 'It would mean that we could stay here in the village. To take a post as a companion or a governess would mean leaving Mama. I'd like above all things to avoid that for the present until she is feeling better.' She raised her head. 'Is the doctor leaving? I thought I heard a carriage. Surely he will speak to us before he goes?'

'It isn't the doctor.' Letty had been gazing through the window. 'We have another visitor.'

'Anyone we know?'

'I don't recognise the carriage. I thought it might be someone who had lost the way, but young Jesse Ekin is pointing to our door.'

'How odd.' India rose to her feet as a thunderous knocking sounded at the door. 'I'll go, Letty. Martha must be upstairs.'

She had no presentiment of what awaited her, but the appearance of the man who stood before her caused her to recoil.

He towered over her, broad as well as tall, and as she looked up at his swarthy face a pair of keen dark eyes raked her figure from head to toe in obvious appreciation.

'Yes?' she said stiffly.

'My name is Isham,' came the brief reply. 'I wish to see Mrs Rushford.'

For just a moment India was too astounded to reply. This was the author of all their misfortunes, and the sheer effrontery of his visit was unbelievable. It was in the worst of taste. Doubtless he had come to gloat over the downfall of his victims. He should not have that pleasure.

'Mrs Rushford is not at home to visitors,' she said in icy tones.

'I see.' The dark eyes studied her face. 'And you are?'

'I am Miss Rushford, and I too am not at home to visitors…'

'On the contrary, you look very much at home, if I may say so. Miss Rushford, what I have to say concerns your family. Will you not hear me out?'

'Nothing you have to say could possibly be of interest to us…' India began to close the door and found a booted foot in the way.

'A rash statement since you don't know what it is. I see that Sir James Perceval's carriage is here. I will speak to him.'

'Sir, you are insolent! Kindly remove your foot.'

'Certainly not! I haven't come all this way to be denied.'

India gave him a freezing look. It had no effect at all. She could not remove him by force, and well she knew it.

'Very well,' she said at last. 'You may see my uncle. I doubt if you will attempt to force your will upon a man.'

To her annoyance his lordship's lips twitched.

'It must be maddening to be a helpless female,' he agreed. 'Now ma'am, if you will lead the way...?'

India's back was ramrod straight as she marched ahead of him. In a moment he would get his just deserts. Sir James would brook no nonsense from this creature.

She was wrong. Much to her astonishment Sir James advanced upon their visitor with an outstretched hand.

'What may I do for you, my lord?' he asked. 'We had not expected you before the New Year.'

'My business concerns your family, sir. I had hoped to see Mrs Rushford, but since she is not available...'

'My sister-in-law is indisposed, I fear. May I not be her proxy?'

'If you would be so good. This is a delicate matter. I should welcome your advice. Perhaps first you will present me to these ladies...?' Ignoring India, Lord Isham turned to Letty with an enquiring glance.

'Forgive me, sir. These are my nieces. India you have already met. This is her younger sister, Letitia.'

Isham bowed politely, but his bold stare brought a blush to Letty's cheeks.

India could have slapped her. Must Letty look so...overcome in this man's presence? She seized her sister's hand, and making their excuses almost dragged her from the room.

'Oh dear! Should we not have been more polite?' Letty looked distressed. 'India, you were giving his lordship dagger-looks.'

'Are you surprised? How he had the sheer effrontery to come here I can't imagine. It is insulting.'

'But, love, we don't know why he came...'

'Most probably he wants his money. There can be

no other reason. Doubtless he has already visited the Grange and feels that he was cheated.'

'Well, it is in a poor state, you know. Nothing has been spent on it in years…'

'That isn't the point. He gambled for it and he won it. That should be enough.'

India was still seething as she hurried up to her mother's bedroom, but her expression softened as she looked at the wan figure lying in the old four-poster. Mrs Rushford's eyes were closed.

The doctor put a finger to his lips. 'Don't disturb her. I've given her a draught. She will sleep now, and should feel better when she wakes.'

'She looks so ill.' Letty choked back a sob. 'Is she…is she dying?'

'Not at all, you foolish girl! Your mother is a prey to nerves. Give her time to recover from the strain of these past months and she will soon be well again.' The doctor picked up his bag and took his leave of them.

'We had best let Uncle know.' India peered through the window, but Isham's coach was waiting still.

'Damn the man!' she cried. 'What can he have to say that takes so long?'

Letty giggled. 'You may be thankful that Mama is sleeping. She would be shocked to hear you swear.'

'I'm sorry, but that creature would try the patience of a saint. Did you see how he looked at us? He might have been assessing prize cattle.'

Letty's colour rose. 'I know it, but, well…you know his reputation. It is the talk of London…'

'Oh, you mean his opera-dancer? The expensive bird-of-paradise? He can well afford to give her a house and carriages and jewels. She's said to be the latest of many, but without his wealth no one would look at him.'

Letty was pink with embarrassment. 'Oliver won't discuss it, but other people do. The matchmakers have given up on Isham. They say that he will never marry.'

'Who would want him? It is no wonder that he tries to buy affection. I never saw an uglier-looking man. Why, he might be a gypsy or a pirate. All that is wanting is a gold ring in one ear.'

Letty was moved to protest. 'He is not ill-favoured, India. He is of a dark complexion, but his eyes are very fine.'

'You are a model of Christian charity, sister dear. Let us say that his reputation must be very bad indeed if even a massive fortune does not attract the marriage market.'

'It isn't that, I'm sure.' Letty was determined to be fair. 'I think he frightens people more than anything. His look is so...so shameless. I felt as if I had forgotten to wear my gown. I wanted to run away and hide.'

'Oh, Letty, must you be so timid? We must not let him see that we care at all for his opinion. I intend to treat him with contempt.'

Letty shuddered. 'Must we go down and take our leave of him?'

'Certainly not! As far as Lord Isham is concerned we are not of the least consequence. Unless I am mistaken he sees women as fit for one purpose only...'

Letty blushed again. Then she gave a sigh of relief. 'Oh, India, he is going. Thank heavens for that.' She stood by the window until his lordship's carriage had disappeared.

'Had we best go down again?'

'In a moment. Letty, Uncle is sure to question us again as to what we mean to do. Have you any ideas?'

'I can't think of anything,' Letty admitted helplessly. 'I couldn't teach, even if Mrs Guarding offered me a post at the Academy. I might take a post as a companion, but that would mean leaving home.' Her lips quivered.

'Dearest, don't distress yourself. You are clever with your needle, which I am not, and you sing so well. You might think of teaching music.'

'I don't know. Mrs Guarding may not have an opening for both of us. In any case, Uncle will not like it…'

'I don't expect he will. He blames Mrs Guarding for Hester's advanced ideas, but that is not quite fair. Hester would be of an independent mind, however she was taught.' India chuckled. 'Uncle wishes me to speak to her and to bring her round to a better understanding of her duty. By that he means marriage, as you know.'

Even Letty twinkled at that. 'I wish you luck,' she said more cheerfully. 'Shall we visit her today? She is such a fund of gossip.'

'Then come with me and enjoy a coze. We could go back with Uncle, since Mama is to sleep for hours. The change will do you good.'

'I'd like that. We have been so dull of late…with nothing but worry and disappointment.' Letty's face grew sad. 'I had hoped to hear from Oliver, although I did say that we must give up all thought of an engagement. He must have taken me at my word.'

'Nonsense, you silly goose! Have you no faith in him? If he loves you truly he will not give up so easily. Now bathe your eyes. We'll go down and hear what Uncle has to say. Isham has probably suggested sending us to the salt mines to earn a crust…'

This outrageous statement finally brought a smile from Letty. Still protesting at the ridiculous notion she followed her sister down the stairs.

'You think Isham capable of anything,' she teased.

Yet even India was unprepared for the news with which Sir James greeted them. He looked so serious that both girls were alarmed.

'What is it?' India asked. 'Is Isham demanding more? We have nothing left to give...'

'Sit down, my dears. It is nothing like that. Now what I have to say concerns each of you. Lord Isham came to offer for you...either of you. He wishes you to decide between yourselves which of you is willing to become his bride.'

Chapter Two

For a few moments India was too stunned to speak. Then she found her voice and began to smile.

'Uncle, I believe you mean to punish us for our rudeness to Lord Isham. You have hit upon the very thing to frighten us. What a fate for any girl! It is a dreadful prospect, even if you mean only to tease.'

Still smiling she looked up at her uncle, but saw no answering amusement in his face.

'India, I do not tease. His lordship has made a serious offer, and I must insist that you treat it as such.'

India stared at him in disbelief. 'You cannot mean it! If this is Lord Isham's idea of a joke it is in the worst of taste. Hasn't he done enough to harm our family? Must he indulge in mockery too? I hope that you ordered him from the house.'

'I did no such thing. This is no joke. I am surprised at you, my dear, though I will make allowance for the shock. Your manner towards Lord Isham left much to be desired. I had not expected such a want of courtesy from any of my family.'

'A want of courtesy?' India cried wildly. 'That man is our enemy. Would you have us fawn upon him?'

'You forget yourself, I fear. Must I remind you yet again that Isham did not force your father to sit at the tables with him? I am disappointed in you. Reason is needed here, not an exhibition of ill-temper.'

His tone was severe, but India was too distraught to heed his displeasure.

'You can't believe that he is serious,' she pleaded. 'I have never heard of such an offer. Are you saying that Isham has no preference? That either of us will do? It is insulting. Forgive me if I question his motives.'

'India, you are not a child. The offer is unusual, certainly, but Isham needs an heir. Should aught happen to him the title goes to his half-brother, and Henry Salton is scarce fit...' He left the sentence hanging in the air.

India struggled to regain some semblance of composure.

'So Isham needs an heir? That I can accept, but why offer for Letty or myself? All the matchmaking mamas in London have been hanging out for him for years. He might take his choice of a dozen girls.'

'I am sorry to see that you will believe no good of him. Perhaps you might consider that Isham has a conscience. He is well aware of your present circumstances.'

'Then this offer is an act of charity? A sop for his guilt? What poor creatures he must think us! I for one will have none of it. He may peddle his offer elsewhere...'

'This is foolish talk. You think only of your own pride. What of your mama and Letty?'

India glanced at her sister and was stricken. Letty

seemed on the verge of collapse, but she struggled to speak.

'Uncle is right,' she whispered. 'If his lordship's intentions are honourable we must not sneer at him.'

'That's right, my dear.' Sir James gave the younger girl an approving glance. 'You should listen to what I have to say before you reject this offer out of hand. Isham is prepared to be generous. He will settle the Grange upon his bride. Your mama may return there with a handsome allowance to enable her to live in comfort. Your own portions will be restored, though much enhanced, and the future Lady Isham will be the recipient of several other liberal settlements.'

'He's trying to buy us!' India cried indignantly. 'Mama will not allow it.'

'Please try for a little conduct, India, and do not get upon your high ropes. I intend to speak to your mama when she is a little restored. In the meantime I shall be obliged if you will restrain your comments. As Letty has pointed out it is quite wrong to censure a man who is trying to make amends for circumstances which are not his fault.'

India hung her head. 'I've been quick to judge,' she admitted. 'But this offer seems so casual. It would appear that any woman will do.'

'That is not so, as you yourself have admitted. Isham must be all of thirty-five. He might have chosen a bride at any time these past fifteen years.'

With all her heart India wished that he had done so, but she would not antagonise her uncle further.

'So what is to happen now?' she asked.

'Isham is staying at the Grange. He will return tomorrow for your answer.'

'So soon?' Letty cried in a faint voice. 'Will he not give us more time to consider?'

'Apparently not. My dears, I must leave you now, but I shall visit you again this evening. By then your mama may be feeling better. We shall speak further on this matter.'

All thoughts of visiting Hester had vanished from India's mind. Her manner was abstracted as she took leave of her uncle. Then she sat in silence for a time. Letty's scared voice recalled her to the present.

'India, what are we to do?' The great blue eyes were wide with apprehension.

'Why nothing, dearest. We must not worry. Mama will be as shocked as we are. She won't consider such a proposition.'

India was wrong. She entered her mother's room that evening to find her parent closeted with Sir James.

More animated than she had been for months, Isabel Rushford greeted her daughters with a radiant smile.

'Now, my dears, is this not a piece of great good fortune? It is all that I had hoped for you. What a match! Even in London I had not thought to aim so high.' She reached out her hands towards her girls. 'Now which of you is it to be? You must have spoken of it whilst I slept.'

'We have spoken of naught else.' India stared at her mother in amazement. 'Mama, pray do not set your heart upon this scheme. It is sheer folly. What do we know of Isham, apart from the fact that he has ruined our family?'

She watched in dismay as her mother's smile disappeared.

'Isham did not ruin us,' the older woman said sharply. 'That was your father's doing. Oh, I know that to you he was a god.' She gave a bitter laugh. 'In your eyes he could do no wrong, but now you know the truth of it. Folly, you say? His was the folly. As to Isham's offer, your uncle welcomes it, and so do I. Will you set your opinion above our own?'

India was silent, but her mother was not finished.

'You are become very high in the instep, Miss, if his lordship is not good enough for you. As I recall you had not offers enough for you to pick and choose...'

It was a cruel gibe and the taunt stung. India bit her lip and turned her head away.

'Isabel, my dear, let us not lose our tempers,' Sir James said mildly. 'Your girls do not know the way of the world as we do and this offer has come as a shock to them. They are entitled to know something of Lord Isham's background before any decision is reached.'

Letty smiled at him. Though terrified at the prospect of becoming Isham's bride, she dreaded further attacks upon her sister. 'Uncle James, I wish you will tell us more,' she said. 'We know so little about his lordship.'

Isabel Rushford intervened before Sir James could speak. Now she tossed her head. 'Very well then, you foolish creatures. Lord Isham's background is impeccable. His is one of the oldest families in the country. You know of his wealth, of course?'

'We do, and we also know of his opera-dancer!' India was moved to open rebellion, and this rash statement brought a shriek of horror from her mother.

'India! Such indelicacy, and before your uncle too!'

'Uncle knows that I am not a child. He told me so this morning.'

'That may be so, but for an unmarried girl to discuss such things! I declare, I am shocked beyond belief!'

'But not by Isham's proposition, Mother?' India plunged on recklessly. She was already in deep disgrace, but now she was fighting for survival, either for herself or Letty. She recognised the stubborn look about her mother's mouth. With all the obstinacy of the weak, Mrs Rushford intended to have her way at any cost. More often than not it was the prelude to hysterics.

Letty had seen the danger too, but before she could speak the bitter tirade continued.

'This is a proposal, not a proposition. Let me assure you that there is a difference. Since you are so worldly-wise I am surprised that you do not know it.'

'Mama, have you ever met Lord Isham?' Letty ventured timidly.

Isabel looked at her younger daughter and saw a ray of hope. Letty was always more amenable than her sister.

'Why yes, my love,' she said more quietly. 'I met him once. Naturally, he was all courtesy...'

Then you must have caught him on a good day, India thought to herself. Most probably he had just succeeded in separating another unfortunate from his worldly goods.

'I wonder that he has never married,' Letty continued in artless tones. 'Especially as he has so much to offer.'

India gave her sister a sideways look. Letty detested confrontation. She preferred to argue in a more subtle way. Sometimes it worked, but on this occasion India felt that both she and Letty were fighting a losing battle.

Sir James bestowed a glance of approval upon his younger niece. 'I doubt if he had the opportunity, my dear. He was with Wellington from the start, you know, and has spent much time abroad.'

'Was that not after Barbara…?' Isabel looked at her brother-in-law, saw the slight shake of his head, and stopped in mid-sentence.

'Isham was wounded at Talavera,' Sir James continued hastily. 'His injuries were such that he was forced to return to England.'

'He must be a brave man,' Letty murmured.

Isabel beamed at her. 'My dear child, that is so. Does this mean that you will accept him?'

Letty was startled. She had not intended her words to convey such a meaning.

The tears sprang to her eyes. 'Oh, no!' she cried. 'I can't. If I can't have Oliver I shall never marry.'

Her words brought on the threatened attack of hysterics. Isabel Rushford threw herself back against her pillows, tore off her cap and gave vent to her feelings of persecution. Hiccuping sobs were interspersed with a diatribe upon the ingratitude of modern children and their evident wish to see their mother starving in the gutter.

India had heard it all before, but it always succeeded in distressing her. Now, faced with tears from Letty and her uncle's acute discomfort, she undertook the belated role of peace-maker.

'May we not speak of this more calmly?' she asked, her deep voice cutting through the pandemonium. 'Perhaps I have been too much the devil's advocate. I have stated my objections. Now, Uncle, will you give us your own opinion?'

There was a sudden silence. Mrs Rushford's sobbing ceased and a wary eye appeared from behind a sodden handkerchief. 'Of course,' she muttered feebly. 'Listen to your uncle, my dears. He will advise you... You know I think only of your happiness... When you have heard him out you will not oppose him, I am sure.'

'It is exactly as I told you, India.' Sir James settled back in his chair with obvious relief. Female vapourings were not to his taste. In the ordinary way he would have absented himself from the scene but this was a matter of the utmost importance. It would not be resolved by cowardice.

'Isham is prepared to be more than generous,' he continued. 'He will make handsome settlements. Even at this present time he is undertaking extensive repairs to the Grange. I believe you should consider carefully before coming to a decision. This match would make all the difference to your circumstances...'

'Surely you won't refuse him?' Mrs Rushford cried. 'He may even be persuaded to do something for Giles.' She glanced slyly at India, knowing her elder daughter's fondness for her brother. 'The happiness of others is at stake, remember. It would be selfish beyond measure to think only of your own.'

India was silent. She knew that statement for what it was. Emotional blackmail was one of her mother's favourite weapons.

Now Letty, desperate, was driven beyond her usual caution.

'Isham is such a black-looking man,' she wailed. 'He frightens me! Mama, don't make me wed him.'

India laid a firm hand on her sister's shoulder, enjoining silence as she squeezed it gently.

'You find him ill-looking?' Isabel returned to the attack. 'Let me tell you, miss, that I was married to the handsomest man in London, and where are we now?'

'I agree that looks are not everything,' India said

quietly. 'Uncle, I think you said that Lord Isham will return tomorrow?'

'After noon—possibly at four o'clock, or so he hoped.'

'Then may I call on Hester in the morning? I haven't seen her in this age...'

Sir James hesitated, searching his mind for some reason to put her off. His eldest daughter, with her radical views on marriage, would be certain to advise against the match. Mrs Rushford too had seen the danger.

'Had you forgot, my love?' she asked sweetly. 'The vicar is to call tomorrow. He would take it ill indeed if you were not at home.'

It was the first that either girl had heard of the proposed visit, but India understood at once. She was to be prevented at all costs from discussing Isham's offer with the forthright Hester. She turned to her uncle.

'You are certain that we have nothing left—not even a single guinea, Uncle James?'

'No, my dear, and I am sorry for it, but there is nothing more to be done.' For some reason the question had disturbed him more than any of India's previous questions. He gave her a sharp look. India was no fool. She must never guess that to pay off her father's debts he himself had had to find the balance. It meant that repairs to his own roof must wait, but this was a matter of family honour.

She did not question him further. Instead she turned to her mother.

'Mama, shall you object if I see Lord Isham on my own tomorrow? You won't be well enough to receive him, and there is no need for Uncle to be present.'

Isabel Rushford looked alarmed. 'Nonsense, it is out

of the question. It would not be seemly. Besides, I am feeling better already…'

'I thought that if I got to know him better…?'

Her mother eyed her with suspicion. 'You are inclined to speak out much too freely, India. Remarks such as those you've made today would cause him to withdraw at once.'

'I promise not to cause him to withdraw…' India was playing for time. She was suffocating beneath the pressure brought to bear upon her.

'That's my good girl!' Isabel beamed upon her daughter. 'You always had good sense, and after all, it is not as though your affections are engaged elsewhere.' She turned to her brother-in-law. 'Sadly poor India did not receive a single offer during her Season.'

'Then that must show a want of taste in our young men,' Sir James replied gallantly. 'Now I must take my leave of you, but, my dear girls, do consider carefully. This could be a splendid match for one of you.'

Letty could scarcely wait until she and her sister were alone. Leaving the radiant Mrs Rushford to her dreams of glory, she seized India by the hand and dragged her downstairs to the parlour.

'What are we to do?' she cried in anguish. 'Mama has set her heart upon this marriage.'

'I don't know,' India admitted. 'Letty, did you see Uncle's face when I questioned him about the money?'

'Oh love, you don't believe that he would lie to us? He would not withhold a penny that was due to us…'

'Of course not, but I suspect that all our assets have not met the debt. I think that he has paid the rest himself.'

'Oh no! That is truly dreadful! But, India, you must not let it sway you. Why did you agree to see Lord

Isham? You dislike him so…you can't be thinking of accepting him?'

'I had to say something. Mama was in a state and getting worse, and Uncle hated all the fuss…' She sighed. 'I suppose that I am hoping for a miracle, but we must have more time. How I wish that Giles were here. He might think of something, and Mama will listen to him.'

'What could he do? Like the rest of us he has nothing now. The loss of the estate has been a bitter blow. He longed so much to manage it.'

'I know.' India was lost in thought. 'Love, shall you mind if I retire? It's early, but my head is pounding.'

Letty was all sympathy, but sensibly she refused to fuss. She knew her sister well. India needed time alone.

'You'll think of something,' she announced with confidence. 'You always do…' Dropping a kiss upon India's brow, she left the room.

India's mind was in turmoil. Letty's confidence, she felt, was totally misplaced. For her own part she could see no solution to their problems other than to agree to this repugnant marriage. The Rushford family must no longer be a drain upon the stretched resources of her kindly uncle.

Her hope now was that Isham would find her unacceptable, but there she was torn with indecision. That might mean that Letty would be forced to wed him. That must not happen. Her gentle sister would be no match for that arrogant creature. He would make her life a misery.

Perhaps she herself could find a way to make him pay for the ruin he had brought upon them. It was a tempting thought, and revenge would be sweet.

There were other considerations. As Lady Isham she

would have her own establishment, with the powers
that an ancient title and vast wealth brought always in
their train. And she could help Giles. Her mother would
live out her days in comfort, and Letty, with her portion
restored, might yet attain her heart's desire. The reasons for accepting his lordship's offer were overwhelming.

Yet every instinct warned her against it. She could
not banish the darker side of the bargain from her mind.
Isham was everything she detested in a man. He was
an inveterate gambler, a roué and above all, one who
had little regard for women. Was this to be her destiny,
and the end of all her dreams of happiness?

She lay awake for hours, staring into the darkness,
but by morning her decision had been made.

Next day her mirror revealed little evidence of her
sleepless night, apart from a trace of shadow beneath
the clear hazel eyes. Her creamy skin glowed with its
usual health. As she tugged a brush through the heavy
mass of auburn hair she sighed. What would she give
now for the services of that fashionable London hairdresser with his gifted way of winding her locks into
a style which emphasised her high cheekbones and the
clean lines of her profile.

She did her best, but the result left much to be desired.

Still, it would not matter to Isham, she decided. He
was not looking for a mistress, merely some female
who would not disgrace his name and would provide
him with an heir.

Well, she would not disgrace him. Her looks were
not in the common way of fashion, but no one would
mistake her for anything other than a woman of breed-
ing. An unfortunate turn of phrase, she admitted to her-

self. It would not be pleasant to be regarded as a brood-mare.

The implications made her stomach churn, and she found that she was trembling. How could she let Isham touch her? Every sense recoiled from the idea. Stifling her fears, she hurried down to the parlour.

There she found the Vicar in conversation with her mother. William Perceval, Sir James's younger brother, held the living, and had done so for many years. A kindly man, he was a favourite with both the Rushford girls.

India kissed him warmly, and asked about his family.

'Your Aunt Elizabeth is well,' he smiled. 'Though she dislikes these cold, dank days of winter. The girls, of course, do not notice. That is one of the advantages of youth.'

India smiled. Her aunt made no secret of the fact that she detested winters spent in the draughty vicarage, try as she might to bear the conditions with Christian fortitude.

The Vicar shot a keen glance at his niece's face. 'Your mama has been speaking of Lord Isham's offer,' he continued. 'I was surprised to receive her message asking me to call so early...'

India did not look at her mama. As she had suspected, the story of the Vicar's proposed visit had been a lie, designed to prevent her visiting Hester.

'We are always glad to see you,' she said truthfully. 'And this offer? How do you feel about it?'

'It came as a shock to us.' India would go no further, but the Vicar was concerned.

He had never had much time for Mrs Rushford—a hysteric and a hypochondriac if ever he saw one. He was well aware of the means she used to get her way. Not for the first time, he gave thanks to heaven that his brother had chosen her sister rather than herself to be his wife.

As for the girls... Poor Letty was looking distraught and India, though controlling her emotions, was clearly under a great strain.

There was little he could do to help them, without appearing to interfere too obviously. For the moment he contented himself with observing that as marriage was for life even the dazzling prospect of this unexpected offer should be given a great deal of thought.

Mrs Rushford frowned at him. 'Why, Vicar, as their uncle I expect you to have the welfare of my girls at heart. What is there to think about? Such a chance is unlikely to come their way again...'

'And do my nieces agree?' he asked lightly, aware of the air of tension in the room.

The ensuing silence gave him his answer, and Mrs Rushford gave him a dagger-look, which she then attempted to hide.

'What do young girls know of these things?' she asked. 'They must be guided by their elders.'

'I see.' It was no more than the truth. He saw very well how matters lay. The girls were to be hounded until one or the other accepted Lord Isham. Well, in the last resort he would refuse to marry an unwilling bride, however wealthy her suitor.

Mrs Rushford saw his set expression and made haste to change the subject. 'Have you heard no more of the Marchioness?' she asked. 'That is a strange business.'

'Indeed it is. Rumour is rife, but we cannot place any reliance on such gossip. So many months have passed since she was seen that we must pray that no harm has befallen her.'

'It is said that Sywell himself has murdered her,' Mrs Rushford announced with relish.

'A rumour entirely without foundation, Isabel. The Marquis is ill-tempered, and capable of violence, but I cannot believe that he would visit it upon his wife. He doted on her.'

'Then where can she be?'

'No one seems able to answer that question. I attempted to question the Marquis, but I am unwelcome at the Abbey. As you know, I was against this marriage from the start. The union of May and December will never serve, and Louise Hanslope was little more than a child when she took it into her head to marry a man three times her age. It could only lead to disaster.'

'You think it important then, for both parties to be in complete accord?' India asked quietly.

'I do.' The Vicar smiled at her. 'Marriage is a difficult state at the best of times. In the first flush of passion most people do not think it so, but it demands self-control, tolerance, and sometimes heavy sacrifice. Such qualities are not common in our society. Best of all, a life partner should also be a friend.'

'It seems idyllic, but almost a fantasy,' she agreed.

'It can happen, my dear. And when it does nothing can be more fulfilling. Well, I must save my sermon until Sunday, but you must come to see me if you feel the need.'

The door had scarcely closed upon him before Isabel Rushford voiced her displeasure.

'Why, I wonder, would your uncle consider that either of you girls might wish to see him privately? Your own mama is the person to advise you.'

'I think he meant only to be kind,' Letty murmured. 'After all, it is his calling...'

Mrs Rushford sniffed. Her regular attendance at the Abbey services owed nothing to religion, but she enjoyed her role as the tragic widow, and the opportunity to gossip. Now she turned on India.

'I must hope that you intend to change your gown before his lordship's visit,' she snapped. 'That bombazine is positively dreary.'

'It is the warmest thing I have,' India told her simply. 'Mama, the weather is so bitter, and this house is very cold. You will not expect me to freeze to please Lord Isham?'

'Must you defy me at every turn? I know that the black silk with the inset trimming has been turned and dyed, but it is more becoming. You will please wear it.'

Delighted though she was by Isham's offer, Mrs Rushford viewed his coming visit with some apprehension. Privately she expected him to choose Letty as his bride, in spite of his suggestion that the girls should decide between them. At all costs India must be prevented from seeing him alone. She had given her promise not to cause him to withdraw, but would she be able to keep to it?

She now felt that she must play her highest card. 'Think of your brother,' she coaxed. 'He is sure to learn of something through Isham. His lordship must have several livings in his gift.'

Even Letty giggled. 'Giles as a parson, Mama? He would not hear of it!'

'Hold your tongue, you foolish child! Giles will decide for himself.'

'Most certainly he will!' India gave her sister a

speaking glance. The transformation in their mother was extraordinary.

Vanished was yesterday's shrinking invalid. Mrs Rushford was already relishing her position as mother of the future Lady Isham. Naturally, her influence would be welcomed by her powerful relatives.

'Isham does not strike me as a man who will be easily persuaded,' India murmured.

'Perhaps not at the moment, but a wife is in a privileged position. Then it will be different, mark my words!'

The prospect gave India no comfort. The sinking sensation in the pit of her stomach was increasing by the minute as the dreaded interview approached. Now she prayed that his lordship had reconsidered his outrageous proposal. He had had time to sleep on it. Perhaps he had already changed his mind.

She could not rely upon such a happy outcome, and she could do no more than pick at the simple meal of cold meats which awaited them.

'Eat up, my girl!' her mother urged. 'A lack of food will cause you to feel faint. Isham must not believe you to be subject to fits of the vapours and you are already much too pale. It is such a pity that we are still in mourning. I wonder if you should change again… perhaps the grey?'

India rebelled at that. 'Mama, it cannot matter. What we wear is not of the least importance. Lord Isham met us yesterday, when we wore our plain round morning-gowns. He can be under no illusion as to our looks.'

'Do as I say!' came the furious retort. 'Letty must change too. At present you remind me of nothing so much as washerwomen.'

There was nothing more to be said, but when they

reached Letty's room she seized India's hand and looked at her with anguished eyes.

'India, I beg of you! Do not go through with this! You should not sacrifice yourself for me.'

'I don't know what you mean,' India lied gallantly. 'Nothing has been decided yet. You know that I hope to win more time...'

'Pray don't try to deceive me. I know you too well... You mean to take him, don't you?'

'I mean to talk to him. As I said, we do not know him. Possibly he is more reasonable than we imagine. I may be able to persuade him to wait, at least until Giles returns.'

'But how will that help us?'

'Giles may have heard of some position which would restore our fortunes...' Privately, India thought this unlikely, but she refused to give up hope. 'Meantime, I must see Isham on my own. Mama will not hear of a delay. One of us will be handfasted to that insolent creature before we can blink an eye.'

Letty still looked troubled. She only half believed her sister, but she promised to talk their mama into allowing India a private interview with his lordship.

'But only if you will give me your word...?'

'Letty, I am not the stuff of martyrs. If all else fails I might agree to an engagement. I could break it later.'

'I suppose so.' Letty gave her a watery smile. 'I feel so selfish, dearest, to have refused outright.'

'Never that.' India looked at the clock. 'Help me now. Isham is sure to be on time...'

She was right. They had not long to wait. As the clock struck four Isham was announced and shown into the parlour.

As he bowed to her mother India stole a critical look

at him. He had exchanged his riding garb for more formal garb, but the perfect tailoring of his plain blue coat served only to emphasise his massive, heavily muscled frame. There was nothing of the dandy about him and she guessed correctly that once dressed he gave his attire no further thought.

His manner was correct, his bow perfection, but his presence shattered the genteel atmosphere in the parlour. India had the impression that a strong wind had blown away all the conventions of polite society.

There was no obvious reason for this. An aristocrat to his fingertips, like many big men he moved with ease and grace. To her relief she was spared his penetrating stare on this occasion.

Instead, he engaged her mother in conversation. 'I hope I see you much recovered, ma'am,' he murmured. 'I was distressed to learn of your indisposition.'

'It was nothing, my lord.' Mrs Rushford waved aside all mention of her previous ailments. 'Merely a headache brought on by this bitter weather. Sir, it is a pleasure to welcome you to Abbot's Quincey.'

Isham bowed again. 'You know this part of the country well?'

'I was born here, and so were my girls at…at the Grange.'

'Ah, yes!' Isham betrayed no trace of embarrassment at this mention of his recently acquired property. 'I have just come from there. There is much to be done, I fear. Perhaps you will be good enough to advise me?'

India glanced at her sister. His lordship had found a sure way to her mother's heart. For the next half-hour she was forced to listen to a discussion about the necessary improvements to the Grange, and the merits of the various workmen in the village.

She glanced down at her hands and found that they were trembling. She hid them at once in the folds of her gown but nothing could remedy the leaden feeling in the pit of her stomach. She had summoned all her courage for the coming interview but it was deserting her fast. Now she longed only to get it over with.

It seemed an age before her mother rose and summoned Letty to her side.

'Will you excuse us, sir?' she said. 'India would like to speak to you.'

Isham merely bowed and held the door for them. As it closed he turned and leaned against it. For a panic-stricken moment India felt trapped. Once again she was forced to suffer that long, assessing stare.

'So you are to be the sacrificial lamb?' his lordship drawled at last. 'What a fate, my dear!'

Chapter Three

It was an unfortunate beginning, but India kept her eyes fixed firmly on the carpet.

'You speak in riddles, sir,' she said. 'Won't you sit down?' Her shaking hands she kept well hidden. It was impossible to think with that large figure looming over her.

Isham sank into a chair. 'Demure, Miss Rushford? The role does not suit you. I prefer the termagant who barred my entrance yesterday…'

India longed to tell him that his preference was not of the slightest interest to her, but she refused to be drawn. There was too much at stake. 'You wished to speak to me, I believe?'

'Oh, I thought you wished to speak to me.' The lazy eyes roved over her, and she was reminded of Letty's comment. Now she too felt naked beneath this creature's gaze. Anger stiffened her resolve. The man was impossible. Well, he should find her a worthy adversary.

'My uncle tells me that you seek a bride,' she said in icy tones. 'I understand that you have offered for me.'

'For either of you, Miss Rushford,' he corrected. It
was a deliberate insult and India's rage increased as his
mocking voice continued.

'Your sister is the more conventional beauty, of
course, though admittedly you have a certain something. In London I remarked it often.'

'In London?' India stared at him. 'I think we have
not met before...'

'I did not say that we had met. You did not frequent
the gaming rooms, but your height alone attracts attention.'

India coloured, which added to her feelings of mortification. She bit her lips upon a hot retort, but he gave
her no time to answer him.

'Pray do not feel embarrassed,' the maddening voice
continued. 'It is not a fault. Often I have observed that
tall women have a certain elegance and style which
must be the envy of their shorter cousins.'

'You are too kind!' India gritted out. 'Have you
other views on my appearance, sir? My nose, is perhaps, a little too long, and my mouth too wide?'

He was beside her in an instant. Then, to her horror,
a large hand cupped her chin and turned her face to
his, 'No, no! Don't underestimate yourself. Those eyes
are well enough, and your skin is flawless. As to the
hair? Well...not quite in the common way, perhaps...'

India struck his hand away, 'I could always wear a
wig,' she cried in fury.

'That's better!' Isham was laughing down at her.
'Now you are more yourself. We shall deal well together, my dear, but only if we are honest with each
other. I can't bear missish ways.'

India did not answer him. This interview was not

going as she'd planned. He'd teased her into losing her temper and shedding her cool composure.

Now she tried to remember what she had meant to say. 'You go too quickly, my lord,' she murmured. 'I do not know you.'

'But you know of me, do you not? Now where is the stumbling-block? Is it the gambling, or the opera-dancer?'

It was too much. India rose to her feet and faced him squarely. 'Are you trying to be offensive, sir? If so, I must wonder why you are here.'

'I'm here to offer for you,' he grinned. 'Will you take me, ma'am? I promise to forget the opera-dancer.'

His tone had changed, but India would not be mollified. Even so, she chose her next words carefully.

'My uncle mentioned certain arrangements, sir. May I hear them from your own lips?'

Isham's expression hardened. 'If you will have it then, here is what I propose.' In a cool tone he listed details of the marriage settlement. 'Is that satisfactory?'

'Perfectly, I thank you. And your own requirements?' India was aware that her apparently mercenary attitude had angered him, but she did not care. He himself had proposed this contract. In effect, he was buying her as a man might buy a slave in some Eastern market. She would not pretend that anything other than this settlement would persuade her to accept him.

'I need an heir.' His bluntness now matched her own. 'I must also have a hostess, as I intend to enter politics. My wife must be able to receive the highest in the land and entertain them royally.'

India felt a little flicker of interest. 'Shall you go with the Whigs or the Tories?'

'With the Whigs. I take it you have no objections?'

'Not in the least.' Secretly India was pleased. The policies of the Whigs were much more to her taste.

'Then we are agreed?' Isham held out his hand.

'Not yet, my lord. I need more time to consider your proposal…'

'Nonsense!' he said roughly. 'Had you not made up your mind you would not be here. Pray spare me these attempts at maidenly convention.'

India hesitated.

'Come!' he continued. 'You make your decision now, ma'am, or my offer does not stand.'

'But where is the need for haste?'

'I have my reasons. I do not propose to burden you with them at this present time.'

'Then perhaps an engagement…?'

'Which you would seek to break at the earliest opportunity? No, my dear, you must give me credit for some intelligence. If you accept we shall be wed by Christmas.'

'So soon? It is but weeks away…'

He smiled at her discomfiture and it infuriated her further. She had suspected him of being ruthless. Now she was sure of it. She was in no position to refuse him and well he knew it. He must have guessed at the pressure which had been brought to bear on her. Now he had added to it with his threat to withdraw.

'Let us understand each other,' he said at last. 'I shall keep to the terms of our agreement if you will keep to yours. Your feelings towards me need not signify…'

India glared at him and he laughed.

'Will you deny that you detest me, ma'am? I should not believe you. If looks could kill I should now be lying at your feet.'

India was reduced to silence. She had never met a

stranger character. What other man would offer to wed
a woman who disliked him? She should have refused
him there and then, but something held her back, and
it was not only the thought of material advantage. With
this man her life would most certainly not be dull, and
what was the alternative? Letty would marry and she
herself would wither on the vine, reduced to caring for
a petulant invalid who gave her neither thanks nor affection.

Suddenly she held out her hand, rather to her own
surprise. 'We have a bargain, sir.'

Isham took her hand and kissed it, and as he did so
she felt an odd little frisson of excitement. Those warm
lips seemed to burn her skin and she drew back
quickly.

'Shall we tell Mama?' she asked.

As she had expected, Mrs Rushford was overcome
with joy. She would have embraced Lord Isham, but
to India's amusement he managed to avoid this fate.

Her sister was her main concern. Letty looked
stricken to the heart.

India made as if to go to her, but Isham forestalled
her, taking her sister to one side. It was to be some
months before India discovered what was said on that
occasion, but whatever it was removed the troubled
look from Letty's brow.

Oh, he was clever, India thought bitterly. He knew
exactly what to say to ingratiate himself with every
member of her family.

Later she tried to question Letty, but for once her
sister was reticent.

'You have not even reproached me,' India murmured
in surprise. 'I thought you were against this match.'

'I was.' Letty's look was positively smug. 'But you
know best…'

India could not help but wonder. Had Isham promised to help Giles, or Oliver? She would not put it past
him to rally support in every way he knew. She tried
to question the uncommunicative Letty further, but
without success.

From then on she found herself with little time to
think. Preparations for the wedding came upon her
thick and fast. Isham would not hear of a delay, in spite
of Mrs Rushford's half-hearted protests that it was already late November.

In spite of her dislike of Isham, India could only
admire the way in which he handled her mother's objections. She noted wryly that he stifled possible argument before it could begin. Mrs Rushford was given
no opportunity to insist upon her grandiose plans for
an elaborate ceremony.

'I would not place such a strain upon you, ma'am,'
Isham murmured smoothly. 'Your health must be our
first consideration…'

India almost giggled. For once her mother's hypo-
chondria had been cleverly used against her.

His lordship was not finished. 'Time is short, as you
have pointed out. I should not have ventured such a
brief engagement except that of necessity you will wish
to observe the proprieties…'

Isabel Rushford stared at him.

'I see that you agree with me,' he continued. 'Owing
to your recent loss we cannot celebrate in the style we
might have wished. Otherwise the marriage might have
taken place in London. As matters stand a simple ceremony would be best.'

It was a statement of intent, rather than a question, and India could not forbear to smile. It was what he had intended from the first, she suspected, but he had advanced upon her mother in good order, reminding her of the need for decorum, but sweetening the pill with apparent consideration for her health.

She caught his eye and surprised a wicked twinkle. Then he turned back to her mama.

'Ma'am, you will have so much to do, and I am sorry for it, but when the announcement appears in the *Morning Post* you may expect a flood of letters...' He sighed. 'It is always the way upon these occasions, I fear.'

This happy prospect succeeded in lessening Mrs Rushford's disappointment. Smiling fondly upon her future son-in-law, she left the betrothed couple to themselves.

Isham grinned at his bride-to-be. 'Well?' he said. 'How was that? I take it you have no wish for some fantastic circus?'

'Would it make a difference if I had?' India was very much upon her dignity. She regretted that he had seen her smiling at his machinations.

'Not in the least, you prickly creature! Even so, I imagine that you will wish for bride-clothes and a trousseau?'

For an awful moment India thought that he was about to offer her money. That would be the last straw. Already she felt like some commodity in the market-place.

His lazy gaze rested upon her face. 'No matter,' he announced. 'We shall be a law unto ourselves. In this case the bride shall have her trousseau after we are wed.'

'It will be unnecessary, sir. You have pointed out yourself that I am still in mourning.'

It was a brutal reminder of his part in her father's death, and Isham's expression changed. 'As you wish,' he said shortly. 'Though the convention does not apply to a bride.'

India made no reply. She thought she saw a look of impatience in his eyes, but he changed the subject.

'I leave for London in the morning,' he announced. 'I shall be away for several days. Have you any commissions for me?'

'None, my lord, though I wish you a safe journey.'

'Thank you, my dear.' His tone was ironic. 'For that, at least, I must be grateful. India, may we not drop some of the formality? My name is Anthony.'

'Very well, my lord...I mean, Anthony... When do you return?'

'You will be spared my company until Thursday of next week. I have other matters to attend...'

India guessed that these important matters most probably concerned a visit to the opera-dancer, but she thrust the thought aside. It was no concern of hers.

'I hope to return with my half-brother, Henry,' Isham continued. 'He will wish to support me at the ceremony.'

It was an unpleasant reminder of the course to which she had committed herself, but now that the decision had been made India was resolved to play her part.

'I look forward to meeting him,' she murmured politely. She was beginning to feel ashamed of her curt manner. Isham had done his best to treat her with civility in spite of her rudeness. On an impulse she held out her hand, but his lordship did not take it. There was something in his expression as he looked at her which she did not understand. For once his manner appeared abstracted.

'Tell me,' he said at last. 'Do you go abroad much in the evenings?'

India stared at him. It was the oddest question.

'No, we do not,' she replied tartly. Isham must know that Mrs Rushford was not in a position to keep horses or a carriage.

'I believe that on occasion you have the use of Sir James's carriage?' he persisted. 'May I beg you not to use it after dusk?'

India stiffened. She was not yet Lord Isham's wife. Why should he think it proper to dictate to her? She would go out as she wished.

He saw her look, smiled, and shook his head, but then his face grew grave. 'There is good reason for my warning, India. You have not heard of the unrest?'

'No,' she answered in surprise. 'What is that, my lord?'

'There is disaffection in this area, and it is growing. Certain men are banding together in large groups. They roam abroad at night, smashing machinery and burning factories.'

'But why? Who are they?'

'They are mostly labourers from the framework knitting industry.'

'But why destroy their means of livelihood?'

'That livelihood is almost non-existent now, I fear. The war with France has reduced demand for their stockings and export of Midlands cotton goods has fallen by a third. The harvest has been poor this year and food prices are extremely high. On reduced wages they cannot afford to eat. Half the local population is on public relief.'

'Then one can hardly blame them,' India cried.

'Their despair is understandable, my dear, but their actions cannot be condoned. The mood is ugly, they are heavily armed with muskets, pistols and hatchets. And there has been at least one death.'

India gasped. 'We have heard nothing of this,' she said slowly. 'But Anthony, they could have no reason to attack a private carriage. We ourselves do not go out at night, but both our uncles come to visit us.'

If Isham was pleased that she had used his given name of her own accord he gave no sign of it.

'I have no wish to frighten you,' he told her gently. 'Yet a mob is sometimes carried away with a strange energy of its own. It needs only a core of hotheads; even a few will serve to whip the others to a frenzy. Then the original reasons for their actions are forgotten. Anyone may become a target.'

She shuddered, but he took her hand and pressed it. 'You will be safe indoors,' he comforted. 'And to date they have not ventured forth in daylight.'

Once again he raised her fingers to his lips. And this time she did not draw away until he took a step towards her. India stood very still. Pray heaven he would not try to embrace her. He was a stranger still. She would need more time to grow accustomed to this man who had come so unexpectedly into her quiet life. Yet again his curious antennae warned him of her feelings. He merely bowed and released her hand.

India felt like a gauche schoolgirl. Would she ever be at ease with him? He was unlike anyone she had met before. In his presence she was aware of the raw power beneath his formal manner. Charm and courtesy could not disguise it. She was about to marry a dangerous man.

He gave her no time to ponder further. With a brief word of farewell he took his leave.

They had expected no more visitors that day, but Isham had not been gone above an hour when Sir James Perceval arrived. He hurried into the parlour eager to hear their news.

'Well, my dears,' he said expectantly. 'How did you go on with Isham?'

'Oh, James, such news!' Isabel Rushford could not hide her delight. 'India is to wed his lordship!'

Sir James took India in his arms and kissed her soundly. 'Well done, my child! Isham is a lucky man, and as for yourself, you could not have chosen a better.'

Forcing a smile, India thanked him. She was not surprised when he turned to her mama. 'If only Hester had some of India's good sense,' he mourned. 'Now, perhaps, as India is betrothed, she will try to persuade my wilful daughter to follow her example.'

Wisely, Isabel said nothing. There was no love lost between herself and this particular niece. India might be difficult at times, but she was a paragon of obedience compared with Hester. She considered privately that the girl had been indulged beyond reason. Now there was no controlling her.

'Well, India, what do you say?' Sir James looked anxious. 'Will you speak to her?'

'With pleasure, Uncle, but I cannot promise that she will pay me any heed.' India smiled up at him.

Hester was her dearest friend, but she made no secret of her views on marriage. She would be no man's chattel. The news of India's betrothal would bring her to Lilac Cottage at the first opportunity. India was sure of it.

* * *

She was not mistaken. On the following morning Hester was announced and, characteristically, she did not beat about the bush.

'What's this I hear?' she demanded. 'Father tells us that you are to be wed.'

'It's true!' India coloured. 'Oh, Hester, I had meant to come and explain to you myself, but it wasn't possible.'

'I can imagine!' Hester said drily. 'It came as a shock to all of us. We had no idea, you see.'

'Nor had I.'

Hester studied her cousin's face intently. 'Then it is as I thought? You were coerced into taking Isham?'

'Not exactly. I made the decision myself.'

'Helped, I make no doubt, by the threat of hysterics?' Hester's opinion of Mrs Rushford matched that lady's dislike of her. 'India, this is too important for you to be swayed in such a way. We are speaking of your entire future. Forgive me if I am too outspoken, but I care about your happiness.'

'I know it, Hester dear, but let me explain. Mama was for the match, of course, but your father too approved of it.'

'He would. Dear Father! He sees no other course for any woman as far as security is concerned.' Hester was indignant, but then her expression softened, and she smiled. 'I fear my parents are biased. Theirs was a love match, as you know. They have been so happy together. I cannot blame them for wanting the same for others, but you can imagine the pressure put on me to wed. I'm sorry for their distress, but I won't agree.'

'Your case is different,' India said quietly. 'There is not the same necessity for you to earn a living.'

'I may have to,' Hester laughed. 'Should Father try to marry me off against my will I intend to run away.'

India returned her cousin's smile. 'That will never happen and you know it. Both your parents adore you.'

'That affection might be strained if I continue to argue for women to have freedom of choice. Yet look at the case of our missing Marchioness. Tell me, if you can, under what compulsion did Louise Hanslope agree to marry an ancient roué three times her age? There's a fate that my father would never have forced on me, nor even your mother on you. You have heard nothing more as to her whereabouts?'

'Not a word. Have you?'

'I've heard a good deal of speculation. You may take your choice of a murder committed by the Marquis, or elopement with a paramour.'

'Most probably she just fled. Her life must have been a living hell.' India turned away to hide her own sadness.

Hester saw it and returned to the matter in hand. 'Why are we discussing the Marchioness?' she demanded. 'What of you? Have you really accepted Isham?'

'I have, but it is not quite what you think. There was so much to consider. I gave it a good deal of thought. Your father cannot continue to support us...'

'Stuff!' Hester exploded. 'He would do so willingly. What is more, he would not forgive himself if he thought such a consideration had influenced your decision.'

India looked steadily at her friend. 'Will you tell me the truth?' she asked. 'I believe that our assets were not enough to cover the debt to Isham. Did Uncle find the balance?'

Hester would not meet her eyes, but neither would she lie. 'There was some talk of it,' she admitted uncomfortably. 'But it is no great matter.'

'It is to me, and then, as you know, there is Letty to consider. Under the circumstances Oliver Wells could not have offered for her. A connection with Lord Isham will alter the matter.'

'And Giles? What has he to say to this?'

'We have not heard from him, but there is little he can do. His own inheritance has gone. Mama is hoping that Isham will do something for him.'

'Well, at least your mother will be able to live in comfort.' Hester's expression mirrored her disgust. 'Have you considered yourself in all of this?'

'Of course I have. Think about it, Hester. What is the alternative? Letty and I had but two choices. Mrs Guarding might have taken one of us to teach at the Academy, but more likely we should have had to become paid companions to some lady, and Mama cannot be left alone.'

'I see.' Hester's tone was grim. 'You will not wonder at my desire to stand up for the rights of women. We are little more than chattels.'

She stopped abruptly at the sight of India's stricken look. 'There I go again!' she confessed. 'Tact is not my strongest point, but I get so angry when I think how little say we have in the conduct of our lives. Now tell me, what do you know of Isham?'

'Very little.' India admitted. 'I haven't spent above three hours in his company.'

'But are you quite determined to wed him?'

'I am. Pray don't try to dissuade me, Hester. I have given my word and I won't go back on it.'

'I see.' Hester looked thoughtful. 'Well, if it must

be, you could do worse, my love. His lordship is no fool. His intellect can only be respected. I have read some of his speeches...'

'He told me that he thinks of going into politics...'

'He should do so. Men such as he are badly needed in Government.'

'Have you met him?'

'No, but I should like to do so. He is sound on conditions in the northern mills. His place is in Cheshire, is it not? He will be aware of the high unemployment in the north. These days trade is almost non-existent, or so I hear. So many have been ruined by Napoleon's blockade of the European ports...'

'But surely the Government must help?'

'The Government will do nothing, India, other than to order in troops to stamp out disaffection. Repression rather than compassion would appear to be the order of the day. Isham opposes this policy, I believe, although I am no expert on such matters.'

India was startled by such vehemence. 'Do you think so highly of him?'

'I do, but from your tone I see that you do not.'

'I don't know him, Hester, but he is the strangest creature. I find him somewhat overwhelming...'

'I hear that he is no Adonis, but surely that will not weigh with you?'

'Of course not. He has presence, but...'

'But you are a little afraid of him? You surprise me, India. In no time he will learn to love you. Then he will realise what a jewel he has won.'

'You are biased, my dear. The plain fact is that his lordship needs an heir. That is his only reason for making me this offer.' India stopped. She had said more than she intended, and her bitterness must be apparent.

'Nonsense!' Hester said roundly. 'The man could have chosen any of a dozen females. I see that you do not find him very lover-like…'

'No! At least he has spared me professions of his undying affection.'

'Very sensible of him! He must have known that you would not believe it. Confess now, you would have despised him for uttering such sentiments?'

She was rewarded with a reluctant smile. 'How well you know me, Hester. I should not have welcomed falsehood. Whatever else, Isham is always frank.'

'Well then?'

'Oh, I don't know. I suppose he injures my pride. He has a most unfortunate knack of putting me in the wrong.'

'How so?'

'Perhaps it's because I am so quick to judge him. Only yesterday I had thought he meant to dictate to me when he warned me not to travel after dusk even close to home. I let him see my anger. Then I found that he was thinking only of my safety. I felt mortified by my own stupidity.'

Hester nodded sagely. 'He was thinking of the Luddites. You would do well to heed him.'

'Luddites? Who are they?'

'He did not tell you?'

'He said something about disaffected labourers. I'll admit I felt some sympathy for their cause…'

'So did I until Father told us of their violence and now, he says, it is gone beyond attempts to destroy the machines and the factories. They are firing barns and hayricks and terrorising the countryside.'

'Could he not speak to them? Uncle James is a reasonable man. If he promised to address their grievances…?'

'What could he do for them? He cannot give them bread or work. Besides, no one knows who they are. They wear masks or blacken their faces, and visit savage retribution on those who inform against them.'

'Can nothing be done?'

'The Government is sending troops. They fear that we may follow France into revolution if these uprisings spread.'

'The Terror? In England? Surely not.'

'It happened in France just twenty years ago, and this movement is growing fast. It is well organised, with secret signs and passwords, and men are "twisted in", or recruited, with special oaths.'

'That does not sound like the work of the ordinary labourer.'

'You are right. So many of them can neither read nor write, but letters have been sent to their employers and even to the Prime Minister, signed "General Ludd". It seems that nothing will stop them, though the penalty for frame-breaking is already transportation and may become a capital offence.'

India shuddered. 'Thank heavens that Mama and Letty know nothing of this as yet. They are gone to the Vicarage this morning to spread the joyous news.'

It was difficult to hide her bitterness. 'I suppose I must tell them?' she asked.

'India, they are sure to hear of it from one source or another.' Hester looked thoughtful. 'You are right about the working men, I feel sure. There is something behind all this—some controlling intelligence which is playing upon their baser instincts.'

'But they must be desperate,' India protested.

'True! They are being forced to starve, but this is more than a plea to right their grievances. Men fighting for a just cause are often joined by those who have private scores to settle. Father is sure of it.' Hester rose to her feet. 'You will be careful, won't you?'

'I doubt if anyone has a score to settle with this family,' India told her with a rueful smile. 'I can't recall that we have injured anyone.'

'Of course not, dearest.' Hester embraced her fondly.

'And shall you attend my wedding? I should like that above anything.'

'You shall have my support, my love, and you take with you my good wishes for a long and happy life.'

India was tempted to tease a little.

'You shall not care to follow my example?' she asked wickedly.

'Great heavens, no! My dream is to have a small house of my own. If my portion remains in my own hands I should write, surrounded by my books.'

'Then that is what I shall wish for you. It sounds idyllic.'

'It is unlikely to happen. Mother insists that I try another Season in the hope that I shall "take" this time. She is such an optimist. My last attempt was a disaster.'

'It was no worse than mine, I think…'

'Oh yes it was! I am too outspoken and the gentlemen fled in droves…' Hester laughed out loud. 'I did make one conquest, you'll be pleased to hear. Can you believe it? I was attacked in the Duchess of Sutherland's library by some ancient lecher who could hardly stand without the aid of a stick. I won't name names, but my admirer was stone-deaf, which must account for it. Hugo had to rescue me. You should have seen his face...'

Her amusement was infectious and both girls dissolved into peals of glee.

Chapter Four

Her cousin's visit had cheered India beyond measure. She respected Hester's judgement and her good sense. It had been pleasant to find that her forthright relative had not reproached her for her decision to wed Lord Isham. She had even expressed her admiration for his lordship's character.

It was strange indeed to find that others thought so highly of him. India wished that she could do the same, but always, at the back of her mind, lay the notion that, however indirectly, he had been the cause of her father's death. That she could not forgive.

Well, she would be spared his company for the next few days. With a sigh she made her way to the kitchen. Letty and her mother would welcome a steaming bowl of soup on their return from the Vicarage.

She'd started her preparations on the previous day, boiling the piece of mutton for a full two hours to make the stock. After straining it, she'd added veal knuckle and her vegetables and herbs, and simmered it again. Now it needed only a further straining and the addition of egg-white to clear it. After a final straining she would add the diced meat, parsley and a glass of sherry.

She was tasting the result when a bustle in the hall announced the return of Letty and her mother.

'Mmm! Something smells good!' Letty had come to find her. 'What is that?'

'It is Mock Turtle soup,' India told her proudly. 'I'm boasting, but it does taste good. Help me carry it through. Then you shall tell me all your gossip.'

'There isn't much, except that the Earl of Yardley hopes to buy the Abbey. What a blessing that would be! We might be rid of the old Marquis for ever.'

'Does Uncle William think it likely that the Marquis will sell?'

'He doesn't know, but he hopes so. It was an evil day for the village when that creature came to live amongst us. Thank heavens that he is now too old to ruin the local girls…'

'Letty!' Mrs Rushford was scandalised at this reference to unbridled lust.

Yet on this occasion even the gentle Letty held her ground. 'Mama, you won't deny it?'

'I do not, but it is hardly a subject for polite conversation. I don't know what girls are coming to these days.'

'Things might have been so different had Yardley not lost everything to him,' India murmured sadly. 'That was a tragedy…'

For once her mother agreed with her. 'The Earl was said to care for nothing after he cast off his heir. Such folly! And just because the Viscount wished to marry a Catholic! As if that signified a jot!'

India hid a smile. Her mother's feeling for religion was not strong.

'Of course she was also a foreigner,' Isabel continued. 'French, I believe, but what could that matter where an inheritance was concerned?'

India felt that she was right, even if for the wrong reasons. 'It was prejudice, I fear, and born of ignorance, but what a price he paid! One shudders to think of the despair which drove him finally to suicide.'

'Well, let us wish the new Earl well,' Letty cried. 'Perhaps Sywell will sell to him. What do you think?'

'There may be a possibility. The Marquis is deep in debt.' Mrs Rushford smirked. 'He cannot pay his bills and the tradesmen will no longer supply him. All his servants are gone, except for his man, Burneck, and certain females whom he hires in town.' She pursed her lips. 'They may or they may not be housekeepers.'

India was no longer attending. Her thoughts were far away. Was Isham really the monster she had thought him? His interests were much in line with her own. She too had been horrified by tales of conditions in the north, where women and children were treated as little more than slaves. Now, it seemed, there were abuses closer to hand.

This was brought home to her three days later, when she heard a commotion in the kitchen. Screams and shouting disturbed the normally quiet household.

'Whatever is it, Martha?' India hurried towards the cause of the disturbance, to find Martha clutching a ragged urchin in either hand.

'Nasty, dirty critturs, miss! I found them hiding in the woodshed.'

India inspected the two urchins. Neither, she guessed, could be ten years old. 'They are children, Martha,' she reproved. Then she addressed the sturdier of the two. 'What are you doing here?' she asked.

The child faced her defiantly. 'We meant no 'arm,' he told her. 'We ain't got nowhere else to stay. They burned the place about us.'

'What place was that?'

'The factory, miss.'

'And when did this happen?'

'Night afore last. We bin walking since…'

India noticed that he seemed unable to take his eyes from the freshly baked bread which lay cooling on the kitchen table. Cursing herself for a thoughtless fool, she cut several thick slices and buttered them with a lavish hand.

'Here!' she pushed the food towards the boys. 'You must be very hungry.'

They needed no persuasion and began to wolf the bread at speed.

'There is no need for such haste,' she smiled. 'There is plenty more…'

They took her at her word, and whilst they were eating she examined them more closely. Stick-thin, they were caked with soot and grime and both were barefoot. The smaller child, in particular, seemed unable to control his shivering.

'Come closer to the fire,' she urged. 'You foolish children! Why did you not knock upon our door for shelter? You might have frozen to death in last night's frost…' Inspecting their tattered rags, she thought it highly likely. 'Martha, fetch me a couple of warm shawls, if you please…'

'Now, miss, you ain't planning to wrap them up in your good shawls? These young 'uns will be covered in lice…'

'I did not ask for your advice,' India said coldly. 'Do as I say.'

'Mistress Rushford won't like it!' Muttering darkly, Martha left the room.

That at least was true. India could only be thankful her mama had summoned Letty and was making a further round of morning calls. She herself had only managed to avoid that tiresome fate by mentioning the likelihood that Isham would return that day. She could imagine her mother's reaction to the discovery of two filthy urchins in her kitchen.

Neither child had answered her question. 'Do tell me who you are,' she coaxed. 'Your parents must be half-mad with anxiety…'

'Ain't got none. We be orphings.' The taller of the two regarded her with a wary eye. He must have felt that he owed her something, for he volunteered the information that his name was Joe.

'And your friend?'

'This 'ere is Tom. 'E be my bruvver.'

There was no reaction from the smaller child and India eyed him with concern. True, he had eaten, but in a curiously mechanical way. Now he was slumped in a corner by the fire gazing into the flames. He had not uttered a word.

'Your brother is very quiet,' she said anxiously. 'Does he not speak at all?'

'Ain't said a word since the burning. Tom were that afeared, miss.' For the first time his bravado slipped and he rubbed a grimy hand across his eyes.

'It must have been a terrible experience. I think your brother is suffering from shock. Can you tell me what happened?' India took the shawls from a sullen Martha and wrapped them about the children's shoulders.

'We wuz asleep beneath the frames when we 'eard 'em coming. They broke all the windows first to get inside. We 'id behind the cotton bales when they smashed up the machines. We thought they'd gone, but then we smelled the smoke. It went up mighty fast…'

'But what were you doing there?'

He had no time to answer, for at that point a burning log dislodged itself and fell into the hearth, creating a shower of sparks. The younger child leapt to his feet and uttered a series of piercing shrieks.

India gathered him to her. 'There, there,' she soothed. 'You are in no danger here.'

'Which is more than can be said for some,' Martha sniffed. 'Don't touch him, miss. I doubt but that you'll catch some nasty ailment.'

'Martha, you are beginning to try my patience,' India said in icy tones. 'Have you no work to do?'

'More than enough, Miss India, and me on my own to do it all. We'll soon see what the mistress has to say…' With this threat she flounced out of the room.

The child had quietened down, and India turned once more to Joe. 'You didn't answer me. I asked what you were doing in the factory?'

'Why, miss, we wuz working there…'

'But surely you are not old enough to lift the bales, or to work the frames?'

Joe grinned at her ignorance. 'We cleans the place. They send us beneath the frames to sweep the floors, but sometimes we 'as to deal with stuff as breaks.'

'Is that not dangerous work, more suitable for grown men?'

'Too big, miss. It's only little 'uns as can get into some places…'

'A likely story!' Martha had returned on the pretext of having forgotten her broom. 'Miss India, these are climbing boys. Look at their arms and legs!'

'Certainly these are burns.' India began to examine the skinny limbs of the child beside her, and was horrified at what she found. 'They must be due to the fire...'

'Nonsense!' Martha was no longer troubling to be civil, sure of her mistress's support. Now she gave a triumphant laugh and, marching over to Joe, she lifted away the rags upon his arm. 'Callouses, miss, and old ones at that. These are not fresh burns.' She bent down to reveal Joe's battered knees. 'I've seen enough climbing boys in my time to know that these come from climbing chimneys. Why, he smells of soot and grime, the little liar! It's my belief that these two have run away from their master...'

'We didn't, and I ain't no liar!' Joe was stung into an angry denial and was cuffed about the head for his pains.

'Touch him again and you will lose your place!' India was furious.

'Some loss!' Martha stalked away.

India turned back to Joe. 'Don't be afraid,' she said. 'You may tell me the truth. Are you climbing boys?'

'We wuz, but even without our clothes we got too big.'

India gazed at him in horror. 'Are you telling me that you were sent into the chimneys naked?'

'Yes, Miss. They only want little 'uns, you know.'

'But there is nothing of you. You are both so thin, and so very young. How old are you, Joe?'

'Dunno, miss, but I think I might be ten. We are both too old for the chimneys...'

'But Tom is even younger, is he not?'

'Not as young as some. Master said that four years old is best. ''Small boys for small flues,'' he said.'

India felt sick. It took her some moments to recover her composure.

'Barbarous!' she murmured. 'What a monster! Did you run away from him?'

'No, Miss, he sold us to the overseer at the factory.'

'He sold you!' India could scarcely believe her ears, yet it was clear that the child was telling the truth. 'Who is this man?'

But Joe had become uncommunicative. She set about trying to regain his confidence, but now, she noticed, he kept a wary eye upon the door.

'No one shall harm you further, Joe,' she promised. 'Tell me his name…'

It took some coaxing and the offer of more food, but at last she got her way.

'You won't send us back to him?' Joe pleaded.

'Certainly not! It is my intention to have him brought before the magistrate. You have nothing more to fear from him, but I cannot proceed without his name.'

'It's Meester Bates,' Joe said reluctantly.

It was at this point that the back door opened to reveal a red-faced man upon the doorstep. He was a burly individual of unprepossessing appearance.

Tom gave a shriek and hid behind India's skirts, whilst even Joe retreated.

'You have not heard of the practice of knocking for admittance?' India enquired coldly.

'Beg pardon, ma'am, but I wuz sent a message that the lads wuz 'ere.'

It was at this point that India promised herself that Martha would most certainly have to go. She drew herself up to her full height.

'And you are?'

'Haddon, miss, the overseer from the mill.'

'So you are the man who trades in flesh and blood?'

Haddon didn't like her tone, but she was gentry. It would behove him to keep a civil tongue in his head.

'It wuz good of you to take them in, miss. I wuz that worried about these lads.'

'So worried that you left them sleeping in an empty mill? They might have been burned to death.'

'That weren't my fault. How wuz I to know what was afoot? Now I'll take them off your hands...' He moved purposefully towards the boys, but India stopped him with a lifted hand.

'What do you intend to do with them? The factory is gutted, I believe.'

'Aye, our livelihood is gone, ma'am, but I can sell them on... They cost me a guinea each, and a poor man can't afford to lose so much.'

'You will do no such thing,' India retorted hotly.

'They are my property.' The man was growing sullen. 'You ain't got no call to rob me!'

With an impatient gesture India moved over to the cupboard and reached out for a small bowl. She emptied the contents on to the table and counted out two guineas.

'There!' she said contemptuously. 'Now take your money and go!'

'India! What are you about? Have you quite taken leave of your senses?' Mrs Rushford bustled into the room, followed by Letty and a triumphant Martha.

At her appearance both children had scuttled beneath the table, but Mrs Rushford had seen quite enough. She clutched at the back of a chair and professed herself about to swoon with horror.

'We shall be murdered in our beds,' she announced dramatically.

'By two young children, Mama? I think not!'

'I won't have them here! This man shall take them away…'

'Nay, missus, they ain't mine no more. I bin paid, you see…' The overseer sidled towards the door, anxious to depart before he was asked to return the money.

'What?' The shrill voice rose to a shriek as Isabel caught India by the arm. 'You wicked girl! Have we so much that you can spend it upon two guttersnipes?'

'Mother, he was going to sell them…'

'Well, now he has done so, and to you.' Mrs Rushford tottered and raised a hand to her brow. 'This is the last straw!' she moaned. 'You'll be the death of me!'

Martha hurried over to her mistress. 'Poor lady! Shall Haddon take them after all?' She looked round, but the overseer had vanished.

'He shall not!' India said sternly. 'Martha, since you have taken such an interest in these children, perhaps you will step over to the Vicarage and ask my aunt for some suitable clothing from her stock?'

Martha ignored her.

'I'll go,' said Letty quickly.

'You will do no such thing, miss. Stay where you are!' Mrs Rushford cast an inimical look at India. 'Pray don't think that you deceive me. I see it all now. You had not the least intention of wedding his lordship. From the first you have tried to cause him to withdraw. This piece of folly will be the last straw.'

This unjust accusation stung India into a hot retort, but her own words surprised her.

'If Lord Isham can find no compassion in his heart for two starving children he is not the man I think him,' she cried.

'Do I hear my name?' The deep voice cut through the hubbub and India spun round to find his lordship standing in the doorway.

He crossed the room in two long strides and bowed to her mama. 'Forgive us, ma'am,' he murmured. 'Your door was open. We knocked, but there was no reply, so we took the liberty of entering.' He gave her a charming smile. 'No need to ask how you go on,' he murmured. 'I am happy to see you in such blooming health...'

India caught her sister's eye. Letty was having great difficulty in keeping her countenance, and India looked away in an effort to hide her own amusement.

Mrs Rushford gave Isham a sharp look, but his expression was one of bland insouciance.

He bowed to Letty and then he turned to India and took her hands in his, dropping a light kiss upon her cheek.

'Well, my love, and how do you go on?'

India murmured something, but she felt uncomfortable. He must be aware that he had walked in upon a family quarrel. He squeezed her hands and turned back to her mother.

'Ma'am, I must hope that we do not inconvenience you, but I'd like to present my brother, Henry Salton.'

Mrs Rushford was on her feet in an instant, all smiles as she walked towards Isham's companion. At a first glance he appeared to be a most eligible *parti*. Perhaps an opportunity for Letty?

'What must you think of us, my dear sir, to be receiving you in the kitchen? It is not our usual custom, I assure you...'

'A pleasure, ma'am, no matter where we meet.' The young man's bow was perfection.

To India's relief he engaged her mother at once in polite conversation, following her into the parlour.

Looking round, India saw that Letty had disappeared and Martha too had made a hasty retreat.

'India, what has happened?' Characteristically Isham did not beat about the bush.

'Haven't you guessed? I am in disgrace once more.'

'Not with me. But why?'

'You had best not champion me until you hear the story.'

He smiled. 'I'll be the judge of that. Won't you tell me?'

India kept her story short. She was not looking for approval.

'And where are the boys now?' he asked.

There had been no sound from beneath the table, but India was encouraged. Isham had heard her out in silence, but his face was calm.

She bent down. 'Joe, you can come out. His lordship will not hurt you.'

There was silence for several moments. Then a grimy face appeared.

'Come to me,' she coaxed. 'We wish to speak to you.'

Joe rose to his feet. She guessed that it had taken all his courage to leave his hiding-place, and though he came towards her she noticed that he was careful to keep himself behind his champion.

'Mr Haddon has gone,' she confirmed.

'So now we belongs to you?'

'Well, yes, I suppose you do, although I should not put it quite like that.'

'We don't mind,' Joe said magnanimously. 'Will the old lady let us stay?'

India hid a smile. Her mother would have taken a turn for the worse had she heard herself so described.

Isham began to question the child. India had not thought that he could be so gentle, and Joe answered him readily enough.

Joe had, in fact, moved closer to the massive figure and now he regarded Isham with admiration. He turned to India.

''E's a big 'un, ain't 'e?'

'Joe, that is a rude remark. You must be more polite...' Then she saw that Isham was laughing.

'Fair comment, India. I'm not exactly a dwarf.' He bent to examine the child more closely, and his smile vanished. 'Fetch your brother to me, Joe. I'd like to meet him too.'

India stared at him. 'Is something wrong?'

'I don't like the look of those sooty warts, my dear. Pettifer should take a look at them.'

'You know our doctor?' India was surprised.

'He came to the Grange last week. One of the maids had burned herself. Does he call upon you?'

'Great heavens, he will come today! I had forgotten to advise him that Mama is so much better.'

'Then let him examine the boys.'

'These warts? Can they be dangerous?'

'They can become malignant, my dear.' He lowered his voice. 'In the worst instances they can kill. These children are never washed, and the risk of infection is high.'

'My lord, I had not imagined...'

'That I should know so much about them? I was instrumental...well, let us say that some years ago a sweep and his wife were charged with murder.'

India's face was ashen. 'Then it was not folly on my part…'

'To rescue them. I think not. There is little to choose between life in a factory or as a climbing boy.'

'But what am I to do with them? Mama will not allow them to stay here. I doubt if she will let the doctor see them.'

'Then let us send them to the Grange. It is now fully staffed and they will be well cared for.'

'Oh, would you do that?' India felt a warm rush of gratitude towards her betrothed. She gave him a brilliant smile. 'It would be so kind of you.'

'Has my stock gone up?' he grinned. 'Would it be worth a kiss?'

India coloured, and was relieved to find that Letty had returned. Her sister entered the kitchen with a big bundle of assorted clothing.

'Right!' Isham took the parcel from her. 'Joe, you and your brother are to take a ride in my carriage.' Without more ado he shepherded the two children out of the kitchen, and to India's astonishment Joe made no demur.

'I thought he'd rescue you,' Letty smiled.

'Yes, he has been very good.' India was thoughtful. 'I suppose we must join Mama?'

'Indeed! By now Mr Salton will have no secrets from her. She will have discovered his marital state, and very likely his income…'

Whatever it was that Mrs Rushford had discovered, it appeared to be satisfactory. As they entered the parlour she beamed upon her daughters.

'My dear girls, you shall make Mr Salton welcome. He is a stranger in this neighbourhood, you know.'

'A sad omission,' her companion stated gaily. 'Had

I but known what beauties you hide in this part of the country I should not have stayed away.'

'So kind!' Mrs Rushford murmured. 'India, as you know, is already betrothed to your brother, but may I make you known to our dearest Letty?'

Her intentions were obvious, and Letty looked ready to sink with embarrassment.

With exquisite courtesy Henry Salton appeared to be oblivious to Letty's discomfort. Somewhat to Mrs Rushford's annoyance he turned to India.

'Will you forgive us?' he said in a low voice. 'I fear we arrived at an awkward moment, but my brother could not wait to see you…'

He had not intended his words for other ears, but Mrs Rushford had been attending closely. She had no way of knowing how much of the quarrel the two men had heard. Now she saw a way of turning the situation to her advantage.

'Nonsense!' she interposed gaily. 'Pray, sir, you must not excuse yourself. You will always be welcome in this house. We treat you as family already…'

Henry Salton bowed.

'We have our little misunderstandings, of course.' Mrs Rushford paused, knowing that she must tread carefully. Then she continued in a sentimental tone. 'Mr Salton, my elder daughter is all heart. She has not yet learned that one cannot change the world alone.'

'To try shows great nobility of character, ma'am.' The young man smiled at India.

'That may be so, but not when it involves taking in two filthy urchins who may be harbouring heaven knows what diseases. You will not wonder at my objections, especially when I learned that she had actually bought them from their master. What she will do with them I can't imagine...'

'Pray do not trouble yourself.' Isham had arrived and had been speaking to Letty. Now he turned to her mother and though his tone was perfectly civil there was an edge to it which India had not heard before. 'You are quite right. This is not the place for those two boys. I have sent them to the Grange.'

Mrs Rushford looked at him in shocked surprise. 'My lord, have you seen them? They are wretched creatures. Pray consider their condition...'

'I have done so.' Isham's expression was grim. 'They need attention from the doctor. I have already sent for Pettifer.'

Mrs Rushford subsided. Isham's look did not encourage further argument. 'India is happy with that arrangement, are you not, my dear?'

India nodded in silence.

'Why, sir, you are too indulgent. India is to be sadly spoiled, I fear.' Mrs Rushford was torn between clear relief at the departure of the boys and displeasure to learn that his lordship supported India's actions. She had expected Isham to give his bride-to-be a sharp set-down for her folly. She could not resist a final gibe.

'We must hope that no ill comes of this. You will not care for India to be questioned by the magistrates, I think, if either of the boys should die.'

Her words were a mistake. Isham did not raise his voice, but suddenly it was full of menace.

'I intend to question them myself,' he said softly. 'That is, after I have visited the workhouse and spoken to the sweep. India, you will accompany me?'

'With pleasure.' India smiled at him. Her mother's face was dark with anger, but Isabel made no further objection. In any confrontation with his lordship she must be sure to come off worst. She was beginning to revise her opinion of him. This charming suitor had an ugly side. Well, let the fool pander to India if he would. It was enough that he had not cried off.

She turned her attention to Letty. Had the girl lost her tongue? Here was an eminently suitable young man and Letty had made no attempt to speak to him. Frowning, she signalled to her recalcitrant younger daughter, but Isham intervened with a tactful request for her advice.

An enquiry as to her preferred choice of new furnishing for the Grange diverted Isabel at once, much to Letty's relief.

'What a splendid influence you are, Miss Rushford! My brother is a different man already.' India turned to find Henry Salton regarding Isham with amusement. 'I do not recognise him.'

'Indeed, sir? I feel that you must know him well.'

'Oh, I do, ma'am. I do.' Her companion looked at India's face. 'But now I have offended you. My remark was not intended as a criticism of Anthony. It was a compliment to you…'

'You flatter me, Mr Salton.' In spite of his disclaimer India sensed that behind the smiling manner there was a certain tension.

'Oh, please!' Salton said quickly. 'Won't you call me Hal? We are now family, you know. I meant only that my brother can be a little stiff upon occasion. But there, you will not have seen it. He is a lucky man and your mutual happiness must be evident to all.'

India bowed her agreement, but she felt uneasy and a little annoyed. How much did Henry Salton know of the circumstances which had led to her betrothal? Was there a touch of sarcasm in his last remark? She looked at him sharply, but his expression was bland. Then he began to laugh.

'Put it down to jealousy, India. I may call you India, may I not? I had thought myself the more likely to marry first since Anthony showed no inclination, but you have swept him off his feet...'

India coloured, but he gave her an impish grin.

'The green-eyed monster has consumed me,' he announced. 'Can you suggest a remedy?'

His frankness was disarming, and India returned his smile. 'Only that you consider marriage yourself?'

'But who would take me? A younger son, with no claim either to the title, or to the family's rolling acres? It would take a miracle, I fear, unless I return to India and come back as a nabob.'

'You have considered it?' she asked in some amusement.

'Oh, yes. It may come to that, but I must not trouble you with my problems. Shall you go into Cheshire for your honeymoon?'

'We have not discussed it,' India told him shyly.

'Really?' Still laughing he turned to his brother. 'Anthony, you have been remiss. Won't you let us into the secret? Where will you spend your honeymoon?'

'It shall be wherever India wishes.' Isham seized her hand and raised it to his lips, pressing a kiss into her upturned palm and closing her fingers over it. 'Cheshire, London, Brighton? What do you say, my love?'

India found herself blushing deeply. As always, the touch of those warm lips against her skin had disturbed her. For once she was thankful when her mother intervened.

'My lord, will you set out in December? Is that wise? The roads may be impossible after these heavy rains. Letty and I were hoping you would stay on at the Grange, at least until the start of the London Season.'

'Ma'am, you are too good. I thank you for your concern.' Isham was apparently untroubled, but his tone belied his words It was clear that he did not welcome interference. 'My horses, you know, are accustomed to travelling in all weathers, and you need have no fears for India. I am persuaded that she is capable of coping with any emergency.' His laughing gaze held a hint of mockery and India stiffened.

Henry Salton was aware of it at once.

'You must not mind if my brother teases you a little,' he murmured in a low voice. 'It is his way. I suffer from it too you know. Perhaps we should be allies.'

'I am accustomed to his lordship's manner,' India said with dignity. 'It does not trouble me at all. I must suppose that it amuses him.'

'Ouch!' Henry raised a hand in pretended self-defence. 'I see that you are more than a match for him. May I beg that you do not reduce him to a gibbering wreck?' His eyes were twinkling. 'In reality he is the best of men.'

India smiled in spite of herself as she studied her companion. There was some family resemblance between the brothers. Both were tall and dark, but there the similarity ended. Beside his lordship's massive figure Henry seemed too slight in build, though he moved with athletic grace.

There was a difference in the features too. Henry's nose was short and straight, rather than aquiline, and a pair of merry blue eyes showed to startling effect against the tanned skin.

A handsome creature, India decided. He had the looks which his brother lacked, and a much more appealing personality.

'India, my dear, you are quite monopolising Mr Salton.' Mrs Rushford softened the reproof for the benefit of the assembled company with an artificial little laugh. 'The dear child is such a chatterbox,' she tittered. 'I must hope that she has not bored you, sir.'

'Far from it, ma'am.' Henry caught his brother's eye. He was surprised when Isham took his leave with rather less ceremony than might have been expected.

'I wish you joy of your mama-in-law,' he confided as they rode away. 'What a harridan!'

'But manageable, Henry! Perfectly manageable!' Isham's face was grim.

'I don't doubt it for a moment.' Henry spurred his horse into a trot.

Chapter Five

India was in disgrace. Not only had she neglected her betrothed in favour of his brother, but she had prevented Letty from engaging Henry Salton in conversation.

'But, Mama, I had no wish to do so,' Letty protested. 'What could I possibly have to say to him?'

Mrs Rushford cast up her eyes to the heavens. 'I wonder at you, miss, indeed I do. Your sister appeared to have no such difficulty.' She shot a suspicious look at India. 'What was the subject of your conversation?'

'We were speaking of Lord Isham...' India replied truthfully.

'Indeed! I must hope that you were not bold enough to question Mr Salton about his brother's...er...way of life.'

India understood her mother perfectly. She was referring to Isham's mistress. How could she imagine that her own daughter would be guilty of such a lack of taste? India's colour rose, but she bit back an angry retort.

'Mr Salton assures me that his lordship is the best of men,' she said in an indifferent tone.

'Indeed he is! He tells me that I am to choose the furnishings for the Grange without regard for the expense...' Isabel preened visibly.

'Was not India to be given the Grange as part of her marriage settlement?' Letty murmured. 'Perhaps she will wish to choose.'

This rash statement brought a tirade of abuse upon her head, which ended only when India assured her mother that she was happy to leave such matters in that lady's hands.

Well satisfied, Mrs Rushford turned to another matter. 'I had meant to mention your bride-clothes to his lordship,' she announced. 'The cost will be beyond me.'

'Oh, pray do not, Mama!' India was horrified. 'I shall need so little. The clothes which you bought me for the Season are still wearable.'

'Last Season's gowns? Are you out of your mind? You would be a dowd in such dated garments, and you have your husband's position to consider.'

'But, Mama we are still in mourning.'

'Must you remind me of our sad loss?' Mrs Rushford reached for a handkerchief. 'Unfeeling girl! You defy your mother at every turn. Why, only this morning you persuaded Isham to interest himself in those two nasty urchins though you knew that I should not like it.'

'It was his own decision to visit the workhouse and the sweep,' India protested.

'Nonsense! He could see that you were set on it. Otherwise why should he trouble?'

'Hester tells me that he is known to take an interest in the condition of children throughout the country...'

'"Hester tells me?"' her mother mimicked sarcastically. 'It is high time that you rid yourself of this ridiculous habit of quoting your cousin as if she were some sort of oracle. Why, her own parents despair of her.'

'Mama, that isn't true!'

'Much you know! Here is your dear uncle, so kindly suggesting that you must be wed from Perceval Hall when we all know that it is his dearest wish that Hester should do the same.' She touched her handkerchief to her eyes. 'I don't know what the world is coming to.'

'Uncle may still get his wish,' Letty ventured timidly. 'Hester is to have another Season. She told me so this morning.'

'So that is why you kept me waiting in the draper's this morning? You were gossiping with your cousin? I wonder that she had not the courtesy to come and speak to me.'

'She was in the company of Mrs Guarding. I expect she felt that you would not like to renew your acquaintance with that lady.'

'She was right. The woman is a pernicious influence. I have told your uncle many times that if he wishes to seek the reason why so many of you girls have such outlandish notions he should look no further than the Academy. Preaching independence? I never heard of such a thing!'

With her mother embarked upon her favourite topic India knew that further argument would be useless, but at least her visit to the workhouse had not been forbidden, if not forgotten.

'When does his lordship propose to come for you?' Isabel asked finally.

'He did not say, Mama. Possibly tomorrow?'

'I cannot like it, but I suppose that we must fall in with his wishes. You must take care to cover up your mouth and nose and carry something to ward off infection. Perhaps a vinegar-soaked sponge?'

With great resolution India refused to catch her sister's eye. The prospect was too much for her, but laughter at this moment would bring down fresh tirades upon her head. Mrs Rushford had not finished.

'I must warn you, India, not to try his good nature too far. At this moment Isham is overly indulgent. That will not always be so. Men do not care for bold, opinionated females. You are much too ready to speak out.'

India was silent, apparently accepting the reproof, but it was clear that her betrothed had kept his own notions to himself when speaking to her mother. What had he told his bride-to-be? True, he had referred to India as a termagant but he had made it sound like a compliment. To his mind, it was infinitely preferable to missish ways, as he termed them.

That was something. She was thoughtful as they sat down to a late nuncheon.

It was not until their mama had retired for her customary nap that Letty mentioned the gist of her conversation with Mrs Guarding.

'I hope that I was tactful, India, but I did ask her about staffing at the Academy.'

'Why did you do that, my love?'

Letty gave her an earnest look. 'I thought it was important. Oh, India, I must be sure that you are happy about this marriage. If not, I should have offered to go to Mrs Guarding.'

'But Letty, you know that you would hate it. Besides, if either of us went to her it would not be enough to keep the three of us. Believe me, I thought about it, but we cannot continue to be a charge on Uncle James.'

'I cannot bear it.' Letty was close to tears. 'I know

that you agreed to take Lord Isham because of us. How will you go on? You have made no secret of your opinion of his character... You do dislike him, don't you?'

'I could be mistaken,' India said cautiously. 'It would not be the first time that I have judged too quickly, and Hester thinks well of him.'

'She has met him?' Letty was surprised.

'No, but apparently his fame has spread. I am not referring to the opera-dancer.' She managed a faint smile. 'To quote Hester, though I am forbidden to do so, his intellect is to be respected, and he is the type of man who is needed in Government.'

Letty's face cleared. 'Then perhaps you will grow to love him. I am so glad. He does seem devoted to you...'

'How can that be?' India told her reasonably. 'He does not know me. Besides, you heard Mama. I am bold and wilful and opinionated...'

'So is he!' Letty began to laugh. 'I am so thankful, dearest, that you don't find him repulsive. Mrs Guarding had nothing to offer. Most of her teachers are still with her, and she has hopes of attracting a person whom she holds in high regard, although she did not give the name.'

'Perhaps it is as well. I should not wish you to give up your plans to marry Oliver. It will be so different now.'

Letty looked uncertain. 'I don't wish my happiness to be at the expense of your own...'

'It won't be! Just think, my love, I shall be the mistress of my own household—of several households, in fact.'

'As if you would care for that!'

'But I do, my dear, I do!'

Letty smiled at last. 'And your children, India, think of them! Children trust you. I have often noted it. You will make a fine mamma.'

India felt a twinge of panic. It was true that she was beginning to think more kindly of her betrothed, but he was still a stranger. His kisses, brief as they were, had disturbed her. Could she bear any further intimacy?

She would have to do so. There was no help for it. That was part of the bargain. Even so, she could not repress a feeling of anger that she was to be treated as a brood-mare.

She thrust the unpleasant thought aside and changed the subject.

'Was Hester in good spirits?' she asked.

Letty giggled. 'She was full of gossip. Where she gets it from I can't imagine but now she has learned that Louise, the Marchioness, accepted Sywell in accordance with the dying wish of her guardian, John Hanslope.'

'Oh, how could she?' India cried. 'The Marquis is a revolting creature.'

'But decrepit, thank heavens! Apparently he did not…could not…' Letty's face grew rosy with embarrassment. 'I mean, there was no chance of children.'

'Then Louise was fortunate,' India observed drily. 'Is there any news of her?'

'Not at present. Is it not the oddest story? For her to be brought to Steepwood Abbey as a child, and under such mysterious circumstances? No one could discover why the bailiff fetched her to his wife.'

'Many believed her to be John Hanslope's love child.'

'No, I cannot believe it,' Letty said firmly. On this occasion she was too intrigued to suffer from embarrassment. 'He was such an upright man. There is something else behind it.'

'Letty, you are a saint,' her sister teased. 'Must you always believe well of everyone? Even Isham himself seems to be in your good books. What has he been saying to you?'

'I don't know what you mean.' Unusually, Letty was evasive.

'I wondered only why you seemed to have lost your fear of my betrothed. That is true, is it not?'

'I was behaving foolishly in thinking him a monster. When one gets to know him better… Well, he is kinder than I thought.'

Yet you did not answer my question, India thought to herself. It was but one more mystery to add to those which surrounded the man she was about to marry.

He was an enigma. Since she had agreed to wed him he had dropped much of the mocking manner which she disliked so much, and which had characterised his behaviour at their first two meetings. Now he seemed anxious to please her, and was all civility. She wondered why. He had no need to do so. The bargain had been struck and neither party would go back on their word. Of that she could be sure.

She shrugged. She had enough experience to know that menfolk hated scenes. Perhaps that was the reason. She would never know, but it did not matter. With Isham in his present mood life was much more comfortable. As he had suggested they might yet deal well together.

India sighed. Perhaps it was a sensible arrangement but it was far removed from the romantic love she'd dreamed of as a girl.

Letty recalled her to the present. Her sister had returned to the subject of the missing Marchioness. 'Where do you suppose she has gone?' she asked.

'I've no idea, love, but if she has run away, as seems most likely, it's to be hoped that she has some money with her. Poor girl! What a life she must have had!'

'I felt sorry for her even as a child,' Letty said slowly. 'We had each other, you and I, and Giles and all our friends and relatives. Louise was such a solitary little creature. I never saw her playing with the village children.'

'I expect the Hanslopes did not wish it. Perhaps that was why they sent her away when she had reached thirteen or so. It could not have been to get an education. As an ex-governess Mrs Hanslope was well qualified to teach her. Possibly she was apprenticed to some trade. Hanslope must have worried about her when his wife died.'

'Indeed!' Letty shuddered. 'To think of a girl of that age, unprotected, and within reach of the Marquis! Hanslope did well to send her out of harm's way for seven years, but I wonder why she returned?'

'Hanslope was dying, Letty. He must have longed to see her just once more.'

'That I can understand, but far better that he had not done so. She was wed to the Marquis within weeks of her return.'

'Letty, that must have been from choice. Hanslope was not the man to force her...'

'Possibly not.' Letty sighed. 'I can only wish her well and happy wherever she is.'

'Don't let such matters weigh with you, my love. We have problems enough of our own. I suspect that Mama intends to add to them. What did you think of Mr Henry Salton?'

'I found him charming. He seemed not to understand that Mama was trying to throw me in his way.'

'He understood well enough,' India said grimly. 'I'm afraid that it was all too obvious, but he is too well-bred to put us out of countenance.'

'Well, *I* was put out of countenance,' Letty admitted. 'I longed to sink through the floor. I was so ashamed. It drove all conversation from my head. I hope that he will not feel obliged to pay me much attention.'

'You need have no fears. He was at pains to explain to me that he is in no position to marry. He did not say so, but I imagine that he will hang out for a rich wife.'

'Isham's brother, and he has no money?'

'His lordship's half-brother, Letty. The title and the property went to Anthony. Doubtless Mr Salton's mother has been well provided for, but she is still alive.'

'Does Mama know this?'

'Not yet. I felt unwilling to gossip about the young man, even to save you more embarrassment, but when she does it will certainly change her attitude towards him.'

'Didn't you like him, India?'

'I haven't decided yet. His manners can't be faulted and his face is frank and open. I won't deny that he has charm, and also a sense of humour. Yet there was something... Perhaps it was more what he didn't say than what he did.'

'Now I am mystified. What is it that worried you?'

'I don't quite know. No doubt I am being fanciful, but I felt that he was trying to warn me against his brother.'

'And you resented it?' Letty was smiling. 'I had not

thought to see you so ready to champion your betrothed, but I am glad of it.'

'I see that Isham has another champion, Letty. Let
me assure you that his lordship has no need of any
such. I suspect that he is a law unto himself. And that
reminds me. Will you try to persuade Mama that Isham
has insisted on a quiet wedding? He has told her so
himself, but she is full of plans for show.'

'Poor Mama! She longs for the marriage to outshine
that of Beatrice Roade on the twenty-second of
December. It is to be the wonder of the neighbourhood,
though as yet she has been able to inform only the
friends who can be reached on foot.'

'Uncle James will have told so many others,' India
said in gloomy tones. 'Mama has already sent a note
asking for the loan of his carriage to take us into
Northampton to buy bride-clothes. I've tried to explain
that there is no need.'

'Let Mama have that pleasure, at least,' Letty
pleaded. 'You will need a wedding-gown and a new
bonnet if nothing else.'

'It seems all wrong when we are still in mourning,'
India told her quietly. 'Oh, Letty, I miss Papa so much.
We must never forget him.'

'We shan't,' Letty comforted. 'But I think he would
not like to see you still so sad. He wished so much for
happiness for both of us.'

Yet it could not stop the gambling fever India
mourned privately. In spite of all she could not bring
herself to blame him for an addiction which had grown
beyond his control. She tried to thrust such troublesome
thoughts aside.

'Have you settled upon your wedding date?' Letty
murmured shyly.

'Uncle William is to let us know. Anthony has been to see him and the banns are to be called next week for the first time.' India felt a twinge of panic. Events were rushing upon her.

'Then you will be wed before Christmas?'

'I believe so. I cannot see the need for haste, but Isham is determined on it.'

'And when is he to take you to confront the sweep? That is well done of him, I think.'

'Indeed it is!' India smiled at last. 'What I should have done without his help I can't imagine, and I am so thankful that the man is to be stopped from injuring other children. I expect that we shall go tomorrow.'

Yet by mid-morning of the following day she had given him up. Northampton was several miles away and the winter evenings drew in fast. She doubted if Isham would risk his bloodstock in darkness on roads already badly rutted in the autumn rains.

India changed into her oldest gown and walked into the kitchen. Relations with Martha had been strained after the maid had been sharply reprimanded for her unwanted interference on the previous day. Now Martha was nowhere to be seen and the kitchen fire was burning low.

India threw some sticks upon the embers and set a pot to boil suspended from a hook set at shoulder height within the chimney-breast. Then she went into the scullery. They were not overly well stocked with food, she noted in dismay, but there was still a piece of pork which she might roast. She placed it on an iron skillet and set it close to the flames. A clear, brisk fire would crisp the crackling. Then she spied the last of the apple crop. In the depths of winter dumplings were always welcome. She set out flour and dripping upon the kitchen table and began to make her pastry.

Absorbed in her task, she was unaware that the kitchen door had opened.

'Something smells good,' a deep voice announced. 'I believe I shall invite myself to dine…'

Horrified, India spun round to find Lord Isham lounging in the doorway.

'You?' she cried. 'I had given you up.'

'Always a mistake, my dear. Did we not have an appointment for today?'

'At this hour? Shall you wish to set out now, my lord? It will be dark by four o'clock.'

'So it will.' Unconcerned he wandered over to the table to examine the dumplings, already encased in their pastry covers, and wrapped carefully in muslin bags. The discarded cores were lying to one side.

'Apple dumplings?' He began to smile. 'They were always a puzzle to our late sovereign.'

'How so?' India was intrigued.

'King George could never understand how a whole apple got inside its covering.' Isham reached into his pocket for a snowy handkerchief and cupped a hand beneath India's chin. 'Spit!' he ordered.

Too astonished to refuse, India did so, and Isham scrubbed cheerfully at her face.

'You had flour upon that charming nose,' he explained. 'Now, ma'am, may I beg you to fetch a cloak. I do not care to keep my horses waiting.'

'You mean we are to go now…at this moment?'

'I do.'

'But, sir, I cannot leave…' She gestured towards the dumplings. 'Besides, I am not dressed for such an expedition.'

For answer he strolled over to the cauldron.

'Boiling,' he said with satisfaction. Without more ado he picked up the muslin-wrapped parcels and dropped them into the water. 'Twenty minutes at the most, I believe. Martha shall retrieve them.' Then he inspected the sizzling joint upon the skillet and nodded. 'Your family will not starve today…'

'But Anthony, my gown…?'

He turned to her then, a large hand resting upon each shoulder. 'India, you have a choice. Which is the more important to you, a toilette of the first stare, or the welfare of urchins such as those you rescued yesterday? It is up to you. We go now, or we do not go at all.'

India looked up into the dark face and felt ashamed. 'You are right, of course,' she said quickly. 'Will you give me ten minutes?'

'Ten minutes *only*,' he replied, smiling. 'Can you be ready in that time?'

'Letty will help me. It will not take long.' She could not resist a little joke, partly to cover her disgust at her own behaviour. She had made difficulties about mere trivialities. 'You need have no fear. I do not own a toilette of the first stare.'

'You will, my dear, you will.' Isham took out his watch. 'One minute has already passed.'

India hurried past him. Then a thought struck her.

'Mama? Anthony, will you speak to her? I think she does not know that you are here.'

'Else I should not have been allowed to find you at your task? You are right. Letty opened the door to me and smuggled me to your side. Your mother has a morning caller and must have been engaged in conversation. Off you go! I will make it right with her.'

He strolled towards the parlour as India fled upstairs.

She found Letty in her room, laying out her most becoming walking-dress.

'You might have warned me of Isham's visit,' she smiled. 'He found me with flour upon my nose.'

'He would not mind that in the least.' Quickly she drew India's old gown over her head. 'Besides, he would not have it. He wished to present Mama with a *fait accompli*. I think he felt that she would delay you with more objections.'

India stepped into her walking-dress, her fingers stumbling over the buttons at the neck and wrist. Then she glanced in a mirror. 'Oh, Lord! My hair is coming down and there is no time to dress it.'

'Your bonnet will hide it, love. Shall you take your cloak?'

'I think so. The weather is still bitter. Letty, his lordship put the dumplings on to boil. Will you see to them, or make sure that Martha does so?'

'He did what?' Letty gazed at her sister in blank astonishment.

'It surprised me too, especially as he knew how long they take to cook. Anthony seems to be a man of many parts.' With that dry remark she picked up her cloak, straightened her bonnet and ran down the stairs.

'Ah, there you are, my love!' Isham strolled towards her, seized her hands and kissed them. 'A woman of your word! Your mama has quite forgiven me for stealing you away at such short notice, and I have promised to take the greatest care of you.'

India avoided her mother's eye as she curtseyed to their other visitor. Their nearest neighbour, the normally voluble Mrs Horton, was, for once, reduced to silence in the presence of the formidable Lord Isham.

He was all civility, but there was a touch of the autocrat in his manner. She guessed that it was deliberate, as much for the benefit of her mother as for Mrs Horton.

'Shall we go?' he asked pleasantly. 'We have much to do today...' He bowed to both ladies and ushered India from the room.

She was still smiling as he handed her into the carriage, wrapped a fur rug about her, and pushed a hot brick beneath her feet.

'Something amuses you?' He had seen the expression on her face.

'Sir, you are behaving very badly. I fear that you have frightened Mrs Horton into fits.'

'Really?' Isham was all innocence. 'India, you must make allowance for a rough ex-soldier. I had imagined that I was behaving with great courtesy. It seems that I have much to learn.'

'Don't gammon me, my lord! You knew what you were doing. Poor Mrs Horton! You must understand that your character will be under the most minute discussion at this moment.'

Isham tucked her hand beneath his arm. 'Are you warm enough?' he asked. 'Our journey will not take long. I have bespoke our luncheon at the local hostelry.'

'Sir?'

'Feeding the inner man, and woman! We cannot undertake our task upon an empty stomach.'

'Food is important to you, sir?'

'Naturally. Is it not to everyone?' His eyes were twinkling as he looked at her. 'Ah, I see! You wonder at my skills. Let me assure you, my dear, that my experience is vast. In Spain we lived off the country when our supply lines were stretched beyond their limits. A single pot would hold a rabbit, pease pudding in a cloth and whatever else we could find.'

'You had no servant then, that you should undertake the task yourself?' India looked at him in disbelief. 'Am I to believe that you slaved over the fires whilst your batman took his ease?'

'He was forced to, India. We were separated from the rest of our command, and my man was badly wounded.'

'Oh, I'm sorry.' It was an inadequate apology. Once again a hasty judgement had put her in the wrong. 'I did not know...'

'How could you?' Isham was untroubled by her comment. 'But even now I would not have you think of me as a man who is unaware of the whereabouts of his own kitchen.'

'You would not be the first,' she murmured, thinking of her own father and her uncles.

'I expect not, but at least we have one thing in common, so it would appear.'

India let the comment pass. 'Was your brother with you in the Spanish campaign?' she asked.

'Did I not mention? Henry is my half-brother. My father married twice.'

'So you have a stepmother?'

'Yes!' Isham's voice was noncommittal. 'She lives in London, but you will meet her at the wedding.'

'I see. You did not answer my question, sir.'

'Henry has no taste for army life. He has but recently returned from India...' Isham's tone did not invite further questioning, but India persisted. She was anxious to hear more of the enigmatic young man who had so strangely puzzled her.

'You and your brother are very different, are you not?' she murmured. 'Is he to stay in England now?'

'Possibly!' Isham's lazy gaze rested upon India's face, but he did not pursue the subject. 'I have been wondering, my dear, if your mother is not right in advising against a trip to Cheshire in the winter. Shall you be afraid to travel then?'

'You would go yourself, would you not?'

'Of course, but...'

'Then pray do not change your plans on my account. I am no fragile creature to be handled with kid gloves.'

Isham grinned at her. 'In that case I shall promise to remove my gloves...'

India coloured, much to her own annoyance. He had left her in no doubt of his meaning, and the thought disturbed her.

'How do the boys go on?' she asked quickly.

'The doctor has examined them. They are in worse case than we had at first imagined, and covered in wounds and bruises as well as burns, some of them infected.'

'Oh, Anthony, they must survive.'

His lordship's stern expression lightened and he smiled at her. 'You need have no fear. Your protéges have courage. Joe's spirit will carry him through, and he supports his brother. I winced myself when they were delivered over to the grooms for washing, but my men are gentle and neither boy made a sound.'

'Your men?'

'Joe made it clear that he was not a baby, to be handled by a nursemaid. Had you noticed their feet?'

'Why no! Is something wrong?'

'Both boys were limping badly. Briggs had a few expedients for forcing them up the flues. He thrust pins into their soles. If that was unsuccessful he lit the fire beneath them.'

India's anger threatened to consume her. 'Oh, I cannot wait to get my hands on him!' she cried. 'We must stop him before some child is killed. I pray that we shall find him.'

'Don't worry!' Isham told her smoothly. 'We have an appointment with the fellow. I doubt if he will disregard it.'

'But...but he may make excuses. He may claim that these wounds are none of his doing. He sold them to the factory, you know.'

'That was but four days ago. Their work there could not account for their condition.'

'It was still dangerous...'

'Agreed, but these are not fresh injuries. We shall bring him to account.'

India was silent. For her own part she would have liked to roast the sweep over one of his own fires. She could think of no punishment severe enough for him. Then she stole a look at Isham's face and felt comforted. From his expression she guessed that Briggs would rue the day that he had taken up his trade.

'I wish you will tell me about the Spanish campaign,' she murmured. 'Here in England I fear that we have no idea of conditions in that country.'

She had succeeded in surprising her companion.

'Pray do not feel the need to make polite conversation, India. You cannot really wish to know...'

'Of course I do, else I should not have asked...' India was annoyed by his dismissive tone.

Isham stared at her. 'Extraordinary! We ex-soldiers are accustomed to a glazing of the eyes whenever we are foolish enough to mention our experiences.'

'You must be mistaken, sir. We are all of us aware how much we owe both to our army and our navy.'

'The navy, possibly, since Nelson's victory at Trafalgar, but our armies are not held in high esteem. On land, Napoleon is held to be invincible, and we have had reverses.'

'But also victories, I believe. Were you at Talavera?'

Isham smiled. 'That battle was the end of my army career, though I had been with Wellesley since the campaign in Holland.'

'And do you miss the life, my lord?'

'In part. I enjoyed the comradeship and the chance to outwit our enemies by strategy, but you cannot imagine the din of battle, the cries of the wounded, the primitive surgery with no relief for pain, and the bitter cold which struck through the bone.'

'I had thought that Spain was a hot country.'

'In summer the heat is suffocating, but in winter the cold is such as you have never known.' Isham stopped. 'I must not go on. I shall destroy your rosy picture of army life…'

'Do you think me a fool, sir?' India said quietly. 'We lead comfortable lives far away from danger, but I have not lost my imagination.'

Isham gave her a long look. Then he took her hand. 'How you continue to surprise me!' he said lightly. 'My apologies, my dear. I underestimate you.'

As he spoke the coach turned off the highway and into the courtyard of the Angel. Their arrival was expected, for as they stopped the door to the hostelry flew open and the landlord bustled towards them.

India was ushered inside with bows and exclamations on the honour done to mine host by the patronage of Lord Isham. Their private parlour was the best he had to offer and the meal would, he assured them, be ready before they had time to throw off their cloaks.

India was amused. Isham's presence was, it seemed, enough to ensure the best of service. She was right, but the dish of breadcrumbed smelts, followed by a fine roast duck, did little to tempt her appetite.

'The food is not to your taste?' Isham enquired. 'Would you care for something else?'

'It is delicious,' she said truthfully. 'But, my lord, I cannot help but wonder how we shall go on with Briggs.'

'Don't you trust me, India?' Isham's eyes were twinkling. 'And will you let him ruin a quite excellent meal for you? Forget him for the moment and tell me about Letty and her hopes of Oliver Wells.'

Chapter Six

'She told you?' India was amazed.

'She did. We are good friends you know, your sister and I.'

'I see.' India was unaccountably annoyed. Letty had always been her ally. It was hard to come to terms with the fact that she had moved into the enemy camp. She was tempted to ask what Isham could possibly have told her sister to give Letty such a good opinion of him, but she held her tongue.

'Letty is sure in her affections?' Isham persisted.

India hesitated. 'Letty has set her heart on Oliver Wells. I think she will not change.'

'And the young man himself?'

'He adores her, as who could not? Letty is so kind and gentle. She sees the best in everyone.'

'Unlike her elder sister?' He was baiting her deliberately and India did not disappoint him.

'If you wish to understand my character, sir, you should speak to my mama.'

'My dear, she has already assured me that you are the most biddable of women—meek almost to a fault! I put down most of her remarks to a certain partiality…' Isham's face was solemn, but India could hear the laughter in his voice.

Try as she might, she could not keep her countenance and she began to smile. 'You need not fear partiality, my lord. My mamma is well aware of my shortcomings.'

'You have some? You astonish me!'

'Now you are making game of me again. You know quite well that I am neither meek nor biddable. Did you not call me a termagant?'

'So I did! Had you not best advise me of your other faults, so that I may be prepared? It would be hard indeed to discover them after we are wed.'

Isham was enjoying himself, but India would not be drawn. She laughed and shook her head. Somehow even this reference to her nuptials seemed to have lost the power to disturb her.

'I think we were speaking of my sister, sir.'

'So we were. Where is the sticking point which prevents her marriage? Letty did not tell me.'

'She would not. It is a great sadness to her, but Oliver's family have other plans for him.'

'You have met them?'

'I met Lady Wells,' India told him stiffly. 'She was not kind to Letty.'

'A disagreeable woman, and something of a laughing stock, I fear.'

'How so?' India was astonished. Her ladyship's queenly manner had given the impression that she enjoyed a position of unchallenged leadership among the Ton.

'She is an ill-bred creature, India. Her efforts to appear more royal than the royal family give rise to much amusement.'

'Letty did not find her amusing.'

'She is a trying creature,' his lordship observed. 'But tell me about your brother. Giles, is it not? He does not go much into Town, I believe. Certainly, I have not met him yet.'

'Giles prefers the country.' It was a bald statement, but India would not explain that her brother had neither the means nor the inclination to visit the London clubs such as White's, or Brooks, or Watier's, so favoured by men such as Isham and his friends.

'And where is he now?'

'He is gone into Derbyshire.' India looked up sharply. She wondered if Sir James had spoken harshly of her brother's absence. 'Giles hopes to gain employment as an estate manager. His friends may know of something suitable.'

'He is interested in farming?'

'He thinks of nothing else.' India relaxed. There was no trace of censure in his lordship's tone. 'He had always hoped to restore…I mean…' She stopped, aware that she was on dangerous ground.

Isham appeared to be untroubled by this reference to the loss of the Rushford lands. He glanced at his watch. 'Time to go!' he announced. 'Dusk falls early on these winter evenings. I would not have your mother imagine that we have met with some mishap should we return in darkness.'

'Is it far to the workhouse?'

'We are quite close.'

'And Briggs? Have you learned of his directions?'

'You will find him waiting at our destination. I sent a message yesterday.' Isham opened the door for her into the passageway. She walked ahead as he paused to settle with the landlord.

Then, behind her, a door flew open and a laughing couple emerged. India heard a squeal of pleasure.

'Anthony, darling! I have not seen you in this age! Where have you been hiding?'

She turned to find her betrothed in the embrace of a young lady of dashing appearance, whilst beside her a young man was pumping Isham's hand.

'By all that's holy!' he cried. 'We didn't expect to find you here. Surely you ain't been forced to rusticate...?'

'Not yet!' With imperturbable calm his lordship extricated himself from the grasp of his companions. Then he looked beyond them to where India stood in wonder.

'My dear, the landlord will see you to the coach,' he murmured. 'I shall be with you in a second.'

His companions spun round as India turned away. She felt humiliated. It was clear that he had no intention of introducing them to her. Was he ashamed of her? She glanced down at her sombre clothing, unrelieved by ornament. Compared with the stunning creature so recently in Isham's arms she felt like a bedraggled crow. Even so, it showed a want of courtesy on his lordship's part, and it had surprised her.

He was as good as his word. India was barely settled in the coach with a fresh brick at her feet and the rug tucked round her before he joined her and gave the office to his coachman.

She did not speak to him. She could not trust herself to treat him with civility when he had shamed her in front of his friends.

Isham appeared to find nothing amiss. 'Are you ready to do battle with Briggs?' he asked with a smile.

'I am.' India relapsed into silence.

'Oh dear, now I am in disgrace.' With his usual quick understanding he had seized at once upon the reason for her annoyance. 'The young lady is not someone you would care to know,' he told her quietly. 'I could not...would not introduce you.'

'You seemed to know her very well...' India replied in haughty tones.

'My love, did I not know you better I might think that you were jealous!' His eyes were twinkling with amusement. 'And no...she is not the opera-dancer.'

India flushed scarlet. 'I did not think so for a moment,' she said untruthfully. 'And you, sir, are certainly not mealy-mouthed.'

'Have I shocked you? I had not thought it possible!' Isham looked at her averted face and relented. 'She and young Stillington are...er...close friends,' he continued. 'Under the circumstances I could not make him known to you.'

'I see.' India felt a little mollified. 'She is very beautiful.'

'Quite ravishing!' he agreed. 'And also very expensive...'

India coloured again. 'I beg that you will not go on,' she murmured. 'I mean, I know that gentlemen have their...er...friends, but it is no concern of mine.'

'Really?' Isham looked at her with interest. 'That is a very liberal attitude. Clearly, you have given the subject some thought. How refreshing! Won't you honour me with your views upon the matter?'

His casual tone annoyed her, and she stiffened. If he wished for her views he should have them. 'I am told that fidelity is unfashionable,' she said coldly. 'Gentlemen may please themselves, and as for wives...? Well, once the heir has been provided one may take a lover...' If she had hoped to anger him she had succeeded.

Isham sat bolt upright. 'You may disabuse yourself of that idea!' His lazy manner had vanished. 'Is this your notion of marriage?'

'No, it is not!' India recoiled. Something in his look had frightened her, but she attempted to recover her composure. 'Yet, my lord, I'll admit that we cannot compete with such as Mr Stillington's friend.'

Isham's expression changed. 'What a goose you are! She cannot hold a candle to you! Have you no idea of your own beauty?'

India stared at him in disbelief.

'Oh, come!' he said impatiently. 'Will you believe that paint and fine feathers make the woman?'

'They help,' she told him, unconvinced.

'Nonsense! One day I shall convince you...' He paused as the coach drew to a halt. 'We have arrived, I think. Heavens, what a place!'

India could only agree with him. They had drawn up beside a long, low, brick-faced building sadly lacking in windows.

'It looks like a prison,' she whispered.

'We shall not be long.' He handed her down as the groom rang the bell. 'You are quite sure that you wish to be present?' he asked. 'If you prefer I will deal with this alone.'

'No!' she told him quietly. 'I want to see for myself.'

'As you wish!' He followed her inside.

They found themselves in an open hall which did not boast a stick of furniture. India shivered. The cold indoors chilled her to the marrow, but the woman who came towards them clearly did not notice it. She was short and plump, small-featured, clad in innumerable shawls, and smelling strongly of gin. As she reached them she sank into a low curtsey.

'Such an honour, my lord!' In that moment the beady eyes missed nothing. India was aware that every item of her clothing had been noted and priced. She faced the woman squarely and stuck out her chin.

'Briggs is here?' Isham wasted no time upon civilities.

'Awaiting your lordship's pleasure, sir. If you will come this way...' The woman moved ahead of them and opened a doorway at the far end of the hall.

The contrast was striking. Here an enormous fire burned merrily in the hearth, beside which a small thin man was helping himself from a steaming bowl of punch.

'You will take refreshment, sir?' The woman looked hopefully at his lordship, clearly disposed to spend a pleasant hour in such exalted company.

'I thank you, but no, ma'am.' Isham's civility was such as to be insulting. 'We are here upon a serious matter.' A hard eye rested upon the unfortunate Briggs, who had risen to his feet.

'Briggs, is it not?'

'That's right, your lordship, and at your service.' The man made an obsequious bow.

'I doubt that, Briggs. I doubt it very much.' Isham turned to the workhouse matron. 'You have dealings with this man?'

'Yes, my lord. Such a help to us, he is! When the childer are of an age to earn a living Briggs here takes them off our hands.'

'I see. How many children has he taken from you in the last six months?'

'Sir, it's hard to say.' The matron considered for a

moment. 'We do try to keep a tally, but it ain't so easy when they comes and goes so fast.'

'Then Briggs may have a better idea?' His lordship transferred his attention to the sweep.

'Well, sir, it's that 'ard to tell. These young 'uns comes and goes, you know. They comes and goes...'

'And where do they go, Briggs?'

For the first time Briggs scented danger. This polite gentleman was mild of manner, but there was something about him which did not encourage ease of mind.

'Poor creatures, most of 'em,' he announced. 'Too weak to stand up to the work. T'aint surprisin', sir. Orphings, most of 'em, or cast off by their parents with too many mouths to feed. It's right sad!' He shook his head. 'Right sad!'

'You are right! Are you telling me that we shall find them in the churchyard?'

Briggs pursed his lips and nodded.

'Yet there must be some who do not succumb?' Isham suggested pleasantly. 'What of them?'

Briggs was undeceived by the charming manner. This swell had come here for a purpose, and the lady was looking daggers. She'd be at the back of it. He had his own opinion of females who took it upon themselves to interfere in matters which were none of their concern. None of this showed in his servile bowing.

'Poor critters, most of 'em, I say again, but cunning little varmints, in spite of all. Dooty is unknown to 'em. Why, sir, you'd think that they'd be grateful to be given work, but no such thing!'

'Grateful!' India turned upon him with flashing eyes. 'Must they be grateful to be thrust into a burning chimney and forced aloft with pricks and prodding?'

Briggs gave her an inimical look. Had she been

alone he'd have sent her to the right about, but the threatening presence of her companion caused him to think better of any attempt at insolence.

'How else must I persuade 'em, ma'am?' he whined. 'A poor man 'as to earn a living, and these lads is lazy critturs. You never 'eard such moans and cries as they give way to when I arsks 'em to obey their master.'

'Are you surprised?' India cried hotly. 'I am tempted to pluck a brand from the fire here and give you a taste of your own medicine.'

'No call for that, miss!' The sweep removed himself as far away from her reach as possible. He was in no doubt that she would carry out her threat. 'I 'ope I am a reasonable man, but chimneys must be swept. And it ain't agin the law to use these childer, as 'is lordship 'ere will know.' He shot a triumphant glance in Isham's direction.

'You are quite right, Briggs. The law is clear and the penalties for breaking it are severe.' Isham's tone was silky smooth. 'You know it well, I see, so you will be aware that murder, for example, will lead you to the gallows.'

'Murder?' Briggs paled. 'Nay, my lord, you shan't lay that charge at my door. My lads is 'ere, as you may see for yourself. Fetch 'em, Em'ly!'

The matron hurried away, anxious to remove herself from a situation which promised to turn ugly. When she returned she thrust two small boys into the room and prepared to dart away.

Isham would have none of it. 'Come forward, madam,' he said firmly. 'Pray take a seat. I have some questions for you.' His eye rested upon the terrified urchins, neither of whom were eight years old. 'Did these children come from here?'

'No, your honour.' The matron was relieved to be able to deny all knowledge of any misdemeanour committed by the sweep. 'These lads are from the orphanage. We don't take 'em under nine years old.'

Beside him Isham heard India gasp. He turned again to the sweep. 'How long have you had these boys?' he asked.

'Not above a week, my lord. If they be sickly it's nowt to do wi' me...' Briggs smirked. His native cunning had come to his aid once more. The lads were filthy, but that was in the nature of the job, and if they looked clemmed, well, he hadn't had time to feed them up, as he was ready to explain.

Isham stopped his excuses with a lifted hand. 'What happened to your previous climbing boys?'

Briggs was ready with his answer. 'Burned to death, I fancy, sir. When the factory was torched.'

'And how did they come to be working there?'

Briggs was wary now. So those two deaths were at the bottom of this. Still, he was in the clear. He hadn't set fire to the place himself, and he could not be held responsible.

'The overseer took 'em on, my lord. They 'ad to 'ave work, you understand, and they wuz too big to be of use to me.'

'A charitable creature, this overseer! Is he a friend of yours?'

'I 'ardly knows the man.'

'So he did not pay you for the children?'

Briggs hesitated, cursing inwardly. Where had this swell come by his information? A lie formed upon his lips and then he thought better of it. He had no wish to be confronted by the overseer, and there had been a number of other witnesses to the transaction.

'T'overseer might 'ave give me a copper or two, just for my trouble. I'd 'ad those lads for a full six months, trained 'em up, and treated 'em like my own.'

India could contain herself no longer. 'Then it is God help your own,' she cried. 'Those boys are in such case at present that the younger child may not live.'

'Sorry to 'ear it, ma'am. A tragedy…to be caught in the fire, and so young, at that.' Briggs assumed a mournful expression, but he was thinking fast. The young varmints must still be alive, but how had they come to the notice of these toffs?

'They were not injured in the factory fire.' Isham had not raised his voice, but no one in the room was insensible to the underlying menace in his tone. 'Their injuries are of long standing. You have told us yourself that they were in your care for many months. Have you an explanation?'

'Must have been injured in the factory,' came the swift reply.

'In the course of a few days? No, that will not serve. I am speaking of neglect, starvation, beatings and the cruellest of torture. If the child dies you will appear before the magistrates on a charge of murder. In the meantime a lesser charge of cruelty will serve to keep you behind bars.'

Briggs fell to his knees, babbling for mercy, but Isham strode to the door and summoned his groom. 'Take him in charge,' he ordered. 'The magistrate is expecting him.'

There was a scuffle, punctuated by much cursing, but Isham's man had been chosen for his muscular build. The struggle was soon over.

Now it was the matron's turn to beg for mercy. Her tears flowed freely as she tried to justify herself.

'I didn't know how bad he was,' she wept. 'Sir, we are forced to send these children out to earn their bread if anyone will take them.'

'Do you tell me that when they leave you your charges are in the best of health?' Isham demanded.

'My Lord, you heard the sweep. Some of what he said is true. You should visit the orphanage if you doubt me. Babes are left on doorsteps, or in the church porch even in bitter weather. Others have been starved for years before they come to the notice of the parish. We can't save them all. And we can't afford the doctor.'

'In future you will be able to do so.' Isham's voice had softened a little. 'Mrs Witham, is it not?'

The woman nodded, drying her eyes with the corner of her apron.

'Madam, in the future I intend to take a close interest in this place, and also in the orphanage. Miss Rushford, who is soon to become my wife, will also do so. I suggest that you place no more children for the present. The board of guardians, including ourselves, will interview prospective employers. They will also consider the suitability of those at present in charge.' He cast a significant look at the bottle of gin in evidence on the dresser.

'Thank you, sir. What am I to do with the children here? Am I to return them to the orphanage?'

'I think not. You will oblige me by washing them and giving them some food without delay. Sadly, we have not time today to inspect these premises, but we shall return.'

With that dread promise Isham rose to his feet and ushered India out of the room, leaving behind him a much chastened Mrs Witham.

India stopped him as he was about to hand her into the coach.

'Oh, Anthony, should we have left the children with that dreadful creature? She may go straight back to the bottle…'

'I doubt it, my love. I believe I made my views quite clear and she has had a fright. If she does not wish to be dismissed without a character she will change her ways.'

'I hope so, but perhaps we should have looked about the workhouse. Heaven knows what horrors we might have found.'

'I am aware of it. That was why I promised to return without giving her a date. I am persuaded that conditions will improve at once.'

'And the orphanage?'

'I have been there, India. There is…er…a complete change of management.'

India gave him a warm smile. 'You do not waste much time, my lord.'

'Not when my heart is set upon a certain course of action.' Isham twinkled at her. 'You have not wondered why I offered for you in such haste?'

He knew at once that his words were a mistake. India retreated into her shell.

'You offered for either of us, I believe,' she said austerely.

'Why, so I did! I had forgot!' Isham returned to his normal teasing tone. 'Does it still gall you, India?'

'It never did!' she replied untruthfully. 'I understand your motives, sir.'

'Do you, my dear? I wonder!' He left it there and India did not pretend to understand him. A silence fell between them.

India was the first to break it. 'What will happen to Briggs?' she asked.

'He'll be left to cool his heels for a week or two. These cases are difficult to prosecute, you know. There are no specific laws to protect these climbing boys...'

'But you told him...'

'I told him that he might not murder them, which is true. As to a charge of cruelty which might lead to death...well...it is a fine point, and must be proved. The doctor will support the case, but even so...'

'That is so wrong!' India was appalled. 'Why, the two we have just left are little more than babes. So you tell me that the law will not protect them? What can the Government be about?'

'There are moves afoot to bring in a bill to prohibit the use of climbing boys. It may pass the Commons, but it will not pass the House of Lords.'

'Your peers?' India did not trouble to hide her contempt. 'I must suppose that rich men take no interest in the young and helpless.'

Isham was watching her closely. 'They have a strong self-interest in this matter, India.'

'How can that be? There must be other ways of sweeping chimneys.'

'There is another way. Let me tell you a story. Some years ago certain individuals formed a Society for Superseding Climbing Boys. We...they...offered a reward to the inventor of a machine which could replace the boys and girls.'

'Girls too?'

'Oh, yes, it is not unknown.'

'And did anyone come forward?'

'The prize was won by a Mr Smart. His machine is now in use throughout England.'

'So where is the problem, sir?'

'Mr Smart's invention works well on ninety-nine per cent of chimneys. The others, which it cannot reach, are in the country homes of the rich.'

India stared at him in disbelief. 'You believe that the Lords would defeat a bill to outlaw this wicked practice for the sake of a few chimneys?'

'Nothing is more certain. My friends assure me of it.'

'Then I despise the pack of you!' India felt close to tears.

'Steady on, my dear. I did not say that I agreed with them.' Isham took her hand and held it in his own. 'I had hoped that you would think better of me.'

India looked up at him. On this winter evening dusk was already well advanced and even within the close confines of the carriage she could not see the expression in his eyes.

'Is it to take a lifetime to prove myself to you?' he asked softly. 'On this matter, at least, I thought we were agreed.'

India did not withdraw her hand. She felt ashamed, and knew that she had been unfair. Isham had done all that she might have asked of him in preventing the sweep from injuring other children.

'I'm sorry!' she said quickly. 'I spoke in haste. It is a fault of mine to lose my temper when I am upset.'

'I have noticed,' he said drily. 'I begin to think that only when I anger you do I get your full attention.'

'Oh, that is not true! I always know...I mean, I am always aware...' India stopped in confusion. She attempted to withdraw her hand from his strong grasp, but Isham would not release it.

When he spoke there was a new warmth in his voice.

'From the moment I first saw you I was aware of you, India. It was at Almack's, I believe. You sailed through that gaggle of silly girls like a graceful swan through a flock of geese. Since then I could always sense when you were in a room even when I did not see you.'

India stiffened. Was Isham making game of her? It would serve her right, she admitted to herself. She had been less than civil to him when she owed so much to his interest in the children. Well, if he had hoped to disconcert her he had succeeded. Suddenly she felt shy.

'Sir, you have already commented upon my height!'

Unaccountably disturbed, and fearing mockery, she spoke more coldly than she had intended. She drew her hand away from his, only to find that he had slipped an arm about her waist.

'I was not referring to your height. Prickly India! Am I not to be allowed the pleasure of paying you a compliment?'

To her own annoyance India found that she was blushing. Thankfully he could not see her clearly in the darkness. To struggle would be undignified and also fruitless. She could feel the strength in that encircling arm, and knew that if he chose to hold her she could not break away. Words could be her only weapon against him.

'A compliment is welcome only when it is sincere,' she retorted.

'And you think I do not mean it?' She could hear the laughter in his voice. To her surprise it was mixed with something else. Had she not known better she might have thought it was tenderness. 'What a goose you are! Has no one ever written a sonnet to the beauty of your eyes or wondered at the bronze gleam of your hair?'

Now she was sure that he was mocking her and she felt a surge of indignation. All her old dislike of him returned. It was clear that he intended to taunt her.

'I have already apologised to you, my lord,' she said coldly. 'Was it not enough?'

'Not nearly enough,' Isham replied in solemn tones. 'I shall demand much more than an apology.' The arm about her waist had tightened, and now he drew her close. 'We have not yet sealed our betrothal with a kiss,' he murmured.

India sat very still. Physical contact was what she had been dreading from the first. Isham was still a stranger to her and she had not been given time to get to know him. She was under no illusions. He was well experienced with women, and he would be sure to find her gauche. She had no wish to be humiliated further, but she had agreed to wed him and her person would belong to him, to do with as he willed. Summoning all her courage, she raised her face to his.

Then she heard a low chuckle. 'Believe me, my love, this will not be unpleasant...' Then his mouth came down on hers so gently that the first touch of his lips was soft and warm and undemanding.

His tenderness was unexpected, and India was confused. She did not struggle, sitting within the encircling arm a prey to a mixture of emotions. The first was a sense of excitement. There was wonder too, and a strange feeling in the pit of her stomach which she could not define. She had to admit that he was right. His kiss was not unpleasant, very much the opposite in fact. She began to relax.

'Surely you did not expect brutality, my dear?' Isham sounded concerned.

India had no time to answer him. As he released her,

the coach came to a halt so suddenly that she was torn from the shelter of his arms and thrown forward on to the opposite seat. She heard the thunder of approaching hooves and the squeals of terrified horses.

The carriage began to rock so violently that they might have been in a storm at sea. Then she was pushed flat, her shoulders pinned to the leather seat as Isham lay on top of her.

She began to struggle violently as a dark shape passed the windows, looming out of the darkness, but she was helpless against Isham's strength.

'Lie still!' he warned. 'Do you wish to lose your life?'

Chapter Seven

India was terrified, convinced that the coach must overturn. Outside, all seemed to be confusion as the horses stamped and neighed, the driver cursed, and the dreadful rocking continued. Then she heard a dull thud as if someone had fallen from the box.

The motion stopped at last and a bloodstained face appeared at the window.

Isham raised India to a sitting position. Then he turned to his groom.

'Watson, are you badly hurt?' he asked.

'Just a tumble, my lord. Yourself and the lady?'

'Unharmed, I believe.'

'Then I'll go to the 'orses' 'eads, sir. They've had a nasty fright. That perishin' lunatic! Drivin' fast, without a light, and so close that 'e might have taken the paint off our doors.'

'And Hickey?'

'Swearin' something 'orrible, sir, but he ain't 'urt.'

'Then we'll go on, but tell him to take it slowly.' Isham turned to India.

'Forgive me for treating you so roughly, my dear. I

was afraid that you might break your neck, or at the very least a limb, being hurled about like that.'

'I am not hurt.' India was still trembling, but she was determined that he should not think her a coward. 'Is my bonnet straight?'

There was a long silence. Then Isham laughed aloud. 'I suspect that I am destined to become your slave,' he said. 'Extraordinary! You neither screamed nor fainted. And yes, my love, your bonnet is restored to its former glory. I'm glad to see that that was your only fear.'

She could hear the admiration in his voice, and hurried to change the subject before he chose to kiss her again. She needed time to try to understand the feelings which had troubled her on the last occasion, pleasant though it was.

'I wonder who that was?' she mused. 'You did not see, my lord?'

'No more than you, India. I suppose it might have been the doctor, on his way to an emergency...'

'No!' India shook her head. 'It must have been a stranger. No local person would take the chance of driving so fast at dusk in an unlit coach and on these narrow country lanes. The roadside ditches are so deep, you see. There have been some serious accidents.'

'Then possibly some foolish youth pursuing his hobby of driving to an inch? On occasion they pay the drivers to take the ribbons of the mail coaches...'

India swallowed. 'Then not a Luddite?' she asked in a low voice.

'Certainly not!' Isham began to chuckle. 'The followers of General Ludd do not aspire to travelling by coach. They are factory workers, India, as you know.'

A silence fell between them. Then Isham took her hand. 'Don't trouble yourself, my love. Even so, I feel it might be wise not to mention the incident to your mamma. No harm was done, and there is no need to alarm her.'

India looked up at him. 'Are we very late?' she asked. 'She may be wondering even now.'

She found that her fears on that score were groundless. Moments later the coach stopped at her door, and Isham helped her down. 'One second, India!' He stopped her beneath the light of the carriage lamp, brushed her down, and twitched gently at the brim of her bonnet.

'That's better!' he announced. 'We must not give the wrong impression.' His grin left her in no doubt of his meaning.

India found that she was blushing furiously. She summoned all the dignity she could command and stalked past him into the house. Why must he always try to put her out of countenance? As if anyone would imagine that she would so far forget herself as to allow intimacies in the back of a coach. He *had* kissed her, of course. The memory did nothing to restore her composure, and Letty gave her a long look as she walked into the parlour.

Her mother noticed nothing. 'There you are, my dears. My lord, will you take some refreshment?'

'Sadly, ma'am, I must be on my way, but if I may call on you tomorrow?'

Mrs Rushford wagged a finger at him. 'No, no!' she cried. 'Tomorrow I must have India to myself.'

India was startled. She gave her mother a look of enquiry.

'Your wedding-clothes, India! Dear me, what a girl it is! One might think...' Mrs Rushford stopped, suddenly aware that it would not be wise to criticise her daughter in Isham's presence. She must raise no doubts in his lordship's mind.

'Your uncle has offered us the use of his coach to go into Northampton to the mantua-maker.' She turned to Isham. 'You understand, my lord? There is so little time, you see.'

'I understand perfectly, ma'am.' Isham's tone was smooth. 'No doubt you will travel in daylight?'

India gave him a sharp look. Surely he did not expect further trouble on the road?

'We shall leave at an early hour,' her mother assured him. 'The coach is to come for us at ten, and we shall be back before dusk.'

'I am glad to hear it. These are worrying times. One never knows…' He left it there and took his leave of them.

'What a strange remark! What could Isham mean, I wonder?' Mrs Rushford turned to India.

'He may be thinking of the mob, Mama.'

Her mother looked at her uncertainly, torn between anxiety and the delightful prospect of a visit to the most expensive mantua-maker in Northampton.

'Those ruffians burn the factories,' she said at last. 'No one else has been attacked. Besides, they will not venture forth in daylight.'

With the matter settled in her own mind, she returned to the subject of India's bridal clothes.

'Mama, it won't be necessary,' India protested. 'I have the gowns which you bought me for my Season, some of them still unworn. Isham has offered…I mean, he suggests that I buy my trousseau after we are wed.'

'You must have a bride-gown. And what of Letty and myself? We have no wish to disgrace you…'

'We can't afford it,' India said stubbornly.

'Nonsense!' her mother's voice was sharp. 'As Isham's future bride your credit will be limitless. I thought of Madame Renaud.'

'You considered her much too expensive when we were buying for the Season.'

'Great heavens, how can I make you understand? Things are different now. Cost need not be our first consideration. You have your position to think of...'

'Isham dislikes excessive show, Mama. He feels that it would offend all notions of decorum under the present circumstances.'

Her words were disregarded.

'Gentlemen know nothing of these matters, India. You will learn in time that they do not always say what they mean, or mean what they say. Isham will wish to see you looking at your best on your wedding day.'

India would not argue further over such a trifling matter, but in the event she enjoyed her visit to the French modiste.

The day had started with a surprise. They had not travelled above a mile before Isham and his brother fell in beside them, both on horseback.

'How charming!' Mrs Rushford exclaimed in sentimental tones. 'India, you are so lucky. His lordship cannot bear to let you out of his sight. Now Letty, wave to Mr Salton. He is bowing to you.'

India shot a despairing glance at her betrothed, only to find that his eyes were twinkling with amusement. She felt ashamed and then annoyed. It was not pleasant to find any member of her family a figure of fun. He read her mind, as always, and shook his head as if to dispel the notion.

It was only when he helped her down at the mantua-maker that she understood.

'Cheer up!' he murmured. 'Your coach is not a tumbril, India, though from the expression on your face you might be on your way to execution.'

'I don't know what you mean,' she said with dignity.

'Come now, my love. We have no secrets from each other, or so I thought.'

She looked up at him. 'I told Mama that you had said...I mean, that there was no necessity to buy bride-clothes. She would not have it.'

A large hand came up to caress her cheek. 'Don't allow it to trouble you,' he soothed. 'Let her have her way. It will not be for long...' With that he remounted, signalled to his brother and they rode away.

India was pleasantly surprised by the charming French modiste. Madame was not effusive. There was no trace of the sycophant in her manner, though she welcomed her new customers with a delightful smile.

India liked her at once. This was a woman who was well aware of her own ability to transform the ugliest duckling into a woman of fashion. In her own case India felt that the task might be difficult, but she was mistaken. The little dressmaker saw at a glance that the future Lady Isham was a woman of commanding height and voluptuous figure. It would be a pleasure to dress her in the latest style.

India could only admire the tact with which Madame was able to counter Mrs Rushford's fancy for excess.

'The gown must be white, I feel,' her mother announced at once. 'White is so fashionable at this present time, and is the perfect background for French lace and satin ribands...'

'Mama, I can't!' India protested. 'We are still in mourning...'

Mrs Rushford had expected the protest, and had her answer ready. 'Giles tells me that in the East white is the colour of mourning...' she said severely.

'But this is England,' India murmured helplessly. 'Besides, in lace and ribands I should look like a birthday cake...' She caught Madame's eye and realised at once that she had an ally. Her own wishes would be paramount. From then on she was wise enough to hold her tongue. Madame had long experience of dealing with difficult customers and could handle them with ease.

'Mrs Rushford is correct in that belief,' she murmured tactfully, 'but in these days we have so much choice. I defer to your good taste, madame. Will you give me your opinion on these latest fabrics before we settle upon the exact shade?'

Mrs Rushford preened herself. After all, the fashionable dressmaker was known to import materials from all corners of the globe, silks from China, muslins from the Indian sub-continent, and even, so it was whispered, laces and satins from France, in spite of Napoleon's blockade.

Madame Renaud's clientele was exclusive. Her prices alone ensured that, but she did not agree to dress all those persons who approached her. Some were turned away with a plea of too much work in hand. Mrs Rushford had made her appointment with some trepidation, although she had guessed that India's future status would ensure her standing as a customer. Now it was very pleasant to be deferred to as the mother of the bride.

'I will look at them,' she conceded. 'Come, India, this concerns you more than anyone.'

Madame Renaud's storeroom was a treasure-house

of delights, with bolts of fabric covering the shelves from floor to ceiling. The myriad of colours dazzled the eye, but India noticed a bolt of fine grey silk, figured in a lighter shade. She stroked the material lovingly. 'This is so beautiful,' she murmured.

'But dreadfully dull, my darling.' Mrs Rushford was examining a length of bead-encrusted satin.

Much to India's alarm, Madame agreed at once with Mrs Rushford's choice, but the little modiste had matters well in hand.

'I see that you are *au fait* with the latest styles, madame. Now for yourself that would make a striking tunic. Beneath it you might wear an undergown of a harmonising shade.'

Mrs Rushford brightened. 'Ah, yes. You are right. This is so much more suitable for a sophisticated woman than for an inexperienced girl.' She pointed to a length of pink brocade. 'India, you might consider this.'

'Not with my hair, Mama.' India moved away, content to leave to Madame Renaud the onerous task of persuading Mrs Rushford that the grey silk would make a delightful bridal gown.

How Madame did it she never knew. Possibly it was the tactful suggestion that perhaps India's choice might be considered too expensive by her mother. Whatever the reason for that lady's acquiescence, India found herself being measured whilst her mother studied pattern books for the latest styles.

'Something simple, please,' she said quietly to Madame Renaud.

'But of course, Miss Rushford.' Madame studied her latest customer with interest. The girl had taste. She had chosen well. That flaming head would show to great advantage against the fine grey silk, and her height would enable her to carry off the most elegant of creations.

She sighed. How her former apprentice would have loved to dress this customer. Miss Rushford was in mourning now, but later she would be one of the few women who could wear to the best advantage the rich colours which were the trademark of her young protégée. With her quiet dignity the future Lady Isham might become one of the most striking figures of her generation.

She herself was skilled in her profession, but she was honest enough to appreciate the difference between competence and genius. And genius was not too strong a word to apply to the talents of her former apprentice. It had been a blow when the child had taken it into her head to return to Abbot's Quincey, and then made that most extraordinary decision to marry the Marquis of Sywell.

She herself would never understand it, but that mistake, at least, had now been rectified. Louise had found the courage to run away, but much as she would have liked to keep her, Northampton was much too close to home. With her help the young Marchioness had been spirited out of harm's way.

She gave a little nod of satisfaction. The decision to send Louise to her old friend Madame Coulanges in London had proved successful beyond her wildest dreams. In the space of a few short months the girl had made her name. She was pleased to think that she herself had played some part in that success. Now she could do no more.

'Miss Rushford, may I make a suggestion? You will not think me presumptuous?'

'Of course not, madame. I should welcome your advice…' India gave her a warm smile.

'It may be of use to you when you visit London. Should you require a mantua-maker I would suggest Madame Félice. She is well known to me…'

'She is well known to everyone. So many friends have written to my sister and myself, marvelling at her talents. She is quite the rage. In fact, it is said to be impossible to make an appointment with her.'

'It will not be impossible for you. Just send in my name…'

'That is so kind of you. I hear that Madame Félice is a law unto herself. She will not dress everyone. Some of our friends have been turned away.'

'She will dress you.' Madame smiled up at the tall girl to whom she had taken such a liking. 'You have the height and style to carry off her creations.'

'You flatter me!' India was startled. She had always considered herself something of a plain creature. It was a shock to realise that someone thought her elegant.

'No, I never flatter!' Madame was much struck by the charming modesty of her customer. Clearly the girl had no idea of her own potential. She looked again at the fine head with its wonderful bone structure, the high cheekbones, and the lovely lines of jaw and throat, as yet unflawed by age.

She sighed; her prices alone ensured that most of her clients were older women with wealthy husbands. Their money could not compensate for the ravages of time. Sometimes it took all her expertise to disguise a drooping bosom or a tendency to embonpoint, and to hide those flabby upper arms and wrinkled necks.

This girl had no need of such help. Louise, or Madame Félice as she now called herself, would welcome the future Lady Isham with open arms, seeing in her the perfect model for her striking creations.

Madame put the last few pins into the fabric draped about her customer. Then she turned to Mrs Rushford. A shrewd judge of character, she was unsurprised to find that India's mother had chosen the most expensive items in her collection both for herself and for her younger daughter. It was with some difficulty that she managed to persuade the older woman that true elegance depended more upon simplicity and perfect cutting rather than ornamentation.

As India was quick to agree, Mrs Rushford kept her opinion to herself until they had left the showroom. Then she turned upon India.

'I fear we shall all look very drab,' she complained. 'What Isham and his relatives will think I can't imagine.'

'The size of the bill will convince him that we have spared no expense,' India remarked drily. 'How I wish that we might have paid for our gowns ourselves.'

'Nonsense! That would have been impossible, and you know it. Sometimes I wonder at you, India. You seem to have no notion of our circumstances.'

The unfairness of this remark left India speechless. She, above any member of the family, had put the clear knowledge of their circumstances first in making her decision to wed his lordship.

Mrs Rushford continued to complain as they made their way out to the coach. She had intended that her daughter's wedding should be the envy of the neighbourhood. Now it appeared that the marriage would be outshone by that of Beatrice Roade, which would take place in the following week. She too, would be wed before Christmas.

Isabel did not trouble to hide her dissatisfaction. 'Madame Renaud has surprised me,' she grumbled. 'I cannot understand her reputation. One might think that she had no notion... She does not seem to realise that India must consider Isham's standing in the world.'

'Mama, I'm sure she does,' India soothed. 'We did explain that we are still in mourning, and she respected your own taste.'

'Of course.' Isabel was mollified by the small white lie. 'You notice that she did not argue with my choice for both myself and Letty?'

India hid a smile. The little Frenchwoman was a businesswoman. She must have been delighted with Mrs Rushford's extravagance; the wonder was that she had refused to allow her creations to be ruined by the addition of expensive lace. Even so, the bill was huge, and India felt mortified. Isham would now regard her as both greedy and irresponsible.

It would have been useless to attempt to explain these feelings to her mother, but the knowledge that she was dependent upon Isham's purse was humiliating. She walked over to the coach in silence.

Sir James's coachman was waiting by the door. Now he turned to Mrs Rushford.

'Lord Isham's compliments, ma'am. He begs that you will join him for refreshment at the Angel.'

'Of course, of course!' Isabel turned to her daughters. 'So thoughtful!' she murmured, her good humour quite restored. 'I am quite famished, I declare.'

India was amused. She wondered if Isham's friends had already left the inn. If not, her mother's face would be a study at the sight of her future son-in-law locked in the embrace of a demi-rep.

She was still smiling as she greeted her betrothed, and Isham looked at her in mock amusement.

'Has Madame Renaud succeeded where I could not?' he asked. 'You look vastly entertained, my love.'

India gave him a demure look. 'I was thinking how brave you were, my lord.'

'How so?' Isham was clearly mystified.

'I had expected to find your friend embracing you with enthusiasm here at the Angel. You did not consider taking refreshment at the George?' India's eyes were twinkling, but if she had hoped to disconcert him she was mistaken.

'Minx!' he retorted. 'Do you take me for a coward, India? In any case, the lady has departed, with her friend.'

'I'm glad to hear it,' she said solemnly. 'So difficult to explain away a lady hanging about one's neck! Mama would have been astonished!'

'I expect she would.' Isham began to chuckle. 'Should I have chosen the George, my love?'

'Not at all, my lord. I am persuaded that you are well able to explain away any untoward behaviour in the most unpromising of circumstances.'

'Ouch! India, you terrify me! Excuses wither beneath your gaze.' He was laughing openly as he led them through into the private parlour.

If his guests had expected a simple nuncheon they found that they were much mistaken. Mine host, overcome by his lordship's patronage on two successive days and charmed by that gentleman's largesse, had spared no effort either on his own part or that of his cook.

The company sat down to a fine roast goose, accom-

panied by a number of different stuffings, a selection
of buttered vegetables, and a variety of side dishes.

India looked at Lettty. 'Great heavens!' she murmured. 'The man might have been asked to feed an
army.'

Henry had overheard her. 'Well, I for one am starving, India! We shall do full justice to this feast.' He
made haste to seat the ladies, placing himself between
India and her mother, and leaving Isham to sit at the
head of the table with Mrs Rushford on his right and
Letty on his left.

'Now we shall be comfortable,' he announced as he
turned to Isabel. 'Ma'am, you cannot imagine how I
dreamed of English food when I was in the East.'

Mrs Rushford smiled indulgently. 'Surely there were
compensations, Mr Salton? We hear so much of the
fortunes to be made on the Indian continent.'

'Yes, ma'am, that is true, but they are not so easily
come by. Much of the trade is in the hands of long-
established merchants. A newcomer may struggle for
years to gain a foothold.'

'How long were you there?' India asked.

'Not long enough, I fear.'

'Then why did you return?'

'You will despise me, India, but I was homesick for
England and my family. And I worried about my
mother. Since my father died she has no one else, you
see.'

'Surely your brother…?'

'Oh, pray do not mistake me, ma'am. Anthony is the
soul of goodness, but he is not her own flesh and blood.
Sadly, it makes a difference.'

'I expect it would.' India heard the note of reservation and once again she was puzzled. On the surface

the two half-brothers appeared to be the best of friends. Was there some mystery in their relationship which was unknown to her? It would have been a breach of taste to question her companion. If there were difficulties she would be sure to hear of them in time.

'Did you see anything of the Indian princes?' she asked. 'We are told that their wealth is fabulous.'

'It is beyond belief,' he agreed. 'Rubies as large as pigeons' eggs, enormous ropes of the finest pearls, sapphires, diamonds and chests filled with gold and silver.'

'Then their countries must be prosperous?' India looked thoughtful. 'Yet I had heard that the poverty was extreme…'

'That is the dark side of the continent. Pray do not think of it. It would distress you.'

'But I'd like to know…'

'Are you quite sure? You can have no idea of the depths to which the human race can be reduced.'

India caught her mother's eye. Mrs Rushford was shaking her head vigorously and glaring at her as she framed a sharp rebuke. Then she thought better of it, aware of Isham's presence by her side.

'Dear India! Mr Salton, my daughter is inclined to take upon her shoulders the troubles of the world. Why, only this week she must rescue two of the most ragged urchins imaginable, and foist them upon Lord Isham. As you say, his goodness is beyond belief.'

'Why, ma'am, I believe I foisted them upon myself.' Isham had turned to Mrs Rushford and was smiling down at her, but there was a slight edge to his voice. 'I am glad to see that you are concerned about the lads. Would it please you to come over to the Grange to-morrow? You may satisfy yourself as to their welfare and at the same time examine the alterations to the place. You may have some suggestions?'

India hid a smile. His lordship was a formidable opponent. Once again he had turned aside her mother's criticism in the most tactful way.

Mrs Rushford heard only the invitation, which she accepted at once.

With Isham's wealth at her command she intended to make herself as comfortable as possible. To date he had raised no objections to anything she suggested. For the first time since her marriage the Grange would be transformed to her own liking. From there she could lay her plans and set about finding a splendid match for Letty. Possibly even Henry Salton.

Now she turned to him again. 'I thought perhaps you had come to England to find yourself a bride,' she tittered. 'So many gentlemen return from the East with that purpose in mind.'

'They do, ma'am,' he told her solemnly. 'There are many hundreds of men for every Englishwoman in the East. The ladies have us at a disadvantage in one respect, but it is a fearful country for a delicately nurtured female. The graveyards are filled with those who have succumbed to the climate and disease. Their children often join them.'

The subject was not to Mrs Rushford's taste. With a pitying smile she turned to Isham and began to discuss the alterations at the Grange.

'Do go on,' India said warmly. Henry had surprised her. For a young man he had shown unexpected sympathy for the plight of his fellow human beings in an alien land. 'It is a wonder that any woman would consider such a life.'

'I would not ask it of anyone I loved,' he assured

her. 'Nor would you, I expect. Will you not tell me of the boys in Isham's charge? I have not seen them yet.'

Isham had heard the remark and now he shook his head in mock reproach. 'Brother, take care!' he warned. 'I would not have India believe that I have drowned them in the well.'

This brought a smile from the assembled company, but India felt moved to protest. 'As if I should!' she cried. 'Especially after you gave the sweep in charge and cautioned that dreadful woman.'

Henry threw up his hands. 'I stand corrected, Anthony. You have the staunchest of champions.' He turned to India with a low aside. 'Did I not tell you that he is a different man? It is due entirely to your influence...'

Once again India was troubled. Was Henry hinting at some shameful secret in Lord Isham's past? He must have seen some reservation in her look, for he made haste to dispel her fears. 'Must I continue to assure you that he is the best of men?' he chaffed. 'Who should know better than I?'

Strangely, India was unconvinced, though Henry was smiling. That smile broadened as Isham began to tease him.

'I'm not surprised that you haven't yet met the lads,' he said. 'They are up with the lark whilst you are still abed.'

Henry assumed a penitent look. Then he appealed to India.

'You see my problem, ma'am? I shall never measure up to Anthony's standards. He regards me as a lazy good-for-nothing.'

'I am quite sure that he does not,' India said warmly.

'There is not the slightest reason for you to take an interest in the boys...'

'Yet Anthony has done so. Why is that, do you suppose?'

'I believe it was to please me. The circumstances were so strange...' She went on to explain.

'Great heavens, ma'am! The lads might have been burned to death in the factory fire...'

'It was fortunate that they escaped, but Joe, the elder boy, is quite resourceful. Now I have no fears for them.'

'You think highly of my brother, ma'am.'

'Naturally, since I have agreed to marry him.' India had stiffened. She was not prepared to discuss her opinion of Lord Isham even with his brother.

Henry, as always, sensed her reserve. Now he engaged her mother in conversation and India was at liberty to glance across at her betrothed. It came as no surprise to find that he was fully occupied with Letty. For once her timid sister looked positively animated. There was no trace of reserve in her friendly manner towards his lordship. India felt oddly betrayed and very much alone to think that Letty, of all people, would change sides.

Then she took herself to task. She was behaving like a child. She should be grateful that Isham was doing his best to please her family. It was more than she might have expected, especially in view of her own ambivalent attitude towards him.

Suddenly she was aware of some altercation at the far end of the table.

'No apple dumplings?' Isham was announcing in astonishment. 'My good fellow, you have let me down!'

The landlord wrung his hands. 'My lord, if you had only said...if you had expressed a wish...'

'His lordship is funning,' India said serenely. 'The apple pie and the custard tarts will serve us very well.'

Mrs Rushford looked amazed. 'Hold your tongue!' she hissed. 'It is not your place to speak out in this way.'

India gave her mother a steady look. It reduced her to silence. India had made it clear that from now on she would not be dictated to. That conclusion was confirmed when Isham spoke.

'Quite right, my love. Landlord, you have done us well... I must wait in patience for my apple dumplings.' He laughed across at India as if to share some private joke.

Her daughter's new-found independence was not to be the only shock for Isabel that day. When the two gentlemen insisted on accompanying them back to Abbot's Quincey she found nothing strange in the suggestion, but India had begun to wonder. Was Isham expecting further trouble on the road, perhaps from the Luddite mob? His sudden decision to visit Northampton at a time that coincided so exactly with her own seemed odd. He had not mentioned it on the previous day. On the journey home she was preoccupied.

Then, as the carriage stopped outside their door, she gave a cry of joy. 'Mama, Giles is home!' She ran down the path to greet her brother.

Chapter Eight

Giles hugged her briefly, then disengaged himself and turned to greet Letty and his mother. He stood aside to let the entire party into the house, directing a look of enquiry at Isabel. The two gentlemen were unknown to him.

'Lord Isham, may I present my son?' Mrs Rushford said quickly. 'Giles has been away from us for some little time, but he will be delighted to make the acquaintance of India's future husband and also that of Mr Henry Salton, his brother.'

Giles looked far from delighted. His normally pleasant face had darkened and his bow was stiff. Civilities were exchanged, but on Giles's part they were perfunctory to the point of insult.

India could have slapped him, quite forgetting her own initial reaction to his lordship. Giles had inherited all his late father's charm, but none of it was in evidence. Now Isham would think her brother a country bumpkin who had no idea of how to behave in polite society. She gave him an angry look.

Isham appeared to be unaware of the young man's hostility. Now he drew India aside.

'With your brother so recently returned to you, you will not wish to visit the Grange tomorrow, as we had arranged. Will you let me know when it will be convenient? Mr Rushford will be most welcome to join you, naturally.'

She looked up at him then, and found that he was smiling. 'You are most forbearing,' she admitted reluctantly. 'Giles is...er...not himself today.'

'So I have another hill to climb?' Without waiting for her answer, he summoned his brother with a reminder that they were promised to dine with the local magistrate that evening.

The door had scarcely closed upon them before India rounded upon her brother.

'How could you have behaved so ill?' she asked. 'I was ashamed of you.'

'Ashamed of *me*?' Giles was scowling openly. 'What of you? I was never so astonished in my life as when I heard that you had agreed to wed that loathsome creature. Have you forgotten what he did to us?'

'I have forgotten nothing,' India told him. 'And he is not a loathsome creature. At least he behaved like a gentleman, which is more than I can say for you.' Once again she was surprised to find herself defending her betrothed.

'Oh, children, pray do not quarrel.' Mrs Rushford had begun to weep. 'I will not have a scene. My health won't stand it. Giles, my love, you don't understand...'

'On the contrary, Mother, I understand this matter all too well. India has sold herself to keep us out of penury. She will save this family where I could not. You must be very proud of her.'

India's face was ashen. She could not answer him. His words were too close to the truth.

It was the gentle Letty who flew at him. 'You know nothing of Lord Isham, Giles. You are judging him in ignorance of his character.'

Giles stared at her. Letty's face was pink with anger and her sudden outburst startled him. He recovered quickly.

'Must I bow to your superior judgement? Letty, I am surprised at you. Father's death must be laid directly at Isham's door, to say nothing of the fact that he has ruined us.'

'That isn't true!' The normally timid Letty refused to be silenced. 'Be honest, Giles! It was Father who gambled everything away. Isham did not force him to sit down at the tables.'

Giles began to pace about the room. 'That may be so,' he admitted grudgingly. 'Even so, he can have no place in our family. Great heavens, India, what do you see in him? An ugly fellow, if ever I saw one, and with a reputation to match. If you had to choose a wealthy husband there are others. Could you not have found someone else?'

India had recovered much of her composure. 'I doubt it, Giles. As you know, I had no offers...' She prayed that Giles would not discover that Isham had offered for either of his sisters, leaving the choice to them. In his present mood he was certain to ride over to the Grange and call his lordship out. He was unlikely to overlook the insult.

Mrs Rushford tried to stem her tears. 'My darling

boy, you should not think unkindly of your sister. We all agreed...I mean, India did everything for the best.'

'You should have stopped her, Mother. You could have forbidden the match. In any case, I am the head of this family now. I might have been consulted.'

'You were not here,' Letty replied quietly. She had said all that she intended, and now she retired to the window-seat and picked up her embroidery.

'Should I have stayed here in this house, and lived on Uncle James's charity?' Giles demanded. 'Why do you suppose I left? It was to find some occupation...'

Letty did not answer him. It was India who became aware of his dejected look and understood. Her brother was suffering from bitter disappointment and hurt pride. He loved them all and blamed himself for being unable to help them. She gave him a loving smile, but it was Mrs Rushford who spoke.

'My dear, do try to understand. This is a splendid match for India, and his lordship has been so generous. Why, even now he is restoring the Grange. He has invited us to see it...'

'You may go, but I shall not. I have no wish to see a stranger in my home.'

'But it is to be our home now. After the wedding Letty and I will live there. It is a part of India's settlement.'

'I wish her joy of it, and Isham too.'

'Please don't be cross, my darling. I felt sure you would be glad to share in India's happiness.'

'Are you happy, India?' Giles stopped his pacing and stood in front of her, his eyes looking deep into her own.

India did not flinch. 'Yes!' she said steadily. 'Isham and I have much in common…'

Her brother gave a sarcastic laugh. 'Gambling? Opera-dancers? You surprise me, India.'

'Possibly, but I have given my word. This marriage will take place, and you, Giles, will give me away.'

'Never! I shall not attend. I will not see you yoked to a man who will bring you nothing but misery.'

This was too much for Mrs Rushford. With a feeble sigh she fainted.

'Now see what you have done!' Letty dropped her work and hurried over to her mother, whilst India chafed her hands.

'Bring me some brandy!' she snapped over her shoulder.

Giles hurried to do her bidding. Then he stood by helplessly until his mother recovered consciousness.

'Mama, I did not mean… Oh Lord, I'm sorry!'

India had summoned Martha, and together she and Letty helped the stricken woman to her room.

Then India turned to her brother. 'Don't blame yourself too much,' she murmured. 'It does not take much to overset Mama. She has been under a strain.'

'I know it.' Giles had slumped into a chair. 'I haven't helped, though, have I? I wanted so much to help you all, but it seems that I fail in all I try to do.'

'Nonsense!' India said robustly. 'In these past few years you have restored so much of the estate.'

'But it didn't save us, did it?'

'How could it, love? I haven't been blind, you know. There were so many demands upon you…'

'It's true. Money that might have been used for seed, or stock, or drainage and ditching was all swallowed up…I don't mean to criticise, but if Father could have understood…'

'It wasn't in his nature, Giles, but we loved him for the man he was. I still miss him dreadfully.'

'So do I.' It was true in spite of all his father's failings, though sometimes he had despaired of bringing the estate into a profitable concern.

The present situation of the family was nothing new. Nine years ago he had been summoned back from Italy by his uncle with a suggestion that he take the management of their lands into his own hands. Even then they had been on the brink of ruin, but he had brought things round. This time he could do nothing.

'I so wish you happy, India,' he told her gently. 'If it will please you I'll attend your wedding and give you away.'

'I knew you would.' She gave him a tender smile. 'Now you shan't despair. Won't you give me all your news?'

'There isn't much, I'm afraid. Conditions are disastrous everywhere, partly due to Napoleon's blockade and in part to the failed harvest. No one has need of a manager for their estates.'

'It will come round. It cannot last.'

'I don't know. There is so much disaffection in the country. Martha tells me that there has been trouble here.'

'Yes, they are known as Luddites. The workmen burned a factory earlier this week.' She went on to tell him the story of the climbing boys and Isham's part in their rescue.

'You surprise me,' he said when she had finished.

'From what I heard of him it does seem out of character.'

'You should have heard him with the sweep.' India's lips curved in a reminiscent smile. 'He put the fear of God into that man, and rightly so.'

'A knight in shining armour?' Giles said wickedly.

'Hardly, but he did not hesitate to offer his help when I needed it. Mother, you see, did not want the boys to stay here.'

'I can imagine. Urchins are not her style, I fear.' Giles regarded her with his head on one side. 'You haven't changed, I see. Still battling on the side of justice?'

She bore his teasing with good grace. 'I've never yet learned to stand aside,' she told him.

'And Isham does not mind?'

'I think it amuses him. He was good enough to tell me that he had not time for a milk-and-water miss.'

'That's fortunate. Certainly he has not chosen such a one.' Then he grew thoughtful. 'The trouble is spreading, India. It is rife in Derbyshire and further north.'

'You do not think that it will come to revolution?' she cried in alarm. 'Those horrors in France! I could not bear it if it were to happen here.'

'It is unlikely, love. We grumble in this country, and even riot upon occasion, but we are not given to savagery.'

'I hope you are right. Oh, Giles, you will stay with us now that you are home?'

'If you have room for me. This place is very small.' Giles looked about him. 'Uncle will offer me a bed at Perceval Hall. It may be more convenient for you.'

'No, it won't. You may have my room. Letty and I will share. Then I shall be able to impress you with my cooking…'

He laughed at that. 'Is there no end to your talents, sister dear? What time do you plan to dine? I have promised to visit Uncle William at the Rectory.'

'Shall we say at seven?' India waved him off and went upstairs to change her dress. There was much to do. A meal that might serve quite well for three ladies would do nothing to satisfy the appetite of a hungry man.

She inspected her larder with some anxiety. The remains of the leg of pork would fricassée and there were plenty of winter vegetables. She set Martha to peeling carrots and turnips in preparation for mashing them together with pepper, salt and a lump of butter. A tough old hen would casserole, with onions in the pot, and the eggs would make an omelette to be thickly spread with jam.

She was sorting through her selection of preserves when Letty came to find her.

'Anything I can do?' her sister asked.

'You might beat these eggs. How is Mama?'

'Much better now. Delighted to see Giles, of course, but, India, she is so troubled because you quarrelled.'

'We've made it up. I can't be cross with him for long. Letty, it was so good of you to take my part.'

'I like to be fair,' her sister said calmly. 'Isham is much maligned. In reality, he is the best of men.'

'Those were Henry's words.'

'Oh, were they?' Letty began to beat the eggs.

'Letty, you don't care for Mr Salton. Why is that?'

'I don't know him, India. May I not reserve my judgement?'

'You haven't done so in the case of Isham.'

Letty was silent.

'I must ask you something.' India was aware that she was on dangerous ground. 'You and his lordship? Well, you seem to get along so well. Please tell me! Do you regret that you did not accept his offer? You might deal together much better than he and I.'

Letty stared at her in astonishment.

'Forgive me!' India faltered. 'I could not help but notice that you are always deep in conversation. Letty, it is not too late. If you wish it I can give back word.'

Letty shook her head. 'You must be mad!' she said with conviction. 'Isham is not interested in me. He loves you, India. Have you not seen it?'

'How could he?' India was unaccountably annoyed. 'Had you forgot? He would have taken either of us to suit his purpose.'

'Would he?' Letty continued to beat the eggs. 'In case *you* had forgot, my heart is given to Oliver Wells.'

'Have you heard from him?'

'Not yet.' Letty's smile was mysterious as she went on with her work.

India was growing impatient. Strange undercurrents seemed to be flowing through her life. She neither understood nor liked them.

'Well, Giles at least is home,' she said with satisfaction. 'Letty, I have been thinking. If the Grange is to be mine, to do with as I please, Giles might agree to manage the estate for me. There would be money enough to improve the land and restock it and he could live with you.'

'I don't know. He might regard the offer as coming from Isham. He would not accept his lordship's charity.'

'It wouldn't be charity,' India said indignantly. 'There is so much to do. He would have to work all the hours God sends. I shall speak to Isham about it. Meantime, do not mention it to Giles. He is coming round to the idea of my marriage. I have no wish to upset him again.'

'He has agreed to give you away?'

'Yes, thank heavens! I could not bear a family feud, especially now.'

'I agree. Nothing is more horrible, and Giles too has enough to worry him. Oh, India, he used to be so carefree as a boy. Do you remember? He was always laughing and joking and playing pranks.'

'I know. It was after he returned from Italy all those years ago that we found him changed.'

'Perhaps it was the responsibility of the estate. He was young to undertake it, though Father was happy to hand it over to him. Poor Giles! Life has not been easy for him.'

'That's true. And then, at thirty, to be forced to face the bitterest blow of all? His work apparently gone for nothing? I cannot blame him for feeling bitter.'

'It will all be different now,' Letty comforted. 'Do you think you can persuade him?'

'I don't know. Anthony may be able to suggest how...' India stopped, feeling a little self-conscious, but Letty smiled to herself. Was her independent sister beginning to rely upon the judgement of her formidable suitor?

India was aware of her amusement. 'Letty, you need

not laugh,' she said indignantly. 'Isham seems to have a gift for getting what he wants...'

'He does indeed!' Letty's tone was solemn, but her eyes were twinkling.

'I meant only that as a man he might be able to advise me as to what might weigh most with Giles. Men are the strangest creatures. I shall never understand them.'

'A task for a lifetime!' Letty agreed. 'Shall you speak to his lordship soon?'

'Yes. The sooner the better. Giles is so unhappy at this present time. I would change that if I could.'

'It would be wonderful. He might become himself again.'

'I'm not so sure. Perhaps it is my fancy, but sometimes I felt that there was something else upon his mind, not merely the estate. I did not like to question him and he said nothing, but I wondered if something happened to him whilst he was in Italy.'

'An unhappy love affair? But, India, that was a full nine years ago. He would have forgotten it by now.'

'Would you?' India looked at her sister's face and was stricken. 'Oh, love, I'm sorry. I did not mean to hurt you, but Giles may be no less constant than yourself.'

'You are right. Time does not always heal a wounded heart. I have often wondered why Giles has made no effort to find himself a bride. Mama has been troubled by it.'

'I wondered too, but thought perhaps that he felt himself in no position to offer for anyone.'

'I can't think why. He is so charming and so handsome, although I may be biased.'

'Me too.' The girls looked at each other and laughed, in complete accord in their opinion of their brother.

At that moment the subject of their conversation walked into the kitchen. Giles was looking grim.

'What is it?' India asked in alarm. 'Is someone sick at the Vicarage?'

Giles shook his head. 'They are all well, but there has been more trouble. Last night a man was shot. Uncle William was called to attend his deathbed.'

'Murder?' Letty had paled.

'I can think of no other word for it. He was travelling peacefully about his business when he was fired on from behind a hedge.'

'But why?' Letty was horrified.

'No reason, as far as we know. Uncle thinks that he might have been mistaken for one of the factory owners.'

'Luddites again? Oh, Giles, this is so unlike our local men. They may have grievances, but I can't believe this of them.'

Her brother gave her a sharp look. India was no fool. 'Uncle shares your opinion, but the word is now that agitators are moving in from other parts of the country. They are not weavers. Their purpose is to stir up trouble.'

India grew thoughtful. Isham must have heard of the incident, though he had not mentioned it to her. Was this the reason for his sudden appearance earlier in the day? He and his brother had ridden close beside their carriage on the journey to Northampton, and also on their return. Her mother had ascribed it to his wish to be with India. Now, it seemed, there might be a more sinister explanation.

'Pray do not tell Mama,' she urged. 'There is nothing we can do, and it will frighten her.'

Suddenly she felt an overwhelming wish to see Isham. He would be honest with her and she knew that he would not try to shield her from the stark facts.

She broached the subject of their proposed visit to the Grange as they sat down to dine.

'When shall you like to go, Mama?' she asked.

'I thought it was arranged that we are to go tomorrow. His lordship suggested it himself.' Mrs Rushford looked more cheerful since her family appeared to have resolved their differences.

'He felt that you might prefer to put it off since Giles is home, although, of course, Giles is included in the invitation.'

'No, you shall not ask that of me,' Giles said quickly. A look from India reminded him that he was not to upset their mother. 'I shall, of course, give India away. If you will forgive me, Mother? I spoke in haste.'

'My dear boy, it is perfectly understandable.' Isabel smiled fondly at her first-born. Then she turned to India. 'I suppose it is too late to renew our arrangements for tomorrow. Perhaps the following day if it is convenient to Isham? After that we shall have too much to do. I must speak to your uncle to see if we may have the carriage again. We have not yet chosen our bonnets, though it will mean another journey to Northampton.'

India caught her brother's eye. 'No!' she said at once. 'I mean, we still have unworn bonnets from last Season. Besides, we cannot continue to monopolise the carriage. Uncle James may need it himself.'

Mrs Rushford waved aside the objection. 'Your un-

cle wishes you to do the family credit,' she snapped.
'As to last Season's bonnets, it is not to be thought of.
They will be dated, and in any case they were intended
for summer wear.'

It was Letty who stepped into the breach. 'Would it
not be best to wait until our wedding clothes arrive?'
she asked quietly. 'Without them it will be difficult to
decide upon style, or colour.'

Mrs Rushford gave the matter her consideration.
'You are right, my dear,' she said at last. 'So sensible!
Very well, let us visit the Grange as soon as possible,
though how we are to send word to Isham…?'

'I'll go.' Giles was ashamed of his previous out-
bursts and was anxious to make amends. 'Just give me
a note for him. I shall have no need to stay. I'll ride
over to the Grange tomorrow.'

Giles was as good as his word, but in the event his
absence was so prolonged that India was in a fever of
anxiety. At best he might have quarrelled with Isham,
and at worst he might be lying in some ditch, the victim
of yet another cowardly attack.

It was late in the afternoon when he returned.

'Where on earth have you been?' India demanded.

'Just to the Grange.' Giles was looking thoughtful.
'I say, India, did you know that Isham was with Sir
John Moore at Corunna?'

'No. I knew that he had served in Spain, but I
thought he was with Wellesley.'

'That was later. Great heavens, we can't imagine
what conditions were like out there. My hair was standing on end!'

'He told me a little about it, but he did not go into detail.'

'I'm not surprised. You can have no idea... Still, if he would not tell you I'm sure that I shall not.'

'So you have been discussing military tactics for all this time?'

'Oh no, he took me round the Grange. It will astonish you. Everything is so much improved, and he has plans for the estate. I was surprised by his knowledge of the latest farming methods. He knows Italy, too...' His face clouded, and India's belief that he had unhappy memories of that country was confirmed.

'Farming?' she returned quickly to her brother's favourite topic. 'I had not thought that he would take an interest. Do not most gentlemen leave that to their managers?'

'Isham doesn't think it altogether wise. The man in Cheshire has a free hand, but Isham is in a position to seek the best advice and to pass it on. He knows how to make a profit.'

For the next hour India was treated to a lengthy discourse upon fertilisers, crop rotation and the merits of different types of cattle and sheep. She was only partially-attending, as she did not understand the half of it, but she was pleased. If she could persuade Isham to agree, Giles might yet take over the management of her estate.

She stopped her brother at last. 'So the date of our visit is acceptable to Anthony?'

'Oh, yes! He'll send his carriage. We are welcome at any time.'

'We?' India was smiling.

'Well, yes. I've been a fool. He ain't one half as bad as I thought him.'

'I'm glad to hear it.' Privately, India gave full credit to her betrothed. Not only had he found a place in Letty's affections, but he seemed well on the way to disarming her brother too. How like him to seize upon the topic so dear to Giles's heart.

When they reached the Grange on the following day she found that Giles had not exaggerated. Her old home had been transformed, and Mrs Rushford was in transports of delight.

'Was I not right to choose the colours and this furniture?' she demanded.

India agreed. The crumbling walls and rotted paintwork were now restored and all was light and airy. Not everything had been discarded, and she was glad to find that many of the old family treasures were still in place.

Isham drew India aside. 'Do you approve?' he asked. 'If not, anything can be changed. Perhaps I should have consulted you, rather than your mother, but at the time I thought it politic to apply to her.'

'Very wise!' India said drily. 'You have found your way into the hearts of all my family, so it would appear.'

'Even yours?' He was looking at her intently.

'It is all delightful.' She was quick to avoid the question. 'Pray do not consider changing anything on my account.'

She was surprised to see that he was looking disappointed. 'Anthony, I need to talk to you,' she whispered. 'May we not be private for a moment?'

'Certainly, my love.' He led her into a small room which he had furnished as a study. 'What is it, India?'

'I think that you have heard about the murder, is that not so?'

He nodded.

'Then that was why you rode beside us to Northampton?'

'Not altogether.' He gave her a brief smile. 'I had a natural wish to see you.'

'Be honest with me, please. Do you think that there is serious danger?'

'I doubt it. The Government will send troops to settle the disorder. Meantime, it might be wise to stay close to home. You are in no danger at the cottage.'

'I see.' India hesitated. 'It was kind of you to speak to Giles about his interests.'

Isham grinned at her. 'I am all good nature,' he said solemnly. 'Do I take it that his hackles have died down?'

'You know it.' Again she hesitated, and then she decided to take the plunge. 'I have been wondering...I mean, only if you agree...but would it be possible to let him manage the estate?'

'It is yours to do with as you will, my dear, though I confess that it is what I had in mind. I hear good reports of him from all the workers.'

On an impulse she laid her hand upon his arm. 'That is good of you,' she said warmly. 'You will have no cause to regret it if only...'

'If only he will accept? Leave it to me. I shall make severe conditions and ask his leave to doubt if he can manage the place. If that does not spur him into action I do not know what will.'

'Oh!' she uttered. 'I am so grateful to you.'

'I do not want your gratitude, my dear.' Isham's tone

was oddly harsh. 'Come, you will wish to see your
protégées...' He took her arm and led her down the
passage and into the kitchens.

She could hardly recognise Joe and his brother.
Scrubbed clean and clad in warm but serviceable clothing, they were seated at the table devouring a hearty
meal. As India entered the room they stood up and
bowed.

'Mrs Dowling, you are not feeding them again?'
Isham murmured in mock horror. 'These lads will
burst.'

'Now, my lord, you said as they were to 'ave all that
they could eat.' The plump cook was untroubled by her
master's teasing. 'Clemmed, they was, poor lads!'

'They look so much better now.' India smiled at the
woman.

'Thank you, ma'am.' Mrs Dowling bobbed a curtsy.

'This is your new mistress. She is Miss Rushford
now, but in two weeks time she will be Lady Isham.'

'And much happiness I wish you, ma'am, and you
too, sir. Now Joe, take those plates, and see that they
are properly washed. Then you can fetch me some po-
tatoes.'

Obediently, Joe slid off his stool, followed by his
brother. India stopped him as he passed.

'Joe, are you happy here?' she asked.

The look in his eyes was answer enough for her, as
was the glance of dumb devotion which he fixed upon
his lordship. Then he nodded and hurried off to carry
out his orders.

'Are they behaving themselves?' she asked the cook.

'Yes, ma'am. Trouble is, they tries to do too much.

That Joe now, 'e's a grand little chap. Looks after the young 'un like a mother.'

'Thank you for looking after them.' India held out her hand.

'Nay, ma'am, no call for that. I'm covered in flour as you can see, but thank you kindly all the same.'

'You have made another conquest, India.' Isham chuckled as he drew her away. 'I suspect that in future all my staff will respect your wishes rather than my own.'

'Then let us hope that they coincide, my lord.' India gave him a demure look.

'Witch! I doubt that they will do so, at least not upon all subjects.' He looked up as Giles and Henry came towards them.

'Anthony, do you have the keys to the gun-room? Giles would like to see your latest pair of shotguns.'

'It was not your idea, of course?' Isham chaffed. 'India, my brother cannot wait to get his hands upon my latest purchase. Will you excuse me for a few moments? I prefer to handle the guns myself.'

India nodded. She was glad to see her brother looking so relaxed.

'Perhaps you would care to inspect the upper rooms?' Isham suggested. 'Let me know if you think of anything we need. I shall join you shortly.'

Letty and her mother were nowhere to be seen, so India climbed the staircase to her old room. She found to her surprise that it was the one apartment in the house where nothing had been changed at all.

This was clearly another example of Isham's thoughtfulness. He was determined, she guessed, that change was to be her choice and hers alone, in this room where she had spent so much of her childhood.

She moved on through the upper rooms, noting how tastefully the faded curtains and upholstery had been replaced. Even the tattered bed-hangings had been taken down and the new ones were a perfect match for the other fabrics in the room.

She found herself reflecting upon the curious character of the man with whom she was proposing to spend the rest of her life. Would she ever understand him? Since he had won her hand he had been kind and thoughtful, determined to please her in every way.

Yet he had a darker side. She could neither forget nor forgive the fact that the choice of a bride had been a matter of indifference to him. She or Letty? Either sister would have suited his purpose.

She shrugged. It was fortunate that her own affections were not involved. Then she heard her name. Someone was calling her from below.

By now she was close to the doorway leading to the back stairs. She opened the door and gave a cry of terror as she stepped out into space. The stairs had gone and she was hurtling towards the stone-flagged floor twenty feet below.

Chapter Nine

In a frantic effort to save herself, India flung out her arms towards the banister rail, twisting as she did so. As her fingers closed about the solid oak she flung herself bodily over the rail and, resting on her stomach, she began to slide towards the ground.

When she was a child the newel-post at the foot of the stairs had always stopped her reckless progress, but this was no childish game. She was heavier now and found that she was sliding fast. Glancing towards the end of the rail, she saw that the newel-post had been removed. She slipped off the end of the banister and landed on the ground with a dull thud.

It was enough to drive the breath from her body, and for several seconds she lay there winded, unable to move or to call for help.

Then she heard the approach of footsteps from behind, but no hand reached down to aid her. Next moment a childish scream rent the silence of the room and Joe was on his knees beside her.

'Say you ain't dead, miss...not you!' The boy was

sobbing wildly. India opened her eyes to see a look of terror on his face.

'I've had an accident, that's all,' she reassured him feebly. 'Will you fetch his lordship?'

'No, miss, I ain't leaving you.' Joe signalled to his brother, who shot out of the room at speed.

'Don't look so frightened, Joe. I am not much hurt, I think. Nothing seems to be broken.' Cautiously India tried to move her arms and legs. She had skinned her knees against the banister rail and grazed her elbow badly as she hit the ground, but otherwise she seemed to be unharmed.

'Can you help me to sit up?' With Joe's aid she managed to raise herself a little, and suddenly she felt sick.

A strong hand forced her head between her knees. Then Isham's arms were round her. 'Are you able to move?' he asked.

Conscious that she must present a sorry spectacle, India attempted to get to her feet.

'No!' he said decisively. 'Stay where you are for a moment!' Gently, he began to explore the extent of her injuries. Then, satisfied that none of her limbs were broken, he cradled her head against his shoulder.

'Can you tell me what happened?' he murmured.

For answer India looked up at the open door above the missing staircase. 'It was my own fault, Anthony. I did not look where I was going. I had no idea that the stairs had been removed.'

The swarthy face paled. 'My love, you did not fall from there?' His eyes were filled with anguish.

'Not all the way. I caught hold of the banisters. They broke my fall.'

There was a scream from the open doorway, and Mrs Rushford fainted.

Isham did not even spare her a glance. 'India, can you put your arms about my neck?' he asked quietly.

Obediently she did as she was bidden. Then, without apparent effort, he lifted her in his arms and carried her into the salon. There he laid her gently upon the nearest couch and rang the bell for his butler.

White-faced, the man appeared at once. 'Send someone for the doctor,' Isham ordered. 'And then come back to me.'

'Anthony, there really is no need to fuss,' India protested. 'No harm has been done...'

'None whatever, except that you were lucky not to break your neck.' Isham's face was grim, and it grew even darker when the butler reappeared.

'Tibbs, did I not give orders for the door above the kitchen staircase to be kept locked at all times?'

'You did, my lord. It has not been opened.'

'Really? You will find that you are mistaken. Please fetch me the key at once.'

When the man returned he looked nonplussed. 'My lord, the key has vanished.'

'Sometimes I wonder why I pay you, Tibbs. Have you an explanation?'

'None, my lord. There are so many workmen about the place. One of them may have taken it.'

'For what purpose, pray?'

'I cannot tell you, sir. Oh, my lord, I would not have had this happen for the world.' The man was badly shaken. Someone had clearly acquainted him with the story of the accident. 'Madam might have been killed.' Beads of sweat stood out upon his brow.

'She might indeed! You will now go at once and have the door nailed up. I shall have more to say to you later.'

When the man had gone India tugged at Isham's sleeve. 'Don't be too hard on him,' she whispered. 'It was not his fault.'

Isham's expression did not soften. 'I pay my staff to do their duty,' he announced. 'Tibbs knows that he must check the Grange each day.'

'He could not take up residence outside that door,' India pleaded reasonably. 'To remove the key would take no time at all. Anthony, a strange thing happened whilst I was lying on the ground. Perhaps I was confused, but I thought that someone came to me and went away again.'

'Possibly one of the workmen, afraid of the consequence of his mistake?'

'I don't know. I thought he might have tried to help me, but the first face I saw was that of Joe.'

'You gave the boys a terrible fright, to say nothing of us... Joe looked petrified. Will you just say a word to reassure him?' He crooked a finger to summon the two lads, who were crouched in a corner of the room.

India managed a smile for them. 'I am not hurt, my dears. You shall not trouble yourselves on that score, but Joe, I'd like some water, and do you think you could find my reticule?'

Both boys sped away and India chuckled. 'They will feel better if they have something to do.' She looked up as Giles and Henry entered the room.

'How is Mama?' she asked.

'Recovering,' Giles told her briefly. 'India, what on earth were you about? Why did you choose to use the staircase to the kitchen quarters?' Anxiety caused him to speak more sharply than he had intended.

India stiffened, and beside her she could sense that Isham was about to reprimand her brother for his obvious anger. She laid a soothing hand upon his arm.

'Why should I not?' she said lightly. 'I was at that end of the house. Besides, someone called to me. At least I think they did...'

'From where?'

'I thought it was from the ground floor, but I may have been mistaken.'

'Did you recognise the voice?' Isham's tone was casual.

'No, but it was certainly a man...'

Isham rose to his feet as the doctor entered the room, accompanied by Letty.

'My lord, I was on the premises attending one of the maids. Now what's all this...a convention of some kind? Small boys, gentlemen and altogether far too many people in this room! I can hardly see my patient. You will leave us, except for Miss Letty, if you please.'

India winced as he examined her battered knees and the bleeding graze on her arm. Letty was instructed to wash her injuries thoroughly. Then, as he bandaged the wounds, Dr Pettifer pronounced her fit to undertake the journey home.

He shook a warning finger at her. 'But that is on condition that you rest for the next few days. You'll be mighty stiff tomorrow, but you've had a lucky escape.'

He looked at Letty. 'The shock will be considerable too. Warmth and rest is what your sister needs. Can you guarantee it?'

'I will guarantee it.' Isham had re-entered the room. 'She will stay here.'

'No!' India's face grew rosy with embarrassment. 'Mama would not permit it. I must go back to Lilac Cottage.'

'Very well. I'll call on you tomorrow to make quite sure that you have taken my advice.' The doctor picked up his bag and departed, accompanied by Isham.

Letty tucked a rug more closely about her sister. She looked badly shocked herself. 'Isham blames himself, I think. Oh, India, what a thing to happen! Dearest, we might have lost you.'

'But you didn't! Now, Letty, may we not have an end to all this fuss? The fault was mine, and it must be a lesson to me. In future I shall look where I am going.'

Isham had returned and was gazing down at her. 'India, won't you reconsider?' he pleaded. 'Stay here, and I will promise you the best of care.'

She smiled up at him. 'You will smother me with attention, I suspect. I shall be treated like some feeble invalid, and it is unnecessary. Is Mama recovered enough to make the journey back to Abbot's Quincey?'

'Quite recovered.' Isham's face was severe. 'You will find that she blames the boys for opening the door…'

'No, no! She can't think that! You do not believe it, do you? Anthony, for them your word is law.'

'I don't believe it, India. I've questioned them and both deny it. Neither is a liar.'

India sighed with relief. Joe had looked terrified as he sank to his knees beside her prone figure, but she hadn't thought at any time that either he or Tom were responsible for the accident.

Isham rang the bell and ordered the carriage to be brought round to the entrance. Then he seated himself beside India on the sofa and took her hands in his.

'I won't forgive myself for this. Oh, my dear, I would not for the world have had it happen.'

India squeezed his hands. 'Try not to think about it,' she advised. 'You shall not blame yourself. It is over, and all is well again.'

'You are very good, my darling. Even so, I shall make enquiries...'

'Will it serve any purpose? We may never find out who removed the key after opening the door. In any case, it cannot signify...' She looked up at him and was surprised to see a look of speculation in his eyes. 'Do you know, or suspect who did it?'

'Not at all!' His face was expressionless. 'As you say, it may be a mystery for all time.'

At that moment Giles and Henry re-entered the room. Between them they supported Mrs Rushford, who tottered feebly to her daughter's side.

'Not dead, thank God!' Mrs Rushford swayed and seemed about to faint again.

'Far from it, Mama! Dr Pettifer assures me that in a few day's time I shall be fully recovered from the fall.'

'And India is to be spared all excitement and worry,' Isham said significantly. 'She is to have warmth and rest to counteract the shock.'

'I understand! He has prescribed the same for me. My constitution will not stand alarms...'

'Then, ma'am, my carriage shall take you home without delay. We shall accompany you.'

He was as good as his word, but on arriving at Lilac Cottage he and his brother could not be persuaded to stay. With a promise to return the following day they left for the Grange at once.

Mrs Rushford sank into her favourite chair and glared at India. 'You are to blame for all of this,' she accused. 'Perhaps in future you will pay more heed to your mother's warnings.'

India stared at her in astonishment. 'What have I done, Mama? I know it was thoughtless of me to have opened the door without thinking, but...'

'Stupid girl! Who do you suppose unlocked the door and took away the key if it was not those two limbs of Satan? Nasty, dirty urchins!'

'Anthony does not believe it, and nor do I.'

'At this present time Lord Isham will say anything to please you, but this time you have gone too far.'

'I trust his judgement.'

'Bah! At times I think he is as big a fool as you.'

'That will do, Mama!' Giles bent a severe look upon his mother. 'I had thought that you were pleased with his generosity and the improvement to the Grange.'

'Well, of course!' Mrs Rushford gave her son an uneasy look. She did not care to upset him. 'But, Giles, this is quite another matter. India has behaved so foolishly in persuading his lordship to interest himself in those two frightful creatures.'

'Lord Isham did not seem to think so.' Letty spoke quietly, but there was a determined set to her chin. 'And there is another thing. Both he and Dr Pettifer insist that India is not to be worried in any way.'

'I see! Only her mama is to bear the brunt of all this trouble. And now my children too are turned against

me. Oh, how sharper than a serpent's tooth is base
ingratitude!'

Weeping bitterly, Mrs Rushford allowed herself to
be supported from the room by a grim-faced Martha.

Giles smiled at his sisters. 'Don't tell me that you
believe that nonsense?' he said lightly. 'Mother should
have tried a career upon the boards. There is nothing
she likes better than a drama.'

'She *was* upset,' Letty reminded him.

'So were we all.' He glanced at India's face and
decided not to pursue the subject. 'Tell me, what did
you think of the improvements to the Grange?'

'I liked them,' Letty said at once. 'In a way I was
dreading going back in case I should remember nothing
but the day we left. We were all so sad, if you recall.'

'I'll never forget it,' Giles agreed. 'I thought our
world had come to an end.'

'In a way it had.' India shifted slightly on the couch
to relieve her aching bones.

'Shall we help you to your room?' Letty had seen
the grimace of pain. 'Would you be more comfortable
in bed?'

'No! I'm not an invalid—just a little stiff—and expecting bruises of every shade by the morning. Letty,
will you speak to Martha? She should set the mutton
on to cook...'

'My God! Are we to have Martha's efforts inflicted
upon us once more? Rather than that I'll roll up my
sleeves and undertake the task myself. Letty, will you
help me?'

'Giles, you are unkind! Martha does her best.'

'Does she? That sour face is enough to curdle the
cream...I wonder that Mother keeps her on.'

'There was no one else,' Letty said lightly. 'Pray set your mind at rest. Isham insisted upon sending along a hamper filled with luxuries of every kind. India is to dine upon cold fowl in aspic with a sallet, and to take both syllabub and fruits in jelly. Those, at least, were my orders...'

'Was there anything else?' Giles was reminded that he had not eaten for some time.

'There is enough to feed an army. You will have your work cut out to make the smallest dent in it.'

'That I should like to see.' Giles strolled off towards the kitchen.

'India, I don't mean to fuss, but you are very pale. Will you not rest upstairs for just an hour or two?'

'I think I shall do so, after all.' India struggled to her feet. 'I don't feel quite the thing...'

It was a relief to step out of her clothing and to slide between the sheets. Her cuts and scratches were beginning to hurt quite badly and she was glad of the draught which Letty gave her to still the pain.

'Shall I make you a tisane?'

'No, love, just allow me to sleep.'

Letty nodded and slipped away, but India found that sleep would not come. She began to tremble violently as she recalled the full horror of the accident—the terrifying sensation as she fell—and the certainty that her body would be broken on the flagstones far below.

It took a supreme effort of will to thrust those thoughts aside. The worst had not happened, so she must not dwell upon what might have been. Apart from a few bruises she was unharmed. At last the opiate began to take effect and she slept.

Isham himself was granted no such respite from his troubled thoughts. Back at the Grange he assembled all his staff and every workman on the place.

Yet his enquiries as to the identity of the culprit met with no success, in spite of a promise to consider extenuating circumstances.

Finally he gave up in disgust and stalked into his study. Henry followed him.

'Anthony, are you not making too much of this?' his brother remarked unwisely. 'Accidents happen every day. They can't always be avoided.' He recoiled a little at Isham's savage look.

'This one might have been,' his lordship snarled. 'It was sheer carelessness to leave that door open. We might have had a corpse upon our hands...' He turned away as if ashamed of an emotion which threatened to overwhelm him.

'But India is unharmed,' his brother soothed. 'She will soon recover her spirits, if I am not much mistaken in her.'

'Oh, she has courage enough. I saw it earlier this week when we were almost driven off the road on our way back from Northampton. I was sure that we must overturn, but her only concern was her bonnet!'

Henry did not smile. 'You did not tell me of this? Why not?'

'We decided to forget it.' A curse escaped his lips. 'Damn it! I bring her nothing but ill luck, and have done so from the first.'

'But how can that be?'

'You do not know?' The firm lips curled in a bitter smile. 'She blames me for her father's death.'

'That is ridiculous!' Henry was quick to protest.

'You did not force the man to sit down at the tables, nor did you run him over.'

'I think that India knows it in her heart, but she isn't yet ready to admit it. I believe she loved her father dearly.'

'Even so...'

'No, I must defend her! India has a brave and loyal heart. I only wish that I could win it.'

'You will do so,' Henry laughed. 'I never saw the woman yet who did not yearn to pick up your handkerchief.'

'You have met one now.' Isham was thoughtful for a few moments, but at last he shrugged. 'Come!' he said abruptly. 'Let us ride out for an hour. I want to inspect the ditching by the boundary fences.'

It was clearly an attempt to divert his thoughts from the near-tragedy of that morning and Henry made no protest, but it was not until the following day that his brother's black mood lifted.

At Lilac Cottage India and her sister were busy with their correspondence, whilst Mrs Rushford checked off the list of wedding guests. As he bowed to her Isham's eye fell upon the list, and he twinkled as he looked across at India. Then he walked over to her and took her hands in his.

'How are you today, my love?' His voice was tender as he raised her fingers to his lips.

Annoyed by his pointed lack of enquiry as to her own state of health, Mrs Rushford sniffed.

'India is feeling better than she deserves,' she announced. 'Such folly! And to give us all a fright like that? It might have been the death of me!'

The thought occurred to all three of her companions

that the accident was far more likely to have resulted in the death of India, but it was Isham who answered her. He gave her a brilliant smile.

'I'm glad to hear that India is better, ma'am. She must continue to obey Dr Pettifer's instructions—no worries or alarms, and plenty of rest, I think he said?'

His gaze rested upon Isabel for a long moment and his message was clear. He decided to reinforce it. 'I trust that she will not suffer a set-back. In such a case our marriage would have to be postponed.'

Isabel stared at him. Was he trying to warn her not to upset India? Her eyes fell before that level look. The more she saw of his lordship the less she liked him. Generous he might be, and he was always courteous, but in her heart she knew that tantrums, hysterics, tears and swooning fits would never sway this man. India was welcome to him. In the meantime she would moderate her tone.

'Mr Henry Salton is not with you, sir?' she asked.

Isham accepted the olive branch, cheered by a look of gratitude from India. She had suffered more than one tirade that morning.

'Henry is returned to London,' he said cheerfully. 'He will accompany his mother to Abbot's Quincey for the wedding.'

'Oh, dear, yes! The happy day is growing close. In fact, this very morning Sir James is to send his carriage for us. My sister wishes to discuss the arrangements for the celebrations.' Isabel looked with satisfaction at the pile of envelopes beside her. 'So many acceptances!' she marvelled. 'There is certain to be a crush, and the villagers are sure to attend. I had hoped that

India would make the effort to come with us, as it concerns her more than anyone.'

'Out of the question!' Isham said firmly. 'I must forbid it, ma'am.' He too had begun to marvel, but it was at Mrs Rushford's lack of concern at her elder daughter's welfare.

'I shall go with you, Mama, since his lordship is here to bear India company.' Letty gave her future brother-in-law a smile of complicity. Then she glanced at the clock. 'We must make haste to fetch our cloaks. It is almost eleven, and Uncle will not care for us to keep his horses waiting in this weather.' She swept her mother out of the room.

Isham drew his chair up to the sofa and possessed himself of India's hand. 'Was I masterful enough?' he grinned.

'More than enough,' India said demurely. 'You terrified me, my lord.'

'Now that I shall never believe. You are roasting me, my dear. Now tell me, are you really feeling better?'

'I am a little stiff, but that is to be expected.'

'And otherwise?'

India laughed. For once she felt at ease with him. 'My bruises have appeared in all the colours of the rainbow, but I think I shall survive.'

Isham's smile had vanished. He made as if to draw her to him, then, afraid of hurting her, he thought better of it. 'I still blame myself,' he said bitterly.

'But that is foolish, Anthony. It was an accident.'

'I suppose so. I questioned the staff and all the workmen, but no one will admit to taking the key or opening the door. Joe, I feel, knows something, but he will not speak of it.'

'You don't suspect him, I hope?'

'No, I don't. Neither he nor his brother opened the door, but I think he knows who did.'

'He was looking very frightened,' India said thoughtfully. 'Perhaps he is too terrified to speak.'

'Don't trouble your head about it. As I recall, you have been ordered not to worry, though I suspect that you have had a trying time this morning...'

'Yes, Mama was cross with me, but that is nothing new. Oh, I had forgot, I must thank you for the hamper which you sent. We dined right royally last night, but you should not have done it.'

'What! Do you dare to scold me, woman?' he said with mock severity. 'Clearly, I have not been masterful enough.' Then he gave her a guilty look. 'In any case, I've brought another one...'

'Oh, no!' she cried in laughing protest. 'How are we to eat it all, my lord?'

'You might invite me to join you?' he suggested wickedly. 'After all, I have not yet heard the details of your bride-clothes...'

'All of which are sure to fascinate you,' she teased.

He refused to be daunted. 'Then I must study the guest list. It did seem to be growing larger...'

'Shall you mind that, Anthony? I'm afraid that Mama got a little carried away. Many of our friends will be in the neighbourhood for the wedding of Beatrice Roade. She felt that they would expect to be invited to ours...'

'And you were longing for a quiet wedding?' It was his turn to smile. 'I don't mind in the least, my love, as long as you do not.'

'You have not said...I mean, is there no one of your own who must be invited?'

'Just Henry and his mother, and Stillington, who will be my other supporter. You know of him, of course. This time you will be introduced with all formality.'

'Then the lady will not accompany him?' she murmured in amusement.

'Most decidedly not!' Isham frowned at her, but his eyes were twinkling. 'Shall you never forget that episode?'

'It is engraved upon my memory.' Belatedly, India remembered her duties as a hostess. 'Will you take some refreshment, sir?'

She struggled to sit upright, but as she set her feet to the ground she winced.

Isham saw it at once and pushed her back against the cushions. Then, with scant regard for propriety, he threw back the skirt of her gown to reveal a scarred and badly swollen ankle.

'That foot requires treatment,' he announced. He strode across the room and rang the bell.

As usual, Martha did not hasten to answer it. When she appeared at last she did so with no good grace.

'Your mistress requires two bowls of water,' Isham told her. 'One must be hot and the other cold.'

'She is not my...' Martha's objection died away as she looked at the harsh face.

'Yes, Martha? You were saying...?' Isham's voice was silky with menace.

'At once, sir!' Martha scuttled away.

'What a creature, India! Why on earth do you keep her?'

'There was no one else, and she is devoted to Mama.

Don't think of her too hardly. She does try my patience sometimes, but she is an excellent ladies' maid. She is disgruntled at this present time, believing that she has come down in the world.'

'Not far enough, in my opinion. Will your mother wish to take her to the Grange?'

'I fear so, if you have no objection.'

'None whatever, my love, though she must accept that you are the mistress now. I will brook no disrespect, or sullen behaviour.'

India gave him a curious look. 'Anthony, where do you find your staff? They are all so very pleasant.'

'I leave it to my London agent. He knows my views. You will have need of a personal maid yourself. I have taken the liberty...I mean, the girl is already at the Grange. I had thought to let you meet her yesterday, but we shall leave it until you are recovered. If she does not suit you there are others...'

India smiled to herself. She was beginning to know her formidable suitor. That the girl was already at the Grange indicated beyond a doubt that she would be eminently suitable for the post. She guessed correctly that not only would she have been interviewed by the London agent, but also by Isham himself. It might be unusual for a man in his position to do so, but he would not care about that. Isham made his own rules.

She looked up as Martha reappeared with a tray. Not only had she brought the bowls of water, but she had added soft cloths of her own accord.

'Shall I help you to bathe your foot, Miss India?' Clearly, Martha was attempting to make amends for her previous ill behaviour.

'That won't be necessary,' Isham replied firmly,

though his words were accompanied by a smile of thanks. 'Miss Rushford will follow my instructions as to the required treatment.' He waved Martha out of the room.

'Now, my love, take off your stocking.'

This simple request proved impossible to follow. India could not move her bandaged arm.

He pushed aside her skirt, ignoring her feeble protests and her rising colour.

'Don't be a fool!' he said sharply. 'This is no time for modesty! In any case, I am unlikely to be roused to uncontrollable passion by the sight of two bandaged knees and a badly swollen ankle.'

The justice of this remark struck India forcibly. She struggled to keep her countenance, but it was impossible. She laughed aloud.

'That's better!' With infinite care Isham rolled down the stocking and plunged her foot into the hot water and then the cold. As he continued the treatment she looked down at the dark head and the swarthy face so intent upon its task. The long fingers had been surprisingly gentle and almost instantly the pain in her ankle began to subside.

He was drying her foot when the door opened and the doctor was announced.

'Splendid, splendid!' he enthused, as he studied Isham's handiwork. A quick examination convinced him that India's cuts were healing with no risk of infection. 'Now, my lord, if we can keep this young lady off her feet for the next week, I am persuaded that we shall not see her hobbling down the aisle.'

'A fate too terrible to contemplate,' Isham agreed. 'You hear the doctor, India? Either you obey him, or

I must consider crutches. They will add nothing to the splendour of your wedding-gown.'

India laughed again. Try as she might, it was difficult to ignore Isham's sense of humour, which coincided so exactly with her own. There lay the danger, of course. She had heard it said so often. That particular quality was irresistible to women. Men without it would never understand the appeal, but it was there. It was disarming to find a gentleman clever enough to make one laugh. She resolved to guard against it.

'His lordship was about to leave,' she murmured to Dr Pettifer.

'I am in no immediate hurry,' Isham assured her. He acknowledged the doctor's bow of farewell. Then he resumed his seat beside her. 'I believe I heard some mention of refreshments?'

'Oh, yes, I had forgot!' India could see that he was determined to stay. 'Sir, will you ring the bell?'

Martha appeared with surprising speed, removed the clutter on the tray, and returned with a bottle of claret and two glasses.

'You will join me, of course?' Without waiting for her reply he poured the wine.

'Anthony, it is not yet noon,' she protested. 'Mama would not care to see me drinking at this hour.'

'Your mother is not here. Besides, this is for medicinal purposes only. Trust me, my love, this will not develop into an orgy. For one thing, it would be difficult to find an uninjured part of your person which I might kiss with wild abandon.'

India laughed again, this time without embarrassment. Really, he was impossible.

'You may laugh, my proud beauty!' He pretended

to twirl a villainous moustache. 'Those bruises will heal and then you may beware of me...'

'A knight in shining armour may come to my rescue,' she teased, falling in with the joke.

'We've had too much rain just recently. The armour will have rusted. I shall defeat him before the blacksmith can extricate him.'

'By that time I may have run away.'

'No, you shall escape me never!' Grinning, he struck a heroic pose and India warmed to him in spite of herself. She might never learn to love him, but possibly they might be friends.

'You are happy with the arrangements for our marriage?' he asked suddenly. 'Is there anything...any way in which I might serve you?'

This reminder of her coming wedding day struck India forcibly. It was now so close. She fought down a twinge of panic and answered him.

'I think not, sir. All seems to be in hand. My aunt and uncle have been more than generous. They suggested that we move to Perceval Hall before the ceremony, but I prefer to be wed from here. Uncle will send his carriage for me...'

She was clinging to her old life to the last, Isham thought privately, but he made no comment on her decision. Instead he dropped a kiss into the palm of her hand and closed her fingers over it.

Again, the touch of his warm lips sent a thrill of excitement through her, though it was mixed with apprehension. She meant to keep her part of their bargain. Isham should have his heir, but every instinct cried out against this cold arrangement.

If she was to give herself to any man, she had

dreamed of doing so in love, but now it was too late for regrets. Isham would find her gauche and inexperienced in the arts which he understood so well. Doubtless it would send him back into the arms of his opera-dancer.

The thought should have pleased her, but for some unaccountable reason it did not. Nothing of her feelings showed in her face as he rose to take his leave of her at last.

'Until tomorrow then?' He stood looking down at her. 'For dinner?'

'Certainly, my lord. I hope to see you then.'

'Do you, my darling?' Smiling, he left her to her thoughts.

Chapter Ten

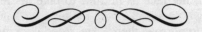

'India, have you run quite mad?' Mrs Rushford was dismayed by the news of the dinner party. 'How are we to feed his lordship? You cannot see to it, and Martha is quite unable to manage on her own. How you came to suggest it I can't imagine. It was thought-less in the extreme.'

'I didn't suggest it,' India told her quietly. 'It was Anthony who insisted. There will be no difficulty. More food has been sent over from the Grange, and knowing him I have no doubt that there is sufficient to provide a creditable meal.'

'And I can help,' Letty offered. 'Mama, you have not told India about the arrangements for her wedding.'

'They are well enough,' Isabel said ungraciously. 'It can be nothing more than a hole-and-corner affair, of course. Had it been held in London the Prince himself might have attended...Isham should take care not to offend the Regent. I hear he is slow to forgive an in-sult.'

'The Prince understands that we are still in mourn-ing. Anthony has seen him already.'

This remark reduced Mrs Rushford to a momentary silence, but she soon recovered.

'Martha tells me that Dr Pettifer has been to see you. What had he to say?'

This unexpected enquiry about her health surprised her elder daughter, but the reason soon became apparent.

'I must continue to rest my foot unless I wish to hobble down the aisle,' India replied. 'It is much easier today.'

Mrs Rushford threw her eyes to heaven. 'That is all we need!' she cried. 'Our wedding-clothes have not yet arrived, we have no bonnets, and now there will be no time to make another trip to choose them. We shall be a laughing stock...positive dowds!'

She was mistaken. Later that day the carrier brought a pile of boxes, and for the next hour Isabel was happily engaged in examining the contents. The gowns were all that anyone might have desired, but Madame, with her usual foresight, had included a number of bonnets designed to match each toilette.

Mrs Rushford turned to her daughters, resplendent in a magnificent turban made of the same beaded satin as her tunic and trimmed with aigrette. 'Does this not become me, girls?' she exclaimed in delight.

India had found another box. 'This is not ours,' she murmured. 'It must have been included by mistake.' She held up a pair of pantaloons, trimmed with fine Swiss lace in one hand, whilst the other held a ravishing negligée, made of pale green silk.

'Of course they belong to you,' Mrs Rushford scolded. 'I ordered them whilst you were choosing fabrics, India. I knew that you had given no thought to the provision of your underclothes, but you must have chemises and petticoats and nightrobes, as well as caps.'

Letty held up a pair of drawers. 'Are not these a little daring?' she asked. 'I thought it was only gentlemen who wore trousers.' She began to blush.

'They are quite the latest thing.' Her mother admonished. 'Letty, it is one thing to be modest, and quite another to be ignorant of fashion. You have seen drawers before. Your brother wears them, as you must have realised on wash-day. Now ladies are to wear them too. There can be nothing strange in that.'

India hid a smile. In the pursuit of fashion all was acceptable to her mama. She closed the box, a little perturbed at the probable cost of all this finery, and even more by the prospect of appearing before her husband in the wispy negligée, which left nothing to the imagination.

When their mama had gone upstairs to rest, India questioned Letty.

'I'm sorry about the dinner. Shall you mind very much? It would have been uncivil of me to refuse such a clear request.'

'I don't mind it the least, though it is sure to be a crush. Isham is so large. He will fill our little dining-room.' Letty giggled. 'We shall have our elbows in each other's ribs.'

'I can't think what possessed him when he might have dined in comfort at the Grange.'

'It could not be that he wished to spend the evening with you?' Letty said slyly.

India smiled, but she shook her head. 'Why are you so determined to prove that he holds me in affection?

It simply isn't true. Isham and I are strangers to each other. Besides, the leopard cannot change his spots. Doubtless he will continue to gamble and to womanise after we are married. I am not fool enough to think that I can change him.'

Letty was looking deeply troubled, but she persisted. 'I was persuaded that you had grown to like him better, India. He has been so very kind...'

'Kind, generous, thoughtful and amusing,' India agreed. 'Perhaps if I could forget the past...? Well, it does not signify.' She shrugged her shoulders. 'Let us discuss our arrangements for tomorrow.'

'No!' Letty's face was pink with determination. 'I will say this, though you may hate me for it. You are being most unfair to Lord Isham. You have not given him a chance to make you love him. Feeling as you do, you should break off the engagement.'

India stared at her normally timid sister in amazement. Letty's outburst was so totally out of character, and the criticism stung, especially as it was justified. 'I won't do that,' she said coolly. 'This marriage will take place.'

Then, as the tears sprang to her sister's eyes, India relented. 'I will be good,' she promised. 'And you are right. Anthony and I are on the way to becoming friends. He makes me laugh, you see. It is difficult to be upon my high ropes for long. Tomorrow I shall make amends.'

It was not to be. The following morning brought Isham's groom with a message of regret. His lordship had been called to London on urgent business.

India's misgivings returned. Anthony had not mentioned such a possibility, and she found herself speculating as to the exact nature of this so-called 'urgent business'. She said as much to Letty.

'Oh, India, will you not trust him for just this once? Must you always believe the worst?'

India was honest enough to acknowledge the justice of her sister's remark. Again, she had prejudged without knowing all the facts. Even so, she was impatient for an explanation.

This was not to be vouchsafed for several days and, confined to her couch, she had plenty of time to think. It was fruitless to try to imagine what could have taken Isham away so suddenly. She would put it out of her mind, but that was easier said than done.

She groaned inwardly at Letty's attempts to interest her in craft-work.

'You might paint a memorial screen,' Letty suggested artlessly.

'It would be a memorial to my ineptitude, my love. Have you forgot my efforts at the Academy? I tried painting on glass, on velvet, in fact, upon any available surface. The results were just the same. Mrs Guarding despaired of me.'

'Oh no, she didn't!' Letty began to smile. 'She prized learning above the more usual accomplishments.'

Visitors were a welcome diversion for the invalid. Her Aunt Elizabeth came over from the Rectory with the girls, but it was Hester who solved the problem of India's enforced idleness.

'Have you read this?' She handed over a book.

'*Sense and Sensibility*? No, I have not. It is a curious title...'

'But a most interesting book. If you do not love it as I do, I shall disown you...'

'Strong praise indeed!'

'But justified. Now where is your betrothed? I made sure that I should meet him here.'

'Isham is called away to London.'

Hester made no comment, but Mrs Rushford did not lose the opportunity to complain.

'So inconvenient!' she grumbled. 'I had a thousand things to ask him about the restoration of the Grange. Let this be a lesson to you, India. Gentlemen are a law unto themselves. They do not consider others.'

India caught Hester's eye and suffered a sudden attack of coughing which forced her to bury her face in her handkerchief. Mercifully, Hester held her tongue.

'How is your foot?' she asked at last. 'Are you able to walk upon it?'

'Dr Pettifer has promised that tomorrow I may try.'

'I cannot imagine why we continue to employ him,' Mrs Rushford complained. 'He is such a fusspot. India might well have been upon her feet a week ago.'

Hester's lips tightened, but in answer to India's unspoken plea, she bit back a sharp reply. 'Is there anything I can do to help?' she asked instead. 'Have you packed your trunks?'

'That task will not take long,' Mrs Rushford sniffed. 'Since India intends to start her married life without a rag to her back.'

'Mama, did I not explain that Isham intends to take me to Madame Félice when we visit London?'

'And until then? How are you to go on in Cheshire?'

'We shall be living quietly, I expect. Hester, it is kind of you to offer to help. If you will lend me your arm I shall manage the stairs. Letty has half filled my boxes, but we could finish them.'

It was with a sigh of relief that she gained the sanctuary of her room. Then she turned to her cousin and shook her head. 'Why do I feel always that we are on the verge of an explosion whenever you meet Mama?'

'Possibly because it's true,' came the unrepentant reply. 'She makes me cross. Tell me, India, what took Isham away so suddenly? Father was hoping that you would dine with us before your marriage.'

'I've no idea,' India told her frankly. 'It *was* unexpected, as you say. He said nothing of such a plan on the previous day. In fact, he was promised here in the evening.'

'And you are disappointed?'

'Not exactly.' India was prepared to stretch the truth a little, though honesty compelled her to admit to herself that she had been surprised.

Surprised? Had that been her only emotion? In her heart she had felt discouraged too. Had Isham returned to London to pay a last visit to his opera-dancer before he took a wife? Possibly the thought of that lady's charms had proved too strong to keep him from her side.

Even now, he might be laughing, teasing, indulging in the banter which she herself enjoyed so much. Well, if this were to be the pattern of her future life she must learn to bear it.

She turned to Hester. 'I am so glad to see you,' she said warmly. 'And, love, the book will be a boon. I have hated the enforced idleness.'

'I know. Let me see, what was I offered when I was recuperating? I believe I had the choice of stencilling, filigree paperwork, creating silhouettes for greeting cards, pinwork or making a bouquet of paper flowers.' Her grimace was so comical that India laughed out loud.

'You may laugh,' her cousin reproved. 'Let me tell you this. Mother thought it preferable to suggesting embroidery in case I had a relapse.'

'Hester, you are impossible!' India felt more cheerful than she had been in days.

'Agreed! There is no hope for me. Now, what are you to pack, my love?'

'Letty has done most of it. We went through all the things I had last season and chose the darker colours and the heavier fabrics. I'm sure it will be cold in Cheshire.'

'Shall you have enough?' Hester began to examine the contents of the half-filled boxes. 'I'd lend you gowns with pleasure, but they would not fit. Shall I send some shawls and gloves? You might find a use for them.'

India was about to refuse, but the offer was so kindly meant that she could not spurn it. 'Are you sure?' she asked. 'Mama would be delighted. She is convinced that I shall be a perfect dowd, and a disgrace to my exalted station. Isham will take one look at me and I shall be sunk beneath reproach.'

'Do you think that likely?' Hester's eyes were twinkling with amusement. 'If appearance is all he thinks about he won't be disappointed in you, but I won't believe it of him.'

'You are right. I doubt if he will notice.' India's face clouded, but she was quick to hide her feelings. It was mortifying to think that she might be right. 'If you will open the chest we might find something else to add to my so-called rags.'

'How about this?' Hester held up a warm redingote in a glowing shade of bronze. 'Perhaps it will serve for travelling.'

'Oh, yes, I had forgot it. It was too heavy to wear it in the summer. I put it away unworn. You do not think it dated?'

Hester began to laugh. 'Of course not. Styles have not changed in these last few months. India, do you intend to take the town by storm?'

'You may believe that when you see it. My destiny is to become a dutiful wife, the chatelaine of several large establishments, and a fond mamma.' She regretted the words as soon as they were spoken. Hester must not think her bitter.

To her surprise her cousin seemed untroubled. 'There will be more than that...much more. With a man such as Isham you will be forced to use your mind, believe me!'

As always, Hester's visit cheered her. 'You may be right,' she admitted. 'Shall I see you again before the wedding?'

'I think not, India. You would not believe the bustle at Perceval Hall. My father is determined to send you off in style, and Mother has a thousand things to do. I've promised to help.' She dropped a kiss upon her cousin's brow. 'Take care of your foot. I won't promise not to laugh if I hear you creaking down the aisle.'

Hester moved towards the door, and then she turned. 'My dear, you go to your marriage with all my love. My hopes are for your happiness. Try not to worry. You have made the right decision.'

These words of comfort were something to hang on to, and for the next few days India was able to crush her own misgivings. Her wedding day was fast approaching and at last she fell into a dreamlike state. Nothing seemed quite real, even when Isham reappeared at last on the eve of the ceremony.

India thought he seemed preoccupied, though he greeted her with his usual pleasant smile. He kissed her hands and then her cheek as he reached into his pocket for a small flat package.

'What is this?' she asked.

'Why not open it, my darling?'

Beneath the packaging, India discovered a box of fine shagreen with an ornate clasp. She threw back the lid and gasped. Against the cushioned satin lay a string of perfectly matched pearls. No expert knowledge was necessary to assure her that they were worth a king's ransom.

'For me?' she asked in wonder.

'One of your wedding presents, India. May I?' Without waiting for a reply, he slipped the pearls about her neck and fastened the clasp. 'Will you not see how they become you?'

For answer she hurried over to the mirror, gazing with pleasure at the smooth sheen of the necklace as it rested against her skin. 'They are quite beautiful,' she breathed.

'And so are you, my love. I guessed at the size of your betrothal ring. Will you try it?' He took her hand and slipped an enormous emerald on her finger. 'I hope it is to your taste.'

'Oh, Anthony, it is a perfect fit, but I shall be afraid to wear such treasures. Supposing I should be robbed?'

Smiling, he looked about the room. 'I see no thieves in our immediate vicinity, but I promise to wear my pistols at all times.'

'Mama was right...you are spoiling me,' she said shyly.

'I haven't yet begun to do so. My dear one, I promise you a happy life. Will you trust me?'

India nodded, too overcome to speak.

'That happiness will start tomorrow. I have a surprise for you...'

'Another one? Please tell me what it is?'

'No, you must possess your soul in patience. There is another matter. After the ceremony, I thought that we should stay at the Grange for just one night. The day will be hectic, and by the time we get away it will be too late to travel far. Do you agree?'

'You plan to make an early start next day?'

'I do. It will take some time to journey into Cheshire. We shall travel in easy stages.'

'Anthony, is something troubling you?' India had not meant to question him, mindful of her mother's strictures as to the horrors of nagging wives, but she had sensed that he was not quite himself.

'Nothing at all, my darling. Until tomorrow then, and the start of a new life?' He held her to him for a brief moment. Then he was gone, leaving India to wonder if he was already regretting his bargain.

India's wedding day dawned bright and clear. Her new maid, Nan, had been sent over from the Grange, and both mistress and maid took an instant liking to one another. The girl was quiet and pleasant and she proved adept at hairdressing. It seemed no time at all before India was being handed into the carriage which was to take her to the church.

Everything about her seemed unreal. Was this really India Rushford, on her way to marry a man she hardly knew? It didn't seem possible.

The church was crowded, rather to her surprise, but the faces were a blur as she walked slowly down the aisle upon her brother's arm.

Then the tall figure at the altar steps turned towards her. Isham's face was radiant with happiness. India smiled up at him and then she gasped. Beyond him she could see a familiar face. It was that of Oliver Wells. So that was the surprise.

Her uncle William motioned the betrothed couple towards him and began to read the order of service. Isham gave his responses in a strong voice but India's replies were barely audible.

After signing the register she found herself upon her husband's arm, moving out of the church through the throng of wellwishers. It had happened so quickly. Just the exchange of a few words, a service and she was now the Lady Isham, handfasted to the man who walked beside her.

The route to Perceval Hall was lined with villagers, many of whom worked on Sir James's estate, and India waved to all of them.

'You are popular, my lady.' Isham slipped an arm about his bride.

'I have known them all since childhood. How good of them to come to wish us well! My lord, Oliver Wells was one of your supporters. How could that be?'

'Stillington was otherwise engaged. He mistook the date...' Isham told her with a twinkle.

India shook her head. 'Now that I will not believe. I had not thought that you were acquainted with Oliver?'

'I wasn't, but I made it my business to become so.'

'You have been to Bristol? You did not tell me,' she reproached.

'That was one of my secrets. Are you pleased with my surprise?'

'I am delighted for Letty's sake. But how did you persuade his mother to agree to this visit to us?'

'Oliver is not in leading-strings, my dear. I found him to be a young man of great determination. However, in the case of his mother, no great persuasion was necessary. On the contrary, she seemed pleased beyond measure.'

'Anthony, you used her own snobbery against her. Is that not so?'

'Something like that.' He was smiling down at her. 'Must we speak of Oliver Wells? I have not told you how beautiful you look today.' He tilted up her face to his and kissed her gently in the lips.

The touch of that warm mouth upon her own was both disturbing and exciting, but India was moved to protest.

'Anthony, everyone will see us...'

'Why not, my darling wife? As from today, this is all perfectly legal.'

'That wasn't what I meant. This is a public place.'

'Very well, my love, but I warn you. I yearn for privacy.'

She blushed and was thankful that he was unable to tease her further, since they had arrived at Perceval Hall.

After that there was no time for private conversation. She and Isham stood at the head of a reception line welcoming friends and relatives for what seemed to India like hours.

One of the first to be introduced to her was the Dowager Lady Isham. As Henry led his mother forward India was astonished. Tall and slender, with huge dark eyes and a finely modelled face, her ladyship was still a beauty. Now she bent forward to kiss the bride.

'I had hoped to meet you before today, my dear, but Henry was delayed. It was late last night when we arrived. You will forgive me?' The prettily accented English told of some foreign ancestry.

India returned her kiss with warmth. 'We are so happy to see you, my lady.'

'Oh, Lucia, if you please. We are to be good friends, I hope.' She passed on down the line with several words of congratulations for Isham.

India had no opportunity to speak to her again until later in the day. When the feasting was done, toasts drunk and speeches made, Lucia came to find her.

'Madame...' she began.

'Oh, please call me India. Is there something I can do for you?'

'I cannot find Henry. You will think me foolish, but I am easily fatigued. I hoped that he would take me to the inn.'

'The inn?' India gazed at her blankly. 'Are you not staying at the Grange? This is out of all reason.'

'No, it is not, my dear. I pointed out to Henry that to newly-weds any visitors are *de trop*.'

'That is thoughtful of you, but quite unnecessary.' Try as she might, India was unable to persuade this charming creature to return to the Grange. 'Then you must promise me one thing,' she said. 'Let Henry take you there tomorrow. My mother and my sister are to live there, and Letty will be glad of company when I am gone away.'

'You are close...you and your sister?'

'Indeed we are.' India scanned the room for Letty and saw her at last closeted in an alcove with Oliver Wells. Perhaps it was her fancy, but she felt that an aura of love surrounded them. When Letty looked at her beloved her heart was in her eyes.

'An enchanting creature!' Lucia murmured. 'Clearly the young man adores her.' Then she swayed.

'Oh, you are not well! Do sit down, I beg of you.'

'It is nothing, India. Please excuse me. I have no wish to spoil your day.'

India looked at her with some concern, noting the tell-tale signs of exhaustion. Now Lucia's few lines were more strongly marked and dark circles had appeared beneath her eyes.

'Come in here. No one uses this small sitting-room. I'll send Letty to you...'

'No, please...'

'She never makes a fuss,' said India cheerfully. 'I will find Henry for you.'

Letty went at once to do her bidding, so wrapped in dreams of happiness that nothing could trouble her. India began to search for Henry. To her own surprise she could not even see the tall figure of Isham in the crowd. Had he and his brother taken a stroll about the grounds? It seemed an unlikely thing to do on this of all days.

Then she saw them, standing at the end of a long

corridor. They were deep in conversation. As she approached she detected a note of anger in Isham's voice.

'I won't discuss it, Henry. This is neither the time nor the place.'

'But you must...' Henry laid a beseeching hand upon his brother's arm.

'No!' Isham moved away. 'And that is final!'

India hurried up to them, aware that she was interrupting a quarrel. She decided to ignore it.

'Henry, your mother needs you,' she said quickly. 'Will you take her back to the inn? She is exhausted.'

Henry looked startled, but he followed her without demur. India waited until they had driven away and then she turned to Isham.

'Lucia needed more time to rest,' she said. 'Henry should have brought her here some days ago, instead of rushing down from London only yesterday.' She looked up at him. 'I'm sorry. I do not mean to criticise, but I cannot like their staying at an inn when we have so much room for them. I have insisted that they move into the Grange tomorrow.'

Isham slipped an arm about her shoulders and hugged her. 'Do you expect me to play the heavy husband and forbid it?'

'I am sure that you will not. I like Lucia very much. Is she Spanish?'

'No, she is Italian. My father met her long ago, during his Grand Tour of the continent. She has been in England for these twenty-five years, but she has not lost her accent.'

'I like to listen to her. I hope she will be company for Letty.'

'Letty is unlikely to need any company other than

that of Oliver, if I'm not mistaken. You must resign yourself to losing her, my love.'

'I shan't mind too much, as long as she is happy.'

Isham dropped a kiss upon her hair. 'We've done our duty by our guests, I think. Shall we take our leave of them?'

He took her hand and led her back through the crowded room to find her aunt and uncle. Sir James brushed aside their thanks as his wife held India in a long embrace. The vicar and his wife Elizabeth added their congratulations to the happy couple, whilst Mrs Rushford ostentatiously held a handkerchief to her eyes. Most difficult of all was to take her leave of Letty. She threw her arms about her sister's neck.

'Are you happy?' she whispered.

'I can't believe it!' Letty said simply. 'Anthony promised, but even then I didn't dare to hope. I told you once before that my dear brother-in-law is the best of men. Oh, India, you will be so happy with him!'

India looked at the shining eyes in wonder. Was this what it was like to be fulfilled in love? She was beginning to understand the reasons for Letty's long conversations with Isham. They had been about Oliver Wells.

Then her husband took her arm. 'Shall we go?' he said.

With a last kiss for Hester and another for Giles, India stepped into the carriage which was to take them to the Grange. As it rolled away from Perceval Hall, she waved until she could see the familiar figures no longer. Then Isham spoke.

'This is the start of a new life for both of us,' he said quietly. 'India, will you be my friend as well as my wife? Together we shall be a team, and I shall do my best to make you happy.'

'You have already done so.' Impulsively, she laid her hand on his. 'Letty is her old self again. I haven't seen her in such spirits since...since last Season.'

'I'm glad of it. She and Oliver will deal well together. They are a delightful couple.' If Isham had noticed her careful avoidance of the subject of her father's death he gave no sign of it.

In her relief India began to tease him. 'Even so, my lord, I believe you to be a dastardly deceiver. Did you not assure me that you were to visit London? Instead, you went to Bristol.'

Isham's expression changed at once, and India felt contrite. 'Oh, I beg your pardon!' she said quickly. 'My remark was intended as a joke...' She could not think how else she might have annoyed him.

'I know it.' He slipped his arms about her and held her close. 'I didn't deceive you, India. I did go to London too.' There was something in his voice which warned her not to pursue the subject, but all thought of it was banished as he found her lips.

It was a passionate embrace, and she was breathless when he released her. 'Will you do something for me?' he murmured against her hair.

'What is that?' She nestled comfortably against his shoulder.

'Don't change your gown when we dine this evening. I want to remember you always as you look today.'

'That is a very small request, my lord.' India laughed up at him, oddly proud that he had approved of her choice. Again he had surprised her. She had not thought him sentimental.

At the Grange the servants had lined up on the steps to greet the happy couple. India spoke to each of them, remembering those names she knew and vowing to herself that she would soon learn the others.

Then she went upstairs to throw off her fabulous fur-lined travelling cloak, yet another extravagant wedding present from Isham.

Out of habit she had turned towards the door of her old room, but Nan forestalled her, peeping from the entrance of the largest suite upon the first floor.

'This is to be your room, my lady.'

'Oh, yes, of course.' India entered the luxuriously appointed chamber feeling rather foolish. She had been forcibly reminded that privacy could be hers no longer. Now she must share her bedroom with Anthony.

A fire was burning merrily in the grate and Nan had unpacked India's nightclothes. Now she looked anxiously at her mistress.

'Which gown will you wear this evening, madam?'

'I believe I shall not change. His lordship prefers that I continue to wear my wedding-gown. Nan, will you do my hair for me?'

Nan turned away from the bed, where she had been slipping something beneath the pillow.

'What are you doing?' India asked curiously.

The girl blushed. ''Tis an old country custom, my lady. Just a lucky charm. I hope you don't mind.'

India shook her head, but the implications were not lost on her. She guessed that it was a fertility charm. She sat in silence as Nan dressed her hair. Then she went down to join her husband.

'Dinner will be served quite soon,' he said. 'Are you hungry?'

'Not very.'

'You must try to eat, my love. This has been an exhausting day for you, and we have an early start tomorrow. I would not have you feeling faint.'

Isham kept the conversation light as the meal was served, sensing that his bride was feeling extremely nervous. His talk was all of Giles and Letty, discussing the management of the estate upon the one hand, and Letty's prospects of happiness upon the other. His strategy succeeded, and India found that she was able to respond to him with no feelings of constraint.

It was as they were about to move into the salon that a thunderous knocking sounded at the door.

Isham raised an eyebrow as he looked at his butler.

'I'll see to it, my lord.' Tibbs disappeared, but he was back within minutes.

'There is a gentleman to see you, sir.'

'Tell him to go away.'

'My lord, he has refused to do so.' Tibbs proffered a card upon a silver tray.

As Isham examined it his face grew dark, He rose to his feet at once.

'Forgive me, India. I shall not be long.' With that he strode away.

Chapter Eleven

India sat alone at the dining-table for some time. What could be keeping Isham? She began to pace the room.

The strain of the last few weeks had been intense, and her nerves were at breaking point. Even the surroundings of her childhood home no longer seemed familiar. All had changed, as her own life had changed.

Only this morning she had been India Rushford. Now, in a few short hours and with the blessing of the church, she had become the Lady Isham, wed to a man who, however kind and generous, was still a stranger. It seemed unreal.

Then she pulled herself together. This had been her own decision. She had accomplished her objective. Her family had fared better than she'd had any right to hope. Now there was just the last, and greatest, hurdle to overcome. Before this night was over she must give herself to Isham.

She rang the bell, asked that tea be served to her in the salon, and left the dining-room.

As she crossed the hall she noticed that the door to the study was firmly closed. Beyond it she heard voices. Isham's late visitor was keeping him well beyond what might be considered a reasonable length of time. She considered making an appearance in the study and then thought better of it.

As she sat down and began to pour her tea the voices grew louder. To her dismay she found that the door which led from the study to the salon was ajar. She moved across the room to close it and then she stopped, fearing that she could not do so without drawing attention to herself.

Isham was speaking and the tone of his voice made her blood run cold. It was icy with contempt.

'You must wait,' he said. 'Tomorrow I go into Cheshire. Your affairs must wait until I return.'

'But they won't wait. Anthony, I have explained at length. If you don't help me now I shall be ruined.'

'You should have thought of that before you embarked upon your present career. I can do nothing for you at this time.'

'Oh, I think you will. Would you bring disgrace upon the family? Your new bride will find it hard to bear.'

'Blackmail, Henry? Don't even think of it. You have mistaken your victim, I assure you. I have listened to you at length. Now you will hear me out.'

India cringed as the inexorable voice went on. She had not thought it possible to flay another human being so completely. Much of it she did not understand. The references to corruption, to deceit, and to bringing disgrace upon compatriots were all a mystery to her. What she could not mistake was the inhuman way in which Isham stripped his brother of all decency and pretensions to honour. Shaking with horror, she covered her ears, but it was impossible to ignore those cutting tones.

At last she could stand it no longer. She threw open the door and walked towards the two men.

'Please don't!' she begged. 'Don't quarrel on this day above any other. Anthony, this is our wedding day.'

Isham spun round to face her, and she recoiled. The dark face was a mask of anger.

'Leave us, India!' he snarled. 'This matter is no concern of yours.'

All colour drained from India's cheeks. She did not recognise the man who stood before her. It did not seem impossible that he would strike her. Without a word she turned and fled.

She was sitting by the dying embers of the bedroom fire when he came to her at last. Nan had undressed her and robed her in her lace-trimmed nightgown and the flimsy negligée. She had been unaware of it.

All her thoughts were upon the man who was now her husband. Tonight she had seen the dark side of his character, and she had been both shocked and terrified. Brute ferocity was the only way she could describe his manner. Her first impressions had been right. She should have trusted them and not allowed herself to be lulled into a sense of false security by Isham's soft words and his generosity. Why, she had actually been on the verge of liking him. She shuddered.

'You are cold?' The deep voice held no trace of anger. 'You should not have allowed the fire to die, my dear.'

He threw some sticks upon the embers. They blazed at once, turning the fiery mass of India's hair into a flaming glory, but no warmth could melt her stricken heart.

Isham knelt beside her and took her hands in his. Then he gave a muttered exclamation and reached down to touch her feet. 'You are chilled to the bone, India. Why did you not go to bed?'

Mutely, she shook her head. She hated his very presence in the room and longed for him to go away.

Isham looked at her averted face. 'Won't you forgive me?' he said quietly. 'I forgot myself tonight. I had no right to speak to you so roughly, but I had been tried beyond endurance. Will you allow me to explain?'

'There is no need,' she said in jerky tones. What could he say that would take away the memory of that dreadful scene? She knew him now. At any time he might turn and rend her with his cutting tongue. It would destroy her just as surely as it must have destroyed his brother.

'Then come to bed, my darling.' He raised her to her feet, but as he slipped an arm about her waist she shrank away. A hand tightened upon her shoulder and he turned her to face him. Then he looked deep into her eyes. His own were fathomless.

'What is this?' he asked quietly. 'Do you find me so repulsive, India?'

'No…I…I'm sorry! I did not mean to flinch.'

'Bravery indeed!' His hands had fallen from her shoulders, and his face was a mask of stone. 'Have I been mistaken in you, my dear? I had hoped to find straight dealing, and although I knew you did not love me, I flattered myself that you were growing to like me better.'

'I was!' India's feelings could no longer be contained. 'I was until tonight! That was a brutal exhibition of anger, sir. I had not thought to see such from a civilised human being.'

'I would not have had you witness it for the world.'

'I am sure that you would not. You have been clever, my lord, in hiding your true nature from my family. How easily we have been deceived...!'

'*You* have been deceived?' He gave a bitter laugh. 'I must claim the prize in that department. Did you not promise to trust me, to be my friend as well as my wife?'

'I won't go back on our bargain,' she told him steadily. 'I will be your wife...'

'You will condescend to share my bed? That is a noble sacrifice, but I shall not take advantage of it.'

India stared at him.

'Surprised, my dear? Believe me, to date I have not found it necessary to force my attentions upon an unwilling partner.'

India stood before him with her head held high, but two spots of colour burned upon her cheeks as she awaited a torrent of vituperation.

Isham said very little to her that night, but when he spoke it was to the point, and his tone was bitter.

'India, you are a cheat! I know your anger for what it is, merely an excuse to refuse me. Was not that your intention from the first?'

She did not answer him.

'You have given me no opportunity to explain the scene you saw tonight. You could not, of course. That might remove your objection to our union.'

Again, she said nothing, and the silence between them lengthened.

Then, abruptly, Isham turned away. 'Don't bother to lock your door. You will come to me of your own free will before I trouble you again.'

The slam of the closing door sounded like a death-knell in her heart. What had she done? Isham's icy words had stung, not least because some of the accusations were true. Had she been unfair? She could not imagine a deed so vile that it would justify his utter condemnation of his brother, but she had not troubled to find out.

And had she used her disapproval of his angry words to cheat him of his rights? Sunk in misery, she faced the truth. He had looked into her heart and found there what she dared not admit even to herself. Her courage had failed her at the last. She would have seized upon any excuse to avoid that ultimate coupling of man and wife. She felt ashamed of her behaviour, but it was much too late to remedy her folly. She was in truth a cheat.

It was long before she sought her bed. The fire had burned to ashes when she slipped at last between the sheets. Then her fingers touched the little token beneath her pillow, and she began to sob as if her heart would break.

When Nan roused her early the next day she felt that she hadn't slept at all, but she was given no time for reflection. His lordship, so she was informed, was anxious to make an early start.

India dressed hurriedly, forcing down the cup of scalding chocolate on her tray.

'My lady, you have eaten nothing!' Nan exclaimed. She had betrayed no surprise at finding India alone.

The gentry had their own queer ways. Husband and wife had separate rooms, or so she had been told.

'It is too early for me,' India murmured. 'I expect that we shall stop to bait the horses. I shall take something then.' She allowed the girl to throw the heavy cloak about her shoulders. Then she picked up her reticule and hurried down the stairs.

Isham awaited her in the hall. She had been dreading meeting him, but his manner told her nothing. He greeted her with his usual courtesy and handed her into the coach.

It was still dark when they left the Grange, and his face remained in shadow as they set off on the road to Derby. Her own comfort had been considered. A hot brick warmed her feet and a fur rug covered her knees.

'You are warm enough?' Isham asked politely.

'Yes, thank you.' There seemed little more to say, so she huddled against the cushions and pretended to be asleep.

The sky lightened only slowly on that dark winter's morning but the weather was dry and clear and they made good time on the first stage of their journey.

Isham was the first to break the silence. 'India, we can't go on like this. Let us at least attempt some semblance of civility, else our lives will be a torment.'

She turned to him then and was surprised to see that the bitterness had vanished from his eyes, to be replaced by an expression which she could not understand. Had she not known better, she might have thought it was anguish.

'I agree, my lord,' she said at once. 'I fear that I spoke to you in ill-judged haste. I should not have refused to listen to your explanations.'

'It is no matter.'

'That isn't true! It is of great importance. Will you not tell me now?'

'To restore your faith in me? Was there ever any such? I think not, my dear. For once I lost my self-control. Now, it must appear, I must pay for it. You see, I had not thought to be betrayed by one so close to me...'

India shivered. 'Please!' she begged. 'You shall not feel that I have betrayed you!'

She had his full attention then. 'You? No, not you, my dear. I have been at fault in all our dealings.'

India frowned at him. 'I cannot understand you.'

'No? Then let me say that I have been a fool. I have rushed you into marriage when you had little or no regard for me, believing that I could win your love in my own way. Such idiocy! You may put it down to my own pride and arrogance.'

India stared at him. 'I did not know that you hoped to win my love,' she faltered.

'How could you? It would have taken a seer to penetrate the reasons for my actions.'

'Oh!' India relapsed into silence. A little worm of doubt was stirring in her heart. Perhaps she had misjudged him. Even now, it seemed impossible, but could it be that Letty had been right? Did Isham truly love her? If so, she had flung his affection back into his face. It did not bear thinking of.

'Why did you quarrel with Henry?' she asked.

'I told you that I had been to London. I was summoned there by a request from the highest level. Whilst he was in India, Henry disgraced not only himself, but also his country. In return for gifts he promised favours which he was unable to grant and sank deeply into debt. I shall not distress you with the methods by which he proposed to clear those debts. He will be lucky not to be impeached.'

India froze. 'Oh, how could he? But Anthony, you will help him, will you not?'

Her husband sighed. 'I have left him a draft upon my bank, and I was able to use my influence to have the worst of the accusations dropped.'

'I have misjudged you,' she said in a low voice. 'I am very sorry.' She was appalled, not only by Henry's behaviour, but also by her own. Why was she always so ready to believe the worst of this man who sat beside her? She did not dare to look at him.

Isham leaned forward and rapped upon the roof of the coach, bringing it to a halt.

'I'll take the reins for a while,' he said. 'Will you have Nan for company?'

India shook her head. Nan was travelling in the second coach with Isham's valet and the luggage. Only yesterday she had teased her bridegroom about his proposal to travel in such state, only to be reminded that she would not find it entertaining to be stranded far from help on a winter's day if they should lose a wheel. Now that friendly banter was a thing of the past. It was clear that Isham had no desire to share the carriage with her.

'As you wish!' he said shortly. He had not even accepted her apology, as she was quick to realise.

The rest of the long journey was a nightmare. When they stopped for refreshment and to change the horses Isham was solicitous of India's comfort, treating her with grave courtesy. It was when they made an overnight stay at Derby that she began to understand how deeply he was wounded. Again she was left to spend the night alone.

She could not fathom her own dismay. It should have been a relief to be spared his attentions, but it wasn't.

They left Derby at first light on the following day, and again Isham took the reins for the long journey north. It was only when they were within a mile of their destination that he joined her in the carriage.

India stole a glance at his face. He had had time to think, to accept her apology for her hasty judgement, and perhaps even to forgive her for her humiliating rejection of him on their wedding night. His calm expression told her nothing. Invariably polite and considerate of her comfort, he was unapproachable. A barrier lay between them, invisible as glass, but almost tangible.

It wasn't from any wish to seek her company that he'd joined her. She understood the reason soon enough as they drove through a small village. A crowd assembled quickly, cheering and waving and running along beside the coach.

'Do you know these people?' she asked in some surprise.

'They are my tenants.'

'Then we are on your land?' It was a relief to think that they were almost at their journey's end.

'We have been travelling across it for the last hour or more. Acknowledge them, India. Some will have stood for hours, awaiting our arrival.'

Obediently, she began to wave and started a fresh round of cheering. It continued in the next village and the next, until at last they turned in through a pair of ornate iron gates, set in a massive wall.

The crowds surrounding the lodge gates were even thicker and the coach was forced to a stop. In the midst of the shouting and the laughter India was surprised to see the horses being led away. As the carriage began to move again she realised that it was being drawn by a throng of brawny men.

Isham gave her a faint smile. 'A traditional welcome for the new bride,' he said.

It needed no words of his to make her feel ashamed. She had cheated her husband on their wedding night. Now she was cheating these good people. A new bride she might be, but she was not yet a wife. The villagers were celebrating the happiness of the newly married couple. How could they know that it was all a sham?

She was roused from her feelings of self-reproach by her first sight of Hambledon. Set in the curve of sheltering hills, the house was enormous.

'You did not tell me that you owned a palace,' she cried in wonder. 'Great heavens! How many rooms are there?'

'Some hundreds, I believe,' he replied indifferently. 'Each generation has added to the place, hence the mixture of architectural styles. The original was an Elizabethan manor house. One wing was added in the time of the second Charles, and another at the start of the last century.'

'Yet they blend together perfectly. What a sight it is, with the sun reflected in the windows! One might almost imagine the place to be afire!'

'Let us hope not, my dear, though it might succeed

in shortening the speeches to which we are about to be subjected. You are not too tired to listen to them?'

India shook her head. 'Not at all. It is kind of your people to wish us well.'

He made no reply and handed her down from the coach in silence. After that India was lost in a sea of faces, returning warm handshakes, accepting bouquets which she realised had not been easy to assemble in mid-winter, and listening intently to halting words of welcome, made by those to whom speaking in public was clearly an ordeal.

Isham rescued her at last, leading her indoors towards the warmth of a blazing fire crackling merrily on a vast hearth in the panelled hall.

He gave her no time to wonder at the sheer size of the room. Instead he led her down the line of servants, greeting one and then another with a joke, a friendly smile, or an enquiry as to their family. India followed his lead, attempting to match his warmth. Would she ever learn to remember all the names, she wondered? It did not seem to matter. A kind word and a handshake brought an instant response.

At last he raised a finger and summoned the house-keeper. 'Her ladyship would like to see her room,' he announced.

'Of course, my lord. My lady, will you come this way?'

India followed the woman through what seemed like miles of corridors. She was shown into a room which had none of the opulence which she had expected.

India sighed with relief. This was a room designed for living. Ormolu and ornate trappings had been banished. Curtains and bed-hangings might even be a little faded, but the chairs were comfortable. There were cupboards and wardrobes in abundance, the huge bookcase was filled to capacity, and the little desk had been freshly stocked with writing-paper and pens. It seemed much less intimidating than the rest of the house, but on closer inspection she realised that the carpets were of the finest quality, as was the bedlinen. She began to study the pictures and realised that they must be worth a king's ransom. The furniture too must have been handed down over several generations. The original workmanship was very fine. Her gilded cage, she thought bitterly, would certainly live up to expectations.

She allowed Nan to remove her cloak and bonnet. Then she sank into a chair beside the fire, bone-weary after the long journey and the exhausting, if well-meant, welcome from the villagers.

'Shall you prefer to dine up here this evening?' Isham was standing in the doorway of the adjoining room.

Tired though India was, she shook her head. She guessed that a celebratory meal had been prepared and she would not disappoint the kitchen staff.

'Then shall we say in an hour or so? I'll wait for you downstairs…' He smiled his approval of her decision, but he did not enter her room again in the weeks they spent at Hambledon. That door stayed firmly closed, though she knew it was not locked.

Life at the great house went on as it had always done, sustained by myriads of servants, and India found that she had little to do. Her mother had warned her that one of her daily duties would be to discuss menus with the chef. India smiled to herself. One meeting with that temperamental genius had convinced her that he would brook no interference, in spite of his Gallic charm.

Clearly, he was in no need of advice from her. The food which graced their dining-table was such as she had never tasted in her life. Invariably it brought compliments from the guests who joined them daily.

Christmas came and went, with the traditional feasting for the villagers, and each day Isham took her to the more outlying parts of the estate to visit the elderly and infirm.

She wasn't surprised by his generosity to those in need. What did astonish her was his intimate knowledge of their circumstances, and the obvious affection with which his people greeted him.

Had his manner towards her softened a little? His courtesy could not be faulted, but the barrier was still there. She sensed it and wondered why it should matter quite so much. Since their first meeting Isham had annoyed her, teased her and puzzled her. Now she was beginning to realise just how much she had welcomed the sight of his tall figure in her home, laughing, provoking and quick-witted. Sadly, that delightful gaiety had quite vanished.

Then the weather changed, cold, dry conditions giving way to constant rain. India missed her daily drive through the rolling countryside, so unlike anything she had imagined in the north of England. Even in the depths of winter she could tell that this was rich farming land, fat and prosperous in spite of poor harvests elsewhere and the depressed state of agriculture. How she would love to see it in the spring and summer.

Her hopes were dashed when Isham came to find her in the library. She had been leafing through the poems of Scott and Byron, unimpressed by the high-flown language. She laid them aside and picked up a book of earlier poetry. John Donne? She had not heard of him. She began to read and her breath caught in her throat. The raw sensuality of his words made her heart turn over in her breast. This was love poetry of the very highest order, and her own emotions brought her close to tears.

What was the matter with her? The answer came as Isham walked towards her. She knew then that she loved him and the shock was tremendous. She rose and went to him, laying a hand upon his arm. It was a bitter blow when he removed it. That slight action was gentle enough, but it threw her into despair. It was clear that he no longer wanted her.

India could not look at him. What had she done? They had not been married above three weeks and her future lay in ruins.

A physical blow would have been easier to bear, but Isham did not seem to notice her dismay.

'I am called to London,' he said quickly. 'India, I do not care to leave you here. The riots are spreading, and to date the military forces have been ineffective against these mobile bands which operate at night.'

'Luddites, my lord?'

'And others. They have been active in Derbyshire, which is not far from here, and also in Leicestershire. Lancashire is on our borders, and already some of our neighbours have had death threats.'

'But Anthony, there are no factories here. I thought that the men were smashing the knitting-frames.'

'Machinery in general is their target. Knitting, spinning, weaving…that would be bad enough. Now they are firing barns and hayricks. It won't be long before they march upon private houses.'

'When do you wish to leave?' she asked.

'Tomorrow…at first light. If you wish it we can go by way of Abbot's Quincey. You will be safe there at the Grange. Your uncle has mobilised a force of volunteers…'

'Shall I not be just as safe with you in London? That is, if you have no objection?'

He looked at her then, hope struggling with cynicism in his eyes. Then the impersonal manner returned.

'I have no objection,' he said quietly.

On the journey south he left the driving to his coachman, and India's spirits rose. Perhaps he was beginning to forgive her.

Isham confined his conversation to remarks about the countryside through which they passed, his concerns for the estate and his assessment of the unrest in the counties.

'Perhaps it will die down,' she murmured.

'I hope so, India, otherwise it may lead to savage repression. The authorities have been badly frightened, and there is much talk of hangings and transportation.'

'You don't agree with that?'

'I don't, my dear. The stockingers, poor devils, were to blame for the fall in exports. That was due to Napoleon's blockade. Now half the population of Nottingham is on public relief. The price of bread is high and they cannot feed their families.'

'Others must think as you do.'

'They do. One of my allies will surprise you. Byron himself has spoken out with a plea for mercy.'

'Great heavens! I thought him naught but a poseur.'

'Another flawed judgement, India?' Isham regretted the words as soon as they were spoken. They drove her back into her shell.

The reminder had distressed her more than he imagined, but India was determined that he should not see it. He should have no further cause for complaint against her. On that lengthy journey she mentioned neither her aching limbs nor the jolting she suffered on certain of the roads.

Even so, it was a relief when they reached the fashionable heart of London and the coach drew up in Grosvenor Square.

After the splendour of Hambledon, India was unsurprised to find that his lordship's town house was sited in the most desirable part of the capital. What did surprise her was the interior. She murmured with pleasure as he led her into the main salon. The simple elegance of colour scheme and furnishings was very much to her taste. His lordship had not bowed to the present craze for Orientalism. The furniture in his home was English, but it did not need the eye of an expert to be convinced that it was the work of a master craftsman.

Everything was immaculate, but that was to be expected, considering the number of staff employed here. She had passed along the ranks, from the butler, housekeeper and chef, to footmen, maids and porter, down to the newest tweeny.

She looked at Isham and smiled, 'What shall I find to do?' she asked. 'This household must run like clockwork.'

He took a turn around the room. 'It does,' he agreed. 'I would not have it any other way. In the Season you will not have time to bother your head with details, but at present you may find London dull. January is not the most popular time to find society.'

'I shall not mind that,' she told him truthfully.

'Perhaps not,' he eyed her thoughtfully. 'There is one thing we might do. You might choose your wardrobe for the coming Season. Shall I make an appointment with Madame Félice?'

'I'd like that.' Even in provincial Cheshire India had become aware of the inadequacies of her present clothing. The need for something more fashionable had become acute.

'I think she will see me,' she murmured. 'Someone gave me an introduction.'

A smile softened the harsh features. 'She will see us, India. You may be sure of it.'

'Us?' India stared at him.

'Of course! I shall accompany you.'

She felt a little spurt of anger. Did he think her such a dowd that she was incapable of choosing becoming clothing for herself? It was a ridiculous notion. Besides, no gentlemen of her acquaintance would be seen dead on the premises of a mantua-maker.

The dark eyes studied her face and then he laughed.

'Shall I tell you why, my dear? In the interests of economy and also to prove your independence you would choose one gown. That will not serve. We shall visit Madame Félice together.'

'My Lord, you have not yet seen the bill from the dressmaker in Northampton,' she said nervously.

'I doubt that will keep me awake at night.' He dismissed the subject. 'India, I have much to do for the next few days. Let us get this matter over with tomorrow.'

If she had had any doubts as to his ability to make an appointment at such short notice, they were soon dispelled. A note sent round by hand brought back an immediate reply. Madame would be happy to see Lord and Lady Isham on the following day.

Next morning India eyed her own reflection in the cheval mirror with some anxiety. The bronze pelisse and bonnet were well enough in their way, but there was no denying that they had been chosen for the previous Season. Madame would find her talents exercised to the utmost if she was to transform this ugly duckling into a woman of fashion. India gritted her teeth against the coming ordeal, but if she had expected anything other than the warmest of welcomes she was to be mistaken.

To India's astonishment she found that this latest star in the fashion firmament was little more than a girl. In place of the formidable tyrant she had expected, the woman who advanced to greet them smiled shyly and invited them to be seated. If anything, her manner was diffident, and India's curiosity was aroused. There must be some mistake, she thought to herself. This slender creature with her pale gilt hair and wondrous eyes was clearly a beauty, but she was much too young to have acquired such a dazzling reputation.

India soon revised her first impression, as a succession of models paraded before her clad in Madame's designs. She knew at once that here was a talent of the highest order. There was so much choice that she found it impossible to make a decision, but she went willingly into a dressing-room to have her measurements taken.

Isham himself had made no comment upon the gowns, but he looked perfectly at ease, and not in the least alarmed to find himself alone with Madame Félice.

India wondered what on earth they would find to talk about, but when she emerged she found them deep in conversation.

Then Madame came towards her, her own gown cut to perfection, and her hair dressed in a style which could only be the work of the finest hairdresser in London, a Frenchman.

'Will you put yourself in my hands, my lady?' she asked shyly.

India nodded.

'Then we shall forget all frills and bows. I see you in jewel colours, rich greens and blues, and sometimes gold. The fabrics themselves will be ornament enough, together with your hair and colouring.' She paused. 'Your height is another asset. My gowns look best on someone of your stature.'

'They are all quite beautiful,' India told her warmly. 'I can't think what to choose.'

'Perhaps you will leave it to me? For the present his lordship thought that you might like these garments to carry you through the spring.' She gestured towards a cluster of girls, who now paraded through the room clad in glowing velvets and pelisses of fine wool.

'All of them?' India glanced at Isham.

'All of them,' he pronounced firmly. 'Now off you go to choose your bonnets. I will not venture into that domain.'

He waited patiently as Madame bore India off into another room. The task of choosing suitable hats was accomplished without delay, as Madame had firm views on those which would complement her outfits.

Then with a word of thanks for Lady Isham's custom she bade her visitors farewell.

As Isham turned his horses towards Grosvenor Square he glanced down at his bride.

'You are very quiet, India. I hope that you are pleased with your purchases.'

'They are more beautiful than anything I have seen before. I am quite overwhelmed, and I must thank you for your generosity.'

'It is my pleasure, I assure you, but I must hope that it has not robbed you of the power of speech.'

'No, it isn't that! But Madame? I must confess that I was surprised. I had not expected a girl.'

'A girl with something of genius, I believe.'

'Yes, I am sure of it, but what do you know about her? Is she French? She had no trace of an accent.'

'She is something of a mystery, my dear. No one knows anything of her background. It is remarkable that she has managed to establish such a reputation within a few short months.'

'That's true. It was only after we came away from London before the Season ended that our friends began to write about her in such glowing terms.'

'Will they be in London still? I shall be happy to meet them if you care to invite them to dine.'

'I'll send round to enquire, but in the usual way they don't arrive in London before April, when the Season starts.'

'I see. Well, my dear, we shall not be here for long.

A day or two will see my business finished. Then we shall return to Abbot's Quincey. You will be glad to see your family again. In the meantime you might take Nan if you should wish to do some shopping. I would suggest Bond Street and the Burlington Arcade.'

She saw little of him for the next day or two. She had not ventured to enquire about the nature of his business and he volunteered no information. At least, she thought with some relief, it did not involve the opera-dancer. Each night his lordship had dined at home.

As he had suggested, she occupied her time with shopping, choosing shoes and gloves, scarves and handkerchiefs, and also a charming reticule which caught her eye. These expeditions were brought to a halt when packages began to arrive for her. They included a fine chinchilla muff and another of sealskin. She had not ordered them, and she mentioned the fact to Isham.

'I thought I would send them back,' she murmured.

'I wouldn't advise it, since I ordered them myself,' he told her. 'Consider the English winter, India. You are like to freeze throughout February and March.'

She thanked him again, and was glad of the fur muff when they set out for Abbot's Quincey at the end of the week.

Chapter Twelve

They arrived to find the family in a bustle, with Letty and Mrs Rushford preparing to set off for Bristol. Giles was to be their escort.

'Is it not wonderful?' Isabel demanded. 'Lady Wells has invited us. I was never more astonished in my life.'

India looked at Letty's sparkling eyes. 'She has withdrawn her objections to your marriage then?'

'It seems so,' Letty said softly. 'We could not go, of course, unless Lord Isham had put a carriage at our disposal.' She beamed at her brother-in-law.

Isham bowed. 'I am very happy for you.' His ironic gaze rested upon India, and she knew what he was thinking.

Oliver's disagreeable mamma would seize the chance to establish a close connection with his lordship. It would give her the entré to the highest circles in the land, as Isham was known to be a friend of the Prince Regent. All other considerations must be set aside. After all, her ladyship was the mother of five daughters, all of whom must find a suitable match.

'We have been awaiting your return,' Letty assured

her sister. 'We had no wish to leave the Dowager Lady Isham alone here at the Grange.'

'Where is Henry?' Isham demanded with a frown.

'We don't know,' an anxious voice replied. 'Oh, Anthony, we haven't seen him since we left the Angel to come here. Do you suppose that he has met with an accident?'

'That's highly unlikely, my dear one. We should have heard of it. Now I must beg you not to worry about your wandering boy. We shall be company for you, India and myself.' Isham took his stepmother's hand, squeezing it in reassurance.

'It's good to have you back,' she said wistfully as she turned to India. 'My dear, you must know how kindly your family has welcomed me.'

'I'm glad to hear it.' On an impulse India kissed the sweet face. Then, leaving Isham in the company of her mother and his stepmama, she went upstairs with Letty.

'You seem to have been gone this age,' her sister told her. 'Oh, India, so much has happened since you went away. I can't believe that my dearest wish is to come true. Won't you wish me happy?'

India threw her arms about the younger girl. 'You know I do. This was what I wanted for you as you longed for it so much. I wish you joy for all your days.'

'As I do for you. We must be the luckiest women in the world!'

India vouchsafed no reply to this remark and Letty looked at her intently, only to see a tear glittering upon her lashes.

'India, what is wrong? This won't mean the break-up of our family. We shall see each other often.'

'Yes...I mean...you must not think me foolish. It is nothing.'

'Then tell me, dearest. Isham has not mistreated you? If so, I shall speak to him myself.'

India managed a watery smile. At that moment her sister resembled nothing so much as a little fluffy chick resolved to tackle a ravening fox. There could only be one result.

'It is the other way about, Letty. I am the one at fault, and we have quarrelled dreadfully.'

'This misunderstanding will not last, my dear one. Isham has loved you for so long...'

'Oh, don't! Please don't! He does not care for me at all. I don't know why he married me...' The tears came then, and India did not attempt to hide them.

'You don't know? Then let me tell you. India, you make me cross, indeed you do. I have always looked up to you and thought you a marvel of good sense. Now I begin to wonder. Have you never questioned Isham's offer for you?'

'He offered for either of us. He would have taken you instead of me.'

'Would he? I suggest that you ask him some time. You silly goose! He has been in love with you for months.'

'That's nonsense! We did not meet until a few weeks ago.'

'You have not heard of love at first sight? He was there when you laughed at Brummell. That was the start of it. Then he watched you unceasingly.'

'So I was under inspection?' came the bitter comment.

'I think you forget. He'd been a soldier. He was

planning his campaign. He'd seen how you frightened men away...that is, those who were rash enough to show an interest in you.'

'They were not many.'

'Of course not. You made sure of that yourself.'

'Oh, I know that I made sport of them, but no one touched my heart as Oliver did yours. What was that to do with Isham? We were not even introduced.'

'And if you had been? Would you not have treated him as you did all the rest?'

India gave a reluctant smile. 'I suppose so, but he might have attempted to find out.'

'He was planning another strategy, by trying to win your friendship first, but there was not time for even an introduction. It was only after Father died that Isham found out that you were his daughter, and we left London at once.'

'You seem remarkably well informed.'

'Oh, India, why do you think I changed my mind about your marriage? Isham told me of his feelings on the day of your betrothal. Have you never wondered what we find to talk about? Our conversation is not all of Oliver.'

'I think you might have told me.'

'He made me promise that I would not, at least before your marriage. In the first place he felt that you blamed him for Father's death and the ruin of the family. He doubted too, if you would believe that he had even noticed you, much less fallen in love.'

'He does not strike me as a man who would be content to worship from afar,' India said grimly. 'This is nonsense, Letty. Had I been a raving beauty I might place some credence upon your tale, but not otherwise.

He needs an heir and that is an end to it, although he will not get one in his present mood.'

'What on earth do you mean?' Letty had flushed a little.

'Pray don't imagine that he cares for me. He will not touch me.' India's voice was no longer under her control. 'I've tried to make it up, but it is useless. When I laid my hand upon his arm he drew away. Oh, Letty, I may be Lady Isham but I am not his wife.' She buried her face in her hands and sobbed.

'Oh, dearest, don't distress yourself! It may be that he thinks himself to blame for rushing you into this marriage, and in such a way. He could think of nothing else...no other way to win you.'

'Then he is a bigger fool than I imagined.'

'No, he is not,' the gentle voice persisted. 'He knows you better than you think. Tell me, would you have received him under other circumstances?'

'No, of course not. Oh, Letty, I wish I could believe you, but I can't. I don't know what to do, and now, you see, I love him so...'

Letty smiled as the tear-drenched face was raised to hers. 'I wondered how long it would take you to find out. All will be well, I make no doubt. Why don't you tell him, India?'

'I can't. I'd die if he turned away from me again.'

'Then give it time, my dear one.' Letty turned to other subjects. 'What did you think of Hambledon?'

'It is a palace, not a house. I don't think even Anthony knows how many rooms there are.'

'And his place in Grosvenor Square?'

'Much on the same lines. We were not there for long.' India grew thoughtful. 'There is some mystery which I don't quite understand. We left Hambledon so suddenly. Isham had received a message from the capital. Yet we spent only a few days in London. He seemed to be anxious to get back to Abbot's Quincey. Do you know why?'

Letty shook her head. 'Nothing that I can put a name to.' Her face clouded. 'The trouble with the stocking-knitters has grown worse, I think, and lights have been seen in the woods at night. Most probably it is poachers.'

'Poachers don't advertise themselves with lights. Were they upon our land?'

'Yes!' Letty's hands were shaking. 'Oh, India, I have been so frightened. I shall be glad to go to Bristol, away from all the violence, though I hate to leave you here.'

'We shall do well enough.' India had recovered her composure. 'The Government is to move at last, sending in dragoons and troops of yeomanry, as well as raising groups of volunteers.'

This news calmed Letty's fears. She turned to less demanding subjects. 'Did you visit Madame Félice when you were in London?'

'We did.' India's eyes began to twinkle. 'Can't you tell?'

'I thought you must have done.' Letty stroked the velvet of her sister's pelisse. 'This is beautiful, and such a glorious shade of green. Tell me, is she as formidable as they say?'

'Not at all! I couldn't believe my eyes. She is just a girl, and rather shy, if anything. I don't think she is French, as she has no trace of an accent.'

'I expect not. It is quite the thing for mantua-makers to give themselves French names.'

'Yes, but…there is something else. She is very lovely, Letty, and was dressed, as you might expect, with perfect elegance, but once, when she turned her head, I had the oddest notion that I had seen her before. It must have been a trick of the light, because that could not be.'

'Possibly in the shops in Bond Street or the Burlington Arcade?'

'Possibly, although we did not frequent them so much during our Season. They were beyond our touch.'

'Well, that at least, can be no longer a worry to you. Did you buy much?'

India chuckled at last. 'You will stare when you see the contents of my trunks. Anthony is no miser, I assure you. Will you believe that he bought Madame's entire collection for next Season? Now, I fear, she will have to start again.'

Letty giggled. 'It must have saved you agonising decisions, love.'

'It did. My only worry now is when I shall find the time to wear so many gowns. Shall you like to borrow some of them for your visit to Bristol? They could be altered for you.'

Letty shook her head. 'No, I won't do that! Come, India, will you help me pack my things? We are to leave as soon as possible, and Martha has no time. Naturally, she thinks of Mother first.'

'She will go with you?'

'Try to stop her! As ladies' maid to a *grande dame* of such impeccable connections, she has been elevated beyond her wildest dreams. I hear that she is given to queening it below stairs.'

'Let's hope that her disposition will improve.'

'I doubt it.' Laughing, the sisters made their way to Letty's room.

Finding that happiness was infectious, India felt much more cheerful as she waved the little party off on the following day. Letty's radiant face beamed at her until the carriage was out of sight. It was reward enough to make her turn to Isham with a word of thanks.

'Letty is so happy,' she said warmly. 'And it is all your doing.'

'My one success, India?' His ironic smile caused her to regret the friendly overture.

Without another word she turned and left him. It was useless to think that he would ever forgive her. She was left to face the prospect of a future life with a man who hated and despised her. She straightened her shoulders. Whatever else, he should not break her spirit. She walked into the library in search of some book which might give her solace. It had been re-stocked, and she picked up a volume by the poet Samuel Taylor Coleridge.

Her attention was caught immediately by the exotic Eastern mysteries of 'Kubla Khan', but when she began to read 'The Ancient Mariner' she was entranced. Swept away by the torrent of magnificent imagery, she rose to her feet and began to walk about the room reading aloud.

Then a small hand tugged at her skirt and she looked down to find Joe crouching by the desk, with his brother close beside him. Both boys looked terrified.

'Why, Joe? What is it? You must not be afraid. This is but a story about a sailor and a great bird…'

''T ain't that, miss. You must go away!'

'But we have only just returned. Are you not glad to see us back again?'

To her surprise he clutched her hand in a painful grip. 'Go! You must go! We seen 'im, miss. We thought 'e'd gone for good, but 'e come back.'

'I don't understand you. What are you talking about?'

Joe's lips set in a mutinous line. 'Best listen up, miss. 'E won't make no mistake next time.' There was no mistaking the panic in his voice.

India sat down and drew him to her. 'What is all this mystery, Joe? Has someone frightened you? Tell me his name and we shall send him to the rightabout.'

He shook his head and tried to pull away, but India would not release him.

'You must obey me,' she said firmly. 'His lordship would not be best pleased to find you disobedient.'

Still the boy was silent, but India found support from an unexpected source.

'Joe, you gotta tell!' His brother was holding tightly to Joe's other hand.

'Won't you trust me?' India coaxed. 'No harm can come to you within these walls…'

Joe grimaced. 'It did to you, miss.'

India was mystified. Then she remembered. 'Oh, you mean my fall? That was just an accident.'

'No, it weren't. We seen 'im, me and Tom. 'E opened the door upstairs and took the key away.'

'But who? Was it one of the workmen? In any case, he may have had a good reason.'

'It weren't a workman.' Joe refused to meet her eyes. 'Miss, we seen 'im before, the night the factory burned.'

'But who?'

Still the boy refused to speak and India shook him gently.

'You are making me cross,' she said. 'Can't you understand? If you know who he is he can be stopped.'

Mutely, he looked at her with tear-filled eyes.

'It were the toff,' his brother said suddenly. 'You knows 'im, Miss.'

'The toff? Tom, who can you mean?'

Both boys looked at her and then the flood gates opened. 'It's 'im they calls Mr Salton. We 'eard 'im givin' orders at the factory...'

India felt that her heart must stop. 'Oh, no!' she breathed. 'You must be mistaken.'

'We ain't.' Joe would not be deterred now that the truth was out. 'When you fell, miss, didn't you see 'im close to you?'

'I thought that someone came to me,' India admitted. 'But he went away again. I couldn't be sure. I was confused.'

'It wuz 'im all right. 'E went off when 'e saw me.'

India felt her throat constrict with horror. She could not doubt that the boys were telling the truth, but it seemed incredible. Had Isham not told her of Henry's previous behaviour she would have refused to believe their story.

Joe tugged at her hand insistently. 'Now will you go?' he begged. ''E's bringin 'em tonight.'

Horror turned to frozen disbelief. 'What do you mean?' she whispered.

'Them strikers, miss,' Joe told her patiently. 'Yon toff told 'em that they'd 'ave rich pickin's.'

'He's bringing them here? Oh, Joe this can't be true. You should not listen to gossip.'

''T ain't gossip. We wuz there. We bin watchin 'im.'

'But how could you? You mean that you have attended one of their meetings?'

'Course we did. They takes no notice of the likes of us. Don't think they even saw us.'

'We must hope not.' India hugged the children to her. 'Now promise that you will not say a word of this to anyone? I must find his lordship.'

The boys still hesitated. 'You are not to worry,' she comforted. 'His lordship will know what to do.'

They were satisfied with that, and slipped out of the room as she rang the bell for Tibbs.

'Have you seen his lordship?' she asked quickly. 'I wish to speak to him.'

'He rode out not half-hour since, my lady.'

'Did he say where he was going?'

'No, madam, but earlier he mentioned business in Northampton.'

'Thank you, Tibbs. Will you let me know as soon as he returns?'

'Certainly, madam.' Tibbs eyed her with some concern. Her ladyship looked pale enough to faint. 'May I bring you some refreshment?'

'Not just now, I thank you.' India dismissed him and sank into a chair. Her thoughts were in turmoil, but her overriding concern was for Isham. How was she to tell him about Henry? Would he believe her? She would not blame him if he didn't. How could he imagine that his own brother would try to harm him? It would be a bitter blow, but the facts were there.

Vainly she hoped that Joe and his brother were mistaken, but in her heart she was convinced that they had told her the truth. Much that had puzzled her was now becoming clear.

From the first Henry had attempted to set her against this marriage with his subtle criticism of his brother. Had he been determined to prevent it? She shuddered. If the fall had killed her he would still be Isham's heir.

Her face grew paler still. What would have happened had Joe not hurried to her side? Henry might so easily have crushed her skull and blamed it on the fall. She buried her face in her hands. Was he indeed capable of murder?

She grew calmer after a time. If Joe was right and the attack on the house was planned for tonight, Isham would need to take some action. The Grange was built of stone and would not fire easily, but the long windows on the ground floor would give easy access to the mob.

The servants? Well, they might arm the grooms and the gardeners, but Tibbs was no longer young. As for Isham's valet, she could not regard him as a fighting man. All in all, they were too few to fend off a determined assault. Even Giles was gone away. Henry had been clever, she knew that now. He had waited until his two intended victims were alone.

Two? Oh, yes, she was convinced of it. Henry planned to remove herself and Isham from his path. How else could he gain possession of his brother's wealth?

She stopped trembling as an icy anger gripped her.

She would fight him to the death. He would find no bleating lamb awaiting execution. Nor would he be able to blame their murders on the mob. If he tried to kill her she would take him with her.

She rang the bell again.

'Tibbs, is his lordship returned?'

'No, my lady. I should have let you know.'

'Of course!' India smiled at him. 'Tell me—do you have the keys to the gun-room?'

'They are kept in his lordship's desk, my lady.'

'Will you find them, please?' She would feel safer with those keys in her own possession.

Tibbs did not question her strange request, though every instinct warned him of approaching trouble. His mistress had heard something, though from what source he could not tell. His fervent wish was that his master would return without delay.

This wish was strongly echoed in India's heart, but the day wore on and still there was no sign of Isham.

India sat through what seemed to her to be an interminable nuncheon with her mother-in-law. She was anxious not to frighten the older woman, but to her own ears the conversation sounded stilted. The Dowager did not notice, though she did remark on India's pallor.

'It is nothing,' India lied. 'Just a slight headache, ma'am. I believe I shall lie down for an hour this afternoon.' She blushed as she encountered her companion's enquiring glance.

'Forgive me if I seem impertinent, but you are not increasing?'

'No!' India almost shouted her reply. Then she remembered her manners. 'It is too soon,' she murmured.

'Not at all. You have not heard of honeymoon babies?'

If anything could have added to India's misery it was this. She nodded, but she bit her lip in desperation.

'It is not that, I assure you, ma'am.'

'My dear, need we be so formal? I feel so old when you address me in that way. My name is Lucia.'

India did her best to respond to the friendly overture but the task was beyond her. In the end she excused herself and went up to her room.

To rest was out of the question, but she needed time to think. The boys had mentioned no hour for the proposed attack. In Isham's absence would she be making a fool of herself if she armed the grooms and the gardeners? The gamekeepers, she knew, already carried guns, and they knew how to use them.

She thought long and hard about issuing firearms to the others. Then she decided against it. A gun in inexperienced hands might cause more harm than good, and an accidental shot might rouse the mob to serious violence.

As the light faded and the day grew into dusk she summoned Tibbs once more. Now she could only ask for his support. Let him think her fanciful if he would. She was past caring.

'I have been warned of trouble, possibly tonight,' she told him quickly. 'The staff is at supper below at this hour?'

Tibbs nodded. 'Yes, ma'am.' His expression was imperturbable.

'This may be a false alarm, and I have no wish to frighten the maids. Will you have a quiet word with the gamekeepers? I'd like them posted along the road to keep watch for his lordship. I...I suppose it would be useless to send them to find him?'

'It would, my lady. We can't be sure of his direction.'

'Then we must do our best without him. The rest of the men must stay close tonight. They might arm themselves with cudgels, or whatever they can find. Above all, they must be alert. At the first hint of trouble you will take the entire staff into the cellars and lock the doors behind you. I cannot think that the mob will harm you. It seeks other prey, but if you are attacked, I shall expect you to defend yourselves.'

'Very good, madam.'

India looked at him and smiled. As far as Tibbs was concerned she might have been giving orders for tea to be served in the salon. Now she began to appreciate his stirling worth.

'There is another matter, my lady. What of yourself and the Dowager Lady Isham?'

'You will take her ladyship with you. I shall follow. You may open the door to me when you hear this signal.' She tapped out a short tattoo upon the desk. 'You will not forget the boys, of course?'

Tibbs drew himself to his full height. 'Her ladyship and the two young boys will be my first consideration, ma'am.'

'Good!' India smiled at him again. 'I shall rely on you. Can you think of any other precautions we might take?'

'We might leave candles burning in many of the rooms, my lady. It might give the impression that you are entertaining and that the house is filled with gentlemen.'

'A splendid idea! Now pray don't alarm the women unless you must.'

Tibbs bowed and retired to carry out his orders, leaving India to wonder if there was anything else she might have done. On an impulse she called him back and handed him the keys to the gun-room.

'You might load two pistols for me, if you please,' she murmured.

For the first time he hesitated.

'I do know how to use them,' she assured him. 'My brother is quite a shot. It was he who taught me.'

Tibbs bowed again. It was not his place to argue, but he doubted if his formidable master would agree to such a request. Nevertheless, he did as he was bidden.

'You will dine at the usual time, my lady?' he enquired when he returned. As he handed over the weapons India was seized with a strong desire to giggle.

She stopped herself at once. Tibbs might see her laughter as the first sign of hysterics, rather than her genuine amusement at his impassive demeanour in the face of what must have been the strangest request in all his long career.

'I think so,' she replied. 'My Lady Isham will think it strange if we change any of our ways.'

Her amusement did not last. Isham's lengthy absence was beginning to trouble her. Had he been waylaid? Her blood ran cold at the thought of it. Nothing could be easier than to fire at a solitary horseman from behind a hedge or a wall.

How trivial their quarrel seemed in the face of real danger. She vowed to put an end to it that night if she was spared.

In the meantime she must behave as if nothing untoward had happened. She bathed her hands and face and went down to the salon.

'Better?' Lucia asked.

'Much better, thank you.' India's expression gave her words the lie.

'My dear, you are still so pale. Won't you tell me what is troubling you?'

'I can't think what is keeping Anthony,' India blurted out. 'It is unlike him to be so long away from home.'

'Do you fear an accident?'

India nodded dumb with misery.

'We all do that, my dear. It is a natural concern for those we love, but it is foolish for all that. Anthony is well able to take care of himself. Have you forgot that he is an old campaigner, and one of Wellesley's favourites?'

This small crumb of comfort carried India through yet another meal which seemed to last for hours. She could only give silent thanks when Lucia announced her intention of retiring early.

'I believe I shall do the same,' she said. She kissed the older woman on the cheek and sought the sanctuary of her room.

There she walked over to the window and gazed across the rolling landscape. It was full dark, but as she watched, the moon began to rise, bathing the countryside in light and shadow. Would Henry bring his followers at full moon? Surely he would not be so foolish, but she could take no chances. When the house was quiet she slipped downstairs again.

The salon was ablaze with light. Tibbs had been lavish in his use of candles, and he had drawn the curtains.

The room looked welcoming and cosy, but she must not be lulled into a false sense of security. India sank into a chair beside the fire, and placed the pistols within easy reach on a low table at her side.

As the hours went by her eyelids drooped, and several times she was awakened only by the chiming of the great clock in the hall. Then she heard another sound as the gravel in the driveway crunched beneath the tramp of many feet.

She slipped into the unlit anteroom next door, giving her eyes time to adjust to the darkness before she peered out through the window. Then she began to tremble. A dark tide of figures flowed towards her across the grounds about the house. She could number them in hundreds.

At a single word of command they stopped, but she heard the tinkle of glass as a volley of stones flew towards the windows. One man took no part in this. He detached himself from the front row of the mob and ran across the terrace.

The locked and shuttered windows delayed him for long enough for India to reach her seat again. She hid the pistols beneath her skirts and looked up as the curtains parted and a masked intruder walked into the room. Raw anger overwhelmed her.

'Henry, you may take off your mask,' she said in icy tones. 'I want to see your face as you fire the shot that kills me.'

Henry laughed aloud. 'Now I wonder how that idea can have entered your head, my dear. Someone must have warned you.' His eyes were alight with feverish excitement, but the hand that held his pistol was quite steady.

'It was not so difficult to discover. I have never fully trusted you.'

'Nor I you, if the truth be known. Oh, I did not doubt your courage, India, but you have one priceless asset which has defeated me till now.'

She would not stoop to question him.

'Don't you wonder what it is? Sheer luck—that touchstone by which the great Napoleon himself has always chosen his marshals!' He perched on the corner of the desk, casually swinging a leg. 'Let us see now, you survived my attempt to overturn you on the Northampton road, or was it on a country lane? I forget. And then the fall? I was convinced I had you there, but it was not to be. Alas, the fates were against me!'

'You are a fool!' she said steadily. 'Give it up now. Would you hang for murder?'

'I have no intention of doing so. In one respect I have had some luck myself. This sullen mob of peasants gives me perfect cover. Listen to them! They are out for blood! Who is to say who sheds it?'

India's hands closed about her pistols. She had never fired at a living creature in her life. Could she bring herself to injure her tormentor? Henry's next words stiffened her resolve.

'Where is Anthony?' he asked pleasantly.

'He's somewhere in the house,' she lied. 'He may be playing billiards with his friends.'

'Now, now, don't lie to me, my dear. The noise alone would have brought him to your side.' He walked over to her then and twined his fingers in her hair, tugging her head back until tears of pain started to her eyes. 'I ask you again. Where is he?'

'I don't know,' she cried. 'Why won't you believe me? I have not seen him for these many hours.'

'Were you looking for me?'

India looked up to see Isham standing in the doorway. To her dismay he appeared to be unarmed.

'Anthony, take care!' she cried. 'He has a gun!'

'I see it.' Isham strolled towards his brother. 'So it is true? You are the leader of these men? I would not believe it.'

'You were always a soft touch,' Henry jeered. 'Not fit to hold the title or the lands. They should be mine. I'd know what to do with them. Why should you have everything and I have naught? It was just an accident of birth. I was your heir. Had you died in the Peninsula War... Well, you did not. Now you have a wife and will possibly beget an heir. I shall be robbed of what is rightfully mine.'

'You are mistaken, Henry.' The soft voice startled everyone in the room. 'You are no kin to Anthony. Your father was killed in the Americas, before I met Lord Isham. You bear his name, but not his blood. You could not inherit.'

'Mother, you lie!' The handsome face was contorted with rage. 'All this is to be mine!'

'No, my dear. That cannot be.'

Henry backed away from them. 'Who is to say me nay?'

'I shall tell the truth, Henry, however it may hurt you.'

'I won't have it!' Henry's voice rose to a scream. 'I'd planned to save you, Mother, but not now.' He half turned and raised the gun as she started to walk towards him. 'Stand back or I fire!'

Lucia did not falter. 'Give me the gun!' she insisted.

India saw his finger tighten on the trigger. All their lives hung by a thread and she had nothing to lose by taking action. She gave a piercing shriek and threw herself into Isham's arms.

'If I am to die, it shall be in your embrace,' she cried dramatically. To her own ears it sounded like a line from a bad play, but she could think of nothing else to do or say. To appeal for mercy would be useless.

'Take the guns!' she hissed. Shielding him with her body she transferred the weapons to his hands and threw her arms about his neck. Then she closed her eyes, waiting for the shot that would smash her spine.

'A touching scene!' Henry was laughing openly, but at least she had diverted his attention from his mother.

Still keeping them covered, he drew aside the curtains with his free hand, allowing the light to stream across the lawn. 'Now!' he shouted to the crowd.

It was his last word on earth. A single shot rang out and Henry fell to his knees.

As his mother ran towards him he made a last attempt to raise the pistol. Then he crumpled to the ground.

Chapter Thirteen

India was transfixed with horror as Lucia cradled her son's body in her arms. Then she released herself from Isham's grasp and ran to the grieving woman.

There was silence in the room, but from the crowd outside she heard a collective sigh, as though a rising wind had stirred a field of corn. She felt the panic as clearly as if she had been among them. Weaker spirits had already begun to drift away, but the dispersal turned into a rout as a troop of dragoons raced towards them at full gallop. She closed the curtains to shut out the shouting and the cries of fear, but Lucia had not moved.

A look was enough to convince her that Henry was already dead. She seized Lucia's hands and tried to draw her away.

'No, let her mourn!' Isham said very gently, as he raised India to her feet. 'My darling, are you hurt?' He gathered her to him and held her close.

India was shaking uncontrollably. 'No! Oh, Anthony, did you have to shoot to kill?'

'I did not fire at all, my love. The shot came from outside.'

'But why? I thought they were his friends.'

'Henry had taken off his mask. They must have thought him one of us. It would have been difficult to tell. He was silhouetted against the light.'

'Thank God that it was not you. We could not have lived with that.' India sank into a chair, feeling that her legs would not support her. She was too shocked for tears.

'You are ill!' he cried in anguish. He lifted her on to his lap. 'What have I done to you?'

India raised a hand to stroke the haggard face. 'I love you,' she said simply. Then her eyes closed and she plunged into whirling darkness.

When she came to herself India found that she was tucked up safely in her own bed, with her hand caught in a firm clasp.

'Anthony?' she murmured. She could not see too clearly, as the candle by her bed was shaded and the room was filled with flickering light from the dying fire. Yet she could not be mistaken in one so dear to her. His nearness was a comfort, and she reached out to touch the smooth cloth of his coat.

'Thank God!' When he raised his head to look at her she could see that his eyes were wet. 'I thought I'd lost you.'

'Don't distress yourself, my darling. I fainted, that is all. It was a foolish thing to do.'

He shuddered. 'Not nearly as foolish as when you tried to shield me with your body.'

'I...I wanted to give you the guns.'

'You took a dreadful chance.' He covered his eyes with his hand. 'When the shot rang out I thought he'd fired.'

'Don't think about it! We are alive and that is all that matters.'

He shook his head. 'No, it isn't! If it takes a lifetime I'll try to persuade you to forgive me. I don't deserve you, India, but I wanted you so much.'

India stroked his cheek. 'There is nothing to forgive,' she murmured. 'Letty told me that you loved me, but I would not believe her.'

'How could you? I never even told you of my love. I let you think that we had entered into some disgusting bargain, and succeeded only in disgusting myself. I must have been mad to offer for you as I did. I deserve to be horse-whipped for my insolence.'

India chuckled. 'You might have been hoist with your own petard. Suppose that Letty had accepted you, rather than myself?'

An unwilling smile crept into his eyes. 'There was no danger of that, my lovely witch. I had studied you more closely than you know. You would not have let your sister make the sacrifice.'

India pretended to frown. 'True! The sacrifice was great, I must admit. After all, who would want a man who pandered to his wife's every whim, fought her family battles for her, saw to her comfort, and showered her with gifts?'

'But it wasn't enough, was it? That you must also admit. Sometimes I thought that you hated me.'

'Sometimes I did, but that feeling did not last. I grew to love you, Anthony, but by that time I felt it was too late. I believed that you would never learn to care for me.'

He kissed her then, gently at first, and then with growing passion as she clung to him, returning the kiss with interest. Her senses reeled as she was swept away on an overwhelming tide of rapture, secure now in his love.

This was what she had dreamed of all her life—not for a union that was just an animal coupling, but for a true marriage where trust, affection and respect played just as large a part.

He released her only to look long into her eyes. In his own she could find no trace of doubt. She raised her fingers to his lips, tracing the outline of the firm mouth as she begged for more.

He kissed her again, but these were gentle caresses, alighting at the corners of her lips, moving to her eyelids and finally to the tip of her nose. They were as light as the flutterings of a moth.

'I should let you rest,' he told her ruefully. 'This must have been the worst day of your life.'

'Oh no, the worst time was when I thought that you would never grow to love me.'

'I never stopped, my darling. I loved you at first sight. My problem then was how to win you.' Tenderly, he pressed a kiss into her palm. 'I was a clumsy fool, India. I curse myself when I think of how I've wasted these past weeks, and then…to put you in such danger!'

'That was not your fault,' she told him quietly. 'How could you have known that Henry was behind these so-called ''accidents''?' Then she remembered Lucia. 'Oh, his mother! Where is she, Anthony?'

'She's resting. The doctor has given her a sedative, and Nan is with her.'

'You found the servants then? I sent them to the cellars. They were not to come out until they heard my signal.'

Isham laughed. 'My voice was enough for Tibbs. I bellowed loud enough to bring the walls down.' His eyes were teasing as he looked at India. 'What a strategist you are! Wellesley has much need of you. He could have done no better himself.'

India shook her head. 'I don't believe I'll offer him my services. I was so very frightened without you. You were away so long.'

'I went to ask for troops, my love. You see, I had been warned of a possible attack.'

'But by whom? You did not tell me…'

'Not all the local men approve of rioting, my dear.' He sat on the bed and slipped an arm about her shoulders. 'I didn't want to alarm you. I had intended to be back with the troops much earlier, but there were formalities…I had not guessed that you would be in serious danger, thinking only that we might suffer broken windows, or lose a barn or two. I was assured that they meant no harm to women.'

'What will happen to them now?'

'I won't seek vengeance against the starving. Most of the men will escape, but if any are taken I'll do my best to speak on their behalf.'

'And the murderer? He who killed Henry?'

'We may never know his name.'

'Poor Lucia! Will this mean a dreadful scandal, Anthony? It would break her heart.'

'I think not. Strangely, his own plan has prevented

that. His death will be blamed upon the mob. I can't imagine that he mingled with them openly. More likely he was always masked, so none would know his name.'

'Then thank heavens he removed that mask before…before…'

'Don't,' he said softly. 'The dragoons will find nothing amiss. To them he will be Henry Salton, a brave man killed in defence of his family. The charges I mentioned to you are certain to be dropped.'

'I am glad of it for your sake, and also for his mother's.' India had been toying with the buttons of his shirt. Now she slid her hand through the opening and began to stroke the smooth skin of his chest. She heard a sharp intake of breath and then he caught her wrist in an iron grip.

'Don't try my fortitude, India! I'm not made of stone. When you touch me I forget my worthy resolutions.'

'And what were those, my lord?'

'You know them well enough. I swore that you should not be my true wife until you came to me of your own free will.'

India's smile was demure. 'You feel that I am resisting your advances?' She released her hand and continued with her stroking. In that moment Isham had told her why he had pulled away from her so hurtfully. Then her gentle fingers encountered a slight puckering of the skin.

Curious, she opened his shirt further to reveal a long scar, white against the tanned skin, running from his shoulder to his waist. It was clearly the result of a sabre cut.

'Oh, my darling, how you must have suffered!' She pressed her lips against the scar.

Isham held her away from him. 'India, this is not the time,' he said thickly. 'You are not yourself. These last few hours must have been a torment.'

'They were indeed. One moment was worse than any of the others, in fact.'

'When was that?' He gathered her to him, encircling her with his arms, as if to protect her from any further hurt.

'It was when Lucia asked me if I was with child. To deny it was torment.'

Isham sat very still. Then he slipped a hand beneath her chin and raised her face to his. 'Seductress!' he said softly. 'Wife, you are a shameless hussy! You are not even blushing.'

'You asked for the truth,' she whispered. 'I cannot blush to tell it.'

'You are sure?' He looked deep into her eyes.

'I was never more sure of anything in my life. I love you, Anthony. I want to bear your sons.'

His mouth came down on hers, and in that lingering kiss all their misunderstandings vanished like snow in summer. India's senses began to reel as his lips became more insistent. She clung to him as if her very life depended on it.

He released her at last, rose to his feet, and walked across the room to lock the door.

'Anthony!' Her soft cry brought him round to face her.

India was standing by the bed. As he watched she

tugged at the ribbon fastenings of her nightgown. The
fine silk whispered to the ground. Then, proud and con-
fident, she walked into the arms and the heart of the
man she loved.

A Companion of Quality
by
Nicola Cornick

Nicola Cornick is passionate about many things: her country cottage and its garden, her two small cats, her husband and her writing, though not necessarily in that order! She has always been fascinated by history, both as her chosen subject at university and subsequently as an engrossing hobby. She works as a university administrator and finds her writing the perfect antidote to the demands of life in a busy office.

Chapter One

November, 1811

The room faced south-east and in the morning it was
full of sun and the light off the sea. Now, in the dark
of a November evening, the curtains were drawn
against the night and the room was lit by lamp and
firelight. The sound of the sea could still be heard, a
faint echo through the dark. Lewis Brabant rested his
head against the back of his chair and closed his eyes.

'So you're not in any hurry to go home, then.'

Richard Slater put two glasses of brandy on the
table between them and resumed his seat opposite
Lewis. His tone had been mildly questioning and for
a moment it seemed he would receive no answer.
Then Lewis opened his eyes and smiled a little reluctantly.

'No, Richard. I'm damnably sorry to be going
home at all! Given a choice, I'd rather be at sea. But
there was no choice...'

'That holds true for both of us—for different reasons,' his friend said, the tiniest shade of bitterness in his voice as he cast one rueful glance down at the injured leg that still caused him to limp a little. He picked up the brandy glass and held it up in an ironic toast.

'To the landlocked!'

They clinked glasses. 'You have done your prison out well,' Lewis observed, his keen blue gaze travelling around the study approvingly. The walls were panelled like the wardroom of a ship, a brass sextant shone on the table by the window, and over by the bookcases was a fine telescope in a battered leather case.

'At least I still have the smell and sound of the sea,' Richard commented, 'unlike you! Northamptonshire's a dashed odd place for an Admiral to retire! What made your father choose the county in the first place?'

Lewis shrugged. 'My mother had family connections in the area and indeed, they seemed happy enough there.' He took a mouthful of brandy and paused to savour the taste. 'This is very fine, Richard! French, isn't it? Was it smuggled in for you?'

Richard grinned. 'Devil a bit! A favour from a friend.'

'I know what you mean.' Lewis stretched. 'Never fear, I won't outstay my welcome here, despite the excellence of the brandy! You and your sister have been most hospitable, but I'm for London tomorrow and from there it's but a day's drive to Hewly.' He grimaced. 'I suppose I must call it home now.'

'Fanny will be sorry to see you go so soon,' Richard murmured, 'as will I. If you feel the need to see the sea again—'

'I'll be working too hard on the estate to spare any thought for my past life!' Lewis ran a hand through his thick, fair hair. He gave his friend a rueful grin. 'But perhaps you will both visit me? It would be good to see old friends…'

'Delighted, old chap!' Richard shot him a quizzical look. 'Not looking forward to life amidst a parcel of women?'

Lewis put his empty glass down gently on the table between them. 'Not a flattering description, Richard, but I take your point! M'sister writes that not only is she joined by our cousin Julia, but now there's some spinsterish companion to do the knitting and fuss over the flowers! Of all the things I need—some Friday-faced female at the dinner-table!'

'Mrs Chessford could hardly be described in such terms,' Richard said slyly. 'You must be eager to see her again!'

Lewis gave his friend a hard stare. 'Julia's always welcome at Hewly, I suppose, though I would deem it a little slow for her tastes!'

Richard nodded. His sister had been in London during the previous season and had returned with plenty of gossip about the dashing widow Julia Chessford. It seemed unlikely, however, that Lewis would appreciate a rehearsal of Mrs Chessford's amours. There had been a time, Richard knew, when Lewis was more than a little smitten with Julia himself.

'How long is it since you were there?' he asked neutrally, steering the conversation away from areas that were clearly not for discussion.

Lewis sighed. 'It was in '05, just after Trafalgar. Father's health had already started to decline then, but it was a slow process. It is only since his recent attack that he has been bedridden and incapable of directing his affairs.'

'Does he show any sign of improvement?' Richard limped over to retrieve the brandy decanter and refill their glasses.

Lewis shook his head slowly. 'Lavender writes that he is occasionally well enough to sit downstairs, but he recognises no one and speaks not at all. It's a damnable shame for so active a man.'

'Isn't Hewly close to Steepwood Abbey?' Richard asked. He leant down to stoke the fire. 'Dashed rum place, as I recall. My Uncle Rodney was a crony of Sywell and Cleeve years ago, before he forswore the drink and the gaming tables! The tales he told!'

Lewis laughed. 'I don't believe that Sywell has ever forsaken the drink and the cards—nor the women! Yes, Hewly is close by the Abbey, but I've never met the Marquis. By all accounts he continues to scandalise the neighbourhood. M'sister wrote that he had married his bailiff's ward less than a year past!'

Richard looked amused. 'Perhaps Cupid's dart will

strike you too, Lewis! Just the thing to help you settle down and rusticate!'

Lewis raised one eyebrow in a disbelieving grimace. 'I thank you, but I do not look to take a wife! Not until I find a woman who can match my last ship!'

'The *Dauntless*?' Richard laughed. 'What were her qualities then, old fellow? I thought she was a leaky old tub that no one else would dare put to sea in!'

'Nonsense!' Lewis grinned mockingly. 'She was a beautiful ship! She was elegant and courageous and she would risk all to gain all!' His smile faded. 'And until I find a woman to rival her, Richard, I shall stay single!'

Miss Caroline Whiston put her leather-bound book of Shakespearean sonnets to one side with a sigh. No one had ever compared her to a summer's day, and if they had she would probably have boxed their ears, knowing their intentions could not be honourable. She knew of too many governesses who had made the mistake of believing in romance and had lived to regret it. Even so it would have been pleasant for once—just once—to meet a man who was neither a rake nor a worthy.

Ever since she had become a governess companion some ten years previously, Caroline had secretly classified all the men that she met into these two groups. The rakes predominated. They could be the fathers, brothers, relatives and friends of her youthful charges and they generally considered themselves irresistible, believing that Caroline should feel the same way. These she dealt with using a mixture of severity and hauteur, resorting very occasionally to physical violence to deter their advances. None of them ever persisted. Caroline was not pretty enough to make it worth their while, and she made sure that she concealed rather than accentuated those features that did give her distinction. Her beautiful chestnut hair was ruthlessly drawn back and confined into a bun. She wore drab, shapeless clothing. Her manner instilled respect into both her pupils and their parents alike.

'I say,' the elder brother of her previous charges had complained with feeling, 'Miss Whiston has a dashed cutting way with her! I'd sooner kiss a snake than try for some sport there!'

Then there were the worthies. These were not as dangerous as the rakes but had to be deterred all the same. They might include a tutor or curate who would imagine that Caroline would make a suitable helpmeet. To these she was kind but firm. She had no intention of exchanging the drudgery of an upper servant for that of unpaid maid of all work in a vicarage, not even for the respectability of a wedding ring.

Caroline sighed again. She was growing cold, for the November mornings had turned frosty recently and not even the thickness of her winter cloak was proof against the chill that seeped up through her boots and was currently spreading through all her limbs. Her scarlet velvet dress, a most impractical present from the kind-hearted mother of one of her charges, was more for show than warmth. Caroline knew it was an affectation to wear an evening gown when she was out walking in the forest in the dawn, but after all, there was no one to see and it was the only time she could indulge in a little luxury. Still, she should be getting back. She shivered. It was cold, and she would be late, and then Julia would be as sharp and scratchy as only she could be.

Caroline tucked the book into her pocket, picked up her basket and started to pick her way through the undergrowth towards the path. The frosty twigs crunched under her boots. Spiders' webs whitened with ice shone like spun silver in the sun. It was very quiet. These early mornings were the only solitude that Caroline could find at present, for she was at Julia Chessford's beck and call all day long and even at night, if Mrs Chessford were suddenly struck down with insomnia. Caroline, who had at first interpreted Julia's invitation to stay at Hewly as a request from a friend, had been quick to realise that she was in fact nothing more than a servant. The days when the two of them had been schoolgirls together were long gone.

Then there was Admiral Brabant, who required constant nursing and whose illness cast a shadow like a pall over Hewly Manor. His latest attack had occurred some three months previously, before Caroline had come to Hewly, and had left him incapable of running the estate any longer. The servants whispered that the Admiral would not outlast the winter snows and their gloomy predictions added to the general air of misery. Hewly Manor was not a cheerful place.

Life for Caroline might have been very different.

She and Julia Chessford had studied together not fifteen minutes' walk away, at the Guarding Academy in Steep Abbot. In those days, Julia had been Admiral Brabant's god-daughter and ward, and Caroline had been the daughter of a baronet. A spendthrift baronet, as it had turned out. Caroline could only be grateful that he had staved off his ruin until she was old enough to earn her own living. He had died when she was seventeen, the title had devolved on a distant cousin, and the estate had had to be sold to pay his debts.

Caroline stepped out of the trees and on to the path, and almost immediately heard the sound of horse's hooves striking against the frosty earth. Whoever was approaching was riding quickly. It sounded like a single horseman coming from the west rather than from the Northampton road to the east. Caroline hesitated. She had no wish to be found alone and loitering in the middle of the wood, and fortunately there was a woodcutter's tumbledown hut set a little way back from the track. She hurried to take cover there. She did not fear poachers or highwaymen—that would have been foolish imagination—but there was no sense in courting danger by making herself obvious.

As the horseman came around the corner of the path he slowed his mount to a walk, affording Caroline the chance to get a good look at him. She peeked through the broken doorway of the hut and heaved a silent sigh of relief. Here was no rake, she was sure. He looked far more like a worthy, with his fair, fine-drawn looks and air of abstraction. He was neatly but plainly attired in a black coat and buff breeches, and his boots were scuffed from hard riding. No London rake, then, but a sober country gentleman. Medium height, medium build, altogether unremarkable. Perhaps he was a poet enjoying the morning air just as she had been. Caroline kept quite still and waited for him to pass by.

It seemed, however, that the gentleman was in no hurry. She watched as he sprang down from the saddle and pulled the horse's reins over its head. It was a fine animal, a high-stepping grey with intelligent eyes, and she saw the man stroke its nose and speak quietly to it as he led it along the path towards her. The horse was limping a little and had obviously gone lame. Caroline held her breath and hoped that its rider would not decide to stop for a rest.

It was the mouse that was her undoing. She considered herself an indomitable female, but ever since Julia had put a dead mouse in her bed at school, Caroline had had a fear of tiny furry mammals. This one ran across her foot and she made an involuntary movement, sending the dead leaves swirling through the doorway of the hut and frightening a pheasant that was scratching around outside. The bird flew off giving its harsh cry and the horse, no doubt still unsettled by the incident that had turned it lame, reared up and almost knocked the gentleman to the ground.

Caroline drew back hastily into the shadows but she knew she was too late. Her abrupt movement had revealed a flash of scarlet velvet and it was useless to just stand there pretending that she was invisible. As she hesitated, the gentleman regained his balance and turned sharply towards the hut. For a long moment he stared straight at her, then he dropped the horse's reins and took a step towards her.

Caroline's heart was racing suddenly. She knew that the sensible course of action would be to step forward and apologise, but even as she thought this, she was turning to scramble through a gap in the back wall and stumble down amongst the leaves and brambles on the other side.

Her legs were shaking as she tried to steady herself and tear her cloak from the grip of the rough masonry that snagged at the material. She heard the scrape of loose stone behind her and was filled with a heady panic. Surely he was not following her! He had looked so harmless, so very worthy...

It was at that moment that Caroline discovered the extent of her mistake. A hand caught hold of her wrist and pulled her round to face him with a force that almost knocked the breath from her body. The hood of her cloak fell back and her hair tumbled all about her shoulders. She grasped instinctively at his arm for support, and felt the hard muscle beneath her fingers, the indisputable evidence of a man in excellent physical condition. So much for her thoughts of a dreamy poet with more interest in pursuits of the intellect than those of the body! Caroline raised her gaze to his face and discovered that the far-seeing eyes that she had imagined were dwelling on some piece of verse were a hard blue, cold as a stormy sea. For a long moment they stared at each other, and then Caroline saw a hint of laughter lighten his face and for some reason she felt her legs tremble again.

'Well…' There was lazy amusement in the man's voice. 'Not the poacher I'd expected, but I cannot find it in me to be sorry! Hold still, sweetheart—' He had felt her struggle and held on to her with insulting ease. 'You owe me something at least for frightening my horse!'

Not a worthy but a rake, Caroline found herself thinking, as she felt him shift his grip a little so that he could pull her into his arms. This had to be the first time that she had made such an error of judgement, and she was not the only one.

'You are making a mistake—' Her words were lost as she found herself being thoroughly kissed. The roughness of his cheek brushed hers; he smelled of leather and fresh air and lemon cologne. It was delicious and she was utterly shocked with herself for even thinking so.

'You were saying?'

The gentleman had let her go sufficiently to look down into her face. Caroline saw his eyes sweep appreciatively over her chestnut curls and linger on the red evening gown. And no wonder. It was cut low and she could feel the sting of the cold air against her bare skin. Drawing her cloak closely about her, Caroline glared at him.

'I was trying to tell you that you were making a mistake…' The words came out with considerably less than her usual authoritative ring. She cleared her throat and frowned slightly. He was watching her with

the same lazy mockery that she had heard in his voice
and it distracted her.

'What I mean is… You should not… I am not—'

'I would hate you to think that I had kissed you by
mistake, ma'am,' the gentleman said politely, and it
seemed to Caroline that he was wilfully misunderstanding her. 'I cannot possibly let you go under such
a misapprehension. Allow me…'

Caroline gave a little squeak of dismay as he pulled
her close again. This was a deeper kiss. Her lips
parted under the skilful pressure of his. He tasted
cold. Sensation swept through Caroline and left her
shivering. She could not believe what was happening
to her and could not begin to understand *why* she was
letting it happen. With a supreme effort of will she
tried to free herself again, and he let her go immediately.

'Listen to me.' She put a hand out as though to
ward him off, although he had made no further move
towards her. 'I am trying to explain to you that you
are making a serious error, sir! I am not what you
think me, and you, sir—' She broke off, unusually
lost for words as she considered his face.

She had been wrong to think his looks fine-drawn.
On a woman, the high cheekbones and chiselled features might have appeared delicate, but there was too
much authority and determination in his face to give
any hint of weakness. Those blue eyes held a disconcerting look of appraisal and the thick fair hair that
Caroline had wanted to touch… She cleared her

throat self-consciously, aware that he was still watching her.

'I believe that you must be Captain Brabant,' she said, with as much composure as she could muster. 'I am Caroline Whiston. I am staying at the Manor.'

A frown had come into the gentleman's eyes, replacing the look of appreciative amusement that had lingered there. This time when his gaze considered her it held no warmth. Caroline drew herself up a little. She dared not think what she looked like, her hair all tousled and her lips rosy from his kisses.

'I beg your pardon, ma'am,' he said slowly, 'but are we acquainted? Or do you include clairvoyance in your gifts, that you already know my name?'

It was on the tip of Caroline's tongue to say that she felt he had treated her as rather more than an acquaintance already, but she knew that there was no point in provoking further trouble. There was no doubt that this could only be Lewis Brabant and she cursed herself that she had not recognised him from the start. His resemblance to his sister was sufficiently strong that she should have guessed his identity straight away, rather than realising only when he was at close quarters. Very close quarters, she amended. And now she was well and truly in the suds, since this man was heir to Hewly Manor and, more to the point, Julia's former fiancé...

She realised that Captain Brabant was still awaiting her response and dropped a slight curtsey.

'No, sir, we have not met,' she said, with tolerable composure, 'but you have a great look of your sister about you so it is small wonder that I recognised you. The household has been expecting you home this se'ennight and more.'

'I see,' Captain Brabant said, and Caroline had the disconcerting feeling that he saw more than was comfortable. She reflected ruefully that she felt much as the cabin boy must have done when Captain Brabant was inspecting his crew on the quarterdeck. Those blue eyes were disturbingly perceptive.

'Forgive me, Miss Whiston,' he said, 'but when you said that you were a guest at the Manor—'

Caroline felt a blush rising. 'You misunderstand me, sir,' she said hastily. 'I am not a guest of your father's but companion to your cousin...to Mrs Chessford.'

'Julia's companion? You?' Captain Brabant took a step towards her and Caroline backed away from him instinctively. One brow arched in ironic amusement as he saw her withdraw. 'My dear Miss Whiston, pray do not be alarmed! You have nothing to fear from me! But—a companion! How very inappropriate!'

'I do not know how you could be a judge of such matters, sir!' Caroline snapped, forgetting that he was to all intents and purposes her host, and giving in to her indignation. 'Upon my word, you have a strange concept of appropriate behaviour! What is appropriate about accosting respectable ladies as they take a walk in the woods? I believe that you must have been away at sea so long that you forget your manners!'

She saw him grin. It seemed an unacceptable response to her annoyance.

'Maybe that accounts for it,' he murmured. 'Deprived of the improving company of the fair sex... Indeed, ma'am, I think you must be right!'

'Fustian, sir!' Caroline retorted, the colour flaring in her face. 'I do not believe that you have been deprived of female companionship! Such freedom of manner argues that the reverse is true—' She broke off, realising that this exasperating man had driven her to express views that should have remained private. Severe Miss Whiston never normally allowed herself a vulgar display of opinion. It was not at all proper for a governess companion.

She bit back her words, trying to ignore the Captain's infuriating smile. 'Well, that is nothing to the purpose!' she finished sharply. 'Good day, sir! I shall leave you to complete your journey alone.'

'That seems rather pointless when we are both travelling in the same direction,' the Captain said politely. 'Permit me to escort you back, Miss Whiston! We may become better acquainted!'

Caroline gritted her teeth. That was the last thing she wanted, and if Julia should witness Captain Brabant's arrival at the Manor with her in attendance... Well, it did not really bear thinking about.

'No, indeed—'

'Perhaps you could explain why you were running away from me,' the Captain continued affably, as though she had not spoken. 'After all, it was your own behaviour that sparked the whole incident!'

Caroline blushed. She knew that he was right, but felt it was not gallant of him to remind her. 'I apologise, sir,' she said tightly. 'I fear I was nervous. You must think it quite odd in me—'

'I do! To startle my horse and then to run off as though you were a miscreant! What was I to do?'

'You cannot truly have thought me a poacher, sir—' Caroline stopped, realising that she was once again being drawn into a ridiculous conversation.

'Not once I had caught you, of course,' Captain Brabant said, with a quirk of his brows. 'When I was holding you, I thought—'

'Thank you, sir, it is best forgotten, I think!'

The Captain seemed undiscouraged. 'This must be yours, I think, ma'am.' He was holding out her book of sonnets to her. 'Shakespeare? Do you also read the romantic poets?'

Caroline practically snatched the book from his hand, thrusting it back into her pocket. Why must the man insist on making conversation?

'I have little time,' she said crossly.

'For poetry or for romance?' Once again he was smiling at her quizzically.

Caroline concentrated on picking her way through the brambles and did not reply.

'You would probably find walking more comfortable in suitable clothing,' the Captain continued, from close behind her. 'That evening dress, whilst most appealing, is not very practical. Though with the boots,' he sounded as though he was giving the matter real consideration, 'it is particularly fetching—'

Caroline set her lips in a tight line and still said nothing. She could not believe how unfortunately everything was falling out. Here was Captain Brabant, authoritative, assured and utterly unlike Julia had described him. Why could he not have been the gentle dreamer of Julia's memory, or at the least a bluff old sea-dog with hair prematurely grey and an everlasting fund of boring tales? She watched him covertly as he retrieved his horse from the forest edge, where it had been happily munching its way through a brambly hedge. She was forced to acknowledge that there was something powerfully attractive about Captain Brabant's loose-limbed grace, something deceptive about that air of abstraction. A thinker as well as a man of action. In Caroline's experience that made him all the more dangerous.

It was the worst possible luck that they were obliged to be under the same roof, but she comforted herself with the thought that she need not see him much. Now that he knew she was not a guest but a servant his interest must surely wane, and any further *unsuitable* interest would have to be discouraged. It was a pity that he did not have enough proper feeling himself to understand the indelicacy of their circumstances. She was sure that she could hear him whistling under his breath, a sure sign that he did not take the situation seriously.

'Your basket, Miss Whiston.'

Caroline jumped. Captain Brabant gave her a slight bow and presented her with the woven reed basket, a few solitary mushrooms rolling around in its base. She had dropped it when she ran away, and she could see the rest of her crop scattered about on the path and in the undergrowth. He followed her gaze.

'We could pick them all up, I suppose,' he mused, 'although in a ballgown it would be quite difficult—'

'Pray do not put yourself to any trouble, Captain!' Caroline said hastily, feeling cross and foolish in equal measure. Would the man never cease to remind her of her idiocy in wandering about in the scarlet dress? Now she was well served for her vanity! The dress would be banished to the back of the wardrobe and never see the light of day again!

She reluctantly allowed Captain Brabant to fall into step beside her as they made their way along the path towards Steep Abbot. Caroline tried to preserve a chilly silence, but found that that seemed to make her even more aware of the Captain's presence at her side. Eventually she was forced into speech by her own self-consciousness.

'Did you have a good journey home, Captain?' she asked politely, picking on the most innocuous topic she could think of. Lewis Brabant smiled at her. It was decidedly unsettling.

'Yes, I thank you. I spent a few nights in London on my way up from Portsmouth. It was strange to be back.'

'Cold as well, I shouldn't wonder,' Caroline said encouragingly, glad to see that he was capable of holding a proper conversation. 'After the Mediterranean, autumn in England must seem very cold.'

There was now a decided twinkle in the Captain's eye. 'Oh, decidedly, ma'am! Cold and wet.'

'It has not rained here for several weeks, although the summer was very wet,' Caroline observed, ignoring the fact that he was now grinning. She knew he was funning her but she was determined to disregard it. She knew how to behave even if he did not.

'I had also forgotten,' the Captain said conversationally, 'how the English are obsessed with the weather! Or perhaps,' he turned slightly to look at her face, 'it is a defence against too personal a conversation? One thing I have *not* forgotten is society's ability to discuss trivia for hours!'

Caroline knew what he meant and she agreed with him. She had spent many a long hour in various drawing-rooms, listening to ladies chatter inconsequentially about something and nothing, gossiping on fortune, connections and scandal. It was galling to think that she was sounding just as hen-witted as they. Yet how to avoid it? She already suspected that Captain Brabant was a man who had little time for prevarication and she felt she had to keep him at arm's length.

She put up the hood of her cloak. The morning was chilly, though the sun was now breaking through the branches. She knew she looked most disheveled, with her hair in disarray, and she was anxious not to arrive at the Manor looking as though she had been dragged through a hedge—or thoroughly kissed.

'Ah,' she heard the smile in Captain Brabant's voice, 'there are other defences, are there not, Miss

Whiston? Hiding away inside your cloak must be one of them! So I suppose that it is out of the question to ask you to tell me a little about yourself? After all, we shall be sharing a roof…'

Caroline did not like the sound of that. The implied intimacy made her blush and she was glad of the concealment of the hood. They had reached the edge of the wood now, and Lewis held the gate for her before leading the horse through. The path crossed the Steep River and approached the village. The river ran in lazy bends here, bounded by trees that in the summer bent down towards the slow, brown waters. This morning, with the sun gilding the frosty branches and glittering on the water, it looked very pretty.

'There is little to tell,' Caroline said, coolly. 'I am a very dull subject. I have been a governess for eleven years, since I left the Guarding Academy, and I am now Mrs Chessford's companion. A paid companion,' she added, to make her meaning crystal clear. For a long moment, blue eyes met blue, then Lewis Brabant nodded slightly.

'No one is ever as dull as they pretend, Miss Whiston! A lady's companion who walks in the forest wearing a ballgown and reading Shakespeare seems extraordinary rather than ordinary to me!'

Caroline could feel her colour rising again. 'Nevertheless… I wish you will not pursue it, sir!'

'As you wish…' Caroline could feel him watching her. 'I did not realise that you were a schoolfriend of Julia's,' he added thoughtfully. 'I do not remember…'

'That is hardly surprising,' Caroline said sharply.

In her experience, the relatives of her old school-friends, particularly the male ones, had no recollection of her at all. How could they, when she paled into invisibility beside Julia's golden beauty?

Captain Brabant raised his hand in a gesture of surrender. 'Very well, Miss Whiston, we will change the subject, since you evidently think it unsuitable! You are the paid companion here—scarce better than a servant!' His tone had taken on a sarcastic edge. 'Far be it from me to overstep the social distinctions that clearly form the boundaries of your life!'

They had passed the Guarding Academy now and had turned down the cobbled lane that led to the Manor, walking at least four feet apart. Caroline clenched her fists in her pockets. She told herself that she had wanted Captain Brabant to observe the proprieties and it was therefore contrary to feel ill-used when he did precisely that.

They approached the gate of the Manor in silence and Caroline's heart sank to see the Captain's frown deepen as his gaze fell on his inheritance. The five-bar gate was rotten and a couple of the spars had broken off. The wall had long ago tumbled into the road and the drive beyond was overgrown with weeds and grasses. It was almost impossible to distinguish the formal gardens from the orchards, for all was a wilderness.

'Much has changed, has it not?' Lewis Brabant said under his breath, and Caroline felt his gaze linger on her as though she were part of a new, unwelcome order. It was not a pleasant feeling.

The clock on the stables read ten thirty, and somewhere in the house Caroline heard the echo of chimes. She winced. Julia might well be awake by now and wanting help with her toilette. She turned to Lewis Brabant, whose face was set in tense lines as he surveyed his home.

'I will go and tell them that you are here, sir. Excuse me—'

She pushed at the wicket gate leading into the gardens, slipping on the damp moss underfoot in her haste to get inside. Immediately the Captain's arm was about her waist, steadying her and holding her close.

'For all your objections, fate seems determined to throw us together, Miss Whiston,' he murmured in her ear.

'The stables are that way, sir,' Caroline said crossly, trying to free herself. He did not remove his arm and she was obliged to push hard against his chest to make him let her go. She heard him laugh.

'I know it. I was brought up here, if you recall—' He broke off and straightened up suddenly, his arms falling away from her. Caroline spun round. One of the upstairs windows of the Manor was open and a figure was leaning out. Her hair was like spun gold on the breeze. She looked like the princess in a fairy story. Caroline bit her lip.

'Lewis!' the vision called out. 'You are home!'

'Julia!'

Caroline heard Lewis Brabant say the name softly and felt a strange pang of envy. She watched with rueful disbelief as he dropped the reins, pushed the gate open and strode towards the main door. Caroline turned away abruptly, took hold of the horse's bridle and led the grey down the lane towards the stables.

'So that is why Julia has been betrothed three times, married and widowed all in the space that I have been governess and companion to three families!' she whispered in the horse's silky ear. 'Alas that I could study for years and never achieve such a result!'

The horse whickered softly and shook his head, as though in agreement. Caroline sighed as she handed him over to the groom, instructing the lad to take a look at the injured leg. That was that, then. It seemed that Julia would have little difficulty in engaging Captain Brabant's affections once again. Perhaps Lewis had never really forgotten her, despite all that had happened since the two of them had last met. As for his behaviour in the wood, it only served to show him to be a man who trifled with the feelings of others and could not be trusted. Caroline thrust her hands into the pockets of the cloak and reflected that the Captain would receive a dusty answer were he to try such shabby tricks on her again.

Chapter Two

'Pray be careful with those curling tongs, Caroline!' Julia Chessford said fretfully, moving her head to one side to admire the fall of golden ringlets about her shoulders. 'I declare, you are as ham-fisted as a scullery-maid!'

Caroline resisted an immediate urge to press the hot tongs against Julia's ear. 'I fear I am no turn at these matters, not being a trained ladies' maid,' she said evenly. 'It is unfortunate that you gave Letty the evening off—'

'Oh, the worst chance imaginable!' Julia agreed, smiling as she considered her reflection in the mirror. 'But how was I to know that Lewis would choose this of all days to return home? Such bad luck quite oversets one's plans, but we must make shift as best we can! Do hurry, Caroline! We are to dine in ten minutes!'

Caroline moved across to the closet to fetch Julia's wrap, watching as her former friend stood up and turned around slowly to consider her appearance.

There was no denying that Julia looked very beautiful. She had huge blue eyes that gave a misleading impression of sweetness and innocence, and the thick golden hair curled lusciously about her rounded face. Her lips were a perfect bow shape, her nose small and straight. Caroline, blessed with a set of features that were less regular, tried to repress her envy. She would not have exchanged her own informed mind for Julia's less enquiring one at any price, but sometimes she could not help coveting Julia's beauty.

'That will do very well,' Julia said with a little, self-satisfied smile. 'I am sure Lewis will scarce be able to resist! After all, he has been away at sea a long time and must be delighted to gain some female companionship!'

Once again, Caroline felt the sharp, irrational pang of jealousy. Judging by Lewis Brabant's behaviour in the woods, she thought that Julia was probably right.

'Miss Brabant told me that Richard Slater has a sister,' she heard herself saying, 'so no doubt the Captain has had time to polish his address in Lyme before coming here!'

Julia gave her a sharp glare. 'I have met Fanny Slater, Caroline, and I do not think I need consider her a rival!' She smoothed the silk of her skirts with a loving hand. 'No indeed, she is a plain woman and has no conversation! And Lewis has already given the impression that he is more than glad to see me again…'

Caroline turned away to hide her face, busying herself by straightening the pots and bottles on Julia's dressing-table. The room, decorated with swathes of pink satin and spindly white furniture, was a shrine to Julia's beauty.

'You are in earnest then, Julia? You wish to rekindle your romance with Captain Brabant?'

Julia shrugged carelessly. 'La, why not? It should provide some fun in this tediously dull place! Besides,' she gave Caroline a sparkling look, 'Lewis is rather attractive, is he not? He has changed since I met him last and I believe he could be quite a challenge! What do you think, Caroline?'

'I have no idea,' Caroline said sharply, bringing forward Julia's wrap. 'I am not accustomed to considering gentlemen in such way!'

'La, I should think not!' Julia's gaze was faintly malicious as it swept over her companion. 'That would be most inappropriate for a governess and could lead to all manner of difficulties! You will not be dining with us tonight,' she continued, taking the wrap without a word of thanks. 'You may take a tray in your room, Caroline. It is bad enough having to share Lewis's homecoming with that little milksop of a sister of his, without augmenting our party further!'

She let the wrap slide over her white arms and sighed. 'Lord, it is so slow living in the country! Now that Lewis is back I hope for some more invitations! I am sure that the Percevals will call, and perhaps even the Cleeves—did I tell you that I met the Countess in Town last year, Caroline, and she was most gracious to me! And now that we are neighbours...'

Caroline let the words flow over her head. She had heard quite enough of Julia's social pretensions in the last few weeks. The Cleeve and Perceval families had shown no inclination for a closer friendship with their neighbours at Hewly. They had been perfectly cordial on the few occasions that Julia and Caroline had encountered them in Abbot Quincey, but no invitations to visit had followed. When Julia had decided to call at Jaffrey House and Perceval Hall, the ladies were apparently not at home. Caroline had seen this as an unmistakable snub, but Julia had shrugged it off airily and persisted in her belief that they would all become great friends in time. For her part, Caroline suspected that the great families of the neighbourhood probably considered Julia encroaching and bad Ton, or even worse, not Ton at all.

'Speaking of the local aristocracy, I heard such a truly diverting piece of gossip this morning, Caro!' Julia spun round to fix her companion with bright, gleeful eyes. 'Only guess what has happened!'

Caroline bit her lip. 'I am sure that you will tell me—'

'Oh, you are so stuffy, pretending to a lack of interest! This is the most prime piece of news! The butcher's boy brought the story from the village—the *on dit* is that the Marchioness of Sywell has run away!'

Caroline stared. She remembered the notorious Marquis of Sywell from her time at the Guarding Academy, for his debauchery and wickedness had been a byword in the Abbey villages. Scarce a week had passed without his depravity being denounced in the local pulpits, rousing much speculation amongst the young ladies of the school as to the precise nature of the Marquis's iniquity. Once she had left the school, Caroline had gradually lost touch with the gossip of Steep Abbot and its environs, but on her return, Julia had been quick to update her on all of consequence. She had related the tale of the Marquis's ramshackle marriage with great excitement, but Caroline, deploring tittle-tattle, had not paid attention to half of it. Now it seemed that an even greater scandal had followed.

'The Marchioness?' Caroline said slowly. 'But surely you told me that they have been married for less than a year—'

Julia clapped her hands. 'I know! Is it not piquant! They said it would all end in tears, what with him being mad and thrice her age, and she being the strange creature she is!'

Caroline sat down on the end of the bed. 'Was she strange? I had not heard so—'

'Oh Caro, you must have heard the old story!' Julia looked eager. There was nothing she liked more than some scurrilous tale. 'Surely I told you already! The Marchioness was ward to the Abbey bailiff—or the bailiff's by-blow, more like! Do you not remember? John Hanslope went off in his cart one day and returned with a child! He said she was his ward and his wife educated her at home, for she had been a governess like yourself! We never saw hair nor hide of the girl—she never came into the village, or visited their neighbours, and you must concede that that is odd!'

Julia paused to adjust the bandeau restraining her curls, then resumed. 'I suppose you would not remember the chit's arrival, for it was just after your papa died and you had left Mrs Guarding's Academy. But surely I wrote to tell you all about it? I would *certainly* have written to relate so choice a piece of news!'

'I am sure you would,' Caroline murmured.

'Of course, at one time I was hoping to marry the Marquis myself,' Julia said brightly, peering into the mirror to view her reflection the better, 'but he was always a drunken old rake and Mrs B., the Admiral's wife, would not let me near him! Anyway, his taste obviously runs to the lower orders for the bailiff's ward to catch his notice!'

She picked up her reticule. 'I suppose the dinner gong will sound in a moment, but I must just finish the tale! When Mrs Hanslope, the bailiff's wife, died, he seemed uncertain of what to do with the girl and apprenticed her to some tradesman in Northampton, I believe, no doubt thinking that she might learn a useful profession! Anyway, she returned when Hanslope was on his deathbed, and made that shocking marriage to the Marquis! Scandalous!'

Caroline, remembering the spiteful delight with which Julia had imparted the tale of the Marquis's marriage, sighed a little. The Abbey villages had always been a hotbed of gossip—no doubt it was the same in any rural community—and probably there were precious few people with a kind word to say about the Marchioness.

'Where do they think she has gone?' she asked dubiously. 'With no friends and no one to help her—'

Julia shrugged carelessly. 'Heaven knows! But she is well served for her folly and greed, is she not! Presuming to marry a Marquis when she was a little nobody and probably quite unpresentable! No wonder that the villages can talk of little else!'

'What does Mr Hanslope have to say on all this?' Caroline asked slowly.

'Why, nothing! John Hanslope died a few months ago, just after the Marquis married his ward!' Julia said happily. 'Is it not the most *engrossing* tale, Caroline! Louise was her name. The bastard child of the bailiff! Each time Sywell did something outrageous they said that he could not possibly do worse, but of course he always did! And no doubt the girl was no better than she ought to have been, so there is one way that she might keep herself in the future—'

Caroline stood up. She had heard enough of Julia's spite. 'Well, it is an extraordinary tale, for sure, but—'

The gong sounded for dinner. Julia gave her golden curls one last, satisfied pat. 'There! I shall not be needing you again tonight, Caroline, for Letty will be back in time to help me undress.'

She swept out of the bedroom and down the curving stair. Caroline followed more slowly. Hewly Manor was a small house, dating in part from the fourteenth century, and whilst Julia deplored the inconvenience of the draughty old rooms and the lack of modern comforts, Caroline admired the style and elegance of previous centuries. The wooden stair led from the main landing directly down to the flagstone hall, where the dinner gong still reverberated softly. The Admiral had always insisted on military precision in his household and it was only recently, when his illness had become so much more severe, that standards had started to slip a little.

Julia grumbled that the food was always late and often cold, the service slipshod, and the servants paid her no heed. She felt was all of a piece with the dilapidation of the house and the estate, but Caroline's observation was that the servants were willing enough, but had no direction and no one to really care about them. She wondered what Lewis Brabant would make of all this neglect and reflected that she would not like to be in his servants' shoes. She already knew that Captain Brabant could be somewhat intimidating.

Caroline paused on the landing, taking care to stay well back in the shadows. She watched Julia descend slowly and saw her pause briefly before the long mirror that hung on the half-landing. Then, apparently satisfied with her appearance, she went down to join the Captain.

Caroline could see Lewis waiting at the bottom of the stair. The light fell on his upturned face as he watched Julia approach, and Caroline caught her breath. In his evening clothes, the dust from his journey washed away, he was elegance personified. The blue eyes that had regarded her so stonily earlier now rested on Julia with warm appreciation. That firm mouth held the hint of a disturbing smile. She saw Lewis straighten up and step forward to take Julia's hand. It was strange, but for a moment Caroline had some impression of restlessness about him, as though he already found the confines of the house chafing on him. It was only a momentary feeling, but it made Caroline wonder. A man who was used to the limitless expanse of the ocean could well find the boundaries of a country estate too restrictive.

'Good evening, Julia.' Caroline saw Lewis press a kiss on Julia's hand. 'Lavender is already down, but does Miss Whiston not join us for dinner?'

Caroline caught her breath. How would Julia respond to that, when she had been the one to forbid Caroline from accompanying them?

'Oh, Caro is a most retiring creature,' Julia said with a ravishing smile, taking Lewis's arm. 'I tried to persuade her to join us but she was positive in her refusal! She is the most perfect companion, you know, so discreet and unassuming. Now Lewis, I want to hear all about your adventures! I am utterly agog, my dear...'

The door of the drawing-room closed behind them. Caroline felt an uncharacteristic urge to stamp her foot. It was not that she had wished to take dinner with the family, but overhearing Julia's misrepresentations was too much. Even as a schoolgirl, Julia had had an uncanny knack of twisting the truth to present herself in the best possible light, and it seemed that this ability had not diminished in time.

Caroline vented her feelings by slamming her bed-room door behind her. It was childish but it made her feel better. Normally she was capable of dismissing the slights and irritations of her working life. After all, she had endured many such in the time since she had left the Guarding Academy. For some reason, however, working at Hewly Manor was proving more difficult. Perhaps it was because she and Julia had once been friends but were now effectively mistress and servant; perhaps it was because of the memories stirred up by being in Steep Abbot again. And now, Caroline thought honestly, it was because of Lewis Brabant. Now that she had met him, she found she did not like the thought of Julia's plans of entrapment, which was odd, since she had dismissed the man as the veriest rake.

On impulse, Caro went across to her bed and pulled out the old carpet-bag that was hidden beneath. In it she kept her most treasured possessions. There were scant few: her book of sonnets, a fine gold pendant and matching brooch inherited from her mother, her grandfather's fob watch. There was also a pile of letters received from Julia over the years.

Julia's communications had been erratic. After she had married and moved from Steep Abbot she had not written for several years, but in her widowhood she had struck up a correspondence again. Caroline often wondered why she had bothered to keep the letters and had come to the conclusion that it was because they constituted a link with Steep Abbot and her childhood. Added to which, Julia's writing, whilst no great prose, was as entertaining as it was malicious.

Caroline turned to the early letters, the ones that Julia had sent when Caroline had taken up her first post as a governess in Yorkshire, and Julia had left the Guarding Academy and was living at Hewly under the chaperonage of the Honourable Mrs Brabant. She scanned the closely written lines until she found the bit that she was looking for.

'...Life is so dull now that you are gone, dearest Caro. Mrs B., whilst very amiable, is the most idle of creatures and will scarce take me anywhere! I am desperate for a season in Town! How else shall I find myself a husband? I shall end up setting my cap at Andrew, though he is the dullest of them all with his hunting and his fishing...'

Caroline raised her eyebrows. Andrew Brabant's dreariness had not prevented Julia from contracting an engagement to him at a later date. But that was not the bit that interested her—at least, not yet. Here it was:

'Lewis is down from Oxford,' she read. 'I believe he fancies himself as a poet, for he is most romantical, with a lock of hair falling into his eyes and a dreamy air. He is forever quoting verse and striking a pose. It would be fun to see if I could make him fall in love with me! That would be just the thing for a poet and might even improve his bad verse! Perhaps I shall try...

'You must remember Mrs Taperley, the farrier's wife? The *on dit* is that her new baby was fathered by none other than the Marquis of Sywell—they say the little boy is the very image! Mrs B. takes great care to keep me out of Sywell's way, as you might imagine, but I should rather like to catch a Marquis!

'The Admiral talks of nothing but this horrid War, and is very dreary…'

There was more. Reams and reams of Julia's news and gossip. Caroline skipped a couple of letters and found another:

'Dearest Caro, the most diverting news! Lewis has asked me to marry him! I knew I could bring him up to scratch and indeed he is head over ears in love with me! He is to go to sea and wished us to become betrothed before he left. He is sure that the Admiral will make no demur, and indeed he might not, for have I not twenty thousand pounds? For my part, I fear that Lewis may be away some time and cannot imagine how I shall go on… I persuaded him that the engagement should remain secret… I saw Hugo Perceval in the village last week and thought him most handsome…'

Caroline sighed. She stuffed the letters back in the bag and pushed it out of sight under the bed. It seemed that Lewis Brabant had only been the first of Julia's conquests. It was not long before the Admiral's ward had transferred her affections to the older brother, and had entered into a more formal engagement. Julia had confided that the Admiral and his wife had not liked the match above half, but that she was determined to cut a dash in the neighbourhood as Mrs Andrew Brabant. Alas for Julia, the plan had been thwarted by the fever that carried off both Andrew and his mother, but it was not long before she had received an offer from Andrew's best friend, Jack Chessford... Jack had been handsome and rich, and Julia had achieved her aim of going to London at last. There had been no more letters until the one telling Caroline that Jack was dead in a carriage accident, the money was almost exhausted and Julia intended to make her home with her godfather, whose own health had deteriorated so markedly in recent years. Of Lewis, there had been no further mention at all.

That was until Caroline had come to Hewly to be Julia's companion. She shifted a little uncomfortably as she remembered how quickly she had got the measure of Julia's plans. As soon as Julia had discovered that Lewis Brabant was returning home, she declared that she intended to set her cap at him once more. Nor did she seem to see anything wrong in her plan to entrap him for her own amusement. Caroline sighed. Natural delicacy gave her an aversion to the idea, no matter how much she told herself that Lewis Brabant probably deserved such a fate, but she could scarcely warn him. Besides, Julia's feelings might be rather shallow at present, but it was not for Caroline to say that a deeper affection might not develop. She felt unaccountably depressed at the thought.

There was a knock at the door and Nurse Prior stuck her head round the door. A diminutive Yorkshirewoman, she had been nanny to all the Brabant children and had come out of retirement on the estate to nurse the Admiral after he was taken ill. Caroline and she had taken to each other quickly, each recognising the other's virtues. Mrs Prior had confided in an unguarded moment that Julia was about as much use as a chocolate fireguard, and had been appreciative of Caroline's help in the sickroom.

'Begging your pardon, Miss Whiston, but would you be so good as to sit with the Admiral for a little whilst I take my meal? The poor gentleman has not been so good today, and I don't like to leave him...'

Caroline jumped up. Over the past few weeks she had become accustomed to sitting with the Admiral whilst Mrs Prior took a rest. Julia never went near her godfather if she could help it, proclaiming herself too delicate for such unpleasantness, but Lavender, the Admiral's daughter, often took a turn to read to her father. Whether the Admiral was aware of any of them or not was a moot point. Often he would lie with his eyes open for hours on end, neither moving nor speaking. Sometimes he was voluble, but the words made little sense and he had to be soothed into a calmer frame of mind. If he were feeling well, he might get up and take a short turn about the garden, or sit in the drawing-room for a little, but he never gave any indication that he knew where he was or what was happening around him. Caroline, who remembered him from her youth as a strong, upright and active man, thought it a terrible pity.

The sickroom was in near-darkness, with only one candle burning on the table beside the bed. The Admiral lay on his back, gnarled hands resting on the coverlet, eyes closed. Caroline sat down beside the bed and picked up the book of naval stories that Lavender had evidently been reading earlier in the day. There was no sound but the Admiral's wheezing breath and the ticking of the clock on the mantelpiece. She started to read very softly.

Afterwards she could not believe that she had fallen asleep, but it had evidently been so, for she found that the book had slipped to her lap and her head had nodded forward. The candle had burned down a considerable way and the door was opening.

'I did not expect to find you here, ma'am.'

Caroline had been expecting Mrs Prior to return, but it was Lewis Brabant who now came forward into the glow of the candlelight. The flickering flame made him appear very tall and cast his face into shadow. He was still in his evening clothes and held a glass of brandy in one hand. Feeling suddenly flustered, Caroline got to her feet.

'Oh! Captain Brabant! Yes, I was sitting with your father whilst Mrs Prior had her dinner, but it seems—' She glanced at the clock in confusion, suddenly aware that it was much later than she had thought.

'The kitchen maid cut herself on the vegetable knife and Mrs Prior has been bandaging her up,' Lewis Brabant said with a smile. 'I am sorry that you have been delayed, Miss Whiston. I am happy to sit with my father for a little now, and allow to join my sister and Mrs Chessford in the drawing-room.'

The prospect held little allure for Caroline, who could not think of many less enjoyable ways to finish the evening. Lewis was looking at his father's sleeping face and his expression was sombre.

'How has he been, Miss Whiston? Mrs Prior tells me that today has not been one of his better days.'

'The Admiral has been asleep whilst I have been here,' Caroline said, a little hesitantly. 'It is true that he has not stirred much today. Sometimes he is quite lively and even takes a walk in the gardens on fine days! And often he will talk to us—' She broke off, aware of Lewis Brabant's gaze resting on her face with disconcerting intentness.

'You must have spent a great deal of time with him,' he said. 'I thank you for that, Miss Whiston. It is kind of you.'

'Well…' Caroline found herself uncomfortable with his gratitude but did not wish to appear so ungracious as to dismiss it. People so seldom thanked her for anything she did. Besides, it was true that caring for the Admiral was not a part of her duties and she had undertaken it to help Mrs Prior and Lavender.

'Mrs Prior is a devoted nurse,' she said guardedly, 'but even she needs a rest occasionally. I believe she would work her fingers to the bone otherwise!'

'She was always the same,' Lewis said, smiling ruefully. 'Did Nanny Prior tell you that she was nurse to us all, and to my mother's family before that? She has always been a tower of strength.'

He moved across to the fire and banked it up. The flames shot up and sent the shadows dancing along the wall. Caroline felt suddenly faint with hunger and grasped the chair back to steady herself. She had forgotten that she had not yet eaten and that the hour for dinner was long past.

'I do believe that you must have missed your dinner, ma'am,' Lewis Brabant said, straightening up and coming towards her, concern showing on his face. He took her arm. 'You look quite pale! Stay here whilst I go to order you a tray of food. We cannot do with having to call Dr Pettifer out for you as well!'

'I am very well, I thank you, sir,' Caroline said, her face flaming with embarrassment. The hard strength of his hand under her arm was strangely disturbing. She felt her head spin with a combination of hunger and mortification, and Lewis gave an exclamation and pressed the brandy glass into her hand.

'Here, take this, Miss Whiston, before you swoon! You will find it most efficacious!'

He was right. The strong spirit burned Caroline's throat and made her cough a little, but the world immediately came back into closer focus. She looked a little doubtfully from the empty glass to Lewis's smiling face.

'Thank you, sir... Your best brandy! I am so sorry—'

Lewis shrugged gracefully. 'It is of no consequence, Miss Whiston! I will fetch another glass.' His amused scrutiny dwelled on her face, which had gone from chalk white to rosy pink. 'I believe that you should retire to your room until I can arrange for a tray to be brought up. For those unaccustomed to strong liquor the result can be confusing!'

'I am not unaccustomed to brandy,' Caroline began, then realised how her words must sound and broke off in confusion. 'That is, I have drunk it before... My grandfather used to promote it as medicinal against chills...' She realised that she was rambling. Lewis had raised one eyebrow and was watching her with a quizzical amusement that disconcerted her.

'I thought for a moment that you must be one of those fabled governesses who was addicted to drink, Miss Whiston!' he said mildly. 'Such an idea seems absurd, but one must always expect the unexpected...'

The colour flooded Caroline's face again. On an empty stomach the drink was proving as much a curse as a blessing. She extricated herself carefully from Lewis's grip and walked towards the door.

'Pray do not trouble yourself to arrange any food for me, sir. I shall go down to the kitchens directly.'

Lewis shrugged, opening the door for her. 'Very well, Miss Whiston. I can see that you mean to be confoundedly independent!' His gaze travelled over her thoughtfully. 'I see also that you have rejected your red velvet for more sober garb! How very apt for a governess companion!'

Caroline looked up at him. The faint light could not hide the mockery in his eyes.

'I am persuaded,' he added pleasantly, 'that it can only be skin deep, however! The dryad who walks the woods reading verse must be the real Miss Whiston! The child who was brought up on brandy-drinking...'

'The real Miss Whiston has a living to earn,' Caroline said tartly, 'and has no time for conundrums, sir! Pray excuse me!'

Lewis Brabant gave her an ironic bow. 'Do not let me keep you from your duties then, ma'am! Good night!'

Caroline closed the door softly behind her and leant against the jamb for a moment to steady herself. It seemed that Lewis Brabant, despite his admiration for Julia, was not above flirting with the companion. Such behaviour was not unfamiliar to Caroline, for she had met plenty of men who thought that governesses and companions were fair game for their advances. Normally such situations gave her no trouble but what was particularly confusing here was her own reaction to Lewis. She should have given him a sharp setdown, but instead she had felt a treacherous attraction, as bewildering as it was unwelcome.

She went slowly down the stairs, through the door to the servants' quarters and along the corridor to the kitchen. The chatter and light interrupted her thoughts, but as she sat down at the trestle table and accepted a bowl of soup, she could not help but wonder just what Lewis Brabant thought of her. Then she thought that perhaps his mind was so full of Julia that he did not think of her at all, and she found that that was more annoying still.

Lewis waited until the door had closed behind Caroline, then took the chair beside the bed, sat back and closed his eyes. It had been a long day and he was bone weary, but despite that, he had to fight a strong urge to take a horse to the Admiralty and demand to be given the first ship available.

His responsibilities dragged him down like lead weights. The house was in poor condition and the estate even more so. His father's man of business had been blunt about the time and effort it would take to get things back into shape and Lewis was not sure that he even wanted to try. He had little affinity with a place that he had only visited once in the past ten years. As Richard had pointed out, it was not even near the sea! If it had not been for his family...

Lewis opened his eyes. His father's breathing was steady but the old man showed no flicker of consciousness. Lewis was aware of a profound sadness. It could only be a matter of time before the Admiral passed on, but he owed it to his father to see that his last days were as comfortable as possible. He would have to talk to the doctor in the morning.

Lewis leant forward and looked at his father's sleeping face. They had never been particularly close, but the Admiral had been a fair man and they had respected each other. Harley Brabant had never understood his son's bookish tendencies but had tolerated them whilst complaining that Lewis took after his mother's side of the family. All the same, Lewis knew that his father had been very proud when he had chosen to follow him into the Navy. It was comforting to think that the Admiral had approved of him.

Which was why... Lewis sighed. Which was why it was difficult to escape the notion that the Admiral would wish his son to continue what he had begun at Hewly Manor. Lewis knew that he could always sell up and move away, but he could not escape the thought that this would be going against the Admiral's wishes.

Then there was Lavender. His sister had only been fourteen when he had gone away and Lewis was uncomfortably aware that she was now a grown woman who must have her own hopes and aspirations. He barely knew her and she was a reserved character who might take some time to understand. He had already seen that she disliked Julia...

Lewis shifted slightly. Julia was just as he remembered her, only more beautiful, sweeter, more desirable. She had been eighteen when he had gone to sea, and he a youth of twenty-two who had thought himself so worldly wise and brave! A faint smile twisted his lips. What a lot he had learned in those first few months, racked by seasickness and homesickness in equal measure, afraid and forlorn! The lowest point had been when he had received his mother's letter telling him of Julia's betrothal to his brother. Lewis had felt sick and betrayed, for had not Julia exchanged the most tender vows with him, promising to wait for him for ever?

He had been prepared to put such youthful folly behind him on his return to Hewly. After all, he and Julia were ten years older and such boy and girl affairs were best left in the past. But to his amazement, there had been a letter from Julia awaiting him on his arrival in London, explaining that she had felt it her duty to return to Hewly to care for the Admiral. She expressed herself delighted to be able to welcome him back to his old home. Her words were well chosen and gracious, and had stirred in him a faint but definite anticipation at seeing her again. And then they had met...

Lewis got up and walked over to the window. The heavy velvet curtains had been drawn against the November dark, and when he pushed them back he felt the cold air rush into the overheated sickroom. The moon was high and cast a silver shadow over the deserted garden. He felt restless and cooped up in the house. With a sigh, Lewis let the curtain fall back into place and moved over to the fire. He had imagined that there might be some initial awkwardness in meeting Julia again, but this had proved far from the case. She had been the perfect hostess, but with added warmth that had been most encouraging.

Thinking of Julia led him to think of Caroline Whiston. There was an enigma. No warm welcome from her! For a moment, Lewis recalled the tantalising softness of Caroline in his arms, her lips parting beneath his. The change from that spirit of the woods into the severe companion in her drab worsted was almost unbelievable. It was as though she deliberately hid a part of herself away. Yet she was not ill-looking. It was almost as though she deliberately sought to efface herself, hiding that glorious chestnut hair, choosing colours that drained all vitality from her pale complexion, concealing her figure. It had not been hidden in that red velvet dress... Lewis smothered a grin. Nor could Miss Whiston disguise the flashing beauty of those hazel eyes. She was a most unusual lady's companion indeed.

Lewis stirred the fire, still thinking of her. What on earth had possessed him to accost her in that particular way? True, he had thought her a maidservant or village girl when he had first glimpsed her, but he was hardly the man to go around stealing kisses from servants! There had been some affinity, some instant chemistry between them that had leapt into immediate life. He was certain she felt it too, for later she had been nervous of him, reserved. Stern Miss Whiston would never allow him within arm's length again!

Lewis sighed, his conscience pricking him. It was little wonder that Miss Whiston had been nervous after his behaviour earlier in the day. Companions and governesses were in a vulnerable position and he had taken advantage. Yet there was something about the girl that drew him on...

'Petticoat government!' Richard Slater had commented, on hearing that Lewis would be returning to a house full of women. Lewis grimaced. He would have to change that. Already he felt stifled by the claustrophobic atmosphere of Hewly Manor, the shadow of the sickroom, the circumscribed life of the country. He would write to Richard and ask him to bring a party to Hewly, then he would throw himself into the management of the estate, visit his neighbours, find somehow, the piece of his life that seemed to be missing. Previously, it had been the Navy that had filled the spaces in his life, occupying his time and energies. It was his main love, but if there was to be another... His thoughts turned fleetingly to Julia again. His first love. The thought of her as a country wife was laughable, but for the time being at least they were sharing a house and he was still not sure if he was glad or sorry. He picked up the brandy glass and looked at it thoughtfully. He must ask Caroline Whiston more about the grandfather who had encouraged brandy-drinking as a cure for chills. Thinking of her once more, Lewis took the empty glass and went downstairs in search of a refill.

Chapter Three

There were no more early morning walks for Caroline. The weather had turned wet and windy and, even had she wanted to venture out, Julia kept her busier than ever with a wealth of trivial little jobs. She saw little of Lewis Brabant, for he spent most of his days immured with his estate manager or riding out to inspect the property, returning only for dinner. Caroline never ate with the family and made sure that she avoided Lewis if it was at all possible. Nevertheless she found herself curiously aware of his presence, as though the house was alive with a new energy.

From what little she did see of him, it struck Caroline that Lewis was a very self-contained man. He listened carefully, spoke sparingly, watched intently and missed very little of what went on. She noticed him taking particular pains to draw Lavender out and was amused to see that whilst his sister's natural reserve kept her quiet to begin with, she was soon responding to his genuine interest. Caroline thought that Lavender had probably been lonely and the return of her brother was just what she needed. Julia had never troubled to befriend her and Caroline had suspected that Lavender did not like her anyway, although Miss Brabant was far too well bred to give any indication of her feelings. To Caroline, Lavender had always been pleasant but very quiet, and because she avoided Julia, Caroline had never had the chance to progress the acquaintance. Now though, under Lewis's encouragement, Caroline saw that Lavender was emerging from her shell.

She found the two of them together in the library one morning when Julia had sent her downstairs to choose her a book. The fair heads were bent close together over what looked like an estate map, and Caroline paused on the threshold, reflecting on the strong family likeness and not wishing to intrude. Then Lewis looked up, tossed her a charming smile and rolled the map up.

'Miss Whiston! How are you, ma'am? My sister has just been showing me her sketches—she has been drawing flora over by Steepwood Lawn. Do you know that part of the forest at all from your walks?'

His tone was suspiciously bland, but since Steepwood Lawn was close to where the two of them had met on his first day home, Caroline knew that he must be teasing her. To her vexation, she felt the faint colour come into her cheeks. Lewis's gaze was bright with amusement as it rested on her face, one brow quirked in enquiry, his blue eyes dancing.

'I believe I know the place a little,' Caroline said stiffly. She saw that Lavender was watching her with a gaze as perceptive as her brother's and tried to overcome her discomfort. 'Will you show me your sketches, Miss Brabant? I should like to see them very much.'

'Of course,' Lavender murmured, gesturing towards the pencil drawings scattered across the table.

Caroline looked, and forgot her self-consciousness. 'But these are beautiful!' she exclaimed warmly. 'I did not realise that you could draw so well, Miss Brabant!' She leant closer. 'And unless I mistake, that is a May Lily! I had no notion that they grew in the woods hereabouts!'

Lavender's eyes lit up. '*Maianthemum bifolium*; you are not mistaken, Miss Whiston, though they are rare. They prefer a light acid soil, you see, and only grow in certain parts of the forest.'

'And oxlip, and squill...' Caroline smiled as she drew the sheets towards her. 'It is a while since I studied botany, but—'

'You studied botany?' Lavender's face was eager. She looked animated and very pretty. Caroline, remembering how Julia had always dismissed Lavender's fair looks as insipid, realised that they had all underestimated the younger girl. She smiled shamefacedly. 'Well, my studies were only for my own enjoyment and most amateur! But I have a delightful book inherited from my grandpapa! It contains all the wild flowers and a wealth of detail. If you would like to borrow it—'

She broke off, aware that Lewis Brabant was watching her, a smile in his eyes. It made her feel as though the room was suddenly overheated. She looked hastily away. Fortunately Lavender appeared not to have noticed.

'Oh, Miss Whiston, thank you! That would be most pleasant!'

Lewis Brabant strode forward with a lazy grace. 'It will be good for you to have another expert to talk to, Lavender, rather than a brother who is a dullard!'

Lavender laughed. 'No such thing, Lewis! You are ridiculous!'

'Well, I assure you I cannot tell a petal from a stamen, but I do know that your drawings are very fine! Now, you must excuse me for I must be about estate business.' He paused with his hand on the door-handle. 'You will not forget the commission at Hammond's for me, Lavender? Perhaps Miss Whiston might accompany you if she has any errands into Abbot Quincey?'

Caroline agreed readily. 'I have some ribbons to buy for Mrs Chessford and a number of small purchases to make. If you do not mind waiting whilst I choose another book…'

She put the two volumes she was carrying down on the table and moved across to the oaken shelves to choose something else for Julia. Lewis picked up the books and perused their spines. He looked at her quizzically.

'*Sense and Sensibility* and *Marmion*! A curious mixture, Miss Whiston!'

'Oh,' Caroline felt flustered. '*Sense and Sensibility* is Mrs Chessford's choice—'

Lewis raised his eyebrows. 'You do surprise me, ma'am! So Julia reads the books on manners and morals, and you read the romance! How singular, when outward appearances would suggest otherwise!'

He put the book in his pocket. 'I should like to read *Marmion* again...' He raised a hand in farewell. 'You must join us for dinner tonight, Miss Whiston. No more skulking in your room!' And he left Caroline feeling confused and annoyed, and suspicious that she had glimpsed more than a hint of speculation in Lavender's eyes.

The walk to Abbot Quincey was very pleasant, though the roads were a little muddy after the recent rain. It was the first fine day of the week, and Julia had roused herself sufficiently to take the carriage and go to visit friends near Northampton. She had dismissed Caroline, telling her that she did not need her when there was other, more congenial company to be had, which left her companion feeling more than ever sorry to be the butt of Julia's bad manners.

Lavender Brabant was a different matter, however, and there was certainly no faulting her courtesy. They talked of botany and art as they walked, and found that they had plenty of interests in common to make the journey pass quickly. Lavender's companionship was stimulating after Julia's trivial gossip, and Caroline felt her spirits lift at being out in the fresh air. They reached Abbot Quincey to find that it was busy, despite not being a market day, and strolled down the main street to pause before Hammond's general store and admire the new frontage. Lavender giggled over the fanlight and huge bow windows.

'Oh dear, it looks a little excessive for a country town! I understand that Mr Hammond has modelled it on his store in Northampton, and is as proud as proud! Only look, dear Miss Whiston—he has festooned the doorway with his muslin and kerseymere! I do so hope he will not get mud on it!'

They were about to enter the shop when they were hailed from close quarters by a cadaverous gentleman with an eager eye. Lavender gave Caroline a speaking glance, ducked under the swathes of drapery and disappeared into Hammond's interior. Caroline sighed and turned to greet the newcomer, trying to compose her face into an expression that was pleasant without being too welcoming.

'Mr Grizel. How do you do, sir?'

Hubert Grizel was curate of a neighbouring parish and had recently preached at the church in Abbot Quincey, on the invitation of the Reverend William Perceval. From the moment Caroline had seen him in church, she had identified him as the perfect example of a worthy clergyman looking for a consort. From the moment he had clapped eyes on Caroline, it was evident that Mr Grizel thought that he had found her. He had called at Hewly, not once but several times, and Julia had made sport of his pastoral visits until Caroline was very uncomfortable. She had no wish to encourage the cleric, but equally no desire to embarrass him.

'Miss Whiston!' Mr Grizel's thin face flushed with

pleasure. He removed his hat, gave a gallant bow and looked as though he were about to topple over. 'How are you, ma'am? You look very well, if I may make so bold! I had been intending to call at Hewly, but the weather being as it has—' He gestured vaguely towards the muddy road.

Caroline smiled. 'I am very well, I thank you, sir, as are all at the Manor. There has been little change in the Admiral's condition. But you will perhaps have heard our good news? Captain Brabant is returned—'

Mr Grizel had indeed heard all about Lewis Brabant's return. 'I am relieved that the Captain is home safely from the wars,' he observed pompously, 'and am more than ever comforted that you ladies are no longer unprotected. A house full of women is in need of a staunch defender!'

Caroline repressed the urge to tell him that they had scarcely felt in danger before, and a small silence fell. It was clear that Mr Grizel was trying to think of some conversational topic and equally clear that Caroline did not intend to help him.

'Well,' Caroline said brightly after a moment, gesturing towards the shop, 'I must be about my errands! We will see you again soon, Mr Grizel.'

Mr Grizel ardently assured her that she would indeed, and took himself off, still stammering profuse compliments.

Caroline smiled a little as she negotiated the blue spotted muslin adorning Hammond's doorway. Poor Mr Grizel! She hoped that she had mistaken his intentions but suspected that she had read them all too clearly. He could scarcely be blamed for considering a governess companion as a suitable wife and she just hoped she had not been so civil as to encourage his pretensions. She had no wish to hurt his feelings.

The interior of the shop was dark after the sunshine outside, and Caroline paused to allow her eyes to attune. One half of the shop was a grocery and general store, selling everything from candles to teapots, whilst the other half was a drapers. It was clear that Arthur Hammond was not a man to miss a commercial opportunity. He understood perfectly that his country clients could be anyone from the baker's wife to Lady Perceval, and that rich and poor alike required a shop that sold all the bits and pieces they needed to save them making the journey into Northampton. At the same time he managed to give the impression of fine quality. Local gossip said that Hammond was very rich and an inveterate social climber, and Caroline could well believe it. She knew that he owned an emporium in Northampton and a string of other shops in the county, and that other members of his family had also made a fortune from trade. Hammond's children had been sent away to get a fine education, all except Barnabas, his eldest son, who was being groomed to take over the shop.

Caroline ducked behind a bolt of glossy lustring that was resting against the shelves, and looked around for the ribbons. Julia had asked her to match some colours for two new gowns. She had chosen the dress material herself, but had lost interest in the details once the purchase was made, leaving the choice

to her companion. Caroline did not mind. She knew
she had a good eye for colour and style when given
a chance, and if Julia did not like the outcome she
should not have delegated the task in the first place.

Caroline paused before a display of fine stockings
and lace. Would that she had either the opportunity
or the means to wear such clothes! The red dress was
the only luxurious item of clothing that she possessed,
and she had ruthlessly avoided buying clothes she had
known she would never wear. Nevertheless it would
be fun one day... Caroline caught herself in a rosy
dream where she was dressed in green silk and descending a sweeping staircase to a ballroom... She
put it firmly from her mind.

She caught sight of Lavender over by the counter,
purchasing some gold braid, presumably the commission from Lewis. Barnabas Hammond himself was
attending to her, which struck Caroline as interesting
since the purchase was small enough for one of the
assistants to attend her. Lavender's head was bent
over her purse and there was an expression in
Barnabas's eyes that made Caroline's heart skip a
beat. So the draper's handsome son had a *tendre* for
the Admiral's daughter! Caroline watched as
Lavender looked up, met Barney's very dark eyes and
blushed becomingly. She pursed her lips in silent surprise. So the interest was mutual! Caroline could not
be surprised, for any woman could see that Barney
Hammond was a devastatingly attractive man. And
perhaps it was simply a physical attraction on
Lavender's part. She had probably not met many

young men and Barney had a strong, lithe physique, and a dark, intense gaze that was particularly compelling. Village gossip had it that the girls were mad for him, but Barney was quiet and kept himself to himself, almost as much as Lavender did...

Barney looked up, saw Caroline watching and straightened up, taking a step backwards and assuming a more formal expression. Caroline hurried forward with her fabric samples. She liked Barney and did not wish to be thought prying, but she could not help but wonder how Lewis would feel if his sister had developed a genuine affection for the draper's son. For all Arthur Hammond's pretensions, it could not be seen as an equal match.

With ribbons, buttons and braid purchased, and waved on their way by a fulsome Arthur Hammond himself, Caroline and Lavender stepped out into Abbot Quincey's main street once more. There was a delicate flush still on Lavender's high cheekbones and a sparkle in her eyes, but before Caroline could decide whether or not to quiz her, they bumped into Lady Perceval.

Caroline felt a little awkward. The last time she had met Lady Perceval and her daughters she had been with Julia, and whilst they had all exchanged cordial greetings, it had seemed clear to Caroline that the Percevals had no wish to further the acquaintance. This was a little odd, for Caroline knew Lady Perceval to be the kindest of creatures and her generosity was spoken of very highly in the neighbourhood. Caroline had been forced to draw the unhappy conclusion that it was Julia who was the rub and that Lady Perceval did not wish to encourage her. This opinion was now borne out as her ladyship greeted Lavender very warmly.

'My dear! How delightful to see you again!' She took Lavender's hand in hers and bent a friendly smile on Caroline. 'And Miss Whiston! A pleasure!' She turned back to Lavender. 'We were so pleased to hear of your brother's return, Miss Brabant! You must be greatly relieved to have him home.'

Lavender blushed and smiled. 'Oh, Lady Perceval, it is indeed a pleasure to have Lewis back! I have missed him a great deal!'

Lady Perceval patted her hand. 'Very natural, my dear! I hope that he will settle to life in the neighbourhood—we all do! It will be good for the estate.' A frown of concern touched her brow. 'And your father? How is he?'

Lavender seemed to droop a little. 'I fear he is not well, Lady Perceval. I do not believe it can be long—' She broke off. 'It makes me more grateful than ever to have my brother home.'

Lady Perceval sighed. 'Yes, indeed. It is fortunate that you have his support at so difficult a time.' She turned to Caroline. 'It is good to see you back in Northamptonshire too, Miss Whiston. You must see some changes since your time at the school!'

'I do indeed, ma'am, I thank you,' Caroline murmured, surprised at this sign of notice. She had not realised that Lady Perceval even knew who she was, let alone her past history.

Lady Perceval was still smiling at her. 'I knew your mama, you know, Miss Whiston. We were débutantes together, Deborah and I.' She sighed and shook her head. 'She was a good friend and I am sorry that we lost touch with each other. If you are ever in need of any help—' suddenly there was significant look in Lady Perceval's eye '—I beg you to come to me. I should do my best to assist you.'

She smiled at Lavender again. 'Well, I should not keep you. No doubt your brother will have a hundred and one things to do about the estate, Miss Brabant, but Sir James and I should be pleased if the two of you would care to dine at the Hall one evening. I will send the invitation over. Good day, Miss Brabant.' She nodded to Caroline. 'Miss Whiston.'

'How charming of her,' Lavender said, as they set off to walk back to Steep Abbot. 'I must confess that I have little taste for company, but the Percevals have always been very amiable to me.' A cloud touched her face. 'Julia will not be pleased, I fear, but Lady Perceval made no mention of including her in the invitation!'

Caroline hesitated. She would have put it far more strongly and observed that Lady Perceval had pointedly excluded Julia from the invitation to dine. She could hardly say so, however. Julia was her employer and as such she owed her discretion at least.

Lavender touched her arm in a contrite fashion.

'I do apologise, Miss Whiston! It must be difficult enough for you, without my tactless remarks! Let us not speak of Julia and spoil this lovely day!'

Caroline's lips twitched. Despite herself, it was diverting to be sympathised with for putting up with Julia Chessford. More than ever, Julia seemed like the cuckoo in the nest at Hewly, unwelcome but somehow too important to be dislodged. But of course, all that would change if she married Lewis. Mrs Lewis Brabant could hardly be ignored in the neighbourhood. It seemed to Caroline as though the sun had suddenly gone behind a cloud.

'Lady Perceval was very gracious to you too, was she not, Miss Whiston?' Lavender commented. 'I had no idea that she knew your family! But what did she mean by offering her help to you should you need it?'

'I imagine that she thought I might need some assistance in finding a new position one day,' Caroline said neutrally, wondering if that was what had really prompted Lady Perceval's words. 'It is very kind of her.'

'Oh, she is the soul of kindness!' Lavender agreed. 'I suppose that she could be in the right of it, if Julia moved away, or were to marry...'

Caroline decided to change the subject. She did not want to dwell on Julia's matrimonial plans a second longer. Knowing that Julia was making a dead set for Lewis put her in a very awkward position when speaking to Lewis's sister. With a sigh, Caroline reflected that the lot of a governess was preferable to that of a companion. She already felt that she was the repository of too many difficult secrets.

'I am glad you are so pleased to have your brother

back at home, Miss Brabant,' she said warmly. 'Do you see much of a change in him?'

Lavender smiled, and it lit up her whole face. 'To tell the truth, Miss Whiston, I do not really remember what Lewis was like before he went to sea. He was very much the older brother, you see, although not as distant as Andrew, of course!' She gave a peal of laughter. 'I do remember that he was very affected when he returned from University—he used to write very bad poetry and was forever striking a tragic pose until one wished to shake him, but I believe the Navy must have discouraged such foolishness in him! At any rate, he is much more forceful and decisive than I remember him, which is little wonder.' She hesitated. 'I do question how it must be for him to return home, however. Hewly is hardly a happy place with my father so ill and the estate gone to ruin. I wonder if Lewis will not simply sell up and return to sea in time…'

Caroline was startled. 'But Hewly is a sound estate and surely must return a profit once it is in better repair! And your brother would not wish to remain at sea forever—' She broke off, realising that she must sound presumptuous.

Lavender did not appear to mind. 'I may be mistaken, but I do not think that Hewly holds happy memories for Lewis. Besides, it is not as though Hewly is a family home in the sense of Perceval Hall. Papa purchased the house, but you must know, Miss Whiston, that his family seat is in Yorkshire. As a younger son, however, he had his own way to make.

Mama, of course, was one of the Fontenoys, but for all her aristocratic connections she had no money, so—' she shrugged '—Hewly should have become our family home. Fate has decreed that it is not a lucky one.'

'Neither for you nor your brother,' Caroline said sympathetically. 'You do not mention your own situation, Miss Brabant, but I imagine that it cannot always have been happy.'

Lavender coloured a little. 'Oh, I manage as well I might. I have been fortunate in spending time in Town with Aunt Augusta Carew—she even sponsored me in society, you know, Miss Whiston, and was very put out that I did not take!' There was suddenly a mischievous look in Lavender's eye that reminded Caroline forcibly of Lewis. 'It is not fashionable to admit it, but I prefer the country to Town. I had no time for all those fops and dandies, and silly, empty-headed girls who had no interest but to catch a rich husband!'

Caroline burst out laughing. 'And I admire you for it, Miss Brabant! The pleasures of drawing and botany must far outweigh those of balls and parties!'

'Why, so I think!' Lavender said spontaneously. 'Although—' a wistful note entered her voice '—I did enjoy the theatre and some of the balls...'

'Perhaps your brother will take a house in Town for the season next year,' Caroline suggested. 'It would be just the thing for you all...'

'I am sure he will do if Cousin Julia has any say in the matter.' Suddenly there was a different note in

Lavender's voice. 'I do so hope that Lewis will not—'
She broke off abruptly. 'I beg your pardon, Miss
Whiston. I have run on a great deal, which is most
unlike me!'

'Pray do not apologise,' Caroline said with a smile.
'It is very pleasant to have your conversation, Miss
Brabant.'

'Then will you not call me Lavender?' the younger
girl said, a little hesitantly. 'I should so like us to be
friends…'

Caroline was touched. 'Well, only if you will call
me Caroline,' she temporised. 'Since we are to be
friends and we share a home, at least for the time
being.'

'I should like that,' Lavender agreed smilingly. 'Oh
look, I do believe that is Lewis approaching—'

They both spun around at the sound of wheels
along the track behind them. Lewis Brabant was driving towards them and for some reason the sight of
him made Caroline blush, as though she had been
caught out in some misdemeanour. She stepped on to
the grass verge and was about to suggest to Lavender
that Lewis take her up in the gig for the rest of the
journey home, when Lavender said hastily, 'You must
be tired with carrying that heavy basket, Caroline!
Lewis can take you up and I shall cut across the fields
here…' And almost before she had finished, she was
through the gate and away. Caroline stared after her
in perplexity. Lavender, it seemed, had a mysterious
habit of appearing and disappearing like a will-o'-
the-wisp.

Lewis Brabant pulled the gig up beside Caroline a moment later. 'Miss Whiston! I looked for you both in Abbot Quincey, but it seems that I must have just missed you! Is everything all right, ma'am? My sister seemed in an unconscionable hurry to escape!'

Caroline's eyebrows were still raised at Lavender's hasty departure. Neither their conversation nor Lewis's arrival seemed to require such speed and she was at a loss to explain it.

'I think Miss Brabant preferred to walk back across the fields,' she said, lightly. 'I believe she might have in mind some scene for a new sketch!'

Lewis Brabant gave her a rueful smile. He jumped down on to the road. 'No doubt! And in the meantime, you are left with the heavy basket! You must let me take you up, ma'am! It will save you a good half-mile!'

Caroline hung back, unwilling to analyse why she felt so reluctant to join him in the gig. 'Oh, but have you finished your business about the estate? I have no wish to inconvenience you, and the basket is really very light—'

Lewis had already taken it from her arm and now had his hand under her elbow, ready to help her climb up into the cart. Before Caroline could even finish her sentence, she found herself installed on the bench with a rug tucked around her.

'It is not so dashing as a phaeton,' Lewis said with a smile as he swung up beside her, 'but a deal more practical on these roads! I would take Nelson out, but he is still a little lame. Thank you for tending to him the day that I arrived, Miss Whiston.' He flashed her a glance. 'The groom told me that you had given very clear instructions on what was wrong with his leg. Do you ride, Miss Whiston?'

'I used to ride as a girl,' Caroline admitted, trying not to smile at the thought of a horse named after England's greatest Admiral of recent times, 'and I enjoyed it a great deal. There has been little call for it in my various posts, however!'

Lewis encouraged the horses to a stately trot. There was little room on the bench, and Caroline jumped as his body brushed against hers. It filled her with an odd feeling of awareness.

'Have you always lived in the country, ma'am, or did the families you lived with sometimes go to Town?'

Caroline tried to concentrate. 'Oh, I have lived mainly in the country and like your sister, I much prefer it! I had a season in Town when I was young—' she hesitated, not wishing to sound as though she were complaining of her lot '—before my father died.'

'Did you so?' Lewis shot her a quick sideways look. His gaze was frankly admiring and brought further colour to her cheeks. 'I am surprised you did not make a match of it! You must have had plenty of offers!'

The breeze cooled Caroline's hot face. 'I did not take,' she said lightly, remembering Lavender's words of ten minutes before. 'I was a hoyden in those days and the stately dowagers took me in dislike!

Fortunately I did not know what would shortly befall me—'

She broke off, aware that her words were equivocal. She did not wish to imply that she would have made a marriage of convenience, for she would have done no such thing. What she had meant was that she had been a heedless girl who had grown up swiftly when she had been forced to earn her own living. There was no way that Lewis would realise that, however.

'I suppose that an expedient marriage would have been a preferable alternative to having to earn a living—' Lewis too broke off, seeing Caroline's discomfort, and for a moment there was a constrained silence broken only by the clatter of the horses' hooves on the track.

Caroline felt awkward. He had misunderstood her in precisely the way she had feared, thinking that she would have accepted any offer to escape penury. She did not like to think that he would believe her shallow enough to consider such a course of action. For some reason it seemed important to correct his impression, but she hesitated on the edge of explaining, good manners holding her back. Whilst she struggled with her feelings, Lewis spoke again.

'I beg your pardon, Miss Whiston,' he said slowly. 'I should not have spoken thus. I fear I am not accustomed to having to choose my words with such care as society requires. I meant no offence.'

'I imagine that one would run aground if procrastination were the rule at sea,' Caroline said brightly.

She found she could not look at him. Her overriding thought was that now he must believe her superficial indeed. She closed her eyes. Why his good opinion should matter so much was unclear, but matter it did.

'So Lavender prefers the country to the city, does she?' Lewis said, after a brief moment. 'I had guessed as much, but was not sure if she was secretly hankering for another season in Town! I had thought to take a house there next year, but I believe the estate will demand so much of my time that it may not be possible for a while.'

'Has the estate fallen into disrepair so very quickly, then?' Caroline asked, hoping that her interest would not be construed as impertinence. 'I did not think that the Admiral had been ill for so very long—'

'It is true that he only had his attack three months ago,' Lewis agreed, 'but I believe his health has been in decline ever since my mother died. They were most sincerely attached. Then there was the blow of losing my brother as well. I believe he felt that all he had worked for was slipping away and that he started to let it go as of that time.'

'I am sorry,' Caroline said hesitantly, 'and for yourself also, having to return from sea at such a time…'

'Well,' Lewis turned his head and gave her a slight smile, 'I was due to return shortly anyway, although the circumstances were not what I would have chosen. My last ship, *Dauntless*, was to be scrapped and they had not yet assigned me to another. A pity,' he added absently, his eyes on the road. 'She was a fine vessel, brave and true…'

They had reached a bend in the road where the land fell away to the south and Hewly could be seen nestling in its hollow, the village of Steep Abbot curled around. The river lay like a shining ribbon and the forest spread away beyond the fields like a patchwork quilt. Caroline could not help a smile.

'It is so very beautiful, though, is it not, Captain Brabant? If one must be forced to stay on land one could do worse! The house is a little gem—it is full of unique features! Did you know that the plaster representations on the wall in the porch are very rare? I have been reading up on their history, and—' She stopped, suddenly self-conscious, wondering why she was rattling on to him about his own home. No doubt he knew far more about it than she! Lewis was smiling too. He gave the horse the office to move off again. 'You must tell me about the history of the Manor some time, Miss Whiston,' he said pleasantly. 'I confess I know little of it, though I suspect Lavender is well-read on the subject! She seems to have a very well-informed mind.'

'Your sister is a very accomplished girl,' Caroline agreed, secretly glad to turn the subject. She was not sure what was the matter with her, only that she seemed as awkward as a green girl in his company. 'Mrs Guarding's school deserves its good reputation.'

'Yet more than a good education must be required for a cultivated mind, surely,' Lewis observed. 'There must be an interest, a willingness to learn…'

Caroline tried not to think of Julia, who had to be the best example of an uncultivated mind and wasted education that she could imagine. 'I believe Miss Brabant possesses both,' she said carefully.

'And I am grateful that she has sensible company here at Hewly, ma'am!' Lewis gave her a warm smile. 'Lavender was ever a quiet child. The gap in age between the three of us was enough to set her apart, leaving aside the difference of her sex. I had feared she might become a recluse, but I realise that your presence here must be of great benefit to her.'

Caroline felt warmed by his approval and told herself severely not to be foolish. There was nothing very encouraging in being described as sensible. In her own mind she acknowledged that it would be of equal benefit to her to have Lavender's companionship. The girl's quiet but intelligent presence was proving a good antidote to Julia's petty demands and spiteful asides. She could scarcely express such a view to Lewis, however, particularly given that he seemed to view Julia as the perfection of womanhood.

The gig trundled down the hill towards the village. Caroline watched Lewis's hands on the reins, tanned and strong, and repressed a shiver. She would be glad to be out of such close proximity. There was something about him that disturbed her equilibrium, and Caroline was unaccustomed at having to deal with such inappropriate feelings.

They clattered up the cobbled street and into the Manor courtyard. A groom came out to take the reins whilst Lewis jumped down and offered a hand to help

Caroline descend. 'It seems to me, ma'am,' he said slowly, 'that we started our conversation talking of *your* tastes and preferences, and swiftly moved to discussing everything from my view of the estate to my sister's accomplishments! Are you always so adroit at turning the conversation?'

Caroline blushed and tried to withdraw her hand from his grasp, but he did not release her. She thought fleetingly that it was odd that no one else had ever noticed how she tried to efface herself, but then that was probably a measure of her success. Most people who knew her would probably concur that Miss Whiston was good at her job, a little severe perhaps, but that was only to be expected in a governess companion. Of her interests and pastimes they would have no knowledge and express no interest. That was how she had always wanted it to be—until now. She looked into Lewis Brabant's blue eyes, softening now with the smile that was creeping in, and felt a strange pang in her heart. For a moment she entertained the thought that this was a man with whom she would gladly share her ideas, her interests. She dismissed the idea a second later, for it was foolish, painful and, she acknowledged, utterly without future.

Chapter Four

That evening was the first time that Caroline had dined with the family since Lewis's return, and the contrast between her own grey worsted and Julia's confection of silk and lace reminded her forcibly of the difference in their circumstances. She felt a frump in her plain grey dress, very much the companion, paid to be seen and not heard, to fade effortlessly into the background. Small wonder that Lewis could not even see her when Julia was by. She knew she was a fool to imagine that it could ever be any other way.

Such uncharacteristically diffident thoughts made Caroline hesitate in the drawing-room doorway. Lewis and Julia were sitting together before the fire, apparently engrossed in an animated debate about the decoration of the house. The lamplight gleamed on Julia's golden curls and sparkling blue eyes. She looked both elegant and appealingly fragile, and Caroline thought drily that Lewis seemed utterly captivated.

'...Red damask and rose wood,' Julia was saying

in her languid drawl. 'You must let me have the re-
furbishment of this room, Lewis! It could be so
Tonnish...'

'My dear Julia,' Lewis said wryly, 'it will be several years before I can even think of restoring the
house! There are fences to be mended and walls to
be rebuilt so that my father's tenants may prosper in
their business—'

'Oh, pooh!' Julia sounded almost petulant. 'Why
must they come first? You *must* decorate the house,
Lewis! No one will call if they think they are visiting
a mausoleum! Why—' She broke off as she saw
Caroline hovering in the doorway. 'Caro! So you
have finally succumbed to my invitations and decided
to join us for dinner!'

Caroline fought down a prickle of annoyance. For
Julia to imply that she had pressed invitations upon
her was bad enough, but then to be addressed as Caro,
in a pretence of friendship, was too much. She came
forward smiling a little stiffly and already regretting
the impulse that had led her to agree to dine with
them. Lewis rose to his feet politely at her approach
and sketched a bow. Caroline, contrasting his cool
courtesy with the warmth she had just seen him show
Julia, felt a sudden pang of desolation.

'A glass of wine, Miss Whiston?' Lewis asked, 'or
some ratafia, perhaps? It will only be a few minutes
until we dine.'

Caroline accepted a glass of wine and went across
to the window seat, where Lavender was reading a
book and making no pretence of joining in the general

conversation. This segregation seemed to suit Julia, who had already taken up again the theme of restoring the estate at the price of neglecting the house. She was leaning towards Lewis and touching his hand lightly to emphasise some point she was making. Caroline looked away deliberately and was glad when Lavender gave her a warm smile and gestured to her to sit down.

'Good evening, Caroline! It is pleasant to have some alternative company!' There was a spark of humour in Lavender's voice. 'I fear that I have little of use to add to Cousin Julia's discussions on household furnishings!'

They fell to talking about Lavender's book, which was Mary Elizabeth Jackson's *Botanical Dialogues*, until the gong sounded. Lewis gave Julia his arm into the dining-room and Caroline and Lavender followed behind.

Caroline privately thought that the cook had excelled herself with the dinner, but Julia was less impressed and compared the dishes unfavourably with the sort of meals she had experienced in London.

'The banquets were so lavish!' she observed. 'So elegant! Why, I recall an occasion when the dear Prince Regent had served forty-eight dishes in one evening!'

'Enough to bring on a fit of indigestion!' Lavender commented sweetly.

Julia fixed her with a cold blue gaze. Caroline waited to see if she would administer a set-down and concluded that it was only Lewis's presence that held her back.

'Do you remember the hideous meals we used to be given at Mrs Guarding's school, Caro?' Julia continued, shivering artistically. 'Boiled mutton and squab pie! It is a wonder I survived at all!'

Caroline thought that she heard Lavender murmur, 'And a pity!' but she could not be sure.

She applied herself to her food. It seemed safer to say nothing, and as far as she was concerned the meal could not be over soon enough. She had no intention of being used as a foil by Julia, who obviously wished to dominate the conversation with her sparkling wit.

Lavender also bent her head over her plate and did not speak again. Watching her face, Caroline wondered suddenly how Lavender must have felt when Julia invaded her home again. It seemed unlikely that Julia had even stopped to consider Lavender's feelings, and since she made no secret of her rather condescending pity for the girl, Caroline could hardly wonder at Lavender's dislike. Once again, Julia reminded her of the cuckoo in the Hewly nest.

She looked up, and saw that Lewis Brabant was watching his sister with a rather curious expression on his face. Caroline speculated that perhaps he was wondering how to smooth over the antipathy between Julia and Lavender. She was certain that he had already realised just how difficult it would make his life if his future wife and sister did not see eye to eye. Still, that would hardly be sufficient to discourage a determined man, and from what she knew of Captain

Brabant, Caroline suspected that he could be very single-minded in achieving his aims... She looked up to see that his gaze had transferred itself to her. For a moment it seemed that he had correctly divined her thoughts, for he raised an eyebrow in a quizzical gesture, and Caroline stared back transfixed before lowering her gaze again and trying to hide her blushes.

Dinner dragged on. It was one of the most uncomfortable meals that Caroline could remember. She positively jumped up from the table when it was time for the ladies to withdraw and leave Lewis to his solitary port. They retired to the drawing-room and Julia immediately began a patronising attack on Lavender's choice of pale blue for an evening gown. It was evident to Caroline that Julia had only been waiting her opportunity.

'That colour makes you look so pasty, my dear Lavender—so sallow! Not that any colour is likely to flatter, for your complexion is so washed-out! Perhaps a cerise...' Julia put her head on one side thoughtfully. 'No, that would be too strong...or yellow—'

'I like the blue,' Lavender said, in a tight little voice.

Julia laughed lightly. 'Yes, my dear, but what do you really know of matters of style? It does not surprise me that you could not catch yourself a husband when you were in London! Why, most of the gentlemen probably scarce noticed you were there!'

The colour rushed into Lavender's face. 'We are not all concerned with entrapping a husband, cousin Julia! I would as lief catch a cold!'

'Well, but you cannot expect to stay here for ever,' Julia said brightly, and it seemed to Caroline, an embarrassed observer, that she had reached the real point of what she was saying. 'Your brother will marry and will scarce wish his little sister to be hanging about the house—'

Caroline cleared her throat, about to intervene to try to pacify the situation, when the door opened and Lewis strolled in. He took in Lavender's angry face, Julia's smug one and Caroline's strained expression, and raised his eyebrows expressively. Caroline was glad to see him so soon, for his presence could not but ease the situation. On the other hand she was surprised; if she had been in his position she would have taken refuge in the study and finished the whole bottle of port.

'Let us have a round of whist!' Julia exclaimed suddenly, clapping her hands. 'That would be just the thing to cheer us up! Lewis, will you partner me?' She gave him a melting smile. 'It will be so much more exciting if you do!'

Caroline studiously avoided looking at either Lewis or Lavender. Whist was not her interest, though she played competently enough, having been asked to make up the numbers on many occasions. It soon became clear that Julia had deliberately chosen a pastime at which she shone. She won handsomely, mainly through chattering all the time and distracting her opponents. After one round, Lavender excused herself and went to bed.

'Country hours! So dull!' Julia yawned. 'You must

take a house in Town, Lewis! The country is so dreadfully slow! The Percevals and Cleeves do not entertain...and as for Sywell! Well, it is shocking that he should be allowed to be the premier landowner in the neighbourhood when he positively ignores us all!'

Caroline saw Lewis smile. 'I am sure that invitations will be forthcoming soon, Julia! As for Sywell, I confess I would not wish to visit the Abbey even if he invited me!'

Julia shrugged gracefully. 'Oh well, the Marquis is a scandal, I suppose, but the others have no excuse! You must call on them, Lewis! I do not care to be ignored by half the county! I shall quite die of boredom if we do not go out and about a bit more!'

'You have no obligation to stay here if you are so tired of our company, Julia!' Lewis said, moving over to the sideboard and pouring a glass of wine. Caroline thought she could detect the tiniest hint of laughter in his voice. 'If you would prefer to leave us for the social delights of the Little Season—'

'Oh, I shall stay!' Julia said hastily. 'You know how concerned I am to see that dear Uncle Harley is cared for! Besides, it will soon be Christmas and I am sure we shall be as merry as grigs!'

Lewis frowned slightly. 'Father's illness must inevitably curtail our celebrations, I fear. A quiet, family Christmas—'

Caroline saw Julia frown briefly. 'But there is the ball at the Angel in a few weeks! Surely you would not seek to curb our pleasure so severely?' She gave him a reproachful glance. 'Why, Lewis, you are the veriest puritan!'

Caroline got to her feet. The prospect of watching Julia exert her charm was not a tempting one and she had been wishing to retire for the past two hours anyway. She felt a very unwelcome third, and Julia had been looking daggers at her in an unsubtle attempt to hint her away.

'If you will excuse me,' she murmured, 'I believe I shall retire now.'

'Oh, you may go!' Julia waved a hand in lordly dismissal. 'But pray do not lag abed in the morning, Caroline, for I have some commissions for you!'

Caroline smarted with annoyance at the implication that she was lazy and closed her lips tightly to prevent a sharp rejoinder from escaping. She swept out into the hall and was somewhat surprised to find that Lewis had followed her to light a candle for her.

'Thank you for your company this evening, Miss Whiston,' he said politely. 'I hope that you did not find it too much of a trial!'

Caroline met his eyes, which held a distinctly speculative twinkle deep in the blue. She was not sure of his precise meaning and did not intend to pursue it. The honest reply was that she would rather pull her hair out with tweezers than endure another dinner in Julia's company, but that would scarcely be diplomatic. She could not resist a look into the drawing-room, where Julia was drumming her fingers discontentedly on the arm of her chair. The Beauty's mouth drooped petulantly and she darted a sharp glance out into the hall, no doubt resenting that she was no longer the centre of Lewis's attention.

'It was a pleasant enough evening, but I would not wish to intrude on a family event again!' Caroline said neatly, taking the candlestick and evading Lewis's observant gaze. 'Good night, sir!'

She could not be sure, but she thought she heard him laugh as she sped up the stairs. When she reached the landing, however, the drawing-room door was just closing, affording a golden glimpse of Julia, now wreathed in smiles. Lewis was bending close to her, touching his glass to hers in a toast. Then the door shut, leaving Caroline out in the dark.

December, 1811

The month of December crept in with a return to hard frosts and cold blue skies. Julia's mood was poor and she vented her spleen on Caroline. Lady Perceval's promised invitation had arrived and, just as Caroline had expected, it was pointedly addressed to Lewis and Lavender only.

'The wretched woman knows full well that I am living here too!' Julia screeched, throwing her silver hairbrush across the room so that it bounced off the door panels. 'I would hardly expect her to invite you, Caroline, but why should I be excluded, pray? And as for Lewis—' her matching silver comb followed the brush '—he has gone out shooting with a party from Jaffrey House! It isn't fair! They have always been too high in the instep to acknowledge me, whilst

Lavender—' She broke off, almost choking with rage.
'That little nonentity—'

'Pray be calm, Julia,' Caroline said, retrieving the
hairbrush. She had already resolved that the only way
to sooth Julia was to treat her as she would a child
having a tantrum. 'Such passion will make you ill!
Take several deep breaths and quieten down!'

Julia glared at her. 'Calm! Why should I be calm?
Just because my father made his fortune in trade—
why, he could have bought them up ten times over!
And who are the Brabants, after all? The Admiral was
only a younger son, and his wife had no money! Yet
they are invited everywhere whilst I am left to rot!'

Caroline itched to slap her, but reluctantly abandoned the thought. Nor would the truth help at this
stage, for it contained the hard fact that Julia was
more snobbish than any of her neighbours and was
unwelcome more because of her manners than her
background.

'Perhaps the Percevals thought that you would not
be staying long,' she said soothingly, 'and besides,
the situation may work to your benefit in the end.'

Julia stared at her suspiciously. 'What can you
mean, Caroline? What possible benefit could there be
in being ignored by one of the premier families in the
neighbourhood?'

Caroline continued to fold Julia's clothes and put
them into the chest of drawers. Julia had thrown them
all over the floor earlier in her tantrum. 'Only that if
the Captain and Miss Brabant go to dine at Perceval
Hall, they will be sure to invite the family here to

Hewly in return, and the Percevals may not refuse!'
She looked up to see Julia watching her with a calculating look in her eyes. 'That will be your opportunity to act as hostess!'

'As long as that foolish little whey-faced sister of
Lewis's does not think to act the lady of the manor
herself!' Julia said viciously. 'Lewis had rather ask a
milk-churn to host the Percevals than ask Lavender!'

Caroline winced. The more friendly she became
with Lavender, the more difficult it was to bear Julia's
criticism of her, and Caroline was uncomfortably
aware that Lavender Brabant was worth a hundred
Julia Chessfords. Not for the first time, Caroline reflected that she should start to look for another position. She had been at Hewly for barely three months,
but her difficulties with Julia had already convinced
her that a long stay was out of the question. It was
not easy to find a suitable position of course, and it
might take her some time, which was all the more
reason to start at once. There had been Lady
Perceval's kind offer, but that would mean admitting
that there were problems at Hewly Manor and
Caroline shrank from exposing that to the outside
world. Gossip in the villages was bad enough as it
was, with everyone knowing each other's business, or
making it up if they did not. She did not imagine that
Lady Perceval herself would gossip, but word would
get out. It always did.

There was still Lady Covingham, the mother of her
previous charges. She might know of someone in
need of a governess. Caroline sighed silently. Anne

Covingham had been so delighted that Caroline was going to be companion to an old friend that it would be disappointing to have to admit that matters had not worked out. Still, beggars could not be choosers. Caroline resolved to write that day.

'I hear that Lewis has invited a friend to visit,' Julia was saying, preening before the mirror now that her good humour was restored. 'Captain Slater, with whom Lewis stayed when he was first ashore. Apparently the Captain was invalided out of the Navy a few years back and has a house in Lyme Regis—small fry to Lewis's fortune, but he might do for you, I suppose, Caroline!'

Caroline flushed. 'Thank you, Julia, but I am not intending to set my cap at Captain Brabant's friends!'

Julia shrugged carelessly. ''Pon rep, you are very haughty today! Well, I shall not throw him in your way if you do not wish to try your luck!' Her sharp gaze appraised Caroline thoughtfully. 'I suppose there is always Mr Grizel if you prefer a parson! Now, pray send Letty to me. She is to fit my new dresses!'

Caroline left the room feeling very short-tempered. She went first to the library and composed a letter to Lady Covingham, enquiring carefully over the possibility of employment. Then, still feeling irritated, she donned a warm cloak and stout shoes, and went out into the garden, hoping that the fresh air would soothe her annoyance. It was a cold day but the fresh chill of the air was bracing.

The kitchen gardens at Hewly were still tended, and provided fruit and vegetables for both the household and the village, but the Admiral's gardener had been unable to keep up the flower gardens without any additional help and had reluctantly let these run wild. As far as Caroline could ascertain, it was not a want of money that had led to the neglect of Hewly Manor, but rather the lack of a firm hand on the tiller for the last few years. The servants had high hopes that Lewis would now provide that guidance, and Caroline thought that they were probably correct. She knew they all had high hopes of the Captain and could not believe that these would be dashed. Not unless Lewis chose to sell the estate in time and return to sea... Caroline grimaced. That would be viewed as a sad event in the servants' hall, but perhaps not so bad as were Julia to become mistress...

Stifling such disloyal thoughts, Caroline walked briskly past the vegetable beds and into the flower gardens. Now that winter was approaching, she was able to trace the lines of the old garden beneath the weeds and tumbledown walls. Here was the rose walk, the bushes in dire need of a hard pruning, and along the old stone walls were the woody stems of lavender. A faint hint of their scent still hung in the air, taking Caroline back to her youth. She could see her grandmother, a huge apron over her old clothes as she collected sprigs of lavender in the gardens at Watchbell Hall. The tiny scented bags would be placed among the crisp sheets in the linen cupboards and Caroline would go to sleep breathing their perfume.

She had a sudden, painful pang of nostalgia, a

shocking wrench of homesickness that took her completely by surprise. Over the years, Caroline had seldom allowed herself to feel sorry that she had no home of her own, but now her loss suddenly overwhelmed her. She felt as small and lonely as a child.

She blinked back the tears and hurried out of the rose garden, almost tripping over the fallen sundial in her rush to escape her memories. She had no real notion where she was going, but she turned sharply into the topiary walk, where the flagged path gave way to a grassy avenue of yew. Rounding a corner, she collided with a figure standing in the shadow of one of the huge trees. Strong arms immediately encircled her, setting her back on her feet. She swayed a little and the arms tightened, steadying her.

'Miss Whiston?' Lewis's voice was close in her ear. 'Are you quite well, ma'am?'

Being so close to Lewis again felt both disturbingly familiar and confusing to Caroline's already troubled mind. She pulled back sharply.

'I beg your pardon, sir. I…' Caroline broke off. Her voice was still shaky with tears and for a moment she was afraid that it would desert her completely. Worse, she now realised that Lewis was not alone, for Belton, the gardener, was close by and he and Lewis had evidently been consulting over the need to cut the yews down to their original size. A stepladder was propped against the hedge and various gardening tools lay scattered across the path. Feeling foolish, Caroline tried to walk past, but Lewis stayed her by the simple expedient of keeping hold of her arm.

'A moment, Miss Whiston! It is fortunate that you passed this way, for I wonder if you could spare me a little of your time?' He turned to the gardener. 'Thank you very much, Belton. We will talk on this again soon.'

The gardener touched his cap and nodded to Caroline before moving off in an unhurried manner towards his greenhouses. Once he was out of sight, Caroline turned to Lewis and pointedly pulled her arm from his grip.

'What do you mean by restraining me thus, sir? And in front of your servants! I intended to walk by—' Her words came out with more sharpness than she had intended and she stopped, realising that her recent distress was still close to the surface. She had the disturbing feeling that Lewis, whose eyes were moving slowly over her face, was also aware of the fact.

'I realise that,' he said gently. 'That was why I stopped you. I was concerned that there might be something wrong and thought that I might be able to help. You seem a little distraught, Miss Whiston.'

Caroline realised with dismay that her tears had dried on her cheeks, leaving tell-tale marks below her eyes. She felt confused by his perception and brushed them away self-consciously.

'It was nothing, sir. There is nothing the matter.'

Having rubbed her face, Caroline turned her attention to removing some stray leaves from her cloak. She did not look at him. There was a silence.

'I see,' Lewis said slowly. 'That would account for

your tears, of course. Well, if you do not wish to tell me I cannot force you to do so—'

'I was feeling foolishly nostalgic,' Caroline said in a rush, 'and I fear I was not looking where I was going. Pray do not let me take you from your work, sir.'

'Perhaps you might accompany me,' Lewis suggested quietly. 'I am planning improvements to the gardens, as you see, and would appreciate your advice. Will you help?'

Caroline found herself taking his arm and walking slowly down the grassy path. She was not entirely sure how she had come to accept Lewis's suggestion, for her first instinct had been to flee from him. Now, however, he was talking of his plans and she was soon distracted.

'I am hoping that we might eventually re-create the gardens that were here when Hewly was part of the Perceval estate,' Lewis was saying, holding some trailing sprays of honeysuckle aside for Caroline to follow him into the first of the walled gardens. 'There are still designs of the ground plan in the Library. Belton's grandfather tended the gardens here in the early days of George III and he tells me that they were spoken of as very fine. There was a series of walled gardens here with fruit and cold frames, and any number of fine trees in the park. There is much work to do but I feel I must make a start.'

Caroline hesitated. She remembered Lavender saying that she was not sure if Lewis would even wish to stay at Hewly. It seemed strangely reassuring that he was planning a restoration project, for surely he would not trouble to do so if he intended to sell the estate. She looked about her carefully, at the old, tumbledown walls and the trailing strands of honeysuckle and rose. In the summer the walled gardens would be a charming sun-trap, but now they just looked neglected and lost.

'I imagine that such a scheme would take several years,' she said tentatively, 'though it would surely be worthwhile in the end.'

'Why, so I hope!' Lewis smiled at her. He was assessing the state of the masonry with an experienced eye. 'If I am to remain here at Hewly I intend to try to restore it to some of its former glory! Though whether I shall be able to create a lake to assuage my need for the sea, I am not so sure!'

Caroline laughed aloud. 'Perhaps you could design a lake, or at least a small pond! Is there not a stream that runs across the far side of the orchard? It drains into the river and I am sure you could dam it if you wished to emulate the work of garden designers of old!' She brushed her fingers against the wall. 'This seems sound enough, and I believe I have seen some statuary in these gardens too...' She pushed aside a huge clump of nettles with a gloved hand. 'Yes, here is one! I am sure that you will find that the foundations of the garden are still here under all the weeds...'

Lewis had come across to see the statue. It was of a stone cherub, curly-haired and with an innocently saucy tilt to its head. Lewis leant over and Caroline was suddenly sharply aware of his nearness. The wind was ruffling his thick fair hair and he pushed it back from his eyes with an impatient hand. The hard lines of his cheek and jaw were so close that she had to prevent herself from reaching out to trace them with her fingers. He touched the cherub's head lightly and Caroline was shocked to feel the echo of that touch through her own body. She turned away abruptly, afraid that her face would betray her.

Suddenly the cold day seemed as bright and hot as high summer. With heightened awareness, Caroline knew that Lewis was watching her and had sensed her feelings. She caught a stem of honeysuckle between her fingers and cast desperately around for some topic to lessen the tension.

'This is growing wild now, but Belton could soon clip it back into shape—'

Lewis' fingers covered hers on the stem. She could feel the warmth of his touch through her gloves and fell silent. Then his hand came up and brushed a stray strand of hair back from her face.

'Keep still.' His voice was husky. 'You have a briar rose caught in your hair…' He untangled it deftly, the touch of his fingers against her skin making Caroline shiver. She stepped back abruptly and almost fell over a low wall.

'I must go now,' she said, knowing she sounded breathless. Her heart was beating fast and she could not look at Lewis. 'Mrs Chessford…she is having her dresses fitted…she may need me…'

It was as though the mention of Julia's name

caused some kind of constraint between them. Lewis stepped back, his expression unreadable, and Caroline shot through the door in the wall as though the hounds of Hades were at her heels. She turned towards the house, hoping desperately that Lewis would not follow her. She needed some time to calm herself.

'Slow down, or you may trip again,' Lewis caught up with her as she reached the yew walk. He spoke in impersonal tones and when Caroline glanced at his face she saw with relief that it was quite expressionless. That extraordinary moment in the walled garden might never have occurred. Only the slight trembling of her hands betrayed the fact that it had.

'You mentioned feeling nostalgic, Miss Whiston,' Lewis said, after a moment. 'Tell me, where was your home originally?'

'Oh…' Caroline rallied herself to speak normally. She slowed her pace, aware that she was becoming out of breath. 'My family were from Cumbria, sir.'

'The Whistons of Watchbell Hall?' Lewis put his hands in his pockets. 'I had no idea that you were related to that family. Was your grandfather not a famous collector of clocks and watches, playing on the name of his home? I am sure I heard that he had some of John Harrison's original timepieces?'

Caroline smiled. 'He did indeed. I have one of them as a keepsake—only small, but very dear to me.'

Lewis squared his shoulders. 'Forgive me if I speak out of turn, Miss Whiston, but did you not have any relatives who might help you upon your father's death? It seems most singular that you had to go out and earn a living!'

'A distant cousin of my father's inherited the title.' Caroline met his eyes a little defiantly. 'I had no wish to be a burden on a family I barely knew. I make shift as well I can.'

'I imagine so. You seem most resourceful, Miss Whiston, but—' Lewis broke off. 'Forgive me,' he said again, 'it is none of my concern after all.'

A slightly strained silence fell between them. Caroline was profoundly grateful that they were nearly back on the terrace now. The mossy stones were smooth beneath her feet and, mindful of the first day she had met Lewis, she was careful not to slip.

'Perhaps you might help me with my garden plan if you have the time,' Lewis continued, on a lighter note. 'I know that Belton respects your opinion. He mentioned that you had given him advice on treatment for some of the diseased roses!'

Caroline smiled. 'I am happy to help if Mrs Chessford can spare me,' she said. 'Whilst I am at Hewly I should like to be useful.'

Lewis tilted his head. 'It sounds as though you do not intend to be with us much longer, Miss Whiston,' he said acutely. 'Are you thinking of leaving?'

Caroline looked away. She knew she should have been more careful, for she was already aware of Lewis's sometimes uncanny perception.

'I have no other plans at present,' she said truthfully. 'Good day, sir.'

She slipped inside and closed the door behind her,

resisting the impulse to watch Lewis as he strolled off
in the direction of Belton and the greenhouses. It
seemed that she had vastly underestimated the case
when she had imagined that she should be able to
avoid the Captain. What she had not underestimated,
however, was the need to do so. After eleven years
as a governess in households up and down the country, she was in danger of succumbing to the sort of
feelings she had never experienced for any man. It
was dangerous, inappropriate and all the things that
Miss Caroline Whiston was not. It also emphasised
the need to leave Hewly before her feelings made a
complete fool of her. She would do best to leave the
garden lost in time, and her own feelings frozen with
it.

The Admiral's condition worsened the following
day and an exhausted Mrs Prior gladly accepted
Caroline's offer to sit with him for a few hours whilst
she tried to get some rest. The doctor had called earlier and had confided that he thought that the end was
very near, a few weeks at the most. Word had got
around the house, with the effect that unhappiness sat
like a pall over the place. The servants whispered and
tiptoed about, Lavender moped in the library and Julia
was even more irritable than usual.

'I do not see why Lewis feels we must all creep
about like ghosts!' she said crossly to Caroline.
'Much more of this and we shall *all* expire—from
boredom, if nothing else!' She flounced across her
bedroom. 'I did not imagine that this would happen

so soon! If Uncle Harley dies there will be no more parties and no entertainment and then where shall we be! We shall not even be able to attend the Christmas ball at the Angel!'

'I am sure that the Admiral will take that into account when he plans just when to pass away!' Caroline said, for once not trying to conciliate her friend. Julia's blue eyes widened to their furthest extent.

'Why, you are very cross today! What is it to you that Admiral Brabant is about to die? *You* cannot share our distress!'

Caroline held on to her temper with an effort. 'I am naturally upset by such an event,' she said evenly. 'It is true that I do not know the Admiral well, but I can still regret his illness! Why, the servants are all worried, and Miss Brabant is deeply upset—'

'Oh, Lavender!' Julia sniffed. 'Well, I suppose that is not be wondered at! I shall do my best to comfort her, of course, but it is Lewis that I worry over, coming home to all this! I feel I must devote myself to ensuring his future happiness!'

'I am sure that he will be most grateful to you!' Caroline snapped. 'Excuse me, I do not believe I can do anything more here, so I shall go downstairs!'

Julia raised her brows. 'Very well! I shall come down too and play the piano! Some music may banish the blue devils in me!'

Once Julia was settled in the music room, Caroline went to see if she could find Lavender.

The December afternoon was dark already, as

though echoing the sombre mood in the house.
Lavender was not in the Library or the drawing-room,
and Caroline was about to enquire if any of the servants knew of her whereabouts, when the study door
opened and Lewis Brabant came out. He looked cross
and harassed, and Caroline gave him a tentative smile,
aware that he must be feeling as dismal as his sister.
It evoked no answering gleam. To the contrary, there
was a hard light in Lewis's blue eyes as they dwelled
on her and a harsh set to his mouth. Caroline's heart
did a little nervous jump.

'Miss Whiston.' Lewis's tone was clipped. 'How
convenient. I wonder if you would spare me a moment of your time, ma'am?'

'Of course—' Caroline frowned a little, taken
aback. She could think of nothing she had done that
would merit the look of dislike in Lewis's eyes. She
felt like a recalcitrant lieutenant who was about to be
hauled over the coals.

Her apprehension rose as he ushered her into the
study and closed the door very firmly behind them.
He did not invite her to sit down; he himself walked
over to the window and stared out over the darkened
garden for a few moments before swinging round on
her.

'Can you tell me what this is, Miss Whiston?'

Caroline followed his gaze, feeling utterly bewildered. He had thrown something down on the blotter
of his desk and Caroline stepped forward to try to see
what it was that he was talking about. It looked like
a letter, the paper faded, the writing extravagant with

loops and curls. Caroline suddenly recognised it as one of Julia's letters from years before, and frowned as she tried to imagine how it could have fallen into Lewis's hands.

'Why, yes... It is an old letter from Mrs Chessford to myself, but—'

'Do you keep all your old letters, Miss Whiston?' Lewis interrupted her with scant courtesy. 'It seems a somewhat singular thing to do!' He drove his hands into his pockets as though to restrain himself from some more violent action. Once again his gaze raked her with dislike. 'Unless, of course, you have some purpose in mind for them!'

Caroline looked at him in bewilderment. 'I kept Julia's letters only because they reminded me of my time at school here. They were a link with my childhood. But I do not understand... How did you gain possession of this, sir?'

Lewis gave her a scathing look and at the same moment, Caroline remembered. Her hand flew to her mouth as she realised that she must have accidentally left the letter in the book of poetry she had taken down to the library. She had been reading *Marmion* one evening when Mrs Prior had come to ask for her assistance with the Admiral, and she had pushed the letter carelessly inside it to keep her place. Later she had taken the book up again and put her bookmark absentmindedly inside the front cover. So the letter must still have been there when she had returned the book, and Lewis had picked it up himself with some remark about enjoying the work...

Caroline caught her breath, wondering which of Julia's indiscreet observations were recorded in that particular letter. How much of it had Lewis read? There must be something in it, to make him react so. Was it the one about Julia's engagement to Andrew Brabant, or was there some reflection on Lewis himself…?

Caroline became aware of Lewis watching her with a penetrating regard. His scrutiny was thorough, from head to foot, and there was a frown between his eyes.

'Oh dear… I am so sorry…' She stopped. Too late, she realised that Lewis had interpreted her words as some kind of admission of guilt, for he was smiling grimly.

'I confess myself disappointed that you should stoop to so clumsy a piece of subterfuge, Miss Whiston,' he said coldly. 'To conceal a letter in the book is an old ruse and one that can only be designed to stir up trouble! What was your aim? To provoke discord between Mrs Chessford and myself! I had thought better of you, ma'am, but now I think it wise for you to start your packing! You will leave Hewly Manor immediately!'

Chapter Five

Caroline stared at Lewis in fury. She was almost breathless with shock and outrage. The suddenness of her dismissal was almost too much to take in.

'Leave Hewly? How dare you make such a presumption of guilt, sir! And you are not my employer, sir, to dismiss me on a whim!'

'But it is my house!' Lewis leant both hands on the desk and returned Caroline's furious regard with a gaze that was equally angry. 'Therefore I say that you should go!'

'In point of fact, sir,' Caroline said evenly, 'it is *not* your house and I am sure that your father would never behave in so arrogant and high-handed a manner!'

Lewis took a deep breath. He straightened up. 'Leaving aside your aspersions on my behaviour, Miss Whiston, do I take it that you deny you played such a trick?'

Caroline spoke cuttingly. 'I beg your pardon, sir. I fear I do not even understand this farrago of nonsense! Do *you* imply that I left the letter in the book deliberately?'

Lewis looked at her in silence. His anger seemed to have gone and Caroline could discern nothing in his face but resignation and a fleeting disappointment. For some reason this made her even more furious. He made a slight gesture with his hands.

'What else am I to think, Miss Whiston? It appears that you left a damaging letter specifically for me to find! No doubt you hoped I should read it, and that its childish revelations would injure the regard I have for Mrs Chessford! I would not have thought you capable of such a deceit were it not for what Mrs Chessford herself had mentioned to me this afternoon—' He broke off, but Caroline was too quick for him.

'Indeed, sir? Pray do not scruple to tell me! After such an injury as you have already dealt me, further accusations can be as nothing!'

Lewis looked slightly uncomfortable. 'Miss Whiston—'

Caroline was not about to let him retreat. 'Captain Brabant? I am waiting!'

Lewis sat down. It was a disarming move and left Caroline feeling slightly foolish that she was still standing in so rigid a pose. When he gestured to her to take the chair opposite, she had little alternative but to comply.

'Miss Whiston,' Lewis said slowly, 'perhaps it is better that we set this aside as a misunderstanding—'

He got no further. Caroline was still furious and

she suspected that he was only trying to protect Julia. She leant forward threateningly, her hazel eyes flashing.

'Captain Brabant! If you do not tell me at once what it was that Julia said—'

'You will do what, Miss Whiston?' Lewis met her gaze coolly, calling her bluff. A slight smile touched the corners of his mouth. 'Can you not accept that there has been a mistake—'

'Oh, fustian! Do not seek to gammon me, sir!' Caroline gave him a look of disgust. 'I suppose that Julia said that I had left my last post under a cloud or that I had been turned off...' She saw by the way his eyes narrowed that she had hit her mark. 'And you believed her!' Caroline added sharply. 'You have made some fine assumptions, have you not, sir, believing that I have a penchant for malicious tricks and that Julia only employs me through kindness since I am so deceitful!'

She locked her hands together to still their shaking. 'I freely admit to leaving the letter in the poetry book, but I did so in all innocence. If you will recall,' she glared at him across the space between them, 'it was *your* idea to borrow *Marmion* and no suggestion of mine! I could not have contrived such a trick even had I wished! It was the veriest accident!'

Their gazes locked, Lewis's watchful, Caroline's bright with anger and distress. 'As for this other tale,' she continued, 'the one of my apparent untrustworthiness—*that* is the fabrication, not my behaviour! I have references, couched in the highest terms, but since Mrs Chessford evidently believes me unreliable, I will leave her service at once! Leave Hewly? You would have to beg me to stay!'

She saw a flicker of a smile cross Lewis's face. There was a very definite admiration in his eyes now, admiration and something even more disquieting. Caroline jumped to her feet and made for the door. Lewis moved quickly to block her path.

'Miss Whiston! Wait!'

Caroline was already reaching for the handle when Lewis put a hand against the door panels and leant his weight on it to hold it closed. They were very close. Caroline stepped back, his proximity sending a sudden quiver of awareness through her. All her nerve endings seemed to be sensitised by their quarrel, her feelings too close to the surface. Some colour came into her set face. She kept her expression stony and avoided his eyes.

'You would prevent my departure now, sir? By what right—'

'Miss Whiston, do not run away!' Lewis spoke urgently, his gaze compelling on her face. 'Allow me to explain—'

'At your command, sir?' Caroline asked icily, covering her trembling with haughtiness.

Lewis straightened up. He raised an eyebrow. 'At my most humble prayer? Please, Miss Whiston, sit down again and hear me out…'

Caroline could feel herself weakening. She looked pointedly at him until he took his hand from the door.

'Please,' he said again. 'I should be grateful for the chance to put matters right, Miss Whiston…'

Caroline felt trapped. Good manners obliged her to do as he asked, although she had a most ardent wish to escape his presence. She waited as Lewis poured two glasses of madeira, sat down opposite her and put his own glass down on the small table between them. He looked at her thoughtfully.

'First, I believe I owe you an apology, ma'am.' There was a frown between his brows again. 'That was devilish clumsy of me, regardless of what I believed at the time. You were quite right to ring a peal over me for my bad manners. It was only because I felt so surprised—' He broke off abruptly. 'But that is nothing to the purpose.' His expression lightened a little. 'I believe this is no more than a misunderstanding and soon mended. I accept that you never meant to leave the letter in the book and certainly did not intend it for me.'

Caroline gave him a very straight look. 'Besides, what would be the point of such an action, sir? As a gentleman I know that you would never have read a letter addressed to another!'

There was a pause.

'As you say, ma'am.' Caroline thought she could see a glint of amusement in Lewis's eyes. 'I did in fact read a little of the letter in order to ascertain to whom it belonged—'

'Since they are all addressed to "dear Caro",' Caroline said acidly, 'that should not have taxed your intellect a great deal, sir!' She looked across to the desk, where the offending letter still rested on the leather top.

'Dear Caro…' Lewis said musingly, and there was a caressing tone in his voice that brought the colour into Caroline's cheeks. 'You are right, that was the appellation, and very pretty I thought it too…'

'That is beside the point, sir!' Caroline snapped, hoping that he put her blush down to anger not embarrassment. 'The issue here is that you apparently believed me capable of wishing to discredit Mrs Chessford! Worse, I believe you indicated that Mrs Chessford herself had some concerns over my integrity—'

'I must stress that this is all a misunderstanding on my part,' Lewis said smoothly, leaving Caroline almost speechless at the skilful way he was glossing over the situation. 'I must beg you to forgive me for a poor, dull fellow. Julia never implied such a thing, I am sure, and your integrity is unimpeachable, Miss Whiston…'

'But…' Caroline felt as though the rug had been pulled from beneath her. 'That is all very well, sir—'

Lewis shrugged casually. 'I would not wish this matter to cause trouble between you and Mrs Chessford, still less that you would feel it necessary to leave Hewly. Please forgive me for this storm in a teacup, my dear Miss Whiston, and accept another glass of wine as a peace offering!'

Caroline looked down and realised that she had already finished the first glass. She had no recollection of drinking it. She frowned a little, still thinking on what Lewis had just said.

'I cannot imagine,' she blurted out, 'why you should think I would wish to discredit Julia! What possible motive—' She broke off as Lewis turned to look at her, one brow raised quizzically.

'Oh no, Captain Brabant! I fear that you flatter yourself far too much!'

Lewis had the grace to look a little abashed. 'Miss Whiston, I was not really such a coxcomb as to believe that you had a partiality for me—'

'No, I dare say that Mrs Chessford planted that particular idea in your head as well!' Caroline's wrath was growing again, fuelled by the fact that there was more than a grain of truth in the idea. 'Of all the conceited... Have you forgotten, sir, that you were the one who forced your attentions on me when we first met! You do not see me begging for your notice!'

Lewis laughed. 'I most certainly have not forgotten...' He put the decanter down and came towards her. Caroline took one look at his face and felt suddenly breathless. Perhaps it had not been such a good idea to remind him of their encounter in the wood. She got clumsily to her feet.

'I believe I should go now, sir—'

'Must you? I felt sure we were about to have a most interesting debate—'

Caroline felt hot all over. It could have been the wine, or the heat from the fire, but she knew it was more likely to be her own unruly emotions. She moved towards the door, almost stumbling over the hem of her dress in her haste to be away from him. Lewis took her elbow to steady her and Caroline snatched it away.

'Thank you, sir, I am able to manage very well!'

Caroline heard him laugh.

'I see.' He was reaching for the doorhandle and she was inexpressibly relieved to see him open it this time. 'And you will not leave Hewly over this unfortunate misunderstanding?'

Caroline bit her lip, suddenly sobering. Whatever he said, the experience had soured her already equivocal friendship with Julia. She did not doubt that Julia had cast aspersions on her integrity, and Lewis's smooth pretence of a misunderstanding was just that—a pretence. It left a bitter taste in her mouth. Julia had told malicious lies about her and Lewis had believed them. Caroline had been intending to leave Hewly anyway, but this only reinforced her intention to do so as soon as possible.

Lewis had evidently read her answer in her face. He closed the door again.

'Miss Whiston,' he said slowly, 'I must beg you to stay with us, at least for a little.' He leant back against the door, his gaze very sombre. 'This is a bad time for us. I have already observed that my sister has started to rely on you as a friend and I believe she is going to need that companionship very soon. I appeal to you—if you cannot stay because of Julia, stay a little to help Lavender.'

Caroline sighed. She felt trapped by his words. She had already thought of the implications of leaving

Lavender in a house where her father was about to die and her cousin was a silly, vain creature incapable of offering her the support she needed. True, she had her brother, but he would have so many matters to attend to after their father's death. A few weeks ago it would not have mattered to her; a few weeks ago she had not come to like and respect Lavender Brabant. But now…

'I know it is unfair of me to ask you,' Lewis said, smiling ruefully. 'Believe me, I only do it because I feel that it is so important for my sister. But if you truly believe that you cannot bear to stay—'

'No,' Caroline spoke quickly. 'I will stay—for Miss Brabant's sake, at least for a little while.'

'Thank you.' Lewis took her hand and pressed a kiss on it. 'I am truly grateful, Miss Whiston. And for the other—'

'Do not let us speak of it again, sir.' Caroline withdrew her hand quickly.

'If you wish.' For once Lewis seemed oddly at a loss. 'One thing I must say, though, Miss Whiston. I was very wrong to doubt you, and for that I am truly sorry—'

Caroline made a dismissive gesture. She did not wish to pursue the subject, for thinking of it would only make her realise how sore her heart was. She allowed Lewis to open the door for her and walked slowly upstairs, aware of his gaze following her progress. When she had finally gained the sanctuary of her own room she closed the door softly and sat down, dry-eyed, in the chair beside the bed.

She did not wish to stay at Hewly Manor. The oppressive nature of the atmosphere was depressing and, taken with the evidence of Julia's malice, it created an unpleasant feeling in the pit of her stomach. Yet she had promised Lewis that she would stay, at least for a little, and she would keep that promise. She opened her eyes and stared at the black sky visible in the square panes of the window. He had said that he wanted her to stay to befriend Lavender, and she had agreed on those terms. Yet now she found herself acknowledging that she wished he had asked her to stay for himself.

The approach of Christmas was heralded by few of the usual festivities. Lavender and Lewis drove around the tenant farms and cottages, delivering presents and Christmas good wishes, but the atmosphere was subdued and the shadow of Admiral Brabant's illness lay over everyone. When Julia mooted the idea of attending the ball at the Angel, Lavender declined to go and Caroline chose to stay at home to keep her company. She could think of little worse than watching Julia flirt with Lewis all night and sitting on the sidelines whilst she waited for him to notice her and remember to offer her a courtesy dance.

Julia returned in high good spirits and full of gossip.

'The talk in the village is all of betrothals and weddings!' she said at breakfast the day after, looking impossibly fresh in a dress of yellow muslin with a matching bandeau in her hair. 'Beatrice Roade is to marry Lord Ravensden tomorrow and if it wasn't for this wretched snow we could all attend! She has done very well for herself, for Ravensden is an excellent catch!' She stirred her chocolate. 'Really, it is extraordinary how well these girls do when they have no looks or portion! When India Rushford caught Lord Isham it was marvel enough, but Beatrice Roade is an odd, outspoken girl...' Her gaze dwelled on Lavender for an instant.

Caroline buttered a second piece of toast. 'Perhaps Lord Ravensden enjoys Miss Roade's company, Julia.'

Julia's eyes opened very wide. 'Lud, what a strange notion, Caroline! Do you not remember,' she gave a little feline smile, 'that when we were at school we used to say that about the plain girls! The only way they would get an offer would be from some gentleman who thought they had a pleasant personality!' She gave a peal of laughter. 'Of course, in those days you were quite a pretty girl yourself—'

Lewis rustled his newspaper irritably. 'You have forgotten Viscount Wyndham, Julia! Do you not have some comment to make about him?'

'Why yes!' Julia seemed to completely miss Lewis's sarcasm, and turned to the others with sparkling eyes. 'The most piquant piece of gossip imaginable, my dears! They say that he sometimes has girls staying alone with him at his hunting-lodge near here—'

Lavender got up and very deliberately left the room. Julia stared.

'Well, upon my word—'

Lewis folded his newspaper, tucked it under his arm and rose to his feet. 'Excuse me. I shall be in the study if anyone requires me.'

Julia shrugged pettishly as the door closed behind him. 'What can be the matter with those two today? Now, did I tell you about Miss Reeth...'

Caroline sighed and poured herself another cup of chocolate. It seemed so unfair that she was the only one who could not simply get up and leave Julia to her own devices.

Admiral Brabant died three days after Christmas. It was hardly unexpected and all his family was with him at the end. Whilst they assembled at the bedside, Caroline took Nanny Prior down to the kitchens and poured her cup after cup of strong, sweet tea, listening sympathetically whilst she talked of her long association with the Brabant family and her sorrow that both the Admiral and his wife had now passed on. It was late in the evening and eventually Nanny Prior blew her nose hard on a capacious white handkerchief, gave Caroline a watery smile and said, 'Bless you for listening whilst I rambled on, child! It's a sad business, but I suppose there's always hope! When Master Lewis—the Captain, I should say, now that he's the head of the household—when he sets up his nursery, then we shall see brighter times ahead here at Hewly!'

Caroline stirred her tea and wondered whether Nanny Prior thought such an event was imminent.

'News of a betrothal might lift everyone's spirits,' Mrs Prior continued, obviously following the same train of thought herself. 'Though, I suppose, with the house in mourning...' She sighed. 'Then there's those who would not be so happy to see the match. Ah well, matters will resolve themselves in time! It's a sad homecoming for Miss Julia, though, with her uncle taken ill so soon after she arrived, and never in his senses again! Why, she was barely in the house two hours before he was struck down!'

Caroline could see quite easily how Nanny Prior had made the connection between Lewis's nuptials and Julia's presence at Hewly, and her heart sank. She could hardly ask the old nurse whether the servants thought a match between the two was a foregone conclusion, and really Mrs Prior's comments spoke for themselves. With a sigh she helped herself to a piece of rich sponge cake, reflecting that eating for comfort was delicious but a bad idea, and that she would suffer for it when she finally came to try to sleep.

'We found him in the study with everything scattered about him,' Nanny Prior was continuing, with a certain gloomy relish. 'The ink pot had spilled all over the desk and the quill was on the floor—there were reams of paper everywhere! Proper mess it was, and with the Admiral lying insensible in the middle of it all! It's surprising the poor gentleman lasted as long as he did!'

'What was he writing?' Caroline asked, her mouth full of sponge cake.

Nanny Prior stared. She seemed much struck by the

question. 'Well! Now you're asking!' She frowned in perplexity. 'I don't rightly know, miss! Never thought on it again until now! There's a thing! A letter, I think it was, though so blotted and spotted you could hardly read...' She shook her head.

'Ah well.' Caroline drained her cup and wondered whether Lavender might need her. She was about to go upstairs to find out, when a maid stuck her head around the kitchen door, bobbed Mrs Prior the respectful curtsey of a junior to a senior servant, and addressed Caroline.

'Begging your pardon, ma'am, but Mrs Chessford is asking for you.'

Julia was waiting at the top of the stairs, weeping artistically into her lace handkerchief and leaning heavily on Lewis's arm.

'Caroline,' her former friend instructed as she wiped her eyes prettily, 'I require a hot posset to help me get what little sleep I can this wretched night. I *must* sleep, or I will look a hag in the morning.' She gave Lewis a sweet, mournful smile. 'Do you go down to the kitchens again and prepare a drink of milk and nutmeg for me, and Lewis, pray stay with me until Caro returns for I cannot bear to be left alone—' She broke off.

Lavender was coming out of the Admiral's bed-chamber, her face pale and ravaged with tears. For a moment Caroline thought she saw a hint of chagrin in Julia's eyes, but the next moment she was drooping charmingly on Lewis's arm, murmuring that she felt a little faint. Caroline hurried across to put an arm around Lavender, calling to Lewis over her shoulder.

'Captain Brabant, I believe your sister needs you. I will assist Mrs Chessford to her room and fetch her a drink. Then, if I can be of any comfort to Miss Brabant—'

'Thank you, Miss Whiston.' Lewis dropped Julia's arm without a second glance, bestowed a grateful but distracted smile on Caroline, and crossed the landing to take Lavender in his arms. Caroline and Julia watched them walk away together, Lavender's fair head resting on his shoulder.

'Well!' Julia said, straightening up and suddenly sounding much stronger, 'you would have thought that Lewis would at least ascertain that I was quite well before he left me! I can scarce believe—'

'Julia,' Caroline said, in a voice of iron, 'Miss Brabant has just lost her father. Whilst I am sure that your feelings for your godfather were sincere, I do not believe that your loss can compare with hers. Now, I will go down to fetch you your drink, and I will send Letty up to attend you.'

Julia flounced off towards her room. 'You have become quite the managing creature, Caroline! Since nobody cares for me I shall do perfectly well on my own!'

Sighing, Caroline went back down to the kitchens. Cook was already there, stolidly stirring a pan of milk on the stove. She looked up and gave Caroline a faint smile.

'Miss Whiston, I've prepared some milk for my

little lamb and I'll slip a noggin of brandy in with some nutmeg so that she sleeps...'

For a moment, Caroline wondered whether Cook could be a lot more fond of Julia than she had always appeared to be, then she realised that the woman was talking about Lavender, not Julia.

'I will take Miss Brabant's drink up for her, if you wish,' she volunteered. 'I know you must all be at sixes and sevens down here...'

Cook threw her a grateful glance. 'Bless you, Miss Whiston, that we are! What with the housemaids crying in the pantry and John the footman gone to the village with the news and Nanny Prior awash with tea...'

'If there is any milk left, may I take it to Mrs Chessford?' Caroline asked carefully. 'I am sure she would be grateful for a cup—'

Cook sniffed. 'Grateful for nothing, that one! Complaining of us to the master, and queening it about the house as though she were mistress here already! Now the Honourable Mrs B., she was a proper lady. Turning in her grave she'll be to think of that one taking her place!'

Caroline realised that she had made a tactical error in raising Julia's name. She had known that most of the servants disliked Julia because she had complained to Lewis of their shoddy ways almost as soon as he was through the door. And Cook was obviously very upset at the Admiral's death, for she was wiping a surreptitious tear away with the corner of her apron and sniffing over the milk. Caroline patted her arm in a comforting manner and received a weak smile for her pains. Cook filled two cups with milk, handed the tray to Caroline and thanked her once again.

Caroline went upstairs and knocked on Julia's door. Letty answered and took the cup in, leaving Caroline relieved that she did not have to endure another of Julia's diatribes. Through the panels of the closed door she could hear Julia's voice rising and falling like a peal of bells. She went along the corridor, past a huddle of servants, and tapped on Lavender's bedroom door. She could hear a murmur of voices from within, and in a moment, Lewis Brabant opened the door.

'Miss Whiston,' he gave her a faint smile. 'Please come in.'

Caroline's heart ached for him. There were lines of exhaustion and grief on his face and his eyes were tired. She wanted to comfort him and take him in her arms, and the impulse was so strong that it shocked her. Fortunately, perhaps, she was still carrying the milk, and now a spot of the scalding liquid jumped from the cup on to her hand and recalled her to her senses. She carried the cup across to the bedside table and set it down carefully.

Lavender was sitting propped up on her pillows and she gave Caroline a pale smile. 'Thank you so much, Caroline. Will you sit with me for a little? Lewis has so many things that he must do.'

Caroline glanced questioningly at Lewis. He inclined his head slightly. 'If you would be so good, Miss Whiston.'

'Of course.' Caroline waited whilst Lewis bent down and kissed Lavender on the cheek, then she sat down at the side of the bed and took one of Lavender's hands in a comforting grasp.

'I am so sorry, Lavender. Although it was not sudden, it must still be a horrid shock for you.'

The younger girl gave her a grateful smile. 'Thank you, Caroline. Yes, it is hard. For all that I knew father was dying, it is difficult to believe that he is gone. Yet I am glad in a way, for he was not himself towards the end and now his suffering is over.'

She reached forward and Caroline passed her the cup of milk. 'Be careful, it is a little full.'

Lavender drank deeply. Her eyes were already closing when Caroline took the tilting cup from her hand and helped her to settle back on the pillows.

'Try to sleep, now. You are exhausted.'

'In a moment,' Lavender murmured. 'Caroline, do you think that Lewis will marry Julia?' Her eyes flickered open briefly, lavender blue and drowned with tears. 'Oh, I do so hope not! I could not bear it!'

Caroline was startled. It seemed to be the night when everybody's prejudices about Julia were coming to the fore. Either Cook had put too much brandy in the posset, or Lavender's grief had broken down the barriers of reticence, or perhaps both. She patted her hand.

'Do not worry about that now, Lavender.'

'No,' the girl turned her fair head against the pillow. 'Perhaps all will be well. It is just…' She hesitated, yawning. 'I do not like her, you see,' she said simply. 'Nor do I trust her. She was supposed to be marrying Lewis years ago, but as soon as he was gone to sea she threw him over for Andrew! Mama and papa did not like the match, but Julia made a dead set for him! She thought that I was too young to see what was happening, but I knew! It was only because Andrew was the elder son, and Julia was bored...'

'Hush...' Caroline soothed, hoping that Lavender would fall asleep soon and the feverish flow of words would cease. She doubted that the girl would even remember them in the morning.

'And then Andrew died and Julia was most put out,' Lavender said, with some satisfaction, 'but there was always Andrew's friend Jack Chessford—with Julia there is always the friend... I do hope—I do *so* hope that Lewis will see through her, but I fear not...I saw him with her in his arms last night...'

Caroline felt icy cold. She too had secretly hoped that Lewis would see through Julia's outward beauty to the person beneath, for he was hardly a fool and she would have expected him to be a good judge of men. But of women...? Physical beauty could blind a man to much. Caroline had seen that plenty of times before and her heart, which had been in her boots, sank still further.

'I would like it above all things if Lewis would marry you, Caroline,' Lavender confided, smiling a little. 'I shall have to contrive...' and at last, she fell asleep.

Caroline sat beside her for a little, until the fire died down and the cold in the room made her shiver. She got up and moved across to the grate, adding coal and logs to build the fire up again so that Lavender should not awaken with the cold.

'Let me help you with that.'

The door had opened softly and Lewis Brabant came back into the room. He helped Caroline to her feet and bent down to stir up the fire, before straightening up and casting a critical look over her.

'You look cold, Miss Whiston, and tired.' He kept his voice low. 'I see that Lavender is asleep now. I hope that she was not...too...distressed.'

Caroline thought that it was hardly the moment to mention that Lavender seemed most disturbed at the thought of her brother's marriage to Julia. 'Miss Brabant is very upset, of course,' she murmured. 'It is only natural. I believe she will sleep through the night, though. Cook put quite a measure of spirits in the milk...'

Lewis's tired face lightened a little. 'It sounds just the thing. I only hope it did not make her too loquacious first!'

Caroline avoided his eye. 'Not...not particularly, sir.'

Lewis raised an eyebrow and Caroline realised that something in her tone had given her away. She had always found it difficult to dissemble, particularly when she was feeling self-conscious, and the very knowledge that he was such a perceptive man made her feel even more ill at ease.

'I see.' Lewis sounded amused. 'Never fear, Miss Whiston! I shall not ask you to break my sister's confidence! Now, you must be tired. I'll bid you good-night.'

They went out together, Lewis raising a casual hand in farewell as he went downstairs. Caroline went to her room and prepared for bed, but found that she could not sleep. The sponge cake was sitting heavily on her stomach and her mind was full of the events of the day. She took out a book and read for a little, then sat by the window looking out at the dark and listening to the muted sounds of the household. Gradually the house became quiet. Caroline heard the clock in the hall strike one. She cast her book aside with a sigh and decided to go down to the kitchens for a third time, this time for a drink for herself.

Pulling a woollen wrap over her nightdress, Caroline slipped out on to the landing. There was no one about. She was not superstitious, but the shadows and the silence made her suddenly nervous and she averted her eyes from the closed door of the Admiral's room. She hurried down the stairs, her candle held high in one hand, the other grasping the wooden banister. A light still showed beneath the door of the study but there was no sound from within the room.

Caroline was about to tiptoe towards the door to the servants' quarters when a movement caught the corner of her eye. The candle flared as she spun round and she gave a muted squeak of alarm. She thought she saw the faintest of shadowy figures waft away down the corridor, then the light went out as her candle fell from her shaking hand.

Chapter Six

The study door opened with an abrupt crash.

'What the devil is going on there?' It was Lewis's voice, sharp out of the darkness. He came out into the hall, holding his own candle high. 'Miss Whiston? What the deuce—'

Caroline's teeth were chattering with nerves. 'I beg your pardon, sir. I saw… I thought I saw someone in the hall…a figure in grey…'

Lewis caught her arm and pulled her unceremoniously into the study. Caroline's relief at being in the light again was tempered a moment later by the sudden realisation that she was in her night attire and that she was now alone in the room with Lewis. She turned to face him and saw that he too was in a state of undress scarcely suitable for company. He had discarded his jacket and cravat, both of which were cast carelessly over the back of one of the chairs, and his shirt was open at the neck. The candlelight gilded his skin to deep bronze and shadowed his blue eyes. Caroline felt her throat dry with an entirely different type of nervousness. Her gaze moved to the half-empty brandy bottle that was standing on the desk, and at the same moment she heard the door close behind her with a wholly unnerving click.

'Have no fear, Miss Whiston,' Lewis said smoothly, reading Caroline's mind with an accuracy she was beginning to find very disturbing. 'Though appearances may be to the contrary, I am quite sober. Pray take a seat and tell me what has alarmed you.'

He put the candle down on the desk and turned to look at her. Caroline's hand strayed to her throat in a nervous gesture. She could think of nothing but that she was in her nightdress and her hair was loose about her shoulders, and she must look like the veriest cyprian.

'I think I had better not, sir.' She found that her voice was still a little unsteady. 'It was only my foolish imagination. I was feeling uneasy and thought I saw an apparition—'

'The grey lady.' Lewis strolled over to the side table and splashed some brandy into a glass. He held the bottle up. 'Are you sure you will not join me?'

'Quite sure, I thank you, sir.' Caroline knew she sounded prim and heard him laugh a little mockingly.

'Then take a seat at least, Miss Whiston, and bear me company.' Lewis came across and sat down, gesturing to Caroline to join him. He crossed his legs at the ankle and leant back. 'I need some company tonight. I do believe that you have seen our resident ghost.'

'The grey lady?' Caroline sat down a little

abruptly. 'Surely not, sir! Ghosts and spirits—what nonsense!'

Lewis shrugged lightly. 'I am surprised that you have not come across the tale in your reading, Miss Whiston! Apparently the lady in question was the wife of a royalist who lost his life in the civil war. When she heard of his death she was inconsolable and refused to eat. She wasted away until she died, and now she haunts the house and gardens, flitting about like a grey shadow whenever there is a death in the family.'

Despite herself, Caroline shivered. 'Stuff and nonsense!' she said stoutly, wrapping her arms closely about herself as she tried to get warm. 'It is just a fanciful story!'

Lewis laughed. He took a long draught of brandy. 'Practical Miss Whiston! Yet you were the one who saw her…'

Caroline shivered again.

'Come closer to the fire,' Lewis said softly. His eyes were intent on her face, making Caroline feel even more tinglingly ill at ease. 'We should not frighten ourselves with ghost stories on winter nights.'

'I would have thought that you would have no time for such foolishness, sir!' Caroline said astringently, assuming a brisk manner to cover her discomfiture. 'Surely you are more used to dealing with matters of action rather than imagination!'

Lewis stretched. Caroline saw the muscle ripple beneath the white linen of his shirt and tore her gaze away. Suddenly the room felt a lot warmer, rather hot and cold at the same time, which was confusing. Caroline wondered if she was about to contract a chill.

'Surely you have heard that seafarers are the most superstitious breed imaginable, Miss Whiston!' Lewis said sardonically. 'We can always be relied upon to tell the most fearsome tales! But let us change the subject. Tell me instead how you came to be wandering about the house so late.'

'I could not sleep,' Caroline said evasively. 'I thought to fetch myself a cup of milk. In fact,' she jumped up, 'that is what I will do now!'

Lewis looked her over with lazy amusement. His gaze took in her flushed cheeks and seemed to linger on the rich chestnut hair that curled about her face. 'What, dare you brave those dark corridors alone?'

'I am persuaded that I imagined the whole matter!' Caroline said briskly. 'There is no danger!'

'Probably less than staying here with me,' Lewis said. His gaze, dark blue as the summer sea, drifted over her again, making her feel acutely uncomfortable. It was not an unpleasant awareness, Caroline thought a little breathlessly, but rather one loaded with too many unnerving feelings. She did not want to think about it, for already she felt as thought she was straying perilously out of her depth.

Lewis reached for the brandy bottle again. 'Well, if I cannot persuade you to join me in a nightcap—'

'I think not,' Caroline said politely, 'but I thank you.' She retreated towards the door, her sense of relief increasing with every step she took. It was only when her hand was actually on the latch that a horrid thought struck her and made her pause. Supposing the Captain intended to sit here all night and drink himself into oblivion? The loss of his father could well take him that way, and though he had shown nothing but strength in supporting Lavender thus far, how would his sister feel if she awoke the next day and found Lewis insensible with drink?

'You hesitate, Miss Whiston.' Lewis's mocking tones broke into her thoughts. He got to his feet and moved towards her with the loose-limbed grace that was peculiarly his own. There was a teasing glint in his eye. Caroline backed away, her gaze riveted on his face.

'Oh…no, it was simply that I concerned that you might—' She stopped, torn between her anxiety and the realisation that she could be getting herself into trouble.

Lewis smiled a little. 'You are concerned that I am more than a little adrift and that without your restraining influence I will become positively foxed?' His smile deepened. 'Well, you may be correct on the first point, Miss Whiston, but you may also trust me… I shall not let Lavender down.'

'I did not think that you would,' Caroline said, as coolly as she was able. 'I admire you for the support you have given your sister, but often it is those who care most about others whom no one else thinks to comfort—' She broke off, the colour flooding her face as she saw the expression in his eyes, a mixture of tenderness and amusement.

'That is very true, Miss Whiston,' Lewis said slowly, 'for you could be speaking of yourself! For all your brusque façade, you care much about others do you not? But who cares for you? You must have been lonely…'

Caroline felt her grasp of the situation slipping away. He was very close to her now. She could almost imagine that she could smell the scent of his skin, feel the warmth emanating from his body. Such thoughts made her feel slightly faint and she struggled to regain her usual cool common sense.

'You mistake me, I meant nothing so profound,' she said hurriedly. 'I was only alarmed that you might over-indulge—'

Lewis's smile told her that he did not believe her. 'I am touched that you seek to comfort me, Miss Whiston.'

'Such was not my intention!' Caroline said, a little wildly. She turned back towards the door. 'You twist my words, sir! I must go! I am very tired!'

'Not so fast, Miss Whiston,' Lewis murmured. His arm slid around Caroline's waist, pulling her against him. There was no time for her to think; his mouth was on hers, for a moment soft and sweet, then hard and demanding. Caroline felt herself tremble, leaning the palms of her hands against his chest to steady herself. She could feel the beat of his heart, taste the hint of brandy on his lips. A hundred protests came into her head and fled beneath the touch of his hands. He was tangling his fingers in the heavy fall of chestnut hair about Caroline's shoulders, and now she could feel him stroking the nape of her neck so softly that she shivered with pleasure. The gentle touch was acutely at odds with the ruthless skill of his kiss. Caroline's tiredness mingled with a most delicious weakness, creating a sensual lassitude that robbed her of the will to move.

'Dear Caro...' Lewis said softly, when his lips left hers. His vivid blue gaze scanned her face and his eyes darkened with desire again. 'I have so wanted...'

His hand came up to touch her cheek lightly, sliding beneath her chin and turning her lips up to his again. This time the kiss was gentle, the searching urgency held in check. Lewis's grip tightened and Caroline slid her arms about his neck, pressing closer against him. She was dazed and dazzled, swept by such unfamiliar feelings...

A door closed stealthily nearby. It was a small noise, but enough to bring Caroline to her senses. How many people knew that she had come downstairs, that she was alone in the study with the master of the house? Suddenly what had seemed so sweet and precious became sordid. The master of the house and the governess companion... It conjured up all sorts of cartoon images in Caroline's mind, the whispered gossip of the servants, the smirks and knowing looks... She pulled herself out of Lewis's arms and drew her wrap more closely about her, clearing her throat painfully.

'I believe you took more than mere comfort there, sir...'

Lewis's eyes were very dark. He ran a hand through his dishevelled fair hair. 'Miss Whiston, I—'

'Pray do not apologise, sir!' Caroline said quickly. She did not think she could bear it if he made matters worse by telling her it was all a mistake, a drunken error of judgement.

'I was not planning to do so.' Lewis gave her a very straight look. 'I wanted—' He broke off and rubbed a hand across his brow. 'Confound it, this is not as I had intended—'

Caroline pressed her fingers against her lips. Suddenly, like a dose of cold water, she remembered Lavender telling her that she had seen Julia in Lewis's arms only the previous day. Abruptly, Caroline's mortification turned to icy anger within her. She had been in danger of losing her heart, whilst he…

'Embracing several different women in a short space of time must have its difficulties,' she observed coldly. 'May I suggest that you rein in your rakish tendencies, sir? You will find life so much less confusing that way!'

Lewis stood still, looking at her with raised eyebrows. 'Rakish tendencies? My dear Caroline—'

'I did not give you permission to use my name, sir, nor do I wish to be treated as some kind of rival to Julia for your affections!' Caroline said, unable to contain herself. 'It may amuse you, but I consider it an inappropriate jest!'

'A jest? A rival to Julia? Whatever can you mean?' Lewis looked genuinely puzzled and Caroline was incensed at his duplicity.

'Do you deny that *she* was the recipient of your attentions only yesterday? You are somewhat fickle, sir!'

Lewis' blue eyes narrowed on Caroline's face. 'What is this, servants' gossip? I do deny it!'

'The whole household knows of it!' Caroline said, exaggerating wildly, 'and it does you no credit to refute it, sir!'

There was some flash of expression in Lewis's eyes, so quick that Caroline could not read it, then he shrugged and his face went blank.

'Very well, Miss Whiston.' He spoke quietly. 'If that is how you wish it…' He handed her the candle from the desktop, then stepped forward and held the door open for her. There was no mistaking her dismissal. Caroline risked one further look at his face, but it was quite unreadable. He gave her a slight bow, as though encouraging her to be on her way, and closed the door behind her with a very decisive thud.

Caroline found herself out in the dark hall, all thought of a soothing drink fled. She wanted to do nothing more than run up the stairs and indulge in a hearty bout of tears to relieve her feelings. As a governess companion she was accustomed to ignoring slights, ill-natured comments and malicious tricks, but she had no experience of dealing with the kind of feelings that Lewis Brabant stirred up in her.

Caroline lay awake for the best part of the night. By dawn, her first fury with Lewis had abated into a numb acceptance that she was partly to blame for what had happened between them. She was the one who had gone wandering about the house at night and she had gone into the study even when she had seen that he was alone. It was the action of a naïve débutante rather than a sensible woman of eight-and-twenty. More to the point, she had scarcely fought Lewis off when he had taken her in his arms. A part of Caroline burned with shame when she remembered the abandoned fashion with which she had returned his kisses, but another part shivered at the memory of his touch. She could hardly fool herself that she was indifferent to him. She furiously told herself that he was unprincipled and beneath contempt, but her heart told another story.

The truth of the matter was terrifying to her and she tried not to think on it too much. Caroline knew that she had repressed her emotions for so long that they were as dry as a tinderbox, and she was in serious danger of falling ever deeper in love. It was inappropriate and pointless and yet another reason why she had to leave Hewly as soon as possible. Though she had lost her heart, Caroline saw no reason to lose her head as well. She was not one to throw her bonnet over a windmill, and to go to Lewis and beg for his love was out of the question.

She finally fell asleep, to be woken late the next morning by a housemaid with a can of hot water and a tray of breakfast. Since Caroline had never had breakfast in bed in the time she was at Hewly, she was rather startled.

'Begging your pardon, miss,' the maid said in answer to her question, 'but the master insisted. He said that you had been up late caring for Miss Lavender and should have some time to rest.'

Caroline inwardly raised her eyebrows at this evidence of Lewis's thoughtfulness, lay back against her pillows and helped herself to a cup of chocolate. She was aware of a very definite and cowardly urge to avoid him that morning, but she knew it was impossible. With a sigh she got herself out of bed and had a thorough wash. She dressed in her undergarments, then lingered before her dressing-table, considering.

She was forced to concede that her figure was not bad when she did not choose to conceal it beneath drab worsted. She was slim but well-proportioned, although she knew she was considered rather tall for a woman. Society did not think of height as an attractive feature in a female, although for a governess it was a positive advantage as it gave an impression of authority. The rules of fashion did not really apply to governesses, Caroline thought suddenly. In fact, other women seemed offended if an upper servant was too attractive, and with the men it was positively dangerous.

She scrutinised her face in detail. Her lips were too full for beauty, though in repose they curved pleasingly into a hint of a smile. Her nose was snub, or retroussé, as her grandfather had affectionately called it. Her skin was good and her eyes a wide, clear hazel. Caroline let a lock of chestnut hair slide gently through her fingers. Once upon a time it had been dressed in ringlets and curls, falling about her face, or drawn up in circlets and ribbons. Such a very long time ago...

What could it be that drew Lewis Brabant's attention to her? Boredom, perhaps, or a sense of devilment. Caroline shook her head and pulled on a no-nonsense grey dress. She wound the curly chestnut hair into a particularly severe knot, and went downstairs.

The house was very quiet. There was no one in the drawing-room or the library, and Caroline was thinking reluctantly that perhaps she should go and find Julia when a noise on the gravel sweep outside attracted her attention. She walked over to the bay window and pulled aside the heavy curtain.

Lavender was standing some twenty feet away, deep in conversation with Barnabas Hammond. Barnabas had evidently come to deliver the mourning attire, for his hands were full of black silk scarves and crêpe bands, and a basket at his feet contained bonnets, caps, hose, handkerchiefs and other items all trimmed with black. Neither Lavender nor Barney were concentrating on the funeral attire, however, for they were quite engrossed in each other. Caroline drew back, concerned not to be seen prying, but as she turned away from the window there was a step behind her and she swung round to confront Lewis Brabant.

Caroline had had no time to prepare herself and felt at a definite disadvantage. Along with her own embarrassment, however, was a confusion over whether she should try to prevent Lewis from seeing the scene outside the window. If Lavender was gaining some solace from talking to Barney Hammond, Caroline could see no reason to interfere. Her brother might well feel differently, however.

As she hesitated, Lewis said, with rueful amusement, 'Do not worry, Miss Whiston! It would be a harsh brother indeed who wrests from his sister some comfort in the current situation! I am not inclined to intervene.'

'Oh! You knew!' Caroline let her breath out in a long sigh. She moved away, wanting to put some space between the two of them. Once again, she knew that her face had betrayed her thoughts. Still, if Lewis thought that her nervousness arose from concern over Lavender's situation rather than her own, she had at least managed to conceal something from him.

Whatever the ill-effects Lewis might be suffering from imbibing too much brandy the previous night, they were not visible to an onlooker. The stark black of the mourning clothes made him look uncompromisingly severe, and though his eyes were still tired, their gaze was quite steady.

'Before you run away, Miss Whiston, I should like to say something,' he said quietly. 'It will not take much time.'

Caroline's heart sank. Running away was precisely what she wanted to do. She rested her hands on the back of one of the chairs and gripped tightly.

'I imagine that you must believe you have several

good reasons for leaving Hewly after last night,' Lewis said. He seemed to be choosing his words with care but he held her gaze quite deliberately. 'I suppose that I should apologise for my conduct—'

Caroline turned her face away, afraid that her feelings for him would be too obvious. 'You had been drinking—' she began, but stopped as Lewis put a hand over one of hers, forcing her to look at him.

'Not that much. Caroline, I—'

'Lewis?'

Julia's voice came from behind them, sweet but with a faintly puzzled note. Caroline had not heard her come in. 'Excuse me if I intrude—'

Caroline heard Lewis swear softly under his breath. He dropped her hand abruptly and turned, shielding her from Julia's gaze.

'Good morning, Julia. I shall be with you directly.'

'Excuse me,' Caroline murmured. She knew that her cheeks were scarlet with embarrassment and did not dare to look at Julia's face as she brushed past her on her way to the door. As she hurried away, she heard Julia's voice, light and teasing, 'Lewis, my dear, must you be so kind to poor Caro? She has led a sheltered life, you know, and is in serious danger of falling desperately in love with you, poor girl!' And her peal of laughter followed Caroline up the stairs, seeming to echo mockingly around the corridors and pursue her wherever she went.

Much to Caroline's surprise, Julia did not broach with her the subject of the scene in the library.

Caroline could only assume that Julia was so sure of her power and so disparaging of any rival that she felt no need to mention it. As to what Lewis had been about to say, Caroline thought that it must have been an apology and told herself that she should be grateful that Julia had foreshortened so embarrassing a moment. She tried to avoid Lewis as much as possible, but it did not make for a comforting existence.

It was several days later that Caroline received a reply to her letter to Anne Covingham. Lady Covingham expressed her disappointment that matters had not fallen out well at Hewly, but was encouraging that she might be able to help Caroline find a place elsewhere. Friends of the Covingham family had just returned from India. They had a young family and two little girls just approaching the age when they required a governess. Anne would make enquiries on Caroline's behalf. Caroline folded the letter and put it in her chest of drawers, then, feeling a mixture of hope and obscure disappointment, went to find to Julia.

It was the morning of the Admiral's funeral, and Julia was seated at her dressing-table, brushing her hair slowly, whilst Letty shook out the black silk crêpe dress that she had been pressing. Julia's big blue eyes swept over Caroline's plain black bombazine, and she gave a slight nod.

'I should have guessed that you would have some old dress that would be appropriate, Caroline! You must have been in mourning for ever with all those dull families you have lived with! Still, I suppose that does not matter for a governess!' She stood up, stretched gracefully, and allowed Letty to slip the dress over her head. 'I was intending to purchase bombazet for you when the servants get new mourning clothes,' she said over her shoulder, 'but I see it is not necessary!'

Caroline helped Letty to fasten the hooks on the black silk dress, wondering if Julia expected to be thanked for her back-handed generosity.

'Will the crêpe be warm enough, Julia?' she enquired levelly. 'It is a chilly morning and the church will not be heated—'

Julia shrugged airily. 'Oh, it will do! To tell the truth I have a black grosgrain that would be warmer, but it is not near so pretty! And with my cloak and muff I shall do very well!'

She sat down to allow Letty to adjust the delicate black bonnet with its gauzy veil. 'What a gloomy way to start a new year! I declare, it is all silence and long faces! I quite yearn for some excitement! And Lewis has decreed a quiet funeral, so I shall have no one to gossip with!'

'I am sure that all the local families will pay their respects,' Caroline said tightly.

'Oh, surely,' Julia pirouetted about the room, and smiled with satisfaction as she heard the crêpe rustle about her, 'but you know that Lady Perceval scarcely deigns to acknowledge me! That must change when I am Mrs Lewis Brabant of Hewly Manor! I shall be generous, however, and not remind her of her former coldness!'

Lewis Brabant closed the study door behind him and leant against it for a moment in grateful silence. They had buried his father with the quiet dignity that the Admiral himself had requested in his last communication to his son. The Reverend William Perceval had led the simple and moving service, and many of the villagers had come to pay their last respects. Now the house was empty, the last of the mourners departed, and the Admiral laid in the cold earth beside his wife, his grave stark and newly turned amidst the snow.

The Admiral's final letter was before Lewis on the desk, forwarded by the family lawyer with a note to the effect that Mr Churchward hoped to present himself at Hewly within a few days to discuss the matter of the will. Admiral Brabant's instructions for his funeral rites had been quite specific. Since he could not be buried at sea, he would be interred with the minimum fuss and expense. Lewis smiled a little as he reread the close-written scrawl. His father's personality came over strongly; opinionated, terse, but for all that, a man to be respected.

He replaced the letter on the desk top and reached for the brandy bottle, frowning a little ruefully as he reflected that he had consumed more brandy in the last week than in a whole month in the Navy. Perhaps that was what had made his judgement so damnably at fault in the matter of Caroline Whiston. He had known what he wanted but had not thought how best to achieve it, and now he was presented with a whole new set of problems...

'Lewis?'

He turned to find that Julia was in the doorway. The light was behind her, and she appeared shadowy and insubstantial in her black crêpe dress. She glided forward into the room and closed the door quietly behind her.

'Pray do not let me disturb you, Lewis,' she said with a gentle smile. 'I know you will wish for some time alone to think of your father. I merely wanted to say goodnight.' She looked at him with sorrowful eyes. 'Poor Uncle Harley. It made me so sad to see him suffer so much. For all our differences, I loved him dearly.'

Lewis rubbed a weary hand across his eyes. He had no particular desire for a tête-à-tête with Julia, but he knew she was trying to tell him something and it seemed discourteous to dismiss her.

'My dear Julia, whatever can you mean? I had no notion that you and my father did not see eye to eye! What can he have done to upset you?'

He saw her hesitate before she made a gesture of denial, a fluttering motion of the hands that was as charming as it was distressful. Her voice was full of confusion.

'To own the truth, Lewis, I always intended to tell you, but not just yet—' She looked up and met his eyes, and her own were full of mortification. He took a swift step towards her, but she moved away, evading his gaze. 'Oh, let us not speak of it! Not now, of all times!'

Lewis was aware of feeling irritated. He schooled his features to patience and took both her hands in his. 'Julia! If there is something I should know—'

She tried unsuccessfully to free herself. 'Oh it is nothing! I feel so ashamed of speaking of it!' She gave a little shudder. 'It was all so long ago, and no doubt I mistook the situation—'

'Julia!' Lewis gave her a little shake. He was feeling both annoyed and concerned now. What could his father have done to engender such embarrassment? And why should Julia be so wary of telling him?

Julia gave a graceful little shrug. 'Oh, if I must tell you…' She cast her eyes down.

'You may remember, Lewis, that when you went to sea I was quite desperately in love with you and hoped that we might marry.' She raised her gaze to his suddenly. Her eyes were limpid and very blue, and Lewis felt a pang of some emotion he did not wish to analyse. 'Despite the fact that our betrothal was a secret I felt as bound by it as if—' She broke off, biting her lip. 'But that is immaterial. What you must have thought when you heard I was promised to Andrew, I cannot imagine.' Her tone was anguished. 'It was your father's doing, Lewis! He made me agree to marry your brother! He told me directly that it was a business matter, uniting two fortunes and that I was a foolish chit to imagine otherwise! And your brother was as determined as he! Together they wore me down, and I was so very young and alone…'

She freed herself and moved away from him. Lewis watched her as, head bent, she stared into the fire. His first response, a natural anger, was already fading into a cynical acceptance. His father had been an ambitious man whose plans for his children had involved both the augmentation of his wealth and social advancement. It was no surprise to hear that his strategy had involved keeping a grip of Julia's fortune.

Julia was watching him, and for a moment Lewis thought he glimpsed a flash of a strange expression in her eyes, too swift to read. She straightened up and gave him a smile that was both brave and shaken.

'Poor Lewis! I am so very sorry to tell you this when your father is scarce cold in his grave, but I thought it better to be honest…'

He had not noticed until now just how close she was to him. One—or both—of them must have moved instinctively towards the other. Julia's face was tilted up to him, the luscious red lips parted slightly. He could smell her perfume, faint but sweet. After a moment, she said regretfully, 'There is worse I fear, my dear. When your brother died before we could be wed, your father suggested that he take the place of the bridegroom—'

This time, the shock was so sudden that Lewis felt it hit him like a physical blow. He could not imagine what must be showing on his face. Julia was watching him with concern and she put a light hand on his arm.

'Lewis…'

Lewis took a deep breath. 'I cannot believe… You are saying that *my father* intended to marry you when his plans came to naught? But he... My mother had died only days before of the same fever that carried Andrew off—'

Julia evaded his eyes again. A faint shade of colour had come into her cheeks. Lewis knew that his pain and repulsion were clear in his voice, but he could not help himself. He broke away and strode across the room, as though to dissipate the horror with action.

'Good God, the squalor of it! How could he—'

Julia had followed him. He could feel her presence close behind him. In an agony of revulsion he swung round and caught her arms. The first allegation he could well believe, for the Admiral might well have forced her to marry Andrew in an attempt to keep the money in the family. But the second? For all his faults, the Admiral had been as sincerely attached to his well-born wife as she was to him and he had been too scrupulous a man to sink to marrying his own ward. Surely...

Lewis looked down into Julia's clear blue eyes. There was nothing there but anguish and he had an unnerving conviction that she must be telling the truth. Besides, why should she lie? There was nothing to gain.

'I am so sorry, Lewis.' Julia's words were a whisper. 'I would have spared you this, but I needed you to know the truth. It was the reason I married Jack Chessford, you see, and in such unseemly haste... I had to escape. But it was always you that I loved...'

Lewis stared down into the exquisite face so close

to his own. His mind was cloudy with tiredness, re-
coiling from the horror of what he had heard. He felt
Julia press closer to him, softly brushing the length
of her body against his.

A stray breath of wind stirred the letter on the desk
and stirred at the same time some doubt in Lewis's
mind. It had something to do with letters, but the
connection evaded him, slipping away. Nevertheless
he froze. Julia, nestling close, opened her eyes.

'Lewis?' she whispered.

He put her away from him gently, aware of a sudden and extraordinary sense of distaste. Caroline
Whiston's face was before his eyes; the uncompro-
mising honesty of her gaze, the sweetness of her smile
on the rare occasions she could be tempted from her
severity, the softness of her mouth beneath his... He
stood back punctiliously.

'Julia. Excuse me. I am very tired.'

He could see the chagrin in her eyes but before she
could speak the front door bell jangled violently.
They both stood quite still for a moment.

'The mourners have all gone home,' Julia began
crossly. 'Who could possibly wish to call now?'

Lewis went over to the door and flung it open.
'Marston? What the devil's going on?'

The front door was wide and a quantity of luggage
was being unloaded from the carriage outside and
piled on the steps. Lewis strode forward.

'What the deuce—'

'You're not on the quarterdeck now, Lewis,'
Richard Slater's voice said sardonically. 'A fine welcome this is for your old friend!'

Chapter Seven

Caroline splashed through the puddles on the road from Abbot Quincey to Steep Abbot. The first snow-fall of winter was thawing, but local soothsayers were promising another cold snap. In the meantime, Caroline found that her boots were leaking and her cloak was soaked through at the hem.

She had been into the main village to send some letters and pick up a few bits and pieces for Julia, and now she was hurrying back as the winter light faded and the darkness set in across the fields. It had been pleasant to be out of the house; Lewis and Richard Slater had been out on the estate all day, Lady Perceval had swept Lavender away to the Hall for a few hours, and Julia had been cross and scratchy as a consequence of being left behind again.

'Miss Whiston!'

Caroline had just passed the last cottage on the edge of Abbot Quincey when she was hailed by Mr Grizel, who was emerging through a doorway at the end of what had evidently been a pastoral visit. The curate trod eagerly down the path towards her, cassock flapping, his gaunt visage wreathed in smiles. For all her charity, Caroline could not help feeling that he looked like a crow. She organised her face into some semblance of a welcoming smile, and waited for him beside the picket fence.

When Mr Grizel arrived he was somewhat out of breath.

'Apologies for greeting you like that, ma'am,' he puffed, bowing awkwardly. 'I saw you pass by and wished to beg a word...' Here he was obliged to break off for a moment to regain his breath.

'I had a plan, ma'am, an excellent idea,' the curate burbled on. 'Knowing of your undoubted skill in encouraging youth in the ways of virtue and good education, I wondered if I might make so bold—' Mr Grizel temporarily lost himself in his circumlocution. Caroline raised her eyebrows and waited.

'The village school, Miss Whiston!' Mr Grizel waved his arms about enthusiastically. 'Might I prevail upon you to spare a little of your time for the children? The benefits of a sound education for untutored minds, the influence of culture and instruction—'

'I should be delighted, Mr Grizel,' Caroline said hastily, fearing that the curate was about to launch into a lecture. 'If you feel I could be of help—'

Mr Grizel beamed. 'Dear Miss Whiston! I knew I could rely upon you to spread the light! Where there is darkness—'

'Indeed,' Caroline said, seeing an opportunity to

escape. 'Speaking of which, sir, I must be on my way. The evening is drawing in.'

Mr Grizel seemed disinclined to bid her farewell. He came out on to the road and kept pace with her, asking after the household at Hewly and commiserating over the Admiral's sad demise. Caroline responded civilly and it was only where the track petered out into a narrow path that she turned to him and held out her hand in an unmistakable sign of dismissal.

'Our ways must part here, I believe, sir. Good day to you—'

To her amazement her hand was grasped in a fervent grip.

'Miss Whiston!' Mr Grizel's Adam's apple bobbed nervously. 'My *dear* Miss Whiston! I had intended to wait a while longer, but your wholehearted agreement to my plans has led me to believe... I *know* you are the helpmeet I require! Allow me to tell you how ardently I admire you!'

Caroline blinked. She tried to free herself, but Mr Grizel was more tenacious than he looked and hung on to her hand with grim determination. Worse, he suddenly went down on one knee on the path in front of her.

'Be mine, admired Caroline! May I be greatly daring and call you thus? Consent to be my wife and make me the happiest of men! Only say the word—'

'I fear that the word is no, sir,' Caroline began. This was worse than her worst imaginings, comic but sad at the same time. She tried to extricate herself once more. 'I am deeply honoured, but I fear I must decline—'

'But why?' Mr Grizel wailed in anguish. 'Surely it is more favourable than your current situation? I am not without means—'

'Please, sir,' Caroline said quickly, wishing to spare both of them embarrassment, 'say no more! We should not suit! And pray get up! You are kneeling in a puddle and someone is coming!'

'Time,' Mr Grizel pressed on hopefully, covering her hand with moist kisses. 'All ladies need time to consider an offer! I shall—'

'Pray, sir, desist!' Caroline said forcibly. She abandoned all hope of sparing his feelings. He really was an irritatingly persistent man and perhaps he deserved to be snubbed after all. She pulled on her hand; he pulled back. Caroline slipped on the damp grass by the path and managed to twist herself from his grip. And at the same time there was a clatter of hooves on the path, a muffled oath from the approaching rider, and the horse missed the prostrate curate by less than a foot.

Mr Grizel scrambled up, but the rider had already flung himself from the saddle and lifted the unlucky cleric clear of the ground. Mr Grizel was not a small man, but dangling in Lewis Brabant's fearsome grip made him appear rather puny. Lewis let him go as suddenly as he had pounced on him, and Mr Grizel staggered over to the wall and leaned rather heavily against it. Caroline found her voice.

'Captain Brabant! You cannot treat a man of the cloth in such a manner—'

It seemed, however, that Lewis was not moved by a spirit of brotherly love towards Mr Grizel. Ignoring Caroline's comment completely, he stepped threateningly towards the cowering curate.

'What can you mean by manhandling Miss Whiston in that outrageous manner, Grizel? Good God, I would have expected more self-control in a man of your stamp! And to conduct your amorous affairs in the middle of the road at dusk is downright foolhardy, let alone ridiculous!'

'Captain Brabant!' Caroline exclaimed again. 'How dare you, sir!' She was infuriated by his casual reference to amorous affairs, as though she were some tavern wench. She moved closer to the shrinking cleric. 'You are the one who should be apologising! Treating Mr Grizel as though he were some miscreant—'

'The gentleman would have suffered more if I had not been able to stop my horse in time!' Lewis said coolly, looking directly at Caroline for the first time. 'The next time you encourage a proposal, Miss Whiston, pray make sure that you choose a safer place or you will find that you are betrothed one moment and sped on your way to heaven the very next!' He stood back and gave Caroline a heavily ironic bow. 'But tell me, am I to wish you happy?'

Caroline glared at him. She had totally forgotten the cringing Mr Grizel, who was still trying to efface himself against the wall.

'No, you are not!' she said hotly. 'I could have managed the business perfectly well without your intervention, sir! I wish you would take yourself off!'

'I have no intention of leaving you at the mercies of this zealous suitor!' Lewis said derisively, his gaze pinning Mr Grizel to the spot. 'I will take you up with me as far as Hewly, Miss Whiston!'

'Ridiculous!' Caroline said roundly, her temper now as inflamed as his. 'There is no need! Mr Grizel will be on his way home and I can cut across the fields and be back before dark—'

'Whilst you are under my roof you are my responsibility, Miss Whiston,' Lewis said, with icy politeness. 'I beg you not to argue. Your servant, Grizel.'

Before Caroline had any idea what he was about, he had tossed her up on to the horse's back and swung himself up into the saddle behind her. It was all accomplished so smoothly that Caroline had barely drawn breath before Lewis had taken up the reins and turned Nelson's head for home.

'Put me down at once—' Caroline began childishly, but Lewis only laughed.

'What, do you prefer a cold walk home to a little time spent in my company?' he said softly in her ear. 'I thought, perhaps, that we might continue our discussion of your matrimonial plans!'

Caroline suddenly found that she could not have spoken even had she wanted to. His arms were around her, holding her with infinite care against his chest, and she could feel his breath stirring the tendrils of hair about her face. He arranged the folds of his cloak about her and the soft cloth, smelling of him, brushed her skin. The words dried in her throat, the anger draining from her like water evaporating.

'I am surprised that you rejected poor Grizel,' Lewis said, after a moment. 'He is one of the Oxfordshire Grizels, you know, and is accounted quite a catch. Besides, it would be a way out of your current circumscribed existence, so perhaps you, will change your mind when you have had a little time to consider—'

'I think not, sir!' Caroline snapped, her annoyance rushing back at his presumption. 'Not that it is *any* of your business, but I would never make a marriage of convenience just to escape my situation!' She wriggled indignantly. 'A fine opinion you must have of me—'

'Steady,' Lewis instructed quietly, tightening his arms as she started to slide off the horse's back. 'Do not startle Nelson! He is of a most nervous disposition!'

'Nonsense!' Caroline said indignantly. 'I am sure the poor creature is as insensitive as you are, sir!'

She felt Lewis laugh. The sound was warm and disconcertingly intimate in the darkness. He spoke quietly. 'How is it possible that a lady so soft to the touch can have a tongue as sharp as a sacking needle?'

'Stop at once and put me down, sir!' Caroline said furiously, betrayed by the trembling of her own body. His words had stirred the memories in her, the feelings she had sworn to freeze out after their last encounter. It made her all the more angry. 'I do not have to heed your words—'

'Oh, but you do...' Lewis's voice was still little above a whisper. 'You are entirely trapped, are you not, Caroline? A novel experience for so self-sufficient a lady! Dear Caro...' He lingered over the words as he had done once before. 'Be calm. We are having such an enlightening conversation! You would not make a marriage of convenience and I am happy to hear you say so.'

'It is none of your concern, Captain,' Caroline said, trying to sound cold when her whole body was suffused with heat. 'You are unmannerly—'

'Yes, I know.' Lewis's sleeve brushed her cheek and Caroline bit her lip. Here, in the near-dark, pressed so close to him, she felt acutely vulnerable. 'We have spoken on this before,' Lewis continued. 'I have been away at sea too long and have no idea how to go on—'

'Nonsense!' Caroline snapped again. 'You know perfectly well how to behave, sir, you simply *choose* to be ill-mannered! It is shameful!'

'My dear Miss Whiston!' Lewis bent his head and his lips touched the corner of her mouth. They were cold against her cheek. 'I now feel precisely like one of your badly behaved charges! Or perhaps,' his voice changed, 'not *precisely* like one of them...'

Caroline was immensely grateful to see the lighted windows of the Manor approaching. She turned her head away and tried to still the traitorous weakness that swept through her. When they turned into the stableyard she was forced to wait until Lewis had dismounted and lifted her down in his arms, for she knew her legs were too shaky to support her. She tore herself from his grip and walked with head held high towards the door of the house. Lewis caught up with her as they crossed the gravel sweep. She thought that he said something—her name, perhaps—in an undertone shaken with laughter, but then the door was thrown open and Julia stood on the threshold. It was evident that she was in a towering rage.

'Caroline! Where have you been? I have been waiting these two hours past in need of your assistance with a letter—' Her gaze slid from Caroline's flushed face to Lewis's blank one and lingered there thoughtfully. There was a long pause, broken fortunately by Richard Slater's emergence from the library. He seemed blissfully unaware of any tension in the atmosphere.

'Lewis! Did you have a good ride back?'

'Eventful,' Lewis said expressionlessly. 'Would you care for a drink before dinner, Richard? I feel in need of one!' He bowed to Caroline and Julia. 'Ladies, pray excuse us—'

'Well, really!' Julia said, as the study door closed behind them. She seemed uncertain whether to vent her spleen on Caroline or Lewis. 'It's all of a piece as soon as there is another gentleman in the house!' She swung round sharply on Caroline. 'And what were you looking so guilty about, pray? You looked as thought you had been caught kissing in the shrubbery!'

Caroline was feeling decidedly out of sorts. 'I fear Captain Brabant had been ringing a peal over me for encouraging Mr Grizel's attentions,' she said, resorting shamelessly to half-truth and evasion. 'We had a most uncomfortable journey back.'

Julia clapped her hands, her good humour restored. 'Mr Grizel has made you an offer! I knew it! And have you accepted him, Caroline?'

'Certainly not!' Caroline said with dignity.

'I suppose that was why Lewis was so annoyed,' Julia said, with satisfaction. 'Really, Caro, you have no idea how to go on! Only fancy rejecting such a suitor! Why, Mr Grizel has a private income of ten thousand a year!'

'Sorry about last night, old chap,' Captain Slater said ruefully as he and Lewis took port after dinner that evening. 'As I said this morning, I had no intention of intruding on the day of the funeral! Fact is, I'd been up in Bath for a few days and your letter must have passed me on the road. If I'd known about your father's death I would never have come—'

Lewis made a swift gesture and cut him off. 'No apology required, Richard, I assure you. Truth is, I was glad to see you. Things have been damnably difficult here these last few weeks and some different company is most welcome.'

Richard flashed Lewis a grin. 'Well, if you're sure… To tell the truth, I've been waiting all day to hear about your petticoat government! I was uncertain whether I would find you here or decamped to London with the fair Mrs Chessford!'

Lewis gave Richard a look, his eyes narrowing. 'Not sure if I should call you to account for that remark, Richard!'

'Oh, I can do better than that!' Captain Slater said with a cheerful shrug. 'I have a special commission from Fanny to discover whether you are betrothed to Mrs Chessford! The tabbies of Lyme would be taking bets on it if they were not all too genteel to gamble!'

Lewis looked startled. 'How is it that my business is of such interest?'

Richard made a deprecating gesture. 'Fortune, old fellow! Estate! Single gentleman in need of a wife and all that!'

'How is it that you have escaped their attentions then?'

Captain Slater looked as soulful as one of his cheerful countenance could manage. 'Alas, I have a broken heart and am inconsolable!'

'The devil you are!' Lewis looked amused. 'It's the first I heard of it! Besides, surely there is some young lady who plans to cure you? To make you happy again!'

Richard grimaced. 'What a dismal idea! Remind me to develop a new strategy before anyone thinks of it! Anyway,' he cast his friend a sideways look, 'I may not remain heartbroken for ever.'

Lewis got up to stoke the fire. 'You would not be so unoriginal as to develop a *tendre* for Mrs Chessford yourself?'

'Not if you don't wish it, old chap! No, I had more in mind to fix my sights on the fascinating Miss Whiston!'

Lewis stopped in the act of passing the decanter. 'I beg your pardon?'

'Miss Whiston!' Richard Slater's grey eyes were bright with amusement as they dwelt on his friend. 'You referred to her as some Friday-faced female, if I recall correctly—'

'I think not!'

'Well, you did. But now that I have got to know her—'

'That was quick work—'

'Well, I was always renowned for it, if you recall! As I was saying, now that I have met her, I realise that you were fair and far out in your description! I thought last night that she looked like the goddess Juno, and she reads philosophy—'

Lewis swore. He returned the decanter to the desk with a decided thump. 'The goddess Juno? When did you see this apparition, Richard?'

'Last night, old chap, like I said! She was coming out of the library! I introduced myself at once!' Richard smiled reminiscently. 'She had a book of Sophocles under her arm and her hair was loose with the firelight shining through—'

He broke off at the martial light in his friend's eye. 'Your pardon, Lewis! Sits the wind in that quarter then?'

There was a silence but for the crackling of the

fire. Lewis looked up and met his friend's quizzical gaze.

'I believe you said all that on purpose,' he said mildly.

Richard grinned. 'Devil a bit! I should be happy to be at Miss Whiston's feet!'

'Well, don't be!' Lewis's frown returned. 'I have plans—'

Richard raised his hand in a gesture of surrender.

'Point taken! No need to call me out! Now, do you remember Charles Drew? Served with you on the *Neptune* under Freemantle? He was in port last week and called to see me...'

Lewis sat back and allowed himself to be drawn into reminiscence, but half his mind was elsewhere. Richard's words had prompted him to think again about the events of the previous night, but it was Julia rather than Caroline Whiston who occupied his thoughts. Something in Julia's statements about his father had not rung true, but at the time he had not been able to work out exactly what it was. Now he remembered. Julia had claimed that the Admiral had intended to force her into marriage and that she had eloped with Jack Chessford through necessity. Yet in the letter that Caroline had accidentally left in the poetry book, Julia had made some reference to her marriage, and it had been couched in entirely different terms...

If only he had read more of it! If only he could see the others... Lewis imagined Caroline's reaction if he asked her to let him borrow them, and smothered a

smile. Then she would give him the rightabout and
no mistake! Yet he had to know, for if Julia were
telling the truth it would be one of the most painful
discoveries he could make, but if she was lying...

He thought of Caroline then, of the sweetness hidden beneath the severity. What had Richard said?
'Her hair was loose with the firelight shining
through...' Lewis shifted in his seat. Every so often
there would be a tantalising glimpse of that creature
of the woods that he had met on his first day home.
Deny it as she might, Caroline Whiston was an intriguing conundrum.

Caroline was having a peaceful afternoon. Earlier
that day, Julia had revealed a sudden need to travel
to Northampton for some goods that Abbot Quincey
could apparently not supply. Whether this sudden discovery had anything to do with Captain Slater's
avowed intent to visit the town Caroline could not be
sure, but certainly the Captain had declared himself
delighted to escort her. Caroline wondered whether
this was some ploy of Julia's to make Lewis jealous.
Certainly she could not believe that Julia had decided
to give up her pursuit of Lewis in favour of Richard
Slater, who had a comparatively small competence
and was decidedly less good-looking.

Caroline liked Captain Slater. He had a practical,
good-humoured nature and treated her with exactly
the same deference and charm as he did Lavender and
Julia. Sometimes there was a decided look of admiration in his eyes when he spoke to her, but Caroline

found that she was quite comfortable with this and that it did not disturb her in the same way that Lewis's perceptive regard was wont to do. Nevertheless, Caroline found herself hoping that Richard Slater would not fall prey to Julia's blandishments. The idea was a comical one in some ways—how many more of His Majesty's Navy needed protection against Julia's wiles?

Julia had only been gone a half-hour when Lady Perceval and her daughters and the Countess of Yardley came to call on Lavender. Caroline knew that it could only be coincidence that had brought them to Hewly as soon as Julia was absent, but she reflected that her erstwhile friend would fly up into the bows when she heard the news.

The January weather was unseasonably warm, almost springlike, and Caroline had decided to take a stroll along the Little Steep river. She climbed a stile in the hedge and jumped down the other side, enjoying the pale sunshine. Her mourning clothes were not very practical for walking and eventually she took off her bonnet and swung it by the strings, feeling rather like a young girl playing truant.

The path meandered along by the side of the river, which was narrow and deep at this point, running fast and brown with the recent thaw. Caroline rounded a bend, sheltered by coppiced willow, and stopped in surprise, for Lewis Brabant was sitting on the riverbank, his back against one of the trees. He had not seen her, for he was engrossed in his fishing, setting his line, his eyes narrowed with concentration.

Caroline watched him for a moment, undetected. As on that first evening at Hewly, she was struck by how much more relaxed he seemed in the freedom of the outdoors. When Lewis was inside the house it was almost as though there was some part of him that felt confined, held under forcible constraint. That was not to suggest that he did not look comfortable in the elegant drawing-rooms of society, for he had an easy assurance that would no doubt carry him through every situation. Despite that, however, Caroline thought he seemed happiest when he was not restrained by four walls.

She watched as he cast the line with one strong flick of the wrist then sat back against the tree. The fresh breeze ruffled his fair hair. Caroline felt as though a hand had squeezed her heart, then let her go, leaving her a little breathless. She made a slight, involuntary movement and Lewis looked up and saw her.

'Miss Whiston! Good afternoon, ma'am! Would you care to join me for a little?'

'Oh, pray do not get up, sir!' Caroline hurried forward to forestall him as he made to get to his feet. 'You will upset your line and you have just got it settled!'

Lewis subsided back against the tree trunk. 'I do believe that you have been watching me, ma'am,' he said slowly, his eyes travelling over her face with the searching intensity that made Caroline so aware of him. 'How long were you standing there?'

'A few moments only,' Caroline said hastily. 'I had

thought you at the Manor, entertaining your guests, sir!'

'I have left Lavender to do the honours,' Lewis said lazily, his eyes on the water. 'To tell the truth, Miss Whiston, drawing-room chatter holds little interest for me! A little conversation, to recognise the condescension of our noble visitors, and I was making my excuses! There is a short cut from Hewly gardens across the water meadows. It took me but a minute to reach this spot with my rod and line.'

'And now I have disturbed you,' Caroline said, making to walk on. 'I believe that fish dislike riverbank chatter as much as you dislike that of the drawing-room, sir!'

'Stay a moment,' Lewis said, gesturing to the rug spread out on the ground beside him. 'You need not speak to me! But it is pleasant to sit and watch the river run.'

After a moment's hesitation, Caroline sat down in the lee of a pollarded willow. The day was very quiet. Away in the distance she could see the roof of the Abbey, and she wondered idly what the Marquis of Sywell would do now that he was alone in all that splendour. The tale of the runaway wife had been the main gossip in the village for months now, with various wild stories circulating that the Marchioness had been gone for ages without anyone realising and, even more outrageous, that the Marquis had murdered her. Caroline sighed. Her own difficulties seemed to fade into insignificance when compared to the problems that would be faced by the Marquis's poor little wife.

Being alone in the world was a difficult business, as Caroline knew to her cost.

On the far side of the river a heron stood quite still in the shallows and a flock of woolly sheep grazed undisturbed. Lewis stretched, resting his fishing rod on a nearby stone.

'Sometimes it is pleasant to be still and think, is it not, Miss Whiston?'

'It is a luxury seldom allowed us,' Caroline agreed, with a little smile.

'Not everyone has the gift of silence,' Lewis said gravely, and for a moment Caroline wondered if he could be thinking of Julia. She turned her face away, feeling the faint sun warm her skin beneath the brim of her bonnet.

Lewis picked up a stone and idly skimmed it across the surface of the water.

'Miss Whiston, will you tell me something?' He hesitated. 'I wonder... Did Julia ever speak to you of her marriage?'

The question was sufficiently unexpected to make Caroline turn and look at him. He too was gazing out over the fields, his chin resting on his hand, some unreadable expression in his eyes. Caroline felt some of her contentment in the afternoon drain away.

'She wrote to me a little,' she said carefully. 'Why do you ask, sir?'

Lewis picked up the line again. 'I wondered if she had been happy,' he said.

Caroline bit her lip. Almost all her enjoyment of his company had now gone, since it seemed that

Lewis's only aim was to speak to her of Julia. She could have kicked herself for her folly in thinking that it could ever be otherwise.

'You would have to ask Mrs Chessford that yourself, sir,' she said, trying not to sound tart. 'I really have no idea. I believe that she enjoyed living in London and that Jack Chessford was an entertaining enough husband, but—'

'An entertaining husband...' Lewis mused. 'What do you consider would make a man such, Miss Whiston?'

Caroline set her lips in a thin line. Here was another of Lewis's strange, quixotic questions. She regretted ever making the remark.

'I have never needed to consider the matter, sir!' she said, not caring this time that she sounded sharp.

Lewis smiled at her suddenly and Caroline's heart gave a little erratic thump.

'Truly?' he asked. 'Well...' He shifted slightly. 'Tell me, Miss Whiston, have you kept all the letters that Julia sent you during your acquaintance?'

Caroline stared at him in amazement. She could not follow his train of thought at all.

'I believe so, sir. Again, I wonder at your enquiry!'

Lewis shifted again, as though he felt uncomfortable. 'Forgive me, Miss Whiston. This questioning must seem odd to you, I know, but there is a reason... I wondered if Julia had ever given the impression that she did not feel happy...safe...at Hewly?'

Caroline stared. Evidently there was more to Lewis's enquiries than a simple wish to learn all he could about his beloved's past, but she was at a loss to understand the reason for his questions.

'I never gained that impression from her writing,' she said, at length, 'but again I must urge you to apply to Mrs Chessford directly, sir.'

Lewis's gaze came back from some distant point and focused on her flushed face. He smiled at her again.

'You are quite right, of course, Miss Whiston! I should not have asked you. Forgive my importunity.'

Caroline made a slight gesture. She was quite at a loss. 'It was nothing, sir.'

Lewis got to his feet and started to reel in his line. 'The fish are not biting today. I fear the river runs too fast for them.' He looked down at her. 'Will you walk back with me, Miss Whiston, or do you prefer that I leave you to your solitude?'

Caroline stood up and dusted down her skirt. 'I will walk back. Twilight is closing in already.'

'I think we are in for a colder spell,' Lewis observed, his gaze going from the sliver of rising moon to the white mist that was starting to curl across the water meadows. 'I should not be surprised if it snows in a day or so!' He picked up his rod and line and fell into step beside her.

The path followed the river's course for a little way, then cut across the meadow and along the woodland edge until it reached the tumbledown wall that marked the border of the Hewly estate. Now that the sun had gone the air had a chill edge, and Caroline shivered a little as they made towards the lighted windows of the house.

'It will just be the two of us for dinner tonight, Miss Whiston,' Lewis said suddenly, as they passed beneath the old apple trees. 'I believe that Julia planned to stay overnight with the Mountfords in Northampton, for there is a concert and assembly she wishes to attend. Richard,' his gaze was sardonic, 'apparently remains there also, to escort her back on the morrow.'

Caroline cast a glance at his face. It was impossible to tell whether he was disturbed to think of Julia already entangling his friend in her schemes. The twilight was deepening now, the sky pure dark blue overhead, and it cast Lewis's face in shadow.

'And Miss Brabant?' she questioned hesitantly. 'Does she not dine with us?'

Lewis flashed her a grin. 'Lady Perceval was intent on carrying Lavender off to the Hall for a few days! Oh, I know it is soon after my father's death, but I thought it the very thing for Lavender to have a change of scene… When I was leaving earlier—' he indicated the fishing tackle '—she was about to write you a note. I know she hopes you will visit her at Perceval Hall, Miss Whiston, for she would not wish to lose your company…'

Caroline was silent, prey to mixed emotions. Julia and Richard Slater absent, Lavender at Perceval Hall… She remembered the ride back from Abbot Quincey and shivered a little. It did not seem wise to entrust herself to Lewis's company.

'So we shall be all alone, Miss Whiston,' Lewis said gently, holding the garden gate open for her with scrupulous politeness. 'I cannot tell you how much I look forward to it!'

Chapter Eight

'Beg pardon, ma'am,' the little housemaid said nervously, 'but the Master says that he is waiting for you to take dinner!'

Caroline closed her book with a decided snap. Since her encounter with Lewis earlier she had been beset by a number of feelings, none of them comfortable. She had puzzled over his questions about Julia's marriage and her letters, had fretted over the thought of dining alone with him, and had eventually sent him a message to say that she would not be joining him and would take her meal alone in her room. It now seemed, however, that Lewis was not prepared to accept that decision.

'Pray tell Captain Brabant that I shall not be joining him,' she said sharply. 'The Captain already knows that I have excused myself!'

The maidservant screwed her eyes up in an agony of embarrassment and anxiety. 'Beg pardon, ma'am,' she said again, 'but the Captain said to tell you—'

she gulped '—that if you will not go to him he will come up here and dine with you in your bedroom!'

Caroline slapped the book down on her bed and got to her feet. 'Very well, Rosie, I shall come down! Do not look so worried, child—it is none of your fault!'

'No, ma'am!' The servant girl dropped a grateful curtsey and sped out of the room. 'Thank you, ma'am!'

Caroline hastily drew her black silk shawl about her shoulders and swept downstairs before her anger and indignation could desert her. Her outrage carried her as far as the hall, wavered slightly as a blank-faced footman held the dining-room door for her, and almost failed her altogether when she saw Lewis Brabant standing by the window and looking out over the dark garden. He turned as she came in and sketched a bow.

'Good evening, Miss Whiston! Thank you for joining me!'

'Is it your practice to send your servants with impertinent messages, sir?' Caroline asked frigidly. 'I had already sent to tell you that I did not wish to partake of dinner—'

'No,' Lewis corrected her affably, 'you had sent to tell me that you did not wish to take dinner with me! That is different!'

He came around the table to hold a chair for her. Caroline sat down, glaring at him. 'Very well! If we are not to mince our words, sir, it is true that I preferred to dine alone!'

'Thank you for that clarification! Perhaps you would explain why?'

Caroline struggled a little. 'Because it is inappropriate, sir!'

'Inappropriate,' Lewis murmured. 'Pray, Miss Whiston, is that one of your favourite words?'

Caroline ignored him. 'It is inappropriate for us to dine together when your sister and Mrs Chessford are absent—'

She was forced to stop as the door opened to admit a footman with the soup. When they had been served and the footman moved to take his place by the sideboard, Lewis signalled to him to withdraw altogether. Caroline caught her breath. For all that Lewis had listened to her views, he had evidently decided to disregard her feelings! This latest piece of irregular behaviour would have tongues wagging in the servants' hall!

Caroline applied herself to the food in silence. Since her remonstrations had cut no ice, it seemed that this was the only way to show her disapproval. Lewis, however, did not seem particularly abashed, for his smile had a teasing edge to it.

'I cannot really believe that we are outraging the tenets of polite society,' he observed gently. 'No doubt we shall have some pleasant conversation by and by, once you have overcome your annoyance that I forced your hand!'

Caroline glared at him again. Under such provocation, she was fast forgetting that one of her guiding principles was a cool and rational approach to all situations.

'You do not understand, sir,' she said coldly. 'You seem to enjoy deliberately flouting propriety! A governess companion should not—' She broke off again as the footman returned to remove the plates, and there was a heavy silence.

They were served with roast beef, and once again Lewis suggested that the man withdraw, adding a few words that were too low for Caroline to hear. When the door had closed behind him, Lewis looked at her and raised his eyebrows enquiringly.

'A companion should not—what—Miss Whiston?'

Caroline shot him a disapproving look. 'This is a waste of time, sir! You are clearly deaf to all pleas of respectability! I shall save my breath!'

'Ah, that argues a very practical mind! Why waste your time and energy on a lost cause?'

'That describes you very well, Captain!' Caroline agreed crossly. 'Determined, wilful—'

'Once again, I feel like one of your naughty charges, ma'am,' Lewis murmured. 'Do you also let them do as they please?'

'Certainly not!' Caroline frowned. 'I hope that they would be more conformable than you, Captain!'

Lewis laughed. He got up to pour her another glass of wine. 'I have certainly had longer to practise disobedience! But let us avoid such inflammatory topics! Tell me a little of the subjects you teach, ma'am.'

Caroline looked at him suspiciously. Surely no one was ever interested in the details of a governess's life?

'Oh, I teach all sorts of things!' she said. 'Languages and geography and music and drawing. If my charges cannot make landscapes in cut paper and embroider their own counterpanes and cushions, I feel I have failed at my task!'

'Landscapes in cut paper... You must be very accomplished yourself to be able to teach such things, Miss Whiston,' Lewis commented. 'But with Mrs Guarding's excellent schooling behind you...'

'Yes, indeed, I was most fortunate not to be turned out into the world without an education!' Caroline agreed with a slight smile.

'Yet there must be plenty of ill-educated governesses in the world, passing on their own ignorance!' Lewis observed, refilling her wine glass.

'Well, that is a little harsh,' Caroline found that she was laughing, 'but certainly there are those who struggle. And their charges are not always biddable girls!'

The conversation moved imperceptibly on to geography, then to history and politics, with Caroline lowering her guard as she realised that Lewis had a genuine interest in discussing such matters with her, as well as a well-informed mind. She found herself expressing her own views with an openness that was far from her usual demeanour.

When the footman finally returned to serve the dessert, Caroline realised that they had indeed been talking for a long time. She bit her lip. To relax into the intimacy of the situation, to find Lewis's company attractive and stimulating, would be a vast mistake. She refused the pudding course a little abruptly and

hoped that Lewis would take the hint and go off to
drink his port, allowing her to escape.

Lewis was frowning a little, as though he were
aware of her withdrawal. 'I shall not desert you for
the pleasure of the port,' he said, almost as though he
had read her mind, 'for then I know you would run
away! Pray come into the drawing-room for a little,
Miss Whiston!'

Caroline hesitated. Lewis was coming round the
table towards her and she suddenly felt a lot less sure
of herself. With acres of polished wood between them
she had not been so disturbed by his proximity, but
now... He took her elbow in a firm grasp and
Caroline felt a flicker of awareness ripple through her.

'I do not believe that would be quite—'

'Appropriate?' Lewis slanted a look at her.

'Suitable,' Caroline amended. She made a gesture
of appeal. 'I am your cousin's companion, sir! Neither
she nor your sister are at home, so...'

'So you said before! Am I to fear for my reputation? Is that it?'

Caroline looked reproachful. 'You may mock, sir!'

'Upon my honour, I intended to do no such thing!
Is it not possible to be compromised by a governess
companion? I could certainly try...'

'I scarce think so, sir,' Caroline said crossly.
'Though the reverse is undoubtedly true! Which is
why I must have a care for my own reputation!
Indeed, I am thinking of leaving Hewly shortly. Now
that Miss Brabant is so well cared for, I feel free to
take up another post.'

Lewis turned towards her, an arrested look in his eyes. His levity seemed forgotten.

'Must you go quite yet, Miss Whiston?'

'Well...' Caroline could feel a blush rising, 'I have the chance of a new position and I did plan...' She broke off, unwilling to refer back to the unhappy business of Julia's spiteful meddling.

'I suppose there is nothing to keep you here.' Lewis's voice was suddenly expressionless.

'Mrs Chessford does not really need a companion,' Caroline said, a little desperately, 'and you know that she and I do not really suit! I am sure that she has been very upset by the Admiral's death, but I cannot really offer her the solace she needs! She requires amusement and distraction, not someone to write her letters for her! And a change of scene would be useful— It must have been horrible for Julia that the Admiral was taken ill so soon after she arrived—'

Caroline stopped rambling, aware that Lewis's eyes had narrowed suddenly on her face. He had listened in silence as she had rattled on and somehow his intent gaze had made her chatter all the more, but now she fell silent as Lewis frowned.

'After she arrived, Miss Whiston? But surely Julia came to Hewly in response to my father's illness rather than before it!'

'Oh, no.' It was Caroline's turn to frown now. 'Nanny Prior told me that when Julia arrived, the Admiral was quite well! It was a few hours later that—' She broke off as she saw the flash of some extraordinary expression in Lewis's eyes. 'Why, what have I said, sir?'

Lewis was shaking his head slowly. 'Nothing, Miss Whiston. I am persuaded...' He touched her hand briefly, sending another shiver along Caroline's nerve endings. 'I wonder what else you know, however...'

For a moment his gaze searched Caroline's puzzled face. She forced herself to keep still beneath his scrutiny.

'About what, sir?' she asked coolly.

Lewis laughed. 'Pity me that I cannot ask you what is in my heart!' he said enigmatically. 'One thing I can ask you, however, Miss Whiston.'

Caroline raised her eyebrows enquiringly. 'Yes, sir?'

There was suddenly a spark of devilment deep in Lewis's blue eyes. Caroline's heart missed a beat.

'There is one thing that I envy my sister for, Miss Whiston,' he said slowly, 'and that is her friendliness with you where I must be formal—as you perceive, ma'am. May I not have a like privilege and address you by your name?'

'Oh!' Caroline pressed her hand to her throat. She remembered the caressing way in which Lewis had said her name on previous occasions, remembered suddenly the heat of his body against hers, the gentleness of his hands, the touch of his mouth... He had taken what he had wanted before. Now he was asking, but even so...

She moved away from him. 'No, Captain Brabant.

As I shall be leaving Hewly soon there is no necessity, and even were I to stay, that would be—'

'Inappropriate?' Lewis had followed her to the door. He did not touch her but to Caroline's overstretched nerves the caressing effect of his voice was almost the same. 'Unsuitable?'

He put a hand on her arm as she made to escape.

'One day, Caroline,' he said, very softly, 'you will admit that under your very proper exterior is a most *inappropriate* governess. But until then—' he gave her a mocking bow '—I shall continue to address you as Miss Whiston. Goodnight, ma'am!'

He turned away and Caroline, regaining the use of her limbs, hurried out of the drawing-room and away to safety, without even waiting for a candle to light her way.

Caroline sat darning her second-best pair of black gloves and wondering what was to be done. She had spent another night tossing and turning, and for one who prided herself on sound sleep this was a dire sign indeed. The cause of her disturbance was, of course, Lewis Brabant, who had behaved in such an altogether quixotic and disconcerting manner the previous evening. It seemed unfair to Caroline that Lewis had immediately perceived the contradictions in her character that she had successfully kept concealed for the whole of her adult life. He had swiftly seen that there were two Caroline Whistons; the staid governess companion who wore the grey worsted and acted so properly, and the free spirit who read poetry and dreamed of romance. Except that the free spirit was not truly free, for it had always been subject to the practical aspects of earning an unromantic crust. The sober lady's companion had always had the upper hand.

Caroline's thread snapped and she bit back an unladylike epithet. She knew it was her own fault, as she had been taking out her ill temper on the inoffensive darning. Casting it aside, she went over to the window. Her room was at the back of the house and had a view across the walled gardens to the rolling Northamptonshire countryside beyond. She could see two of the maids shaking out a blanket on the terrace below, and away down the gardens, Belton and Lewis Brabant were deep in conversation as they inspected the walls in the old rose arbour. Caroline sighed. It was pointless to wonder what quality had drawn her to Lewis in such a wholly inappropriate manner. Perhaps it was the contradictions in his own nature that had sparked such recognition in her. The authoritative man of action who was also dangerously perceptive… She shivered and drew back from the window, almost as though she thought her regard would draw his gaze.

Mrs Guarding had always said that action was the best cure for the blue devils, so Caroline took up her cloak and set out. She took care to avoid the gardens, walking down the path to the orchard and out on to the lane. It was a bright, frosty winter's day and her heart lifted a little with every step. She decided to make some calls.

Her first stop was the Guarding Academy itself. When Caroline had first returned to Steep Abbot, she had visited the school and had been made most welcome by Mrs Guarding. Her former teacher had delicately made no open reference to Caroline's change in circumstances but had chatted about the changes at the school and the activities of some of the other girls Caroline had known. She had returned to Hewly Manor with an open invitation to visit whenever she wished, but she had not taken this up, perhaps because the school held so many memories for her. When she had first thought of leaving the Manor she had considered Mrs Guarding as a possible employer, but now she knew that that would never serve. The school was far too close to Hewly and therefore to Lewis, and the thought of Julia holding court nearby as Mrs Lewis Brabant was more than Caroline's nature could take.

She rang the bell and discovered that Mrs Guarding was away, but received a very warm welcome from Miss Henrietta Mason, the history teacher. Caroline stayed for a cup of tea and enjoyed a long chat on the trials of trying to imbue young ladies with an interest in history and geography, which seemed to be the same whether taught in a private house or a forward-looking school. She finally left with a promise to visit Miss Mason again soon, and took the track towards Abbot Quincey.

Caroline turned aside from the road at Perceval Hall, as she had letters and messages for Lavender. She had not been intending to stay, but found herself invited to join the ladies in the saloon, and soon they were all chatting like old friends. After a while, Lavender suggested that Caroline accompany her to the church to lay a wreath on the Admiral's grave.

'I hope you do not feel my desertion too keenly, Caroline!' Lavender said as they walked along. 'Lady Perceval suggested that I should invite you to join me here, and if it were not for Julia—' She broke off. 'I am sorry. My tongue runs away with me when I speak of her! Tell me, has she prevailed upon Captain Slater to elope yet?'

Caroline gave her a reproving look that was marred by the twinkle in her eye. 'Lavender! You know you may well be speaking of your future sister-in-law!'

'I know it!' Lavender said gloomily. 'The whole neighbourhood knows it! I have been quizzed on little else!'

They let themselves in through the lychgate and walked slowly up the path to the quiet corner plot. There was a simple headstone and the grave still looked freshly turned. Caroline cast an anxious look at Lavender, but the younger girl, although pale, appeared composed. She bent to put her circlet of berries and winter green on the dark earth.

'There!' She stood back. 'I miss father so much, you know, Caroline! It is odd, for we spoke little and then not on matters of any great import, but I knew that if I ever needed his help, he would be there. He was a good man.' She sighed.

'I am sure that your brother can perform such an

office for you now,' Caroline urged, anxious to comfort. 'He has the same integrity.'

There was a pause. Lavender's blue eyes searched Caroline's face. Her own was troubled. 'I am sure that you are correct, Caroline, but it is not so easy…' She did not need to mention Julia's name again but it hung in the air between them. Then Lavender brushed the stray soil from her gloves and turned away.

'I think that father would have liked you,' she said conversationally. 'He always admired spirit!'

Caroline laughed, despite herself. 'I am scarcely spirited, Lavender! A governess cannot afford such luxuries of temperament! I must efface myself and creep about, quiet as a mouse!'

Now it was Lavender's turn to laugh. She wrinkled up her nose. 'Fustian to that, Caroline! What could be more spirited than having to go out into the world and earn a living? I do not mean spirit in the sense of wilfulness, but I believe you have true courage!'

Caroline was touched and sought to turn attention away from herself. 'I wonder how the Marchioness of Sywell fares, poor creature!' she said lightly. 'She must have had a strange time of it, with no friends either before or after her marriage—'

'Oh, Louise had a friend—' Lavender began, then broke off, the colour rushing into her face. Caroline watched in puzzlement, wondering if Lavender had been about to imply that the Marchioness had run away with a man, but after a moment, Lavender said, in a rush, 'It's just that I saw her several times speaking to Athene Filmer, who lives with her mother in

Steep Ride. I believe they were firm friends.' She shot
Caroline a shamefaced look. 'There has always been
much gossip about Louise Hanslope, I believe, but I
never gave it credence! To suggest that she was the
bailiff's natural daughter was quite foolish and the
tales going about now are even worse! I hate that sort
of spite!' She took a deep breath. 'Oh, I am sorry,
Caroline! I am sure you were not expecting a sermon
from me!'

Caroline was intrigued and a little amused at
Lavender's defence of the mysterious Louise. Perhaps
it was that Lavender felt that both she and Louise
were different, neither fitting comfortably into a conventional society. Certainly, Caroline could see that
Lavender, with her honesty and lack of artifice, would
find hurtful gossip to be nothing but malicious. The
thought inevitably made Caroline see how difficult it
would be for Lavender to live with Julia for any
length of time, and they both made their way back to
the lychgate with slow steps.

It was dusk by the time Caroline left Lavender at
Perceval Hall, with her friend promising to return to
Hewly within the week. Lady Perceval pressed her to
take the carriage home, remarking that the January
afternoons were short and that darkness could come
up very quickly. Caroline thanked her and reassured
her that there was plenty of time, and armed with a
basket full of eggs, fresh churned butter and a loaf of
bread that was still warm, she started to make her way
back to Hewly through the twilight.

The moon was climbing up through the trees and

Caroline drew her cloak closer about her. It was cold, far colder than it had been the previous night, and she thought that predictions of another snowfall could well be true. She began to wish that she had accepted the carriage after all. It was dark under the trees, and although she had strong nerves Caroline jumped a little at the strange rustlings of the undergrowth. She knew that she was almost back at the Hewly estate, but when she saw the flicker of faint lights in the woods up ahead, she froze in near panic. The lights dodged between the trees, glimmering in the darkness as though in some unearthly dance. Caroline inconveniently began to remember all the folk stories she had read about the countryside round and about the Manor, the tales of spirits in the woods, the story of the grey lady…

Abruptly she turned and plunged through the undergrowth, seeking the edge of the wood, and resolved to run across the open fields if she had to. She had barely gone thirty yards when the trees ended and she found herself on a rough track beside a high hawthorn hedge. Panting a little, she leant against a field gate to get her breath back, and jumped a mile when an unmistakable voice said, 'I had no idea that you favoured such strenuous exercise, Miss Whiston! Dashing about in the woods at dusk! You are fortunate that I did not shoot you by accident!'

'Captain Brabant!' Caroline drew herself up and tried to catch her breath. She was not sure whether she was glad or annoyed to be caught out in such a situation. 'Shooting in the dark does not sound a very sensible occupation!'

Lewis Brabant laughed. He let himself through the gate and stood beside her, his shotgun across his arm. 'Do you seek to reproach me, Miss Whiston? Running around on your own is an even less sensible occupation and certainly not an appropriate one!'

'I thought I saw some lights in the wood—' Caroline began, to break off as Lewis's hand closed firmly about her wrist.

'Miss Whiston, come closer to me—'

'What on earth—' Caroline stopped as he drew her deep into the shelter of the hedge. The sharp spikes of hawthorn prickled through her cloak, but still he pulled her deeper into the shadow. And then there was a step on the road, the sound of muffled voices, the rustle of leaves as the wind passed by, and they were left in silence once more.

Caroline realised that she had been holding her breath. She noticed in the same moment that she was pressed against the whole length of Lewis's body, and stepped away hastily. 'What...who...what was that?'

'Poachers,' Lewis said softly, unlatching the gate with the softest of clicks. 'This way, Miss Whiston, and quickly. You can only just have missed them.'

He took her hand and pulled her quickly across the field, so that Caroline was almost running again in the effort to keep up. It was only when they reached a stile on the opposite side and tumbled down into the road that ran by the school that he allowed his pace to slacken.

'I don't understand,' Caroline said, a little breath-lessly, as she followed Lewis through the gateway into the Manor stable yard. 'You had a gun—surely if you had challenged them—'

Lewis gave her a look that silenced her. His voice was low and angry. 'Do you think that I would have dreamed of challenging a gang of poachers when I had you to protect, Miss Whiston? Of all the fool-hardy actions... Please consider what might have hap-pened if you had stumbled on them alone during your wanderings in the wood, and promise me that you will not indulge in such reckless behaviour again!'

Caroline knew that he was right but for some rea-son it grated on her to admit it. 'I am not reckless! I always behave appropriately—'

Lewis flashed her a look of mingled irritation and contempt. 'Oh, spare me the denials! You have no more idea how to go on than an infant in arms! The truth is that you are so bored with your circumscribed life that you get into danger through most unseemly behaviour!'

Caroline glared at him, furious now. 'How dare you so criticise me, sir! At least I have the good manners to know that it is not fitting to argue in public!'

'Then let us step inside,' Lewis said with biting sarcasm, 'so that I may quarrel with you in private! Your conduct is not only improper, Miss Whiston, but downright dangerous—'

One of the stable doors opened and a groom came out into the yard. Caroline bit back an angry retort and waited whilst Lewis handed the gun over and exchanged a few words. She toyed with the idea of leaving him there and stalking off into the house, but there was something in Lewis's demeanour that suggested he would probably deal with her in a summary and unbecoming manner were she to do so.

'I see that Mrs Chessford and Captain Slater have returned,' she said tightly, nodding towards the carriage that was standing waiting to be put away. 'At least we may have some congenial company at dinner!'

'I will allow you to exchange my unwelcome presence for Richard's more agreeable company shortly,' Lewis said, as stiffly as she, 'but not until I have your promise, Miss Whiston. You are too precipitate. You will not go wandering off alone again—'

Caroline felt as though she was going to burst with anger. She started to walk away towards the house. Lewis caught her arm.

'Miss Whiston!'

Caroline was appalled to find that there were tears in her eyes. She had no idea how they could have reached such a pitch of conflict. She had spent her working life soothing the sensibilities of others and it should have been easy to efface herself, give her word, dismiss the quarrel as unimportant. Yet as she looked up into Lewis's angry face, all she wanted to do was to hurt him.

'You are not my employer, to constrain me so—'

Lewis's brows snapped together. 'No, I am not, as you were so good to remind me once before! Yet I must also remind you, Miss Whiston, that Hewly is my house and whilst you are under my roof you will submit to my instructions! Now, your word—'

'Oh, you have it, sir!' Caroline snatched her arm from his grasp. 'Though why it could possibly matter—' She felt a sob rise in her throat and broke off. 'And you need have no fear for my safety! Once I am gone from Hewly I shall be no more of your concern!'

She turned on her heel and walked off, and though she did not look back, she had the disconcerting feeling that Lewis was watching her all the way to the house.

It was largely due to Richard Slater's presence that dinner was so pleasant an experience. Caroline had been dreading having to face Lewis again, but she found that he was perfectly civil to her. His manner was distant and he allowed Julia to monopolise his attention, suggesting to Caroline that he had already dismissed their quarrel from his mind. Richard, by contrast, gave her an amusing summary of the trip to Northampton, asked her opinion on the Luddite riots that were causing so much trouble in towns and cities further north, and engaged her in a lively debate on the merits of the poems of Samuel Taylor Coleridge.

'Lud, poetry!' Julia yawned, when the discussion had finally come to a close. 'What a pity Lavender is not here to converse with you both! She is a frighteningly accomplished young woman!' She smiled at Lewis. ''Tis a shame we cannot have any music, though I suppose with dear Uncle Harley so recently passed on... When do you expect Churchward to be here for the reading of the will, Lewis?'

'In a few days, I imagine.' Lewis reached over to pull the bell. 'He writes that he has been delayed by the unfortunate death of Lord Nantwich.'

'Oh yes,' Julia looked animated. 'Did he not die in a carriage accident with his mistress, whilst on the way to visit the family of his affianced bride? The *on dit* is that he had intended to install the woman in a local hostelry and visit her every evening! Why, did you know that...'

Caroline turned away and closed her ears to the gossip. It was an interesting fact that Julia had often declared herself to have forgotten everything she had ever learned at Mrs Guarding's school, yet she maintained an encyclopedic knowledge of scandal.

They all retired early. Julia declared herself fatigued by the journey from Northampton, then insisted on having Caroline's company in her room and chattered endlessly about Lewis and Richard Slater and which of them was the better prospect.

'For though Lewis is better-looking, Richard is more gallant! I find that Lewis has an odd, ironical way with him sometimes! But then there is the estate, for Lewis is quite a rich man, you know, and I have not been able to ascertain Richard's fortune...'

Caroline had a decided headache by the time that she escaped to her bedroom. She sat down on the bed with a sigh and rubbed her aching temples. The room looked very cosy, with the fire burning bright and the candlelight concealing the worn patches in the rugs and curtains. There had been none of Julia's home improvements here. Caroline reached up to unpin her hair, and at the same moment her eye caught a scrap of white protruding from under the bed. She bent down curiously and saw that it was the corner of a letter.

Dropping to her knees, Caroline lifted the bedspread and pulled out the old trunk that contained her keepsakes and letters. Her grandfather's watch was still there, as was the locket left to her by her mother and the other little bits and pieces she had accumulated over the years. But there was nothing else. Where previously there had been bundles of letters tied with ribbon, now there was an empty space. Julia's letters to her had all disappeared.

Caroline stared in disbelief and mounting anger, going down on her knees again and peering under the bed. There was no mistake. All the letters had vanished. She sat back on her heels and surveyed the room for signs of disturbance, but there were none. That, and the fact that the letters were all that was missing, suggested that the thief had known exactly what he was looking for.

Caroline got to her feet slowly. She did not wish to believe it, but there could be very little doubt that it was Lewis Brabant who had stolen them, and as she thought about it her fury started to grow. Lewis was the only one who knew about the letters, for he had found the one in the book and quizzed her about it. Then he had asked her about them again, only a few days ago. She had refused to discuss Julia's correspondence and had foolishly believed that he had accepted her decision, but it seemed not, and now she would have to confront him about it...

Caroline glanced at the clock and acknowledged that it would be the height of folly to beard Lewis in his room at this hour. The last time she had encountered him late at night, the consequences had been extreme. The matter would have to wait until the morning.

Unfortunately that gave her too long to dwell on the situation. She tossed and turned all night, and by the time the morning came she was equally full of apprehension and anger. She knew that she did not look her best, for her face was drawn from both strain and lack of sleep, and she would have done anything to put off the confrontation. However, she knew it would not serve. She had to see Lewis at once.

She found him in the library, apparently discussing horseflesh with Richard Slater. Captain Slater took one look at Caroline's face and made a hasty excuse.

'Well, I shall go directly to the stables and see what I think, Lewis. Perhaps you will join me later. Good morning, Miss Whiston...'

Alone with Lewis in the unnerving silence, Caroline found her apprehension growing rather than diminishing. Lewis gave her a cool smile that reminded her of their previous quarrel and Caroline's heart sank even further. This was going to be very difficult.

'Well, Miss Whiston? What can I do for you?'

'I have come to ask you to give me my letters back,' Caroline said, in a rush. She could feel the colour rising to her face. 'I must insist, Captain—they are my property and should never have been taken!'

Lewis' smile was fading. 'I beg your pardon, Miss Whiston? To what do you refer?'

'You know full well!' Caroline's overstretched nerves found relief in anger. 'You know that I kept all of Julia's letters over the years—you saw one yourself! Do you deny it?'

'Of course I do not deny it,' Lewis said reasonably, frowning a little. 'Forgive me, Miss Whiston, but I fear I am confused. What has happened to the letters?'

'Oh, do not seek to gammon me!' Caroline snapped. 'The letters have been stolen! I refused to tell you about their contents so you took them yourself! It is obvious who is the culprit!'

There was a silence, but for the ticking of the long-case clock. Lewis' eyes had narrowed. He rested both hands flat on the table and leaned towards her. His voice was very level. 'A moment, Miss Whiston. Do I understand that you are accusing me of theft?'

'What other explanation is there?' Caroline stared at him. 'You were the only one who knew about the letters! You asked me about their contents and I refused to tell you! So—'

'So you think that I went creeping about my own home to wrest from you that which you would not give willingly?' Lewis straightened up and drove his hands into his jacket pockets. With a queer jump of the heart, Caroline realised that he was very angry and that this was different from their quarrel the previous day. He was looking at her with disgust.

Caroline backed away, feeling suddenly intimidated, but Lewis reached her side in two strides and put his hand out.

'Do not hurry away, Miss Whiston! We have not finished discussing this yet!' He pulled her around to face him, his blue eyes hard with dislike. 'We had just reached the interesting subject of your opinion of me! Unscrupulous, devious and a thief, I infer!'

'I...' Caroline faltered. It had not occurred to her previously that she might have made a mistake. It had seemed so obvious; Lewis had wanted the letters, the letters had disappeared and therefore he must have taken them. Part of her anger, she realised now, had sprung from her disappointment in him. She had believed him principled and honourable, only to find that he had stooped to subterfuge and stealing. Or so she had thought. She had acted impulsively, and now it seemed that she might have made a dreadful error...

'I will not waste my time in protesting my innocence,' Lewis was saying coldly. 'If that is your opinion—'

'What else was I to think?' Caroline asked desperately, stepping back and spreading her hands in a gesture of despair. 'You wanted those letters—and they have gone! Someone must have taken them!'

For a long moment Lewis stared down into her face. 'Not merely anyone, Miss Whiston! You believed that I, myself...' He broke off, shaking his head. 'Well, I would restore your letters to you if I had them, but I fear I do not!'

He turned away and strode across the room. Caroline hurried after him.

'I am sorry if I have made a mistake.' She put her hand tentatively on his arm and felt the tense anger in him. She was only slightly encouraged that he did not immediately shake her off. 'I will not seek to make excuses. It was wrong of me to doubt you—'

Lewis turned to look at her. The coldness and dislike were still plain in his eyes. 'Pray do not apologise, Miss Whiston! I thought I had your good opinion, but it seems I was mistaken! Now, I have business to attend to. Good day to you!'

And he went out, leaving the air still humming with his anger.

Chapter Nine

Mr Churchward, of the eminent London lawyers of the same name, arrived that same evening, just before dusk. Lewis sent a messenger to Perceval Hall to acquaint Lavender with the news, and the official reading of the will was set to take place the following morning.

In the meantime, Mr Churchward requested a few private words and Lewis steered him into the study to take a glass of port. If the news of his inheritance was bad, he felt that the lawyer would probably need a stiff drink even more than he would.

They settled in the wing chairs before the fire, but Lewis had noted at once that the lawyer could not be content with small talk, for he fidgeted with the clasp of his document case and rustled his papers at frequent intervals. Recognising these signs of agitation, Lewis decided to cut to the chase.

'Well, Churchward, it seems there are certain matters causing you concern. Would you care to enlighten me?'

The lawyer cleared his throat portentously. 'Thank you, Captain Brabant. There are a number of issues that are a trifle irregular...'

Lewis passed him a glass of port and raised an eyebrow expectantly. 'Yes, Churchward? I must say that you do surprise me. Of all the things my father was, *irregular* could hardly be described as one of them...'

Mr Churchward regarded him with mournful eyes. 'One never can tell, Captain.' He shook his head slowly. 'It is not that the Admiral's affairs are not in order, simply that some of his requests are somewhat quixotic...'

Lewis smiled ruefully. 'It is a character trait I share, sir. Pray do not spare me—let us get straight to business. What are these irregular conditions to which you refer?'

Mr Churchward cleared his throat again and extracted a sheet of paper from the pile. He placed his glasses on the end of his nose. 'Well, sir. The Admiral's will is relatively straightforward, given the fact that the estate is not entailed and there are only a small number of beneficiaries. He altered his will after the untimely death of your brother, of course.'

Churchward paused for a suitably respectful moment.

Lewis nodded briskly. 'Understood, Churchward.'

'You are to inherit the estate of Hewly and the bulk of the Admiral's fortune,' Churchward continued. He gave a small, dry smile. 'The Admiral has made some sound investments over the years, sir. You are to be congratulated.'

Lewis inclined his head. 'Thank you, Churchward. Fortune has favoured the Brabant family, although fate has exacted a high cost with my brother's death.'

Mr Churchward assumed an expression of dolefulness. 'Indeed, sir. The inheritance is not entirely straightforward, however. It is contingent upon two facts, but it is perhaps preferable that we deal with other matters before coming to those. Now, there are the usual bequests to servants and retainers, of course, and two additional beneficiaries.'

'My sister and my father's ward?'

'Precisely so.' Again a hint of uneasiness seemed to enter Churchward's demeanour. He had not touched his port. Lewis noted his discomfiture and wondered. He leant back in his chair and waited in silence.

'Your sister Miss Lavender Brabant is given a dowry of ten thousand pounds. If she has not married by the age of twenty-five the money reverts to her absolutely.'

Lewis raised his brows. 'Very enlightened of my father! There are no other stipulations attached?'

'None whatsoever, sir.' Churchward shuffled his papers again, then looked him straight in the eye. 'Now your father's ward, Mrs Chessford. She inherits the sum of one thousand pounds.'

Lewis pursed his lips in a soundless whistle. That was scarcely enough to keep Julia in the style to which she aspired and he knew she would be deeply disappointed. The Admiral had been both godfather and guardian to her and he was a rich man. She could justifiably have expected more. Lewis shifted a little uncomfortably, remembering the unpalatable story that Julia had told him about his father's behaviour. If the Admiral had proposed to Julia and she had rejected him, this looked very much like a spiteful revenge...

'The bequest is smaller than I had anticipated,' he said carefully. 'Did my father give any reason why he should leave his ward so small a legacy?'

Mr Churchward fidgeted a little. He was looking at his most dry and formal, an expression which gave Lewis to think that even had the Admiral explained at great length, his lawyer was not about to share that with him.

'No, Captain, not precisely. I believe,' Mr Churchward wetted his lips with the port, 'that he felt that Mrs Chessford had a large enough fortune of her own. That is, she did before—' Mr Churchward made a vague gesture and Lewis understood what he meant. Julia had had a substantial fortune of her own before she and Jack Chessford had squandered it about Town. Lewis had heard the rumours and perhaps his father had too.

'I had mentioned that the Admiral changed his will in your favour after your brother's death,' Churchward said dryly. 'It was at this time that he also made a change to Mrs Chessford's legacy. Before that the figure had been...ah...considerably larger.'

Lewis sighed and rested his chin on his hand. The

difficulty was that all actions were open to interpretation when one of the parties was dead and could not therefore state his side of the case. The Admiral had disapproved of Julia's behaviour for one reason or another... Lewis became aware that Churchward's eyes were fixed on his face in the manner of one who has some further, even less appealing news to relate.

'The two contingencies, sir...' The lawyer murmured.

'Oh, of course.' Lewis drained his glass of port and sat back. 'My inheritance is dependent upon two factors. Pray tell me, Mr Churchward...'

Churchward looked gratified at this businesslike request.

'Of course, sir. Your father made the following stipulations. Firstly that you should marry within a twelvemonth of coming into the estate. The Admiral said—' He cleared his throat and quoted: 'There should be no long faces and foolish fussing over mourning. The boy—yourself, I believe, sir—should settle down, marry and produce an heir...'

Churchward broke off at Lewis's crack of laughter.

'I suppose I should just be grateful that my father did not make the inheritance contingent upon the heir as well! Or was that his second criterion?'

'No, sir,' the lawyer said primly. 'The Admiral specified marriage within the year but the heir was—'

'An additional benefit rather than a requirement? Thank you, father!' Lewis raised his glass in mocking toast. 'So, the second stipulation...'

'Was that you should *not* marry your father's ward,

Mrs Chessford,' the lawyer finished. 'In point of fact, the Admiral stated that he could not prevent such a marriage, but if you should do so, the estate would be forfeit and would pass to your sister.'

This time there was a silence. Lewis refilled his glass, taking his time. 'But that is outrageous,' he said quietly, after a moment. 'If I wish to marry Julia—'

'You will lose your inheritance. Yes, Captain, that is precisely the case.'

Lewis ran a hand through his hair. 'But why—'

Mr Churchward had assumed his favourite sympathetic expression, the one reserved for the breaking of bad news.

'I am sorry, sir. Your father was most insistent.'

'And he gave no reason?'

'No, indeed. He gave no reason at all.'

Lewis raised his head. 'I see. Then there is no more to be said, Mr Churchward. You will, of course, be obliged to disclose all of these facts tomorrow?'

The lawyer nodded slowly. 'I will, Captain. You will understand now why I wished you to be apprised of them in advance?'

Lewis nodded absently. 'Yes, Churchward, I thank you for the warning.' He stood up. 'I need some time to think. Now do you care to join the others, sir, or would you prefer to retire? After your long journey…'

The lawyer took the hint. 'Yes, Captain,' he said quietly, 'I think that would be for the best.'

'How could he be so cruel!' Julia wailed piteously, shredding her delicate handkerchief to strips and fixing Caroline with her desolate blue eyes. 'Why, I cared for Uncle Harley like a daughter and how does he repay me? By leaving me next to nothing and separating me from the only man I ever loved!'

Caroline reflected that it was the first time she had ever seen Julia cry real tears. At school Julia had always been able to cry on order if she needed to render a teacher more sympathetic, but she was seldom genuinely upset. Now, of course, she had been denied the two things she wanted most in the world and two huge drops were rolling down her cheeks towards her quivering lips. She dabbed at them ineffectually.

'It is so unjust of him! The money is bad enough—how shall I manage now!—but to be torn apart from Lewis is too cruel!' She peeked at Caroline. 'We had talked a little of the future and both of us knew how we wished it to be. Oh, of course, Lewis could make no formal declaration, with Uncle Harley's death and matters so uncertain, but now!' She gave a sob. 'We have waited so long, and now it is never to be!'

'Perhaps Captain Brabant will disregard his father's wishes if his feelings are so strong,' Caroline said, feeling the words stick in her throat. She had no wish to dwell on the thought, but it seemed possible that Lewis would renounce his inheritance for Julia if he truly loved her. He was not the man to be dictated to or to be tied by worldly considerations. 'Besides, the Captain has his own fortune and need not be dependent on his inheritance—'

'Oh…' Julia sighed heavily. 'I could not ask Lewis to make such a sacrifice. To choose between his love and his duty—no man should be so obliged! Besides, Lewis has money of his own but it is nothing compared to the Hewly estate and fortune! He would be obliged to work for a living!' She wrinkled up her nose. 'Oh, how dreadful! No, I have decided that I shall go away! It is the only solution!' She caught Caroline's sleeve. 'Dearest Caro, you will come with me, shall you not? We shall live in a cottage together and it shall be delightful…'

Caroline could think of little that was less appealing. To hear Julia bemoaning her lack of funds when a thousand pounds was more than she could earn in a lifetime was particularly galling.

'I have to earn a living, Julia…' she temporised, 'and I doubt that you could bear the expense of a companion now—'

Julia patted her hand. 'Well, but I have a little to share! And we are *friends*… My mind is made up! We shall leave Hewly in a few days' time! Now—' she cast her handkerchief aside '—pray send Letty to me, for I must organise my portmanteaux! I will call you in a little, Caroline, to write my letters for me!'

Caroline went downstairs to find that Lavender was just bidding farewell to Mr Churchward. She turned with relief as Caroline came up and closed the heavy outside door.

'Caroline! Thank goodness! Will you take tea with me? I need someone to talk to!' She looked closely at Caroline's face. 'Dear me, perhaps you need a confidante too!'

They settled in the drawing-room with Lavender presiding over the silver pot.

'Lewis and Captain Slater have gone out for a ride,' Lavender said, stirring the tea. 'Poor Lewis, I think he wished to escape for a little! And really, it is monstrous of father to have behaved so, though I cannot but be glad!' She poured tea daintily into the two china cups. 'I confess myself puzzled, however. Why should father do such a thing? I know he did not approve of Julia hanging out for Andrew, but that is scarcely enough...' Her voice trailed away in puzzlement.

Caroline had been wondering this very fact herself. She was not missish, and had even speculated that Julia could be the Admiral's natural daughter and therefore Lewis's half-sister, which would of course have precluded a match. However, she had seen a locket of Julia's with a picture of her father in it, and the fair good looks of the Beechams were unmistakable in father and daughter. There could be no family reason to forbid the banns, so there had to be some other barrier. But Julia, even in her most impassioned railing against the Admiral's decisions, had not identified a reason...

'Lewis was asking me this morning whether it was true that Papa was set against Julia marrying Andrew,' Lavender said, still frowning. 'Then he asked me what happened the night Julia arrived here three months ago! I tried to answer as best I could but I do so dislike mysteries! Still,' her brow lightened a little, 'there is one matter that need concern me no longer! Is it very bad of me, Caroline, to be so pleased that I will not have Julia as a sister-in-law?'

Caroline tried not to smile. 'My dear Lavender! Have you yet considered the possibility that your brother might renounce his inheritance for Julia? Then you would be heiress to Hewly and have Julia as a sister into the bargain!'

Lavender clapped her hand to her mouth, but quickly recovered herself. 'Oh no! But I should not at all wish to be the owner of Hewly! No, Lewis will never give up the estate for Julia!'

'He may put love before duty,' Caroline said, feeling as though she had to point out the possibility even though it wrenched at her own heart.

'No,' Lavender said again, apparently restored to serenity, 'Lewis does not care enough for Julia to do such a thing! In fact,' she raised her lavender-coloured eyes to Caroline's face, 'I do not believe that he cares for her at all! He must look elsewhere for a bride!'

Caroline felt herself blush under her friend's penetrating scrutiny. 'Well, there are plenty of other eligible young ladies in the neighbourhood, and he has a whole twelvemonth—'

'Pooh, Caroline, do not be so foolish!' Lavender smiled at her. 'You would be perfect for Lewis! And I know he likes you! What could be better?'

Caroline reddened even more. 'You mistake, Lavender. Your brother and I would not suit! Besides,

I am scarce eligible! Anyway, I am to go away. Julia plans to leave Hewly in a few days—'

'Well, you need not go too!' Lavender leant forward urgently. 'Please, Caroline, stay here with me instead! I could do with a companion!'

Caroline shook her head. 'Lavender, I cannot. I have written away for other posts—'

'Because of Julia? But you need not worry, for if you stay here with me—'

'It is not just that.' Caroline spoke desperately. She put her cup down. 'There are other reasons—'

'It is because of Lewis, isn't it!' Lavender sat back with some satisfaction. 'I knew it! I knew you cared for him!'

Caroline put both her hands up to her burning cheeks. 'Oh Lavender, pray do not!'

'I'm sorry!' The younger girl looked suddenly upset. 'Dear Caroline, I will not press you to stay if you do not wish it, nor will I embarrass you any further. But,' she hesitated, 'please do not go with Julia! If you must take another post, stay here until it can be arranged! I promise—'

A bell rang from within the depths of the house. 'That will be Julia,' Caroline said evenly. 'She wishes me to write her some letters—'

'Oh, why can she not write for herself!' Lavender said stormily. She sounded more agitated than Caroline had ever heard her. She stood up, almost sending the tea-tray crashing to the floor. 'Oh, it puts me out of all patience to see you at her beck and call!

It is simply not right! I am going to visit Nanny Prior! She will know what to do for the best!'

Caroline sighed as she righted the tea-table and tidied up the cups. Matters suddenly seemed very uncertain. She would dearly have loved to stay at Hewly with Lavender, who was the best of good friends. Her feelings for Lewis precluded such a course of action, however. Then there was Julia, who might still become the next Mrs Brabant were Lewis to renounce his inheritance. Whatever the outcome, her role as Julia's companion had to come to an end.

The bell rang again, impatiently. Caroline smoothed her gown. She knew that the only outcome was to take up another post, away from Julia, Lavender, and Lewis most of all. It was a sensible course of action. It was appropriate. And it seemed a desolate future.

Later, after Julia had dictated so many letters that Caroline's hand positively ached, she finally escaped to the library for a little solitude. It was not yet time for dinner but the lamps were lit and the January evening was drawing in. Feeling strangely restless, Caroline drew near to the fire and stood for a while looking into its glowing heart. She heard Lewis and Richard Slater come in from their ride, and tensed as she waited to see if they would come into the library.

Since her quarrel with Lewis the previous day there had been no time to ask for forgiveness and Caroline doubted that he would accept her apology anyway. Not that it mattered—Lewis had far greater issues to consider than a foolish argument with Julia's companion! Caroline shrank a little at her own presumption in imagining that he would even remember it and resolved that it would be better simply to avoid him until she left.

The voices faded away and Caroline sighed a little and moved over to the bookshelves, looking for something to distract her mind. The books by the writer of *Sense and Sensibility* were not so appealing at a time like this, mirroring as cleverly as it did the trials of everyday life. Instead Caroline's eye was caught by the rows of old estate maps, and she remembered what Lewis had said about the garden designs dating back to the time of the Percevals. It might distract her a little to study the old plans.

She put out a hand and pulled one of the maps from the shelf. The paper stuck slightly, as though caught on another document, and Caroline paused so that she did not rip the old parchments. She took out two or three of the maps, found that they were all stuck together and began cautiously to separate them out.

Something fell from between the folds of one of the maps and Caroline bent down for a closer look. It was a piece of paper, folded roughly, blotched and splotched with ink. Caroline's heart began to race. She remembered Nanny Prior's words about the document the Admiral had been writing on the night he died, the one that had not been seen since and was almost forgotten. Perhaps this could be the very letter, though what it was doing amongst the estate maps was a mystery in itself. Turning the paper over in her hands, Caroline saw that it had Lewis's name at the top.

'My dear Lewis,

I am writing this in great haste lest I never have the chance to tell you—'

Guiltily, Caroline looked away and stuffed the letter into the pocket of her gown. She bundled the maps together again and pushed them haphazardly back on to the shelves, all the time frantically thinking of what she should do. There seemed to be little choice. Although it had only been five minutes previously that she had resolved to avoid Lewis for the rest of her time at Hewly, she was going to have to seek him out. There was no alternative.

She moved over to the fireplace and rang the bell, telling the footman who answered that she wished him to tell the Captain that she requested an appointment. In a surprisingly short time, the man reappeared.

'Captain Brabant's compliments, Miss Whiston, and he will see you now in the study.' The footman bowed and backed out of the room, waiting politely for Caroline to precede him into the hall. Caroline went, feeling distinctly nervous. But then, she told herself sternly, all she had to do was to hand the letter to Lewis and withdraw. Her obligation in passing him the Admiral's last message would then be fulfilled.

'Miss Whiston.' Lewis stood up as she came into the room and waited until the servant had closed the door behind her. His expression was unreadable. 'You wished to speak with me, ma'am?'

'Yes, I...' Caroline cursed herself for her inarticulateness. All her eloquence seemed to have deserted her of late whenever she was near him. She could not believe that she could be so tongue-tied. She came forward hesitantly and held out the letter.

'I found this today, sir—just now—and felt that it should be handed to you immediately. Now if you will excuse me—'

'Please take a seat.' Caroline could not be sure whether Lewis was so preoccupied that he had not heard her, or was simply ignoring her plea to escape. His head was bent over the letter and he did not look at her, but his words seemed unequivocal enough. She sat down gingerly on the edge of one of the chairs and waited whilst he started to read.

'This is in my father's hand,' Lewis said, looking up suddenly. 'You say that you found it recently, Miss Whiston?'

'It was in one of the old estate maps.' Caroline felt uncomfortable, as though she had been prying. 'I was not certain whether or not it was important, sir—for all I know it may be several years old, but as it was addressed to you—'

'Did you read it?' Lewis asked sharply.

Caroline coloured a little.

'Only to find the direction, sir...'

She saw Lewis's mouth twist in a slight smile at her use of the same words he had once spoken to her.

'I see.' He scanned the rest of the letter quickly. 'So you have no notion of the contents?'

'Not in the least, sir.' Caroline held his gaze. 'As

I have said, I do not even know if it is a recent letter or several years of age. The only reason I thought it might be important was that I remembered Mrs Prior saying that the Admiral was writing a letter when he was taken ill. So I wondered...'

'If this was that very letter?' Lewis was watching her intently. 'Did Mrs Prior say that? I had not heard that tale. But then, there is much that I have not heard...'

Caroline frowned a little, uncertain what he meant. Lewis smiled. 'Forgive me for the mystery. But this is odd. There seem to be too many missing letters in this house! Do I take it that you have not found yours?'

Caroline blushed. 'No, indeed, sir. I have searched everywhere.' She got to her feet. She knew she had to apologise and she felt better standing up. 'Captain Brabant, I feel I should—'

'Please, Miss Whiston,' Lewis held his hand up, 'if you are about to refer to our disagreement then I beg you do not.'

'But—' Caroline watched as he crossed the room towards her. Somehow his approach made her feel vulnerable. She toyed with the idea of sitting down again and changed her mind. That would be even worse.

'You must permit me, sir... That is, I wished to apologise...'

Lewis came right up to her. Caroline looked up into his face and completely lost the thread of what she had been saying. There was a smile in the blue eyes that told her more eloquently than any words that she was forgiven. She tore her gaze away from his and realised with horror that her hand was now resting against his chest. She withdrew it hastily.

'Your apology is accepted, ma'am,' Lewis said gently. 'We have both made errors of judgement.' He gave her a smile that sent the blood tingling through Caroline's veins. 'Let us study to do better in the future.'

'I fear that there will be little time,' Caroline said, backing away from him. 'Mrs Chessford and I are to leave for London in a couple of days—' She broke off, remembering that Julia's circumstances might change again should Lewis declare himself.

'Yes, I met Lavender earlier and she told me that you planned to leave Hewly,' Lewis said. He was still watching her. 'Can we not prevail upon you to stay here, ma'am? I know that my sister would be pleased for you to stay, not as a companion, but as a guest—'

'You are both very kind,' Caroline said guardedly, avoiding his eyes, 'but I fear I cannot accept.'

'May I not press you to do so, Miss Whiston?' Lewis had taken her hand now, the pressure of his fingers insistent on hers. 'It would be more comfortable for you to remain here, even if it were only until you took up a new position—'

Caroline's misery threatened to overwhelm her. To have Lewis ask her to stay for all the wrong reasons was particularly disheartening.

'My mind is made up, I fear, sir,' she said, giving

him a tight smile. 'You really must forgive me. I cannot stay at Hewly.' She tried to free herself.

'If it is because of Julia—' Lewis began.

'Please—' Caroline found that her composure was at breaking point. 'I wish the two of you very happy, but I cannot—' She broke off before she could give herself away any further.

'Excuse me, sir,' she said. 'I must go.' And she hurried from the room before Lewis could ask any more difficult questions.

The snow started that night. It brushed against the windows, falling softly, cloaking the woodland in white. Caroline stood by her bedroom window, watching the flakes swirl in the wind and shivering a little to think of the dark night in the cold forest. The same feeling of restlessness possessed her that her dogged her footsteps all day. It was odd; she felt as though the house was waiting for something to happen. She shrugged off the fanciful notion, but even so, she found she was not tired enough to go to sleep.

The clock had struck one when Caroline heard the creak of a step on the landing outside her door. It seemed an odd time to be prowling about, and she wondered whether Lavender was unable to sleep and was needing some company. She opened her door softly. The dark stairs stretched away below and Caroline could just see an insubstantial figure descending into the gloom. Then a stair creaked sharply. Caroline froze. What kind of spectre was it that trod so heavily that the ground shook beneath their feet? Perhaps the sort who had taken her letters?

Caroline slipped out of her room and closed the door soundlessly behind her. All the doors leading off the landing and the corridor beyond were closed and blank. She paused for a moment. There was a sound from below—the noise of a step on stone. The air shivered a little with the draught of an opening door. Intrigued now, Caroline crept down the stairs. The hall was all in darkness, which made navigation difficult, but Caroline thought that she espied a flickering light moving behind the door of the servants' quarters. She hesitated, unsure whether to go in and confront whoever was lurking there, or to wait and see if they emerged again. Whatever they were up to was evidently secret, for the light glimmered erratically and there was no sound.

Caroline put her hand on the door knob and was about to turn it when a sudden sound from further down the corridor made her jump almost out of her skin. Someone was coming out of the study; a different person from the one whose light she could still see behind the closed door, but someone equally secretive and cautious. Without further thought, Caroline dived through the open door on her left. It was the library.

The curtains were not drawn and the sharp moonlight reflected on the snow outside and lit the room with a bright white glow. Without conscious thought, Caroline made for the window and pulled the heavy velvet curtain about her. She thought that she could hear pursuing footsteps on the stone flags of the hall, and suddenly it seemed foolish in the extreme to be creeping about in the dark, particularly without anything with which to protect herself. She was about to emerge into the room to arm herself with a candlestick when there was a sound on the threshold and the door closed with a slight but unmistakable click.

They were in the room with her. Although Caroline could hear nothing, some sixth sense told her that she was no longer alone. She froze as still as a mouse, yet she was certain that whoever it was who was standing inside the door, watching and waiting, could hear her frightened breathing. Telling herself that there could be no danger, that she was no silly girl to be frightened by gothic horrors, Caroline drew herself up to her full height. In a moment, when she had steadied her nerves, she would throw back the curtain and confront whoever was there…

Even as the thought went through her head, the curtain was seized and thrown back, and she found herself looking into the furious features of Lewis Brabant.

Chapter Ten

'What the hell...' Lewis began angrily. He cut off whatever he was about to say and ran a hand through his hair, as though the gesture could help dissipate some of his pent-up fury.

'What the devil are you doing here, Caroline?'

'What am I doing here!' Caroline exclaimed. 'What are *you* doing, scaring me half out of my wits—'

Someone else moved in the shadows and Caroline smothered a squeak of alarm. Lewis clapped a hand over her mouth. 'Quiet! It's only Richard—'

Captain Slater came forward into the moonlight. He sketched an immaculate bow. 'Servant, Miss Whiston.'

Caroline stifled a ridiculous desire to laugh. Here they all were in the darkness of the library in the dead of night, whispering lines like characters in a bad play.

'What were you doing in the servants' quarters earlier?' she whispered urgently. 'I saw you—'

'That wasn't us,' Lewis began, only to break off as Richard put a hand on his arm.

'Don't believe we've time for explanations now, old chap! They're coming...'

There was a sudden noise outside the door. The effect on the men was instantaneous. Lewis stepped back behind the curtain next to Caroline, and Richard Slater moved swiftly across to the other side of the bay window, where he took up a similar stance. It was not a moment too soon. The door of the library opened and candlelight spilled into the room.

'Come along, you foolish girl!'

Caroline heard the edgy whisper as she watched through a crack in the curtains. There was no mistaking those impatient tones.

'We don't have much time! I only got as far as that prosy bore Shakespeare last time! Oh, was there ever such a clunch-headed idiot? Why can you not remember where you put it?'

Caroline heard the other figure mumble something under its breath, only to be cut off sharply.

'Cease this ridiculous whining, girl! We have not the time for it!'

Despite herself, Caroline found herself starting to smile. A moment later, Lewis threw back the curtain and stepped into the room.

'Good evening, Julia,' he said politely. 'Perhaps we may help you find whatever it is you are looking for?'

The maid, Letty, started screaming and it was Julia herself who gave her a sharp slap.

'Be quiet, you foolish creature! Do you wish to bring the whole house down around our ears?'

'It is a little late to worry about that,' Lewis said laconically. He and Richard Slater moved to light some of the candles, whilst Caroline drew the heavy curtains across the windows. Julia, who had been looking from one man to the other with a rather calculating expression on her face, stared at Caroline balefully.

'What is going on here? What is *she* doing here, Lewis? Surely I have not interrupted some tryst?'

Caroline met Julia's sharp blue gaze. 'I heard a noise and followed you downstairs, Julia,' she said quietly. 'I was curious to know what you were doing.'

'Is that so?' Julia scoffed. She seemed to be growing in confidence as the minutes passed, seating herself in the most comfortable chair and arranging her dress about her in precise folds. The candlelight shone on her guinea-gold curls and perfect profile, and Caroline felt a little sick. Julia was so artless, so plausible. Was it possible that she was about to make fools of them all?

Julia's gaze, amused and slightly condescending, went from Lewis' stern face to Richard Slater, who had urged the snivelling maid to take a seat and was now standing, rather ominously, by the door.

'Well, this is a cosy gathering!' Julia said sweetly, her eyes resting on Lewis's face. 'But why the long face, my dear? All I was looking for was a book to ease my sleeplessness—'

'Or, in fact, a set of estate maps,' Lewis suggested

softly. 'The set in which your bungling accomplice here—' he nodded towards Letty '—hid my father's last letter!'

The maid began to sob at once. 'I didn't do nothing wrong, sir! I just thought… They had had a quarrel, and if he had changed his will…'

'Be quiet, you fool!' Julia said venomously. She turned her gentlest smile on Lewis. 'The girl understands nothing! Dearest Lewis, let me explain this to you alone and not in front of all these people!'

Once again her disparaging gaze flicked over Caroline. 'Indeed, I cannot think why we need an audience! My servants and your best friend! Send them away and we shall set all to rights!'

Caroline went across and put an arm around the maid, who was crying in earnest now and grasped thankfully at the clean handkerchief Caroline handed her.

'I didn't do nothing wrong, miss,' she repeated miserably, 'only I couldn't remember where I'd put the letter—'

'Don't distress yourself, Letty,' Caroline soothed. 'The letter is found now, and—'

'The letter is found?' Julia swung round in her seat and glared at Caroline. 'By you, I suppose, you scheming creature! To think that I ever trusted you! Why, all the time you were planning to discredit me and we all know why!' Her poisonous glare turned from Caroline to Lewis. 'I do not know what she has told you, Lewis, but it was all self-seeking!

Insinuating herself into the family, befriending Miss Brabant—'

'That's enough, Julia!' Lewis spoke quietly, but there was a note in his voice that made Caroline jump and Julia fell silent, the colour coming into her face. Lewis continued. 'Miss Whiston found the letter and very properly brought it to me, since it bore my name. So you need not concern yourself any longer that it is lost.'

'Oh well,' Julia gave a casual little shrug. 'I was only looking for it because I remembered that Uncle Harley was writing when I saw him that night, and I thought it might be important. But I daresay it is of no consequence—'

'As it turns out, it is very important,' Lewis said, with a smile, 'though not, perhaps, in the way in which you imagine.' He crossed to the hearth and leant one arm along the mantelpiece. 'You will be relieved to know that the letter contained no change to his will.'

Caroline saw that Julia's face was a study in indecision. Clearly Lewis's words meant something to her, more than they could to Caroline herself, who was quite at sea. Instinct told her that Julia's motive for searching out the letter was not as altruistic as she liked to pretend, and the maid had effectively condemned her anyway. It seemed that Julia had thought that the Admiral had written a codicil to the will and had been trying to keep it quiet. In which case, what had prompted Admiral Brabant to take such a course of action?

Julia shrugged again, carelessly.

'Well, I am glad that the will still stands, but I am not surprised. It was only the tiniest quarrel, after all—'

'Is that so?' Lewis gave her a hard stare. 'Now that must be…the fifth time you have lied? Certainly not the first…'

Caroline gasped, but Julia gasped louder, her face suddenly bright red with outrage. 'How dare you, Lewis? Just what do you imply?'

Lewis shifted slightly. He seemed utterly unconcerned, unmoved by Julia's rage. 'Well, as you have asked me to explain, we shall start at the beginning. The first lie was the one you told me when you said that you had come to Hewly to care for my father. In fact, you arrived before he was taken ill, did you not, Julia? He was hale and hearty—at least for a few hours!'

Julia looked evasive. 'Well, what of it? I did not intend to deceive! I had every intention of staying here to care for Uncle Harley! Why, I loved him like a daughter—'

'So you professed,' Lewis said, and there was a grim note in his voice that sent a shiver down Caroline's spine. Letty heard it, too, and raised her head from the handkerchief for a moment, her eyes darting like a frightened rabbit. Richard Slater looked unmoved, his face like granite.

Julia's face was working like boiling milk. 'I do not see why I should bear this nonsense any more!' she said stormily. 'I never intended to mislead—if I forgot to tell you that Uncle Harley was well when I arrived—'

'It was because you did not wish to have to explain the cause of his sudden illness,' Lewis finished, giving her a very straight look. 'But we shall come to that. For next there was the matter of your…forced marriage…'

Caroline shot Julia an incredulous look. The letters had scarce implied any coercion, in fact Julia had been quite ruthless in setting her cap first at Andrew Brabant and then at Jack Chessford. Looking up, she caught Lewis's eye and saw the cynical gleam there.

'You may remember, Julia, that after my father died you told me a sad and affecting tale of how he had tried to force you into marriage with my brother,' Lewis said smoothly. 'When Andrew died, you told me that my father had put himself forward as a suitor in his place, so anxious was he to keep your fortune in the family. You had been so much in fear…' Lewis hesitated, 'that you chose to elope with Jack Chessford in order to escape him.'

His eyes met Caroline's for a moment, dark and sombre, and it seemed that he was speaking directly to her. 'I confess that I was horrified by the tale. A man in my father's position, a position of trust, to so abuse his ward that she felt she had to flee! It sickened me!' He sighed. 'Of course, I could not ask him if it were true, for he was beyond both recall or confession. I was the one who had to live with the horror of it.'

Julia stirred slightly in her chair. 'Well, I am sorry for it, but truth must out!'

'Indeed!' Lewis said quietly. 'And my father's will appeared to bear this out! It seemed that he had taken his rejection so badly that he wished to punish you, Julia! Not only did he leave you a smaller sum than you had hoped for, but he also expressly forbade that we should marry. He had known, of course, that I was once at your feet—' again, Lewis's gaze met Caroline's, his expression unreadable '—and no doubt he suspected that such sweet feelings might reassert themselves when we were together once more. So he asked me to choose between my inheritance and the woman I had once loved.' Lewis looked away, into the fire. 'That was one interpretation of events. There was, however, another. The true version.'

There was a silence. Even Julia was looking a little frightened now.

'The truth of it,' Lewis said softly, 'is that it was *your* desire to marry my brother, and none of my father's doing. Nor did he ever press his suit on you or make improper advances. You quarrelled with him on the night you returned to Hewly and tried to blackmail him for money. He was so distressed that he had an attack almost immediately. But not before he wrote me the letter…'

Julia was very pale now. 'Lewis, I protest—'

'As you wish,' Lewis said inexorably. 'I know from Churchward that the Admiral vouchsafed considerable sums to you over the years and that your own fortune was finished years ago. Jack Chessford was a gambler, was he not? And I believe you adopted the same expensive vice.'

He looked across at Richard Slater, who had kept silent during the whole exchange. 'There are plenty of people who have seen you run through a fortune in one sitting, Julia! And as always, you applied to my father to pay your debts. Only this time, he refused to help you!'

'This is monstrous!' Julia was looking wildly from Caroline to Richard Slater. 'They are all out to discredit me! Your so-called friends and my companion...' She burst into noisy sobs. 'It is iniquitous!'

Lewis was looking grave. 'So reluctant was Richard to tell me what he knew that I had to confide all my own suspicions first! As for Miss Whiston, she scarcely deserves your censure—'

Julia sniffed furiously. 'Oh, do not speak of her! Treacherous creature!'

'She has spoken not one word against you,' Lewis said, gently, smiling at Caroline. 'But let me finish. You had a quarrel with my father, a bad one. When you realised that he did not intend to give you the money, you threatened to spread slanderous gossip. You told him that you would say he had tried to force you to marry my brother, that he had then pressed his own suit, that he was a satyr who had abused his own position as your guardian to maltreat you! None of it was true, but it would make a good story! My father reacted furiously and you stormed out, intending to leave immediately. Then, you heard that he had been struck down by the attack that would eventually kill him.'

Lewis turned away. His voice was toneless. 'You decided to stay at Hewly. It was a convenient place to hide from your creditors, you knew you might inherit something if my father died, and Lavender told you that I was returning home. There were all sorts of possibilities.' He sighed. 'It was not for a while that you heard the rumour that my father had been writing something when he was taken ill, but then the horrid thought took you that perhaps it had been an alteration to his will, made with the intention of cutting you out altogether!'

Lewis looked across at Letty, who was sitting quietly, head bent. 'Unbeknownst to you, it was your own opportunistic maid who had hidden the letter, intending to come back for it later and make use of it as best she could! She was planning a little blackmail of her own, but you made it worth her while to join forces with you! Unfortunately, however, she had forgotten quite where she had hidden it, and the two of you were obliged to sift through every book in the whole house, and then without success!'

He crossed to the table, took out the letter and placed it down by Julia's side. 'Here it is. *You* were the ghostly figure who was wandering about the house after my father died, but you were on a more earthly quest! You did not wish to lose what little money had been left to you!'

Caroline found her voice. 'But if the letter does not

contain an alteration to your father's will, Captain Brabant, what does it say?'

There was grim humour in Lewis's voice. 'I doubt that my father would have had time to make a legal amendment to his will even had he wished to. But that was not his aim. Angry, outraged by Julia's threats, he cared more about honour than money. My father was at pains to tell me that your accusations were untrue, Julia, and that if you should ever seek to besmirch his memory, you would be telling falsehoods. He told me that you petitioned to marry Andrew of your own free will—both Lavender and Mrs Prior bear this out. You ran away with Jack Chessford because you were bored and Jack had a fortune—before he gamed it all away, of course! So—' Lewis finished quietly '—your lies are ended. Not even the theft of Miss Whiston's letters was enough to save you!'

Caroline looked startled, but Letty, whose nerves were clearly in shreds, started to sob again. 'I'm sorry, miss! I burned every one of them like she told me!'

Caroline shook her head in bewilderment. 'Never mind, Letty. I doubt it matters after all else that has happened.'

'My father had already been disillusioned by you when Andrew died, Julia,' Lewis finished quietly. 'He added the bizarre stipulation to his will to try to dissuade me from ever marrying you. He need not have troubled himself. I have seldom heard such an ugly tale of double-dealing and deceit, and I was already suspicious of it before I ever had his letter.'

Julia leaped to her feet. Her eyes were wild and two bright spots of colour burned feverishly in her cheeks. 'That being so, Captain Brabant, I shall remove from your house at once!'

'You shall!' Lewis seemed amused rather than anything else. 'I am obliged to you!'

'But do not seek to try to cut me out of the will!' Julia added viciously, as she headed for the door. 'I am entitled to that money for tolerating Uncle Harley's tedious company for all those years! And as for you—' she turned on Caroline with a fury that made her flinch back '—with your scheming ways, I wish you happy! I can do much better for myself than a miserable sea captain with no title and a tiny fortune!'

'Which is probably true,' Lewis said cheerfully, as the slam of the library door echoed through the whole house. His eye fell on the maid, who was shrinking in her chair. 'Well, run along, girl,' he said, not unkindly. 'Your mistress will need help with her packing! The two of you deserve each other!'

Caroline sat down rather heavily in the chair that Julia had vacated. There was a silence. 'A glass of wine, perhaps,' Richard Slater said, moving across to the sideboard. 'I believe we are all in need of fortification!'

'She took so many risks!' Caroline said, still thinking of Julia and the enormity of what she had done.

'She's a gambler,' Lewis said shortly. 'Reckless risk has become part of her life. Perhaps it always was…'

Caroline gratefully accepted a glass from Richard and drank deeply, welcoming the reviving warmth. She shivered. 'This is a nasty business, Captain Slater. How did you know that Julia was so deep in debt?'

Richard Slater looked uncomfortable. 'It was gossip only, which was why I was at pains not to pass it on to Lewis. My sister Fanny had been in London the Season past, and commented to me that Mrs Chessford was playing deep and on the watch for a rich husband. I believe she only mentioned it because she knew of Mrs Chessford's connection with Lewis's family...' He shrugged. 'I thought little of it until Lewis told me of the Admiral's letter.'

'Speaking of letters,' Caroline turned her enquiring gaze upon Lewis, 'how did you know that it was Julia who had taken mine?'

Lewis stretched. He gave her a mischievous grin. 'My dear Caroline, when you accused me of stealing your property you had forgotten one important fact! You thought that I was the only one who had known of the existence of the letters, but there were always two—myself and Julia. After all, she had written them and knew what they contained! When I told her of the incident of the letter left in *Marmion*, she immediately realised how incriminating they would be and how they contradicted her own story! So,' he shrugged, 'she took them, or had Letty steal them for her.'

Caroline thought of the artless phrases the young Julia had written when she was planning to throw Lewis over in favour of Andrew Brabant. There was no doubt that they conflicted dramatically with the tale that she had been forced unwillingly into the betrothal and they would have done her much harm had they come to light.

Lewis shifted slightly. 'I have to confess that I read more of that letter than I first admitted, Miss Whiston! It was that that planted the first doubts in my mind when Julia tried to pretend she had not wished to marry Andrew.' He cleared his throat and quoted dryly: '"Of course, Andrew is the elder and so will inherit the Admiral's fortune one day, which is so much more comfortable than having to scratch around on a sailor's income…"'

'Oh dear…' Caroline said, grimacing.

'Well, I have to agree with her,' Richard Slater said with a grin. 'A most practical woman, Mrs Chessford!' He yawned. 'Excuse me, I am worn to a thread with all this Cheltenham tragedy! I will see you both in the morning!'

He drained his glass and sauntered out of the room. Left alone with Lewis, Caroline felt suddenly and unaccountably shy. She avoided his eyes.

'I think I should retire also, sir. It is very late—'

'And you seem to have a penchant for creeping about the house in your night attire,' Lewis observed, his gaze wandering over her in a thoroughly disconcerting manner. 'Miss Whiston, there is something I wish to ask you. It has nothing to do with what has just passed, and no doubt it should wait until the morning, but I find I cannot wait.'

He got to his feet and pulled her up too. Caroline's gaze searched his face, a little bewildered. 'Sir?'

'Miss Whiston.' Lewis kept hold of her hand, grown suddenly cold, in his. 'You must be aware of the regard I have for you. I should therefore deem it an honour if you would consent to be my wife.'

Caroline was not sure how long it was that she stared up into his face. 'You are precipitate, Captain Brabant,' she managed to say, after a pause. 'You have only just cleared your decks—'

'And having done so, I believe in aiming for my goal. It was what I had intended all along. Perhaps I should have waited, but as I said, I could not.'

Lewis was watching her face intently. Caroline looked away, unwilling to give her own feelings away.

'I am honoured by your regard, sir,' she said uncertainly, 'but I must have time to think. After all, I was obliged to hear rather more than I wished this evening of your affections for another lady!'

Lewis's tense expression lightened a little. 'Affection be damned!' He gave her hands a little shake. 'Surely you must see that I cannot bear Julia? Oh, I admit that for a while I was at her feet—impressionable youths must be allowed to make mistakes in their salad days! But she was always a mercenary piece! Even when I went away to sea she asked for a keepsake and took me to task for presenting her with a necklace of pearls rather than one of diamonds!'

Caroline tried unsuccessfully to smother a giggle.

'Alas that your judgement of women is so faulty, Captain!'

'Not this time,' Lewis said.

'And then there is the question of your more recent behaviour,' Caroline pursued. 'You were seen embracing Mrs Chessford, and yet you denied it!'

Lewis raised his eyebrows. 'My dear Caroline, you have already accused me of this once! If you refer to the occasion when Julia cast herself into my arms in floods of tears, then I suppose I must plead guilty! There was nothing in it but if Lavender saw—' He shrugged. 'I suppose she may not know the difference!'

He slanted a look down at her. 'Perhaps you might make the same mistake? Allow me to demonstrate...'

He smiled down at her for a moment, then bent his head and kissed her gently. Caroline resisted briefly, but the temptation was too delicious to withstand. Her lips parted and he deepened the kiss immediately, tasting, teasing, until compelling pleasure sent her mind reeling. She was dimly aware of Lewis pulling her closer, and she slid her arms about his neck, all thoughts lost in the delight of sensation. One could drown in such pleasure...

'Your answer, Caro...' Lewis's words were barely above a whisper. 'Say you will marry me...'

His mouth had left hers and was brushing the sensitive skin just below her left ear, sending shivers of excitement coursing through Caroline's blood. His mouth drifted lower to the hollow at the base of her throat, then down to the soft swell of skin above the lace of her nightgown. Caroline caught her breath.

'Lewis, wait…' She stepped back and tried to extricate herself. 'I must think…'

'Must you?' Lewis loosened his grip a little but did not let her go. 'Just for once, Caro, could you not put aside your customary cool detachment? The romantic Miss Whiston I met in the woods had no such scruples…'

Caroline laughed a little shakily. Cool detachment was hardly the way to describe her feelings. 'I think you took advantage of me then, sir—'

'A delightful thought! But, no—' He had felt her instinctive movement of protest and let her go '—the time and place are scarcely right. I know I should have waited to ask you. I will give you until tomorrow for an answer, but Caro—' she looked up at his tone and met the determination in his eyes '—do not think to refuse me.' He pulled her back to him and gave her a brief, hard kiss that held a disturbing echo of their former passion. 'Now I had better let you go.'

The morning had come. Caroline lay in bed and watched the shadows move on her ceiling, the curious white light that suggested that there was thick snow outside. She had slept late after the events of the previous night, falling into a deep, dreamless sleep as soon as she had tumbled into bed. There had been no time to reflect on either the extraordinary revelations about Julia or the more pressing problem of Lewis's proposal.

Just why was it a problem? Caroline turned on her side and heaved a sigh. She cared deeply for Lewis and had done so almost from the first moment she had met him. She believed him when he said that he no longer cared a rush for Julia, so it was not as though she felt she was living in a shadow of another woman. Their mutual passion was as intriguing as it was explosive, but perhaps she should not think of that, for it was enough to blind her to all else...

Caroline shifted uncomfortably. She had lived her whole adult life without succumbing to physical desire and it was only now that she realised how vulnerable this had made her, affecting her judgement, making her uncertain... For the nub of the problem was that Lewis might no longer love Julia, but that did not necessarily mean that he loved her.

Caroline faced the thought plainly and sadly. Lewis had to marry to fulfil the terms of his father's will. Who better than the convenient companion, a woman with no expectations, sensible, plain, a good manager who would help him turn the estate around? Put in such straightforward terms and shorn of the misleading confusion of physical attraction, it seemed a little bleak.

That did not mean, of course, that she had to refuse him. Caroline got out of bed, washed and started to dress, all the time preoccupied with her thoughts. It was an opportunity that any governess companion would give their eye teeth for. She had only to say yes.

She stared into the mirror, wondering why the

thought gave her such difficulty. Her wan face looked back at her. The reason was not far to seek. She had fallen in love with Lewis Brabant and wanted him to love her too. Anything less was not enough; physical passion, companionship, a home... Caroline shook her head. How foolish, when she had had none of these things a few months ago, and now had been offered the world! Almost all the world. Yet somehow, without Lewis's love, it was not enough.

Caroline was not surprised to find that Julia was not at the breakfast table. Lavender was present and had evidently received a foreshortened explanation of the events of the previous night from her brother, for she was looking shocked and pale. Lewis had finished eating and had progressed to his newspaper; Richard Slater was placidly demolishing a plate of devilled kidneys. It seemed to Caroline that everyone was trying a little too hard to behave as though nothing had happened.

Caroline sat down and returned their greetings a little self-consciously. She was very aware of Lewis's gaze resting upon her, of a contained restlessness about him that was even more noticeable than previously. Caroline could hardly pretend that she did not know its cause and her nerves tightened in anticipation of the interview to come. She accepted a plate of toast, then promptly found that her appetite had deserted her.

Lewis put down his newspaper and got to his feet. 'Miss Whiston, would you grant me the pleasure of your company as soon as it is convenient? In the study. Preferably now.'

Caroline hesitated. Richard continued to eat his breakfast whilst Lavender looked speculatively from one to the other. Caroline capitulated.

It was with some trepidation that she preceded Lewis into the familiar room and waited whilst he closed the door. She pressed her hands together to give herself courage.

'Well?' Lewis spoke softly. He had come to her and taken her hand, and his touch almost undid all her resolutions. Caroline moved away.

'Captain Brabant, I am conscious of the honour you do me but…' She met his eyes and looked quickly away. 'I fear I must decline your offer.'

Lewis was very still for a moment. 'I see. Will you do me the courtesy of explaining why you reject my suit?'

Caroline bit her lip. This was dreadful, worse by far than disappointing poor Mr Grizel, for in refusing Lewis she was going against her own feelings as well as rejecting him. She wrung her hands.

'You seem in some distress, Miss Whiston,' Lewis said quietly. 'Pray tell me what I may do to help you.'

Caroline cast him an agonised glance. 'There is nothing you can do, sir, save not to press me for a reason—'

Lewis gave her an ironic smile. 'Then it seems I must be cruel, for I do most ardently wish to know your reasons, Miss Whiston.'

Caroline's feelings got the better of her like a dam

bursting. She abandoned polite restraint. 'There are one hundred and one reasons why we should not wed, Captain, as you are well aware! The most obvious one is that the dispositions of your father's will mean you are obliged to marry! You can scarcely expect me to feel flattered, the convenient bride!'

'The devil!' Lewis seemed genuinely amused, which only served to irritate Caroline the more. 'My dear Caroline, please do not suggest that I have proposed to you because I am lazy and you are convenient! Such assumptions do credit to neither of us!'

'It is what everyone will think—'

'Who cares a rush about that? *I* do not think it, and now that I have told you there is no truth in the accusation, you may disregard it too!'

'Leaving that aside, sir,' Caroline said hastily, 'there are other considerations! I am—was—Mrs Chessford's companion, and it would be most—'

'I hope you are not going to say that it would be inappropriate!' For a moment, Lewis looked dangerous. 'Caroline, you are a Whiston of Watchbell Hall, if you insist on social distinctions, and even if you were not from a good family, I would not care tuppence! You will have to do better than that!'

'There will be a lot of talk,' Caroline said desperately.

Lewis shrugged indifferently. 'There always is! Let them talk!'

'And then,' Caroline said, grasping at straws, 'there is my age, sir.'

'Your age!' Lewis looked completely incredulous.

'I believe that you should marry someone younger, someone more...' Caroline broke off in slight confusion.

Lewis looked as though he were not sure whether to laugh or lose his temper. 'Caroline, that reason is contemptible! You are scarce in your dotage! Besides, I should run mad if I were married to some brainless débutante!'

'There are some very sensible young girls,' Caroline began, but Lewis stopped her with a gesture. 'Please, Caroline, do not insult my intelligence with any more of your spurious excuses! It is clear to me that there are other reasons, ones that you do not see fit to disclose. Well, I have a solution.'

He reached her side in only two strides. 'The correct course of action is not an appeal through the intellect at this stage. Caroline—' his arms slid about her waist '—I know that you are not indifferent to me, and I, for my part, find you most deliciously attractive! You may have as much time to think as you wish, but please succumb to your romantic side and accept my proposal!'

Caroline gave a despairing squeak. She could feel herself weakening, both literally and metaphorically. Lewis tightened his grip and bent to kiss her. Caroline felt her lips tremble beneath his. Then, to her huge disappointment, he let her go and stepped back.

'You will not accept me and I will not accept your refusal,' he said evenly. 'So, Miss Whiston, until we may come to some agreement, that is the way it will stay!'

Chapter Eleven

'So Julia has gone,' Lavender said contentedly, biting heartily into a slice of Cook's sponge cake. 'Did you hear the fuss she made, Caroline? Still, I cannot envy her having to travel in this weather!'

The snow was no longer falling but it lay thick on the ground in drifts of up to two foot deep.

'I suppose she may not make London by nightfall,' Lavender continued, not sounding much concerned, 'and will have to put up somewhere on the road. Ah well, the house is the more peaceful for it!'

This was odd but true. Caroline had already noticed that a certain tension seemed to have gone from the atmosphere. The servants were smiling more. The cuckoo had gone from the nest.

'You are very quiet,' Lavender said suddenly, fixing Caroline with the perceptive blue gaze that was so like her brother's. 'Is something troubling you, Caroline? It is unlike you to be so silent whilst I chatter on!'

Caroline shook her head. 'No, not precisely. That

is…' She gave Lavender an anxious look. 'I feel a little awkward now that Julia has gone and I am still here! I must make plans…'

'Well, there is no hurry!' Lavender said, gesturing with the cake in her hand. She put it down hastily as a few crumbs scattered on the carpet. 'How unlady-like of me! I suppose I am too old for your teaching, Caroline? You could always stay as my governess rather than my companion!'

Caroline smiled and frowned at the same time. 'Now Lavender, we have had this conversation!'

'I know it!' The younger girl sighed. 'I do not understand why I cannot persuade you! Oh, that reminds me…' She fumbled in her pocket. 'I have a letter here for you! I almost forgot! Perhaps it will be the good news you are awaiting.'

Caroline took the letter with some trepidation. The writing was that of Lady Covingham, and suddenly Caroline was uncertain whether she wished to stay or to go. Impatient with herself, she tore it open.

'Is something wrong?' Lavender asked, a moment later, her gaze resting on Caroline's face. 'You look a little disappointed, Caroline…'

'Yes, no… I don't know,' Caroline pulled herself together and gave Lavender a weak smile. 'Lady Covingham writes that the family she had had in mind for me have already appointed a governess and so will not be needing my services. She says that she will continue to search for a position for me, but…' Caroline's voice trailed away. 'Oh, never mind! I shall just have to change my plans.'

'Capital!' Lavender said, clapping her hands and ignoring Caroline's frown of disapproval at her language. 'You may stay here for a spell instead! That will give Lewis the chance—' She stopped and clapped her hand to her mouth. 'Oh dear...' She looked quickly at Caroline's face. 'Well, it was an open secret...'

'Was it indeed!' Caroline said wrathfully. 'Your brother has not spoken to you of it?'

'Of course not!' Lavender looked indignant. 'He would not! But anyone with any sense can see that Lewis cares for you, Caroline!' She gave a pleasurable little shiver. 'Sometimes when he looks at you—'

Caroline raised her eyebrows and decided that this was not the moment to try to explain the difference between physical attraction and love. Lavender's face was suddenly wistful. 'I wish...' She broke off. 'Oh, I know it is none of my business, Caroline, but if you have refused Lewis because you think he is only interested in marrying to fulfil the will, you are fair and far out! Why, it is plain to me that he loves you and I know you care for him too!'

Caroline smiled a little sadly. 'That is not all, though, is it, Lavender? Only think how people will talk! The Captain and the companion—'

'Let them!' Lavender said robustly. 'Anyway, you are wrong if you think that the neighbourhood would not approve! Why, only last week Lady Perceval said to me that you were a charming girl, just like your mama, and that she hoped that you would find you would be spending longer at Hewly than you had first thought!'

Caroline raised her eyebrows at this sign of approbation. 'Well…'

'Think about it!' Lavender said, patting her hand and suddenly sounding far older than her years. 'I am persuaded that you will find that most of your objections do not truly exist!'

'Perhaps you are right,' Caroline said, getting up. 'I shall go for a walk and give the matter some thought! It is time I cleared my head!'

'Only do not stray too far!' Lavender called after her. 'Belton says that it will snow again later!'

The gardens were completely transformed under their blanket of white. Heavy branches bowed down under the weight of snow and the sun was blinding. The snow crunched under Caroline's boots as she walked. She was wearing a thick winter cloak, a warm scarf, gloves—and the red velvet dress, for if she was to make the most momentous decision of her life she wished to do it in style.

The sunlight glittered on the icy surface of the Steep river and Caroline walked on, deep in thought. Lavender was probably correct and all her objections were insubstantial ones. She would make a good mistress of Hewly, she loved Lewis deeply and if he truly loved her… Well, there was only one way to find that out. She would have to ask him. Caroline squared her shoulders. It was a daunting thought but she would prepare carefully and approach him in a sensible and rational manner. Then, if the answer was not as she hoped, she would be able to withdraw with what dignity she had left and consider an alternative plan...

An icicle dripped from the tree above her head. Caroline jumped and looked around her. She was disconcerted to realise that she had wandered quite far into the forest whilst she had been thinking. The blue shadows were gathering beneath the silent trees and it was almost dusk. She looked around for the path, but nothing was visible beneath the white covering of snow. Her own footsteps stretched behind her as far as she could see. Turning around, Caroline hurried back the way she had come.

Within a half hour she was no nearer the edge of the forest and she was forced to concede that she was lost. Darkness was falling and it had started to snow again, just as Belton had predicted, obliterating her footprints and making it even more unlikely that she would find her way back. Caroline was very angry with herself. Of all the foolish starts, to go wandering off in the snow without so much as a second thought of how she might find her way! Everything was now covered by a fresh layer of snow and she was completely disorientated. Nor were there any lights to guide her. Caroline fought down a wave of panic and continued to pick her way through the trees, taking care not to stumble over a hidden root. It was slow going in the snow, and she was feeling both hungry and tired now. The hem of the cloak and the red dress were both soaking, and Caroline's feet were numb with cold.

She had almost given up hope of shelter when she stumbled across the hut. It was more substantial than the one in which she had hidden on the day she had first met Lewis, for the roof and all the walls were sound. Indeed, when Caroline stumbled inside she found it to be furnished in a rough fashion, although deserted. There was a stump of a candle in a dish and dry brushwood in the fireplace, a pitcher of water and a long truckle bed against the wall, as well as a few other sticks of furniture.

Caroline closed the door against the snowy night and groped her way across to the table. After four attempts she managed to strike the tinder and light the candle, which proved to be tallow and smelled strongly. Caroline did not care. She lit the brushwood fire, stoked it to a blaze and stripped off her cloak and soaking dress. Then, huddled before the fire in her shift, she wrapped the cloak around her once more and tried to get warm.

It seemed that the hut was the base for woodcutters or possibly those engaged in more furtive work. Caroline thought it unlikely in the extreme than any poachers would be out that night, so she counted on having the place to herself. That said, it was draughty, uncomfortable and cold, but it was shelter and she would have to stay in it until the daylight brought either rescue or at least the chance of finding her way back to the path. Caroline thought guiltily of Lavender, who had warned her not to walk too far and would now be beside herself with worry. Lewis would probably be furious... But there was nothing to be done. At last she was starting to feel warm and the warmth made her drowsy. She banked the fire down, lay down on the rough bed and drew the cloak about her as best she could. She blew out the candle and almost immediately fell asleep.

Caroline had no idea how long it was before she awoke. It was still dark, and from outside the hut came the scrape of metal on stone. She sat bolt upright, suddenly terrified. If this was a poachers' hideout and she was here, alone in just her shift in the middle of the night... Even as the thoughts rushed through her mind, there was a crash and the door was flung open. In the aperture stood Lewis Brabant and he looked furiously angry. He held a carriage lamp high in one hand, the candle inside shedding its light over the interior of the hut and shining into Caroline's eyes. Behind him, the darkness swirled with flakes of white. Lewis came into the hut and closed the door behind him, shaking the snow from his cloak. Caroline found her voice.

'Lewis! Oh, thank God, it's you! I had quite given up hope!'

Her words did not appear to have a soothing effect, for Lewis still looked furious. 'Had you indeed, madam? Yet you seem quite comfortable here whilst the rest of us tramp through the snow searching for you!'

His gaze swept over her, taking in the warm firelight, the makeshift bed and Caroline, her hair dried in curls about her shoulders. An indefinable look came into his eyes, one that made Caroline suddenly self-conscious. She started to rise, remembered that she was in her shift, and pulled the cloak more securely about her.

'I was making do until help arrived,' she said hastily, 'but now that you are here, Lewis, we may return to the house—'

Lewis gave her a scorching look. He removed his cloak and arranged it beside Caroline's dress in front of the fire, kicking the glowing embers into life again.

'Return to the house? You must be mad if you think that I would step outside again in that weather!' He came across to the bed and sat down on the edge, grasping Caroline by the shoulders. 'I have sent the others back and I was about to give up and go home myself! Have you any idea what I have been through, Caroline, searching for you from barn to byre, calling your name, looking for footprints until I thought all hope was lost!' He shook her. 'And now that I am here I will not stir again until the snow has ceased and neither will you!'

The cloak had slipped. Caroline folded her arms firmly across her breasts.

'But we cannot stay here—' she began, only to be silenced by the infuriated glare Lewis gave her. She started to realise that he was even more angry than she had first thought.

'Pray do not argue with me, madam!' His tone was as arctic as the weather. 'I suppose you will tell me next that it is inappropriate for us to be alone! All I can say is that you should have thought of that before wandering off and putting us all to an unconscionable amount of trouble!' The fury took hold of him again.

'Good God, you of all people should know that there are poachers in these woods—'

'Well, they will not be out tonight!' Caroline retorted, as angry as him now.

'No!' Lewis stood up and turned away to put more wood on the fire. 'They will not! No one else would be so stupid! Of all the addle-pated little fools! What were you doing—running away from me? If my proposal was so unwelcome you need only have said! I would not have pressed my suit further!'

Caroline frowned. 'Of course I was not running away! How can you be so nonsensical! I went for a walk and wandered from the path by the veriest accident!'

'Hm,' Lewis looked slightly mollified. He straightened up. The fire was burning brightly now, filling the hut with light and warmth and shadows. Caroline snuggled back under her cloak.

'By all means make yourself comfortable by the fire!' she said sleepily. 'If we are indeed to stay here until daylight you must try to rest...'

'Thank you!' Lewis sat down on the edge of the bed and pulled his boots off, sending them crashing across the hut, where they bounced against the door. 'I confess that sleep is not the matter on my mind at the moment.'

Caroline, whose eyes had just started to close, opened them again hastily. She was in time to see him discard his jacket and pull his shirt over his head. She drew back with a gasp of alarm.

'Lewis, I only meant—'

'Yes?' He turned on her suddenly. 'Just what did you mean, Caroline? I believe you gave me your word that you would not stray from Hewly again, yet I find you foolishly walking in the snow, wandering from the path...'

Caroline, totally intimidated by the presence of a semi-naked man so close to her, shrank back against the wall of the hut. 'I was only... I wished to have some time to think... I took my book of poetry...'

Lewis' gaze travelled over her slowly, taking in her flushed face and stormy hazel eyes. He deliberately dropped his gaze to her bare shoulders and the cloak that Caroline was now desperately clutching beneath her chin. Caroline felt the heat come up to her skin, suddenly suffusing her from head to toe. Lewis looked from her to the red velvet dress, draped across the wooden chair before the fire. He started to smile, but it did not reassure Caroline at all, edged as it was with predatory intent.

'Well, well,' Lewis said cordially, 'so you decided to go for a walk... In your evening dress, in the snow... And to think that I have been waiting this age for your romantic inclinations to triumph and when they do they almost kill us both! Yet I find that I am glad, after all...'

Caroline found that there was nowhere further to retreat to, for her back was against the wall and she was becoming decidedly chilly. She tried to wriggle under the cloak, but Lewis was too quick for her. He leant across her and pulled her beneath him in one swift move, trapping her with his weight. Caroline squirmed.

'Lewis, what—'

Her words were cut off as his mouth came down fiercely, violently, plundering the softness of hers. A delicious warmth flooded through her, a trembling and tingling that left her utterly confused. His lips were parting her own ruthlessly, his tongue sliding between them with a merciless demand that left her reeling. Caroline gasped and he took immediate advantage to deepen the kiss, sending her senses spinning. His hands tangled in her hair; his mouth moved over hers in total supremacy.

Caroline came to her senses briefly when Lewis let her go for a moment and she realised that he was removing the last of his clothes. The firelight slid across his hard, muscular body in slabs of red and shadow and Caroline lay still and watched, unable to tear her gaze away.

'Lewis,' her words came out as a whisper, 'is this really necessary…?'

His shadow seemed to stoop like a hawk as he leaned across her, taking her lips in another insistent kiss.

'Yes, my darling Caro, it is entirely necessary.' His voice was very husky. 'But before we go any further there is something I should tell you. The church is booked for Saturday morning—two days' time, or indeed it might only be one day by now, and I shall brook no opposition. I have a special licence. And if you still think that I do not love you…'

Caroline's eyes flew wide. 'You love me? I did not realise—'

'Are you quite mad?' For a moment Lewis looked fierce again. 'How much more obvious does it need to be…?'

Caroline could not answer as he kissed her for a third time. His skin was warm beneath her fingers, intriguingly taut and soft at the same time… She smoothed her hand across his chest experimentally and heard him groan as he slid down beside her on the truckle bed.

'I thought that you were married to your ship,' she said at last, a hint of teasing in the words as she looked up into the blue eyes so close to hers. 'I am sure that you said that she was brave and true…'

'So she was, and I swore not to marry until I found a woman to match her…'

Lewis stripped back the covering cloak and his fingers found the laces of Caroline's shift. She caught her breath as he dealt efficiently with the bows and brushed the material aside impatiently.

'I protest— You have done this before, Lewis…'

He laughed. 'What, do you think I am a rake, then? Prim Miss Whiston will have no truck with rakes…'

He bent his head to her breast and Caroline cried out at once, arching against him. This was a whole new world of sensation, urgent, melting…

'Severe Miss Whiston…' Lewis's voice was rough now as his hands moved softly over her exposed skin '…would never indulge in such inappropriate behav-

iour as this…' He slid the shift down over her hips.
'I am persuaded that she would be quite horrified at
such unsuitable conduct…' He trailed tiny kisses
down her throat and over her breasts until Caroline
was almost crying with need.

'Do you know how much I have longed to find my
own sweet Caro again?' Lewis said softly. 'I knew
that she was only hiding and now that I have found
her I will never let her go…'

'Lewis,' Caroline could barely concentrate, but she
had something to tell him. 'Did I tell you that I love
you too…'

She saw the blaze of triumph in his eyes. 'Darling
Caro…'

Caroline reached out and slid her hands over his
back, gasping with pleasure at the feel of him beneath
her fingers, pulling him closer. Every inch of her was
burning for him and when Lewis brought his mouth
back down to hers she writhed with delight and drew
him to her, aware of nothing but the spiralling desire
that threatened to consume her.

'Please, Lewis—'

'Oh, Miss Whiston—' his eyes were mocking her
but there was a heat there that matched her own
'—pleasure should not be hurried!'

'Later,' Caroline whispered, arching against him,
'later you may take your time…'

She heard him laugh and it was the last conscious
thing that she remembered in the whirl of sensation
that engulfed her. She had no thought for convention

or appropriate behaviour. Prim Miss Whiston was gone for ever.

It was cold in the hut and Caroline burrowed deeper under the covers, closer to the warm, male body entangled with hers. Lewis shifted slightly to accommodate her and drew her to him so that her cheek was resting in the curve of his shoulder.

'Lewis, you say that we are to be married in two days...'

'One day. It is past midnight.' His voice was a sleepy murmur.

'But I have not yet agreed to your proposal...' Caroline was tracing her fingers over his chest. She leant closer and saw the corner of his mouth lift in a smile.

'So you have not. Will you run away instead, then?'

'I might...'

'And I would have to bring you back and tell anyone who cares to challenge me that you are absconding with the family silver...'

Caroline wriggled closer, lowering her lips to within an inch of his. Drowsy blue eyes smiled into hers.

'Is there any?' she whispered.

'Mmm...' Lewis made an effort to stir himself. 'I am sure I could find some to substantiate my claims...'

He reached out a lazy hand and pulled her back down beside him. With one finger, he traced a line down the soft skin on the inside of her arm, pausing as his hand brushed the side of her breast. Caroline started to tremble.

'Do you think that you will like being married to me, Caro?'

'It will be tolerable,' Caroline gasped, as his hand drifted across her bare stomach. 'Of course, you will have to behave sensibly—'

'I have no intention of doing so, I assure you. Is this sensible?' Lewis bent over and kissed the corner of her mouth softly. 'Is this?' His hand cupped her breast, stroking gently.

'Lewis?'

'Yes, Caro?' The gentle movement did not cease.

Caroline shivered. 'It is not really appropriate to repeat your actions so soon—'

Lewis leant over her. 'Yet I distinctly remember you telling me that I might do so. Slowly, as well...'

Caroline abandoned the unequal attempt to think straight. There was no necessity for it. Probably, she thought blissfully, as Lewis started to kiss her again, very slowly, there would never be any need to be strict and prim and appropriate again.

'Caroline, brave and beautiful,' Lewis whispered against her skin. 'My dauntless Caro, the perfect companion. I believe that I have truly met my match!'

* * * *

The drama continues!
Look out for more Regency drama, intrigue, mischief...
and marriage in **The Steepwood Scandals Volume 3**
featuring A Most Improper Proposal *by Gail Whitiker*
& A Noble Man *by Anne Ashley*
Available next month, from all good booksellers.

THE STEEPWOOD
Scandals

*Regency drama, intrigue, mischief...
and marriage*

VOLUME THREE

A Most Improper Proposal by Gail Whitiker

When Desirée Nash is propositioned by Viscount
Buckworth, she is outraged. A year later impossible
circumstances force Desirée shamefully to agree to
become Sebastian's mistress...

A Noble Man by Anne Ashley

To discourage the pampered men her father would have
her marry, Sophia puts out a rumour that she is looking
for a husband outside her class! Could a duke disguised
as a groom change her mind?

On sale 5th January 2007

*Available at WHSmith, ASDA, Tesco
and all good bookshops*

www.millsandboon.co.uk

A young woman disappears.
A husband is suspected of murder.
Stirring times for all the neighbourhood in

THE STEEPWOOD

Scandals

Volume 1 – November 2006
Lord Ravensden's Marriage by Anne Herries
An Innocent Miss by Elizabeth Bailey

Volume 2 – December 2006
The Reluctant Bride by Meg Alexander
A Companion of Quality by Nicola Cornick

Volume 3 – January 2007
A Most Improper Proposal by Gail Whitiker
A Noble Man by Anne Ashley

Volume 4 – February 2007
An Unreasonable Match by Sylvia Andrew
An Unconventional Duenna by Paula Marshall

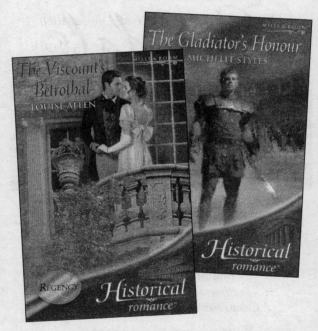

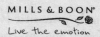

An enchantingly romantic Regency romp
from *New York Times* bestselling author
Stephanie Laurens

After the death of her father, Georgiana Hartley
returns home to England — only to be confronted with
the boorish advances of her cousin. Fleeing to the
neighbouring estate of Dominic Ridgely, Viscount
Alton of Candlewick, Georgiana finds herself sent
to London for a Season under the patronage of the
Viscount's sister.

Suddenly Georgiana is transformed into a lady,
charming the *ton* and cultivating a bevy of suitors.
Everything is unfolding according to Dominic's plan...
until he realises that he desires Georgiana for his own.

On sale 15th December 2006

Available at WHSmith, Tesco, ASDA, Borders, Eason, Sainsbury's
and all good paperback bookshops

Also available from M&B™ by *New York Times* bestselling author Stephanie Laurens

A superb 2-in-1 anthology of linked Regency stories

Featuring

Tangled Reins

Miss Dorothea Darent has no intention of ever getting married, but the disreputable Marquis of Hazelmere is captivated when they meet — and determined to win her heart…

Fair Juno

The Earl of Merton's days as a notorious rake are numbered when he finds himself rescuing a damsel in distress. But the lady flees the scene without revealing her name, leaving the Earl in pursuit of his mysterious *fair Juno*.

M&B™

Enjoy the dazzling glamour of Vienna on the eve of the First World War...

Rebellious Alex Faversham dreams of escaping her stifling upper-class Victorian background. She yearns to be like her long-lost Aunt Alicia, the beautiful black sheep of the family who lives a glamorous life abroad.

Inspired, Alex is soon drawn to the city her aunt calls home – Vienna. Its heady glitter and seemingly everlasting round of balls and parties in the years before WW1 is as alluring as she had imagined, and Alex finds romance at last with Karl von Winkler, a hussar in the Emperor's guard. But, like the Hapsburg Empire, her fledgling love affair cannot last. Away from home and on the brink of war, will Alex ever see England or her family again?

On sale 3rd November 2006

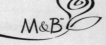

All you could want for Christmas!

Meet handsome and seductive men under the mistletoe, escape to the world of Regency romance or simply relax by the fire with a heartwarming tale by one of our bestselling authors. These special stories will fill your holiday with Christmas sparkle!

On sale 6th October 2006

On sale 20th October 2006

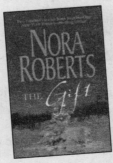